THE CASSANDRA COMPLEX

FRAZER DOUGLAS

Frazer Douglas was born in 1971 and as well as a writer has also been a professional actor and celebrated audiobook narrator. The Cassandra Complex is his first novel. After many years spent in both Europe and the U.S.A Frazer now divides his time between London and France.

For Margaret Elizabeth Stacey, Meg.
The last of the Stacey girls from Chelsea.

'It is made in the size of a suitcase. It is a suitcase actually. You could carry it. You could put it in another suitcase if you want to.'
'. . . One person is capable of triggering this nuclear weapon — one person.'
'I'm saying that more than a hundred out of the supposed number of 250 are not under the control of the armed forces of Russia.'
'I don't know their location.'

- Former Russian National Security Adviser Aleksander Lebed - 7th September 1997

'All men are loyal, but their objects of allegiance are at best approximate.'

John Barth

1

Somewhere on the outskirts of central Moscow, in a small flat owned by Russian Foreign Intelligence, Valentin Baskov became English. It was a balmy Sunday in early May when the black Chaika with official number plates arrived outside the anonymous grey apartment block and sat there with its engine running, belching smoke through their open windows while it waited for the young man to step out onto the curb. When he did, Irena Bushenova from Flat 3 who was opening her mail in the entrance hallway recognised the type at once. They came and went from time to time. Delivered by government car, always wearing a military uniform and the same sad expression. Lost-looking, lonely, she had decided. These were the ones you shouldn't notice, let alone engage with or talk to anyone about because you've been expressly warned not to and no one wants the mistakes of their past to be dredged up again. Of course you'd wonder what on earth they got up to in number 4 for months on end, but then since the loquacious old drunkard Yuri Zykov from the top floor was escorted away by men in leather jackets never to be seen again and his life's belongings burned in the communal area, it had become a widely held belief within the building that some things are better not known. "A warning to us all," Kozlov from Flat 9 called it, face set resolutely against the same fate as they stood around the bonfire watching the flames engulf Zykov's suitcase, blacken his treasured carved walrus bone caskets and melt his black market vinyl records. No one could argue. That was the night everything changed in the building. Before that there was healthy, hushed speculation in the corridors: reports of hearing voices through the paper-thin walls, foreign chatter on the radio, endless repetition of the same unfamiliar words for hours on end and then some. But not since.

This one was awfully handsome though, she noted through the tobacco-coloured glass of the entrance door, unafraid of allowing her gaze to linger when it should have quickly dropped back down to her bill from Central Telegraph. And neither lost nor lonely looking, merely impassively regarding their facade like someone who has detected a bad smell. If the irascible piano tuner on the top floor was as deaf as the hawk-eyed stamp collector in flat nine was blind to such arrivals, there was still one occupant who could be relied upon to throw caution to the wind when a handsome soldier landed on the curb and that was glamorous Irena Bushenova - sable coat even in May and teenage daughter who borrowed her blue eyeshadow and kept ungodly hours.

Baskov swung open the glass door and passed through the cloud of heavy perfume that enshrouded her, a smell he found intoxicating but that by the time he reached the stairwell had been replaced by disinfectant, and that upon entering the second floor flat had given way entirely to damp. To a soldier used to the charmless brick barracks and frozen parade ground of The Forest, the secret intelligence training camp that had been his home for two years, the colourless rooms that greeted him were scarcely an improvement. It was a small, miserable flat, meanly furnished with Soviet-era furniture and with small windows through which too little of the spring light was allowed to enter. The bedroom even had a single army bunk so he wouldn't feel too homesick. Hanging in the wardrobe was a morbid selection of trousers, shirts and jumpers, all of poly-blend fibres in muted shades bearing labels that read Debenhams, above a single pair of black PVC shoes. The contents of the bathroom cabinet suggested he would be shaving with razor blades and washing with shampoo and soap all supplied by a company called Woolworths — of which he had never heard — while the lone bookcase in the living room held tall textbooks in English with titles like *Tongue Position, Breathing, Rhythm and Stress, Intonation Patterns & Connected Speech, Train Your Speech Muscles,* and *Advanced Series 1. Master Mixed Conditionals.*

How many before him had stood here, absent-mindedly wondering who the author D. Philips was, what a Mixed Conditional was, whether he'd be expected to master one, and what in god's name prompted the Ministry of Education of the RSFSR to publish books with such deadening titles in the first place.

Inspection of the kitchen cupboards for food yielded only a one pound bag of Tate and Lyle sugar, so in the absence of either sustenance or any other stimulus Baskov found himself drawn to the flat's only adornment: a watercolour print in the hallway. *Gorky Park at Dusk,* he decided instinctually, having never looked properly at a painting before, was awful, clumsy, the work of an amateur.

A few silent hours in a fabric armchair later a

plain man in a plain suit clutching a Gladstone bag like it contained treasure let himself in, placed a fresh pile of books with equally galvanising titles upon the coffee table and some rectangular-shaped items in the freezer, and introduced himself as Talbot. A curt briefing followed in what sounded like a native southern-English accent.

'You will live alone. I will visit you every day except on Sundays, for eight hour periods. You remain a soldier of the Russian army, therefore while you are here you remain under strict orders. Alcohol, drugs, what not, are forbidden. You will not leave the confines of the flat unless it is to take exercise, which will take the form of an hour-long run twice a day, once at 06:30 a.m. and again at 8 p.m. — there should be a running kit here, if not I'll arrange for one. You will have contact with no one. Everything you need will be brought to you. We begin tomorrow. There's food for tonight in the freezer.'

At 8 a.m. the following day Talbot made a basic appraisal, noting that while Baskov spoke very good English his native accent was thick, before an initial lesson plan was made. Mornings, it was decided, would be dedicated to specific advanced grammatical structures, using the question and answer technique over and over, and to exercises in intensive phonetics with particular attention paid to the sounds unfamiliar to the Russian tongue. To the dreaded Voiced Dental Fricative that students of English the world over know as the *th* sound as in father. *The* not d, *th*is not dis, *th*at not dat, again, repeat, please. *The* not d . . . The *a* as in *bad*. *Bad* not *bed*. The stress of syllables, dip thongs, the *h*, the *w* sound, *why* not vy, *well* not vell. Repeat. The I: Ship, sheep, ship, sheep, leave, live. Repeat, please.

Book vs boot, feet vs fit, Again. Repeat, please. Again.
'Again.'

Lunches were pre-made, deep-frozen, microwavable versions of the English classics: shepherd's pie, toad in the hole, bangers and mash, meat loaf with peas, fish fingers, chips and beans, chicken curry and rice. All rapidly heated, tasted largely of the cardboard trays they came in, and consumed silently each day at one p.m. before the work recommenced. Afternoon sessions were spent reading newspapers, watching television and films (mainly historical newsreel), as well as listening to radio programmes, all broadcast in English and paused often to encourage discussion. Current affairs, football results, the weather, bylaws, politics, customs, and myriad cultural references were addressed and analysed at length, while the young man was constantly encouraged to improve his use of slang phrases and vernacular language in conversation. The tape recorder installed in the bedroom would run for twenty-four hours a day, continuously broadcasting news from the target country, so that at night as he slept he would be inspired to dream in English. Total immersion.

On Sundays Talbot wrote up his weekly report to his GRU superiors that chronicled the young recruit's "extraordinary progress", consistently attesting his advancement to be outstanding. Attention span, memory, mental acumen, information stamina, and noise immunity: all remarkable, while his talent for the target language was exceptional. The reports also noted a "coldness and complete lack of emotion" in the Russian. Baskov was, Talbot wrote, the very best he had encountered, and for three months all ran smoothly until one Monday morning, that of August

20th, when he arrived to find the young man still asleep in bed with two empty bottles of champagne on the floor beside it and a naked girl wrapped around him in it. The report dated 21st August, rather tactfully, read, "An unfortunate relationship has developed with a young female student called Bushenova who lives across the hall in neighbouring Apartment 3 who appears to have developed a crush." Two days later the girl was told she was no longer welcome to attend the Academy for Veterinary Medicine and Baskov was relocated to another flat in a different suburb of Moscow to complete his training.

It was upon seeing this new apartment, identical in every way down to every blind eye turned in the communal entrance hall, every government-purchased stick of furniture, to the print of the park at dusk in the hallway, that the young man's stomach muscles tightened.

Suddenly he felt like a laboratory rat, that he wasn't alone, that there must be more like him.

It was one Tuesday a few weeks later that the two men sat and watched in silence as the television news reported terrorist attacks on the world trade centre in New York. Throughout that afternoon Talbot was chilled to observe that if the young man in his presence felt any emotion while the horror played out in real time, he made no sign.

And so it was that over a twelve month period that saw Muscovites bake in a merciless July heat, plod through a contrasting August that enjoyed the fewest hours of sunshine on record, suffer the Arctic winter that followed only then to be rewarded for their tolerance with a temperate spring, Valentin Baskov, through rigorous, monotonous repetition with a humourless man in a matching fabric armchair, became more and more conversant across an immense range of news and gossip that related to a country in the West the young man had never visited in his life.

One afternoon in May 2002 after watching a news item about the Queen of England arriving in Scotland to commemorate her Golden Jubilee, Talbot, satisfied any last trace of a Russian accent had been ruthlessly erased, stood and switched off the set, declared the immersion phase complete, and for the sake of courtesy only, shook his hand once. No more words were shared, for no bond nor sense of camaraderie had been formed. He simply gathered his books, pushed them into the Gladstone, buttoned his plain jacket, and left.

The following day Baskov rose late and decided not to exercise. In the afternoon another plain-clothes man from the FPS, once the KGB's Ninth Chief Directorate, drove him deep into the countryside to a gated enclave near the Moskva where Russia's elite keep their elegant country houses and whose narrow streets are patrolled day and night by armed FSO men. There, in a dacha nestled deep in a pine forest in luxury he'd never before glimpsed, General Alexei Sorokin, a plum-faced, corpulent chain-smoker of sixty-ish who was then Head of Directorate S, invited him to sit. The old man enjoyed speaking English, and he adopted an informal tone for the occasion.

'Valentin. *Valentin.*' An avuncular hand on the knee as an elderly general might to the blue-eyed boy of his unofficial directorate. '*Patience and labour will do everything.* Is this correct translation? It sounds better in

Russian.' Hearty laughter, not reciprocated. A deep, reverent breath now, grip on the knee tightening. 'Valentin. *Your* patience we now must require. To wait is one of the most difficult things to do. But you must wait. And be sure, Valentin, one day, you will see great reward for your patience. You are special, Valentin. We will choose *you* for a mission of such critical importance that, if successful, will not only fill you with pride, shower you in glory like is reserved only for our nation's greatest heroes, but will deliver promotion *and wealth* few dare dream of. You want to be a rich man, Valentin?'

Inside the Kremlin, some thirty-three kilometres to the east, on that same day, 24th May 2002, the presidents of the United States and Russia were signing The Treaty of Moscow - a mutual nuclear disarmament treaty George W. Bush claimed "liquidates the Cold War legacy of nuclear hostility," a young man was being assured by an elderly general that one day he would be handed the power to change the course of world history forever.

When he had finished speaking, Sorokin reached down and lifted a document from a silver tray, brushing cigarette ash from it. Despite the gravity of the moment the general knew from the instructor's reports Baskov's features would remain impassive, and as he handed him his new identity he was proved correct, for when Baskov opened the British passport not the merest glimmer of a reaction crossed his face. The photograph inside the British passport showed the bearer to be the same stoic-looking young man of nineteen who stared down upon it for the first time: the same evenly drawn features, the same dark brown hair - then closely cropped that had since been allowed to grow out — the same glassy look to the light green eyes.

The name, however, was now foreign.
Russell Edward Blake.

It was almost twenty years later when Dmitri Petrenko stared with wide and unblinking eyes directly into the centre of the sun. The ultraviolet rays may damage his retinas, but as he watched it tremble lower into the blurred white horizon in the distance he was certain that it didn't matter, for it was a sun he would not live to see rise again. With the staff car now deep into the plains of the North West and about to enter the snowy forests of Moscow's barren outskirts, he knew he would never see the ones he loved and who loved him again.

A black dot upon the white sheet of landscape, the Mercedes crunched on heavily through the snow. Despite the absence of road signs for an hour designed to disorient, the prisoner knew exactly where he was being taken, confirmed when high barbed-wire fencing started to appear along the road's eastern side and the outline of the prison camp began to emerge out of the fog. The shape of the perimeter, familiar to him from all the sheaves of plans, photographs, correspondence he'd copied, caused his heart to begin palpitating. Beside him Grushenko took another strong swig from his hip flask and caught the drips with his coat sleeve. Dmitri knew the barbarian would have chosen this grim, brutalist relic of Stalin's Soviet-era justice with only one end in mind — to make him disappear, the way millions had before him. Traitors, *izmenniki.* Men who were weak like him, who would bend and snap like twigs beneath stone cruel barbarism.

The car turned off the road and slowed beneath a rusted hammer and sickle suspended amid tangled barbed wire. A uniformed guard rushed forward, stood stiff to attention and saluted to the man he knew to be Colonel General Ivan Grushenko of the GRU before signalling to a face in a frozen box for the barrier to be swung open. Grushenko slid the hip flask into a fold of his coat, adjusted the brim of his high-arched cap, pulled on thick gloves, and after the black-uniformed FSB driver had walked round and opened the door, stepped out into the freezing evening air.

At the foot of the high stone perimeter walls were piles of long-since felled tree logs, while derelict tools once used to work them lay around corroding in random heaps — frame saws, pickaxes and makeshift wheelbarrows. Contained within the walls a series of low-roofed military huts, simply built oblong blocks with horizontal slits for windows. It was a desolate outpost, and largely unremarkable were it not for the giant radio transmitter in its centre that dominated entirely; a steel lattice mast of two thousand feet that quickly disappeared into the sky. Comprising countless equilateral triangles, the two megawatt tower was powerful enough to both send and receive signals far across the globe while crawling up it was a cluster of radio dishes of differing sizes. Although the place seemed abandoned, Dmitri knew differently, and also that for him to see it now was to have seen too much.

He shut his eyes, and in the centre of the dark orange sun that had burned itself onto his retinas was Natalya. Her beautiful clear blue eyes, her flock of blonde hair, her golden smile. Hers alone would be the last image in his mind's eye and he wouldn't let anything ugly obscure it. He stepped out of the car and felt the freezing air bite at his face.

'In the West they called them Gulags,' Grushenko called over in his slurred rasp, 'labour camps where traitors of the Soviet Union were sent to be punished for their crimes. In some they were made to mine for copper, or for coal, often by hand. In this one it was logging trees. See, the tools are still here.' He gestured to a pile of rusted shovels.

Dmitri stuffed his hands under the armpits of his thin canvas jacket. The general was walking slowly back towards him.

'Of course, many didn't survive the harsh winters. The inhumane living conditions, the brutal punishments. But they were traitors, so it was what they deserved.' He looked down at him. 'Traitors like you.' A heavy, gloved fist swung out at the little man's mouth that knocked him to the icy ground. Grushenko sniggered, then kicked him hard in the chest, breaking two ribs. He liked inflicting pain, and wished he could do it more often — though nowadays he was bound to his office and the dictates of his superior rank, kept far from his beloved battlefield.

With bloodshot eyes he regarded the hunched figure bleeding into the sludge beside his staff car, raised his GSh-18 9 mm automatic pistol and was about to pull the trigger when a noise from above made him look up. The howl of a Kazan Ansat helicopter's two Pratt and Whitney turboshaft engines filled the sleet-swept sky. Swearing, he holstered the gun as the frozen ground became whipped up into a mini-storm. The helicopter bounced once and settled, its four-bladed rotors slowing, swinging in neutral, and the door slid open. *Blyad*, Grushenko swore beneath his breath. Igor Savich, ancient and impeccable in a charcoal overcoat and fur *ushanka* was marching from the helicopter followed by rotund army general, Volkov, Deputy Head of S-Directorate. Behind them was a young bespectacled signalman in uniform carrying a hard leather attache case. His name, not that Grushenko knew or cared, was Krupin. The accompanying radio equipment told him they were here to begin testing the transmitter.

'What brings you here, comrade General?' Volkov shouted as they approached from beneath the rotors.

Savich slowed as he noticed the man lying in the snow. 'What is happening here General Grushenko?'

'I caught this man in my outer office, at my secretary's desk. I'm dealing with it.'

They walked over to the groaning, bloodied man in a soaked plain brown uniform.

'Who is he?' asked Savich.

'I do not know. I've never seen him before.'

Igor Savich, as well as having been chief strategic operational planner for Russian Foreign Intelligence for forty-seven years was also a man who possessed an unnatural ability to detect a lie when he heard it. 'Then would it not be wise to find out before rendering him mute by beating him half to death?'

'I said I'm dealing with it, Igor Mikhailovich.'

Volkov lifted a thick arm in a signal to two men who were unloading equipment from the helicopter — simple, bored-looking thugs whose necks were like bull's and with brains to match. Dogs, as they're known, one of whom upon receiving the command abandoned the cases and ran over, grabbed at the back of Dmitri's collar and dragged him towards one of the larger huts, the heels of the prisoner's shoes carving two lines in the snow behind them.

Grushenko scowled. If anyone finds out I'm related to this piece of shit, he thought, I'll be finished. The face of his brother appeared in his mind as he followed them inside. Georgi - long-since dead but still surfacing from the depths to haunt him. Georgi, whose only daughter Katya had married this idiot only then to turn up unannounced begging him through floods of tears to give her pathetic husband a job. In the end he succumbed, thinking it would shut her up if he had his secretary march Dmitri down to the cleaning department. But some hope. There was a daughter, Natalya, with some rare form of leukaemia that only the most expensive drugs could help treat - more than a cleaner's salary could afford anyway - and that *Uncle Ivan* was expected to pay for. Like it wasn't enough that he'd arranged for her useless husband whose career until then was as a toilet cleaner in the Leningradsky station to walk the hallowed corridors of Lubyanka. No, Katya wanted more. "Natalya is your flesh and blood," she'd yell, still hysterical, still begging like a vagrant and leaving tears and mucus on his office carpet after he'd had her thrown out.

But no one will know, he told himself resolutely as he watched the two dogs tie his unwanted nephew to a chair in the low-ceilinged interrogation room, not unless he talks. Georgi's name isn't on her birth certificate. Nothing to tie her to me. And if Katya starts shouting her mouth off then she can also be silenced.

Grushenko sneered down at him from the

control room as the dogs gave the still unconscious man a couple of slaps for starters. *Leukaemia*, pfft, he dismissed. To him it confirmed only that the Petrenko genes were riddled with weakness, plagued by frailty and infirmity. Biting his lip, tasting blood, he wished he'd taken Petrenko down to the basement prison in Lubyanka earlier that day and shot him dead there.

'Your name, please,' a voice echoed out from above through a badly wired speaker.

A sudden explosion of pain. Blinded by light. Unsure if he is awake or asleep, alive or dead and on his way to heaven or more likely hell, Dmitri's brain attempts to take stock. He immediately senses he is seated and his wrists are tied behind his back, fingers of both hands crushed, mouth throbbing badly, body trembling with fear that he cannot control. The stench is foul. He remembers now, the gulag. How long has passed since he arrived? He doesn't know, only that he's been heavily beaten whilst unconscious. Heavy boots pace about on the stone floor and the sound of rubber hoses hum through the air as they pass. More bruises on his trunk, cold clawing at the broken skin on his back.

Think.

The dark orange sun throbs in the centre of his vision. His thoughts are scrambling — fragments of jarring violence. Somewhere inside the pain, emerging like a poppy on Flanders Fields, is Natalya's face. But the poppy wilts, she is crying, holding her belly, and the sight and sound of his daughter's distress is more than he can bear.

'Your name, please.'

The voice again. Cracked, ancient.

In the control room somewhere above him, Igor Savich took his finger off the button of the old Bakelite tannoy microphone. He was frowning, which caused the already deeply drawn lines in his forehead to crack further as he watched the prisoner come to. Why had Grushenko had him beaten so badly he couldn't speak? What didn't he want him to say? Savich had long-regarded Grushenko as nothing more than a common criminal who used the military merely as an outlet for his cruelty. Like one of Hitler's Nazi thugs — specifically Oskar Dirlewanger, that cruel commander of the SS - amoral, alcoholic, sadistic. A trench-rat who stank of sweat and liquor. Slovenly was the way the elegantly clothed and highly disciplined Savich had always regarded Grushenko, both in appearance and in duty.

Finger back on the button. 'Your name, please?'

Think. How did I get here?

It is four hours earlier, Dmitri remembers. The afternoon snow is falling inaudibly in the Moscow streets as he enters the double-sized outer office on the third floor of the FSB headquarters, shoves his janitor's cart and mop bucket against the wall and rushes to the desk clutching the miniature camera. He knows he has six minutes. He knows because he's called Grushenko's secretary away under a false pretence like this many times in the last six months. He starts pounding the shutter, feverishly photographing the contents of the desk when something in the corner of his eye makes him freeze. Lowering the camera he feels his stomach sink. The woman's handbag. Why would she leave it? It is the moment he knew would come. Then the silence is broken by a sound that may just as well have been a gunshot to his head.

'Hello, Dmitri.' The voice comes from the shadow in the office doorway. The rasping voice of the general he has been betraying for the last six months.

'I think we should take a drive.'

His patience expired, Grushenko lurched for the confiscated camera and held it up like a child's toy in his strong fingers. 'Ah, let's kill him and forget it,' he spat. 'The camera card is empty. There is no breach. You really think I would risk everything by leaving anything of value on a secretary's desk?' The rage was rising in him. 'You think this vermin is a safe cracker? He is just a clumsy thief,' he laughed, too desperately. He knew Savich and Volkov would be compelled to report the breach to Defence Minister Sotnik, who as head of the new Top Secret Directorate would in turn be compelled to act, but if the cretin talks, Grushenko thought, biting deeper into his lip to taste more blood, breathes a word of this ridiculous, this vile family connection - I'm a dead man.

Click. Mild feedback. 'Help him.'

The dogs hit him across the face with wide slaps from calloused hands.

'Your name, please?'

'Dmitri Petrenko,' he manages through the blood that's sticking to his tongue.

The time had arrived for some kind of confession.

For over an hour Igor Savich has let the prisoner speak. Time has taught him the valuable lesson that to listen is to learn, and the only sound that has left his lips has been to tell the ever reddening Grushenko to be silent.

From the beginning Dmitri is scrupulous in his detail, as if he believes being meticulous about his betrayal will forgive it and exonerate him. He has described the day they received the terrible diagnosis that burrowed a hole in his heart. A daughter's illness, a mother's despair, a father's feeling of helplessness, the desperate need for money the likes of which few men ever see. How for weeks afterwards he spent what little they had in pubs and bars close to the British and American embassies until he managed to befriend a young Russian who claimed to know someone who worked as an attache at the British mission.

He has described how a week later he sat coughing on shisha tobacco on a faux-leather settee in the tacky setting of a neon hookah bar called The Blow Lounge on Smolenskiy Pereuloka, close to the eastern banks of the Moskva, while an Englishman in a good suit told him he might be able to introduce him to someone. Then of how another long week passed before he found himself in the greasy office of a back-street mechanic coming to an agreement with a man who calls himself Carlo.

Here, Dmitri pauses as the memory of the meeting returns. Grushenko, Carlo is saying through thin lips that seem set in a permanent smile but one that isn't at all friendly, is of interest to the British. Dmitri skips this and moves on to their second meeting.

The artillery courtyard of the State Historical Museum on Red Square is the location. As they wander around the courtyard, blithely regarding its canons and shells, details are exchanged. Carlo assigns him the codename Jackdaw and makes him memorise a long number, that of a bank account into which he tells him ten thousand dollars has already been deposited. Realising he might now be able to save his daughter's life, Dmitri recounts how he became unable to contain himself, how the tears spilled out of him, which made Carlo uncomfortable as there were people around. Carlo is angry, he says, orders him to compose himself at once, then makes him memorise dead-drop sites, various dates and times, what seem to him overly elaborate fallbacks, an emergency telephone number, email address, and the location of a safe house, all of which he soon forgets except the primary dead drop site.

Careful not to mention Grushenko by name, sure that this omission will save his life, Dmitri falls silently back into the memory of that day: *Grushenko is not in the office most mornings,* Dmitri tells Carlo under his breath, *and I know that two or three times a week he visits a prostitute on the Kamergersky Lane – it is a quiet side street in the Tverskaya suburb. I study his routine. When I see the staff car disappear north up Ulitsa Bol'shaya Lubyanka, I will place a call to the secretary to call her away. Then I will enter Grushenko's outer office with the electronic key tag the cleaning staff have. I know the password to her computer – I watched her use it once — so I will insert a memory stick into the tower and download many documents and folders while at the same time photographing everything on the desk.*

'My plan was to get into any office I could and copy whatever was on desks and in drawers. I would like to be able to tell you it was better planned than this but it was not. Carlo gave me a miniature Leica camera to use and he warns me "No cell phone cameras, *ever*. Nothing that can be intercepted."'

There is silence in the stale room. He looks down at the floor. It is filthy. The dogs are bored. One is gnawing his thumbnail, the other can't stop scratching. Dmitri recalls internally how he ended the meeting with Carlo with that day: They are about to part when a strange thing happens. A sudden downpour prompts Dmitri to burst into tears again. Through misted spectacles and helpless sobs he confesses they are tears of elation, due to his new found wealth. Also, he confesses emotionally, he 'just loves the rain'. Unused to such outpourings of emotion the Englishman retreats back to his embassy, probably wondering what he's got himself into, and Dmitri rushes home and dances Katya around the living room until they are both ragged.

'But it is only for a few months am I photographing and passing to the British. I love Russia, I never wanted to betray her.' The tears rise again as he thinks of Natalya. He sees himself through their eyes: crying like a baby, convulsing on a chair like this in this God-forsaken room, wrists still bound and with a head still fried and feeling like he's been struck by lightening. But he can't help it.

Still silence from the tannoy.

He sniffs back the tears, swallows. It is okay. It will be okay, he tells himself. He has told the old man everything. Now he will work for his own side, feed false intelligence to the British, be a double agent. Carlo would still pay – Natalya's health would still improve. And every word of it was true, every detail accurate except for the one crucial detail: that he had targeted Grushenko at random.

This lie by omission of the family connection

surely would buy him his life.

Savich left the room to splash his face. A clumsy amateur, he concluded to the cracked face in the cracked mirror above the filthy bathroom sink, a walk-in, in over his head. But something wreaked. Grushenko was hiding something, he could smell it. He dabbed his face with a clean handkerchief, then from his pocket took out a sterling silver filigree pill box, removed a tablet, and swallowed it.

Back in the observation room, the bloated Volkov scratched at the folds of skin that formed his wide neck. He had also long-regarded Grushenko as a sloppy operator, yet he was eager to begin the radio testing so he could fly back to Moscow and to a bucket of fried chicken in bed. 'Why not report him? Why go to the trouble of bringing him here?'

Grushenko raised the mic to his lips. 'No trouble,' he said before pushing the button.

In the room below the familiar voice echoed out, 'Kill him and bury him in the forest.'

'No. No – please . . . Natalya - '

At 8:17 p.m. one of the bored-looking thugs shot Dmitri in the side of the head with a PSS-2 silent pistol and he died.

Grushenko smiled. He liked watching life leave them. He wiped his brow, drunk with relief as well as vodka, while the dogs untied Dmitri's wrists and hauled his limp body off the chair. They then dragged him out into the freezing night where, two-hundred yards away among some poplar trees, the way so many men had done before them in that place, they began the arduous task of digging the frozen soil with two simple pickaxes.

2

The following morning two and a half thousand miles to the West, a middle-aged man stepped off the first Eurostar train of the day from London's St Pancras and began walking along a chilly platform 2 of Brussels' Gare Du Midi. He was rather donnish in appearance, wearing a blue raincoat over a suit made of a winter fabric, and while perhaps taller than average he was otherwise unnoticeable as he passed the front of the train with the other travellers and headed towards the escalator. His angular features remained fixed as he exited the Eurostar terminal onto the main station's concourse, and as he crossed the passageway underneath the tracks that spans the width of the station his hooded eyes hadn't once left the young woman's back. She was walking briskly, dark hair bouncing upon her shoulders and dressed in a slim raincoat and carrying a briefcase with one hand while pulling a small suitcase on wheels with the other. She was completely unaware she was being followed by two MI6 officers. Another of the morning's early commuters, a plainly — dressed woman called Zoe Taylor, whom although was wearing earbuds and the centred stare of an audiobook listener, also remained completely focused upon the target.

Exiting the station on the North side into bright sunlight, the woman turned right towards the taxi rank where a line of black cars with yellow chequer stripes was waiting, and got into the first one, a Skoda SUV. The drivers of the first three taxis in line were members of the Watcher team. As the car pulled away the man following crossed the street, slid open the rear door of a plain van and climbed in. Without speaking the driver pulled out into the morning traffic, circled the station, and turned right onto Avenue de Stalingrad where the van crawled along the pretty tree-lined street at a safe three-car distance behind the Skoda. At the van's wheel a local man of thirty-six called Stef passed a Motorola hand-held radio and small plastic box to his new passenger and said, 'Channel nine.'

John Henderson placed the earpiece in his left ear and the tiny dot of a microphone beneath his shirt collar. Back at the taxi rank, Zoe Taylor got into the next taxi in line.

Ten minutes later the Skoda taxi had come to rest in front of a pretty corner hotel on a cobbled side street called the Hotel Amigo that was tucked away behind the opulent La Grand Place. The woman got out and asked the driver to wait. Sitting beneath a cafe canopy opposite, a young man looked up from an opinion piece in the Brussels Times, folded the newspaper, stood, and walked towards the hotel. The van parked up, and its occupants watched the man cross the wet cobblestones in front of them and follow her inside.

Henderson sat back and allowed his heavy eyelids to close. Operation Domino had been five days and nights of watching, listening, waiting — the usual routine — but if Charlotte Fisher hadn't waited until the ungodly hour of 1 a.m. to book her Eurostar ticket then there's a good chance he would have managed to get some sleep the night before. But when the balloon goes up at that hour it sparks the same rapid flurry of preparation as it always does — in this case meaning an hour on the phone with the office and with the Belgian VSSE instructing them to lay on a whole welcoming party in Brussels in a few short hours time, followed by a quick wash and a shave before leaving his house in West Kensington. Twenty minutes of the dark amber pavements of the North End Road later and he found the van parked a few houses along from the target's flat in a Fulham side road.

'Morning, John. You look like you haven't slept either,' Godwin said, deadpan as ever as Henderson climbed silently into the back of the unmarked van. 'Makes me feel better, cheers.'

'Glad I can help, Keith. Jane moved?' In Watcher-speak the target is always John or Jane.

'Not a muscle. She can snore though, here.' He said, passing over the headphones and zipping up his anorak.

Godwin left him to settle back into what passed for home these days: the back of a panel van whose only light source was the few LED's from the monitoring equipment on the nearside wall. Since Sarah had left him, the house in Kensington was just that, a house, while home was in the shadows. It was where he was most content, a place that allowed him to reflect on the past and to consider an uncertain future. Almost three decades before the future had seemed so certain, when the newcomer from Cambridge, so keen and sad, some said, but born for Section 'S' thought most, arrived inside the department whose single acronym denotes its geographical area, in this case 'Soviet' — an etymological hangover from a time John Henderson would doubtless have more comfortably inhabited. Earlier that spring, Moorehouse his history professor asked him what he planned to do for a career.

'Not sure, sir. Thought I might write something,' he replied, leading the man to enquire if he had ever thought of working for his country. Soon after, an envelope appeared in his pigeonhole from an anonymous government department inviting him to interview in London. It was after a two year stint in Moscow during that chaotic period in post-Soviet history when he arrived at Vauxhall Cross, where in no time he became regarded as resident Russian expert, a shining red star who seemed to live his work, spoke the language like a native and whose knowledge of Soviet-era intelligence networks seemed so encompassing that when the post became available he was the natural choice for head of section.

Though ever more distant a memory of late he could still remember the relative calm of the waters before the storm — a storm that, like they all do these days bore a name. Stephen Jones-Cooper had rolled in from the corporate world, had been appointed Assistant Chief, and appeared to have been given a mandate to restructure and rebrand the service with teams of lawyers, PR consultants and employ a new breed of officers who would fall in line with modern expectations and "bear the public scrutiny intelligence agencies face in a changing, more accountable world." But that wasn't enough for Stephen. His ego demanded more, so he also rebranded himself. For years, perhaps a quarter of a century, there had been quiet rumblings in the higher echelons of British Intelligence that there was a mole, a double agent at work, and once Jones-Cooper got a sniff of that he decided he would be the one to smoke him, or her, out. *The Mole Hunter* - who in reality was someone who was satisfied replacing anyone who didn't fit his mould. Unfortunately his arrival three years ago had coincided with the submission of Henderson's *Overture* report, which its author knew had contributed to the man's targeting of him. An absurd work of fiction, the new AC had labelled it. Findings baseless, conclusions crackpot, sensationalist. The Cold War is over, John. Fantasise for it by all means, but do it in private like a good chap, had come the reply. He'd handed Jones-Cooper the excuse he needed to be rid of him, neatly bound and numbered and only missing a bowed ribbon. The submission of that one report had left him clinging to a life-raft ever since. These days John Henderson felt like a drowning man. Early retirement had been mooted, which, since he had long held a desire to pursue a more comprehensive literary effort in some form or another wasn't inconceivable to him, though for now he had to accept the constant threat of his own extinction from within his own service as a way of life.

Another day, another van, while at the oak-panelled desk inside the Hotel Amigo's elegant lobby, the target, Charlotte Fisher, parliamentary assistant to Morris Jacques MP, took the plastic key card from the clerk and walked over towards the lift. She hadn't noticed the young man standing next to her with that morning's copy of The Brussels Times beneath his arm, and she couldn't have known that within its folded pages rested an RFID reading device that had just cloned her room key.

A crackling came into Henderson's ear, forcing

his eyes to open. 'Room forty-three,' the voice stated. It belonged to the man with the newspaper, an ex-policeman from Ghent called Thomas who had been with the VSSE for four years who was now walking towards them. With invisible skill he brushed past the van and tipped the newspaper towards the open window. Stef picked up the RFID reader from the passenger seat and handed it back to Henderson, who pocketed it. Two minutes later Fisher exited the hotel's ornate doors, climbed back into her taxi and instructed the driver to proceed onto the Rue de la Violette. Thomas, now astride a cream Vespa scooter next to the cafe, pulled down the visor of his full-face helmet, kicked the starter down and followed.

'Stay with her until she gets to Charlemagne and if she gets out of the car before then and comes within three feet of anyone, Thomas, you break off and tail them. Zoe will pick her up inside the foyer of the building. Wait for me here, Stef,' he instructed the driver before he climbed out of the van and began walking along the narrow pavement towards the hotel.

The journey to the European Commission's Charlemagne Building in the European Quarter of Brussels is less then four kilometres but until the SUV crossed Rue Royale at the entrance to the Theatre Royal du Parc, dense traffic meant it didn't get above five miles per hour. Fifty metres back, the Vespa puttered dutifully along at the same snail's pace.

In the corridor Henderson plugged the RFID reader into the key slot, waited for the red light to turn green, and slipped inside. Room 43 had plain, cream-coloured walls and red velvet curtains hanging at large, south facing French windows. It was as the maids had left it save for the suitcase on the bed. After a cursory visual sweep he went to the closet and smiled when he saw the safe on a low shelf — a Stalwart – the ubiquitous, ineffective hotel safe of choice — just as he'd hoped for. Without hesitating he lifted its front an inch from the shelf, and slammed it back down while twisting the locking knob to the left. Immediately the pin inside dropped back into the knob and the door opened to reveal a two-and-a-half-inch Intel solid state drive. He retrieved a mini laptop from the inside of his jacket, plugged in the device via a cable, and pressed the key to begin the upload. It was 10:45.

Hugging the park's perimeter, the taxi turned right, then a sharp left onto Rue Belliard. It was now entering the area that is home to the administrative centre of the European Union.

Less than a kilometre away, in the foyer of the European Commission's fifteen storey, glass-fronted Charlemagne building, Zoe had arrived and was waiting among the sober-suited throng of civil servants who were gathered to continue seemingly endless deliberations as to the uncertain future of the Russian-Eurozone co-operative venture: the Nord Stream 2 Russian gas pipeline to mainland Europe. The talk was already all business. Lobbyists keen for the completed pipeline to be activated huddled in small groups with those more wary who saw Russian gas supply nowadays predominantly as a dangerous political weapon. Three minutes later Fisher arrived, registered at reception where she was issued an obligatory plastic ID card with magnetic stripe and photo, and was pointed towards the airport-like security control while inside her hotel room Henderson watched the progress bar pull gradually to the right and the seconds count down on his screen as the encrypted bug infected every document on the Intel. Once the upload was complete he left a small listening device in the smoke alarm, gave a final glance around, and stepped back into the corridor as silently as he had entered.

Amid the large group of delegates, Zoe followed Fisher up to one of the giant conference rooms, a high-tech amphitheatre with stadium seating. On the street outside the grey van parked up at a safe distance. It was eleven o'clock when the three men began their wait with pre-packed sandwiches Stef pulled from a Carrefour bag in the footwell.

Zoe took a seat two rows behind Fisher, who opened a laptop. An awkward German took to the stage beside a six-foot plastic tree and the flag of twelve five-pointed stars on the blue field that represents the unity of the countries of the European Union, tapped the mic and began his introduction.

'Ladies and gentlemen, good morning and welcome to this high level conference to continue discussions on the Nord Stream 2 Russian gas pipeline to Europe. My name is Tim Sauer, I'm the European Commission's spokesperson on action and energy. So to recap: In addition to existing Turkstream and Nord Stream 1 pipelines, The Nord Stream 2 gas pipeline is 1230 kilometres long and stretches along the sea bed from the Gulf of Finland in Russia to Lubmin in Germany. Forty-five percent of the EU's gas is supplied by Russia . . . '

Far from the European seat of power in the attic room he'd long ago converted into his own personal listening station in the small village of Brottby in the Swedish province of Uppland, a fifty-two year old man with headphones around his neck was busy fielding emails from across the globe. As editor of his humble magazine he felt compelled to respond to every message, yet he'd been up all night doing so and by now was barely able to spell. The iMac whose keys he was tapping nestled incongruously in the centre of the whole wall of vintage listening devices: wooden and aluminium boxes that featured toggle switches, sliders and dials, and small screens of green waveforms; equipment designed to detect high frequencies from 3–30 MHz that are reflected and refracted from the ionosphere. The odd perturbations of morse, spoken numbers, or even the faintest drone of buzz they produce could provoke levels of elation in him other men usually only find in more sensorial pursuits.

But this was something else entirely, the cause for real excitement in the short wave community. For suddenly during the usual gale of noise that inhabits the murky high frequency band, at precisely 7 p.m. the evening before, for the first time since 1989 on the 4625 kHz frequency, UVK-71 began transmitting again. It was incredible news, almost unbelievable. It lasted less than half a second, sent from a military mast somewhere northwest of Moscow that he picked up on his own home-made antenna — a two-hundred foot length of copper wire he'd strung up over to the next apartment block many years before. It was a squirt, a brief data-burst that unless slowed down substantially would make no sense to the listener. But his iMac's software had made short work of that. The morse now decoded, he was left with the following series of letters in his notebook:

GUDLD FPSWQ BHJCD SDALR HDKBS

Every one of his fellow enthusiasts agreed that this was a most exciting development. Had his magazine possessed a press it would surely have to have been held. Neither he, nor any one of his likeminded hobbyists knew what on earth the message meant of course, and they were twice as ecstatic precisely because of the mystery of it all.

The receipt of the same transmission at six o'clock the evening before had been received in other, more official, quarters, however, with rather less enthusiasm.

Deep in the English countryside inside a steel building shaped like a doughnut just outside Cheltenham the transmission triggered a flashing icon upon a screen, and the man who first caught it inside the cryptanalysis section of GCHQ was called Rashid. The icon indicated Top Priority. A quick click told him it was data-burst from a long-dormant Russian transmitter. Morse. And unbreakable. Both he, his superiors and anyone who knew anything about UVK-71 and even the most basic of codebreaking techniques knew that to even attempt to crack the code was futile. Futile because despite his deep understanding of the most advanced cryptanalysis techniques and with the world's most mathematically sophisticated computerised algorithms at his disposal, young Rashid knew that no technology existed that was sophisticated enough to decipher the simple morse-coded message from UVK-71. What was required to do that was a pen and paper, or to be more precise, a pen and the same one-time-pad as the Russian sender.

A few seconds after the broadcast ended and the

airwaves settled back into static, such a pad was being unwrapped from a dusty pack of twelve not a hundred miles from Cheltenham. It had been wrapped in cellophane at the end of the last century somewhere in Russia and kept hidden inside the false bottom of a suitcase that had been stored in the top of a closet in a London apartment since the owner had bought it some years before. The man unwrapping the pads had been waiting almost two decades to receive such a signal, whose content once decoded would be known to only eight other men in the world, as well as himself, Russell Blake.

Having stared at the back of the woman's head for hours to the soundtrack of endless bureaucrats drone on about energy supplies, Zoe suppressed another deep yawn. Like John, she too had been deprived of sleep before the same early train, yet her reason was less operational responsibility and more a restless three-year-old called Joe who was having nightmares about red-eyed monsters appearing uninvited out of the walls. Domino was her third only field operation, the first alongside Henderson, and she was warming to Six, as it was to her, despite her being confused by just about everyone for an American. This was despite her parents' best efforts, for although they were English she had grown up in the coastal city of Everett in North Washington State after her father had taken a job for Boeing there in 1990, aiding in the design of the twin-engined 777. At the university of London she'd scraped a first in Russian and Politics at Queen Mary then fallen into the civil service and spent thirteen years in Whitehall as senior administrator for the Ministry of Justice until applying for MI6 in July

2018.

She rolled her wrist to see her watch again and wished she was back staring out to sea on the banks of Port Gardner in the silence of a golden evening, watching the sailing boats bob gently on the calm emerald waters of Possession Sound.

The image vanished with the snapping shut of laptops and sudden gabble of goodbyes. Outside in the van, John Henderson gave the order to stand-by.

With Zoe close behind, Fisher weaved herself through the suits, caught the first lift to the ground floor, stepped into a waiting taxi, and was driven back to the Amigo.

Outside on the street, in the back of the van on his uncomfortable bench seat, Henderson listened as Fisher made two phone calls from her room. The first was to Jacques, whose tone made it obvious his wife was present in the room. After she had hung up he continued bumbling awkwardly, 'quite, well, absolutely, yes, thanks for letting me know. Yes, we can discuss it further tomorrow. Goodbye, Charles.'

The second was to a number registered in Lille, a first since the intercepts had begun. A woman's voice answered with a simple 'Oui?'.

'I'm thinking of booking a gîte for next July.'

'I have vacancies for August between the twentieth and thirtieth.'

'All right, I'll try somewhere else, goodbye.'

'An address in Prague old town,' Stef said from the front seat as he pulled the phone away from his ear. 'Nothing on file.' The rear door opened and Thomas climbed in, followed by Fisher's first taxi driver, then Zoe.

It was an hour after the sun had gone down

when she appeared at the hotel's front entrance. Henderson tailed on foot as she entered La Grand Place on its south side and crossed the shining cobblestones towards the grand neo-Gothic Musée de la Ville. Without warning, she broke away and disappeared into a small dark alley to the north. Zoe, facing the window of a lace shop, picked her up. She doubled back again, entering the narrow Rue de la Colline, lined with chocolatiers, cafe tables, small pubs and jewellery shops. Thomas was at the end of it. She walked at pace for twenty minutes making abrupt changes of direction in attempts to shake any tail she may have picked up. At the apex of the busy T-junction on the corner of Rue de la Colline and Rue du Marche Aux Herbes she stopped and smoked two cigarettes next to a Roman column at the entrance to the luxury Galeries Royales St Hubert arcade, studying every face for the slightest stolen glance of her. She paid no attention to the man sitting with his back to her on a whicker chair beneath a burgundy awning belonging to Island Ice Cream parlour. He was eyeing her reflection in the window while stirring his pot of salted caramel. The moment she moved, the man, Thomas, spoke into his collar.

Le Faucon cafe's three rows of pavement tables were overflowing with patrons at eight o'clock when she arrived, shouldering her way past and moving quickly towards the bar on the back wall where she pulled up a stool and ordered a pastis. Outside, a creeping van stopped at the kerbside. Behind the tinted window, John Henderson was pointing a Canon 5D camera with 600 mm telephoto lens and polarising filter. He pulled the focus. The frame remained mostly unobscured for the ten minutes Fisher sat sipping her drink until a man in an anorak approached. He was closing an umbrella and seemed to be asking if he could sit beside her.

'Hello, who's our friend?' Henderson murmured with the press of the shutter.

Mid-forties with a wide, determined face, and the classic horseshoe pattern of red hair atop it, he scanned the menu too closely for a few minutes then got up to leave. Out on the street he flagged down a taxi, and it was as he was climbing in that Henderson noticed the faint outline of something small and oblong-shaped bulging out from inside the bottom of his umbrella.

'That was it, that was the pass,' said Henderson into the radio. 'It must have happened when he approached her with his back to us.'

With the van following, the taxi drove six kilometres south out of the city until it came to Avenue De Fré 66, 1180 Uccle, Belgium. By night, visibility to the property and its grounds was completely obscured from the road by a hundred yards of thick trees. But John Henderson knew exactly where they were.

MI6 had their answer.

With her head pressed against the window of her fifth floor apartment in the Koptevo district of Moscow, Katya Petrenko tried to blink away the tears. Natalya was sitting with a ragged teddy bear on the patterned carpet in front of the television and she didn't want her to see her in such distress, so she turned away when she felt the tears prickle her swollen eyes again. It was the second night he hadn't returned home, and the knot of fear in her stomach was tightening. She blew her nose and looked out across the communal area of the housing complex. In the last hour its perpetual bleakness had been disguised by night and now wore a sepia tint courtesy of the settling snow and cheap yellow street lamps. The rusted swings were still, the line of parked cars undisturbed, and other than a solitary hunched babushka sweeping a path to a door on the ground below, there was no sign of life at all.

There were four Khrushchyovkas that formed the complex: low cost, sixty-apartment blocks of grey, prefabricated concrete panels built in the 1960s under Nikita Khrushchev, each with five stories but no lift. The Petrenkos' basic living space measured just twenty-two square metres and consisted of a living room that doubled as a bedroom, a separate kitchen, and small bathroom. The ceilings were low, the walls were damp and, due to the nature of the construction, sound insulation was poor. In the stairwells, mothers like Katya would steer their children carefully around used needles as if through a minefield as they climbed the urine-smelling concrete stairwells.

A rapid-fire round of expletives erupted from next door. Katya squeezed her eyes shut. The Zelenkos were at it again - an elderly couple she knew had taken to drinking Boyaryshnik, a methanol-based bath lotion that replaced cheap vodka, which made them violent. She reached over and turned the television's volume up full to protect Natalya's innocent ears from the language. A rerun of a Victory Day parade blared out from the portable's speaker, but the massed military bands could barely compete with the threats and screams blazing through the thin walls. Katya looked over at the small cluster of Dmitri's plastic model aeroplanes that hung on fishing wire from the ceiling and imagined his long, pianist's fingers holding sections together waiting for the glue to set, or softly brushing paint in delicate swirls onto their noses and tails. *Where are you?*

In the kitchen she tried again. Still no reply. Tomorrow she would take a bus into the city to visit her uncle on Lubyanka Square. She didn't want to, but she was desperate.

3

A handful of early visitors were placing passports into sliding metal trays, being patted down with plastic paddles, and having their bags, wallets and briefcases X-rayed by joyless staff behind armoured glass as he swiped his card at the barrier. It was seven sharp when he stepped into the lift and pressed the button for the third floor inside the ochre granite Mayan temple-like building on the Albert Embankment.

Henderson often wondered what it would have been like to arrive for work at 54 Broadway, the home of the SIS between 1926 and 1964, feeling he belonged more to that secret past than to the more public present. He found it ridiculous that MI6 headquarters today was a tourist attraction, a highly conspicuous Fortress on the Thames, famous around the world, whereas during the second world war the only way of identifying the inhabitants of Broadway Buildings to those in the know was a brass plaque stating Minimax Fire Extinguisher Company. Security then meant the janitor in his box knew your name and you knew his. Where after his greeting you'd rattle up in one of the ancient cage lifts or climb the creaky wooden staircase towards a labyrinth of secret rooms, offices divided by wooden partitions and frosted glass, all connected by hallways and corridors with fish-eyed mirrors on the walls. Where the fog of cigarette smoke mingled with the smell of hair lotion, ink, and tea, and the soundtrack was the constant clatter of typewriters, the squeal of heavy filing cabinet drawers opening and being slammed shut, the clinking of china cups on saucers, and the tapping of secretaries' heels across floorboards.

Yet no amount of longing for the dusty cloaks and decayed daggers of the Service's past could change what greeted him every morning: A building whose eleven above-ground floors were populated by anonymous, antiseptic meeting rooms of leather and steel, open-plan offices and conference rooms identifiable only by acronyms on doors and whose five floors below ground (whose corridors he rarely darkened) housed the command centre, central processors, data wiring stations and computer mainframes, various laboratories, workshops and technical areas, security systems and cipher and communications area.

He reached his office, once spacious, now crammed with heavy bookshelves whose bulging folders and files surrounded and threatened the office's only vestige of the present — a desktop computer. Columns of books had performed a gradual invasion of the floor, led by Marx, Lenin, Gorky and Gorbachev - their spines displaying subjects such as Imperialism, Revolutionary Theory, Capitalism, Trotskyism, the Cold War, and the KGB - and were keeping uneasy company with Intelligence memoirs by Kalugin, Litvinenko, and Navalny. The once bare green baize board was now a thick forest of haphazardly pinned paper, while still managing to peek through was the Christmas card with the Russian proverb "the quieter you go, the further you'll get" printed on its front in Cyrillic letters and signed inside some years before by members of a department long-since disrupted by progress. His office reminded him of his politics professor Chapman's study at St Anthony's that was so overburdened with books the old man would insist you took a pile with you each time you left. How it looked to others inside such an otherwise slick, automated, minimalist building, he could only guess. Fusty and anachronistic, probably. Of course he knew how it looked to Stephen Jones-Cooper. Perhaps it was the masochist in him but he was tempted to hang a *Lenin Lives* poster behind his desk, just to seal his fate and be done with it.

He turned over a newspaper. "Russian Submarines Constantly Circling Britain's Coastline" announced the headline, as if he didn't know. He pushed it aside and began to finger the fresh pile of papers a staff officer had left for him the night before while he was on the Eurostar. With the train in the tunnel he'd considered S-Section's latest recruit, wondered how long she would last under the current regime, counting in his head the officers his section had lost so far in the cull — those who had been relocated, retired, replaced, in the name of 'restructuring'. He had few allies left. Kesterton the long-standing loyal comrade, Faulds too at a push, but the rest had gone. Quibell: sent to Tottenham. Knowles, Maddox: snatched up by the cousins in Langley and testicular cancer respectively — no one was sure which was worse. Pelletier: Washington, then dead under a Berlin tram only weeks before retirement. All that remained were Jones-Cooper's crawlers — the 'new strain'. Classroom-bred, risk-averse graduates whose instincts had been trained out of them. Encouraged to spy by the book from desks in the air-conditioned glass castle. Zoe Taylor was different. She was strong-willed, independent, but moreover she knew her history, which had immediately attracted her to him during her recruitment.

She'd been heavily pregnant on that afternoon they'd strolled along the Thames Path on the Albert Embankment with Vauxhall Bridge behind them. He'd asked what she knew of the Illegal's network. Passing another Dolphin lamp on its granite plinth, she'd responded without hesitating. 'The most prized of all intelligence officers. Sleeper agents operating in deep cover in all walks of life on both European and American soil. Seemingly ordinary men and women deeply ingrained into society — legally documented, law-abiding, invisible. Since the USSR's collapse in ninety-one, with the days of hazardous journeys through Asia or the Middle East to arrive in Europe over and the availability of direct flights from Moscow to Heathrow in what, just over three hours, their numbers have increased exponentially. A network that was estimated to be a few hundred in the mid-eighties is now thought to be into the many thousands.' She needed to sit. They continued talking on one of the swan benches, pausing only when joggers or passers by came within earshot. With one hand cradling her swollen stomach while the other gripped the cast iron swan-shaped arm she'd continued, and it wasn't just textbook stuff learned by rote either, she'd displayed a true understanding of the Illegal's Program and believed it as germane today as it had been thirty years ago. Many of the new strain would scoff at the suggestion that something so anachronistic as an Illegal was still relevant in today's high-tech, digital world of espionage. Others knew better, however.

Knew they were still out there in even greater numbers, woven deeply into the fabric of society but that exposing them often meant political fallout and public scandal that did more harm than good. Something Jones-Cooper wouldn't comprehend.

Spies were for turning, not for exposing, after all.

Her university Russian was excellent if rusty, but he was persuaded that she could be the ally he needed in his own section. Jones-Cooper would likely try to turn her against him of course, but Henderson had a feeling Zoe Taylor was no-one's pushover, and that with her he would fail.

He picked up a document — an email from a senior analyst friend over at GCHQ.

From: D. Hedges
To: J. Henderson
Subject: squirt

Hello John,
Trust you're keeping well. Thought I'd bring it to your attn as head of S that we intercepted a transmission today at 18.00 that may be of interest. Came from an ex-Soviet transmitter - Kolikovo. Seems it's gone active again for the first time since 1989. Broadcast on the 4625 kHz frequency, one you probably remember more fondly as good old UVK-71!!! No prelude or identifier like before in the good days of old, just a single data burst in morse. Nothing since — in the event we'll keep you updated of course.
Message reads: GUDLD FPSWQ BHJCD SDALR HDKBS
We've run it through everything but, as predicted, drawn a blank.
Do drop by the next time you're in our neck of the woods.

All the best, David.

Kolikovo. That was a name he hadn't thought about in years. The old gulag. Abandoned, like they all were after Stalin's death in the early fifties. But Kolikovo was where the GRU built a giant transmitter in the sixties — used all the way up until eighty-nine. UVK-71 was the original identifier when the frequency was a number station. Stuff of legend, he smiled to himself, before filing it away in his head and getting on with preparing the Domino brief.

Zoe pushed two photographs across 'C's wide polished table for the assembled heads to view. The chief's office was on the same floor as Henderson's but the only thing the two spaces shared in common was the sealed, triple-glazed green windows. This was a vast art-filled room dominated by a huge work by the abstract expressionist artist Patrick Heron that hung on the far wall. One of the perks of chiefdom was being able to take your pick from the government's art collection.

'Charlotte Fisher,' Henderson said, 'aged twenty-seven. Parliamentary assistant to Morris Jacques MP. Last night she passed top secret intelligence to this man, Yuri Bosnik, known SVR agent in the Brussels rezidentura.'

There was a collective sigh of exasperation. To the letter this was what 'C' didn't want. "Don't give me another scandal to bury," the Cabinet Secretary had bemoaned on the phone only minutes before, "there's no more room in the ground." Sir Humphrey's weak heart couldn't handle much more unwelcome news. Squinting down through his half moon titanium glasses, 'C' considered how to break it to his friend.

Like many a Thorpe male ancestor from his

distinguished military family before him, the chief of the secret service, most agreed, possessed the appearance of a grey eagle: the knotted bridge to the nose, sharply angled eyelids, and the flat, slate coloured hair. Going back centuries Thorpe men were Oxford men, Marlborough College in his case, from which he graduated after a childhood spent in The Black Forest under the tutelage of a succession of nannies with names like Griselda, hired for their directness, respect for structure and organisation, linguistic ability, and love of swimming and the outdoors. A proverbial tap on the shoulder in an oak-panelled study would later lead to stints in Central Europe and South America where he recruited networks under cover as a lecturer, and then the Middle East and Afghanistan, before becoming head of counter-intelligence in 2008, Assistant Chief in 2011, and Chief in 2015.

To 'C's left was Sir Nigel Williams, Chair of the Joint Intelligence Committee, and to his right Sir David Hall, Director General of MI5, Six's sister service that from Thames House on the opposite bank of the Thames deals with domestic intelligence and security. He was only really present as Jacques had recently been photographed with the leader of a group of far-right activists called Andrew Bullen - someone the papers dubbed Bulldog and described as a "Muslim-hating extremist"; a former Tory activist banned from the party after allegations he tweeted Islamophobic comments online only days before the stabbing of a man during the call to prayer in a mosque near Regents Park. Hall was a new broom, a silk-shirt keen to demonstrate how serious he took the stirring of racial hatred by being here this morning despite his dislike for those he like many of his ilk privately called TSAR, Those Shits Across the River.

The egg-shaped man with sunken, jealous eyes and wispy ginger hair next to Sir David was Six's Assistant Chief, Stephen Jones-Cooper. He was jowly, but not noble-looking like the bloodhound he imagined himself to be, merely fleshy. He was rolling his expensive pen and regarding Henderson with a scurrilous eye that he would swap for an obsequious smile when any other man around the table spoke.

'Jacques, as well as being MP for North East Somerset,' Henderson continued, 'is a member of the Common's Defence Committee and the European Security and Defence Assembly so he's party to highly classified material. Fisher's been working him, sorry, Freudian slip, working *for* him, since June. Six days ago the amount of sensitive information requested by his office suddenly surged. Discrepancies in both the photocopying and the session logs flagged it up.'

Zoe took over, pushing several folders across the desk. 'Information such as inventory of Britain's nuclear arsenal, details of plutonium and enriched uranium outside of international safeguards, locations of submarine bases worldwide, and the future of Trident.'

In concerned silence the three mature men in their finely cut suits leafed through the logs, the irregularities in which were highlighted by circles of red ink.

Modern methods for modern times, Zoe remembered her instructor saying during the New Entry Course at Fort Monckton training centre two summers before when in a chilly classroom on the edge of England she had learned of the rigorously meticulous electronic and physical access records that exist to protect against the theft of sensitive material. The Crypto-Intelligence class had been taken by an instructor called Crowther, whom in Tattersall and corduroy looked for all the world to her like he'd stepped right out of a BBC Bletchley Park biopic. Presiding over an overhead projector he'd pronounce in clipped English, 'Every document marked top secret or above that requires a physical printed copy inside the building is printed with a laser printer that secretly embeds tiny yellow dots onto it so it can be traced back to its source.' She couldn't help but smile remembering the slide that showed three enlarged yellow dots on the screen. 'These *tiny* dots,' he'd say, 'although invisible to the human eye, contain a serial number, and *that* number contains details of where and when the document was printed. This information must match the number on the electronic log taken by the printers and photocopiers inside MI6, and this also means that every physical document created also has an electronic trace.' Then a slide showing a shredder, she remembered, as if without the visual aid they'd all be left in the wilderness. 'Once viewed, hard copies are shredded, an action that is electronically logged by the shredder. Meaning if a stray top secret document leaves the building, it flags up as a discrepancy for investigation. And if more documents are printed or photocopied than are shredded, this also means there's an obvious breach. If, on the other hand, an officer with the appropriate clearance wishes to view the file electronically, first he must log on and pass security before beginning the session. His sessions are logged and recorded — this may include the downloading of a PDF from a sensitive server or sharing emails between cleared parties — but these electronic files too carry metadata that can trace them back to the source.'

What each man was looking at now beneath heavy frowns was the irrefutable evidence that someone in Morris Jacques' Common's office had illegally downloaded twenty-four documents marked 'TS' onto an external hard drive over the six day period in question.

'Damage?' ventured Williams.

'The breach was noticed almost straight away, Sir Nigel, thanks to the technology in place, so we were able to scramble quickly and feed her false documents after the initial four were downloaded on the sixteenth — that was last Friday. Those four were very sensitive, however. They outlined strategic weapons systems to be used in the Dreadnought Class subs. So we contacted Lockheed Martin, who builds the Trident D5's, and worked with a team there and with the MoD over the weekend to try to muddy the water, so to speak. As a result, when the downloads resumed on Monday the intel she was getting was all false. Luckily we didn't have to wait for very long for her to make her move. We put round the clock surveillance on both her and Jacques last weekend, four teams of watchers, phone taps and internet, and last night in Brussels she made the drop.'

'I thought it wise to sanction surveillance right away, Sir Clive.' Jones-Cooper interjected, attempting to claim any glory that might be in the offing. Actually his tight grip on S-section's budget meant he'd been against such surveillance from the beginning.

'God, not another one,' groaned Williams, 'aren't these people vetted?'

'She was, her background's impeccable,' said

Zoe, passing the file across the table for him to read. 'Charlotte Fisher, born in High Wycombe, Buckinghamshire, 2nd April 1993, only daughter of Alex Fisher and Suzanne Lander - both died in a car accident in 1997 in Aylesbury. Brought up by her aunt on her mother's side, Hayley Lander, in Guildford, Surrey. Graduated with English BA (Hons) from the University of Leicester in 2013 then an MSc in International Public Policy at University College London in 2015. Assistant to various MP's before joining Jacques' office in June.'

'C' studied her photograph. She was pretty, this traitor. Easy to see how Jacques with his reputation in the halls of Parliament would be inclined to employ her. The old letch had narrowly escaped public disgrace by the deft wielding of Sir Humphrey's shovel on more than one occasion already. He opened the MP's file. Morris Jacques: 58, married in 1982 to Lady Cecilia Forbes-Bailey, daughter of Major-General Cecil Forbes-Bailey, Viscount of Ascott, whose own mother was lady-in-waiting to Queen Elizabeth, the Queen Mother. Two children: Michael - a barrister, Sarah — BBC television chef, author of a bewildering amount of bestselling vegan cookbooks and media darling.

Christ, he thought, sliding the file back into its folder, another bloody dagger in the belly. Minor royals, resignations, political scandal, a blood-thirsty press, tarnished legal reputation, the BBC . . . it went on. The MP was in it up to his salmon and cucumber all right. He looked like a Garrick man.

'And they're definitely . . . ' Sir David looked for the least incorrect term, and, as a lady was present, chanced upon, 'at it?'

'The surveillance logs contain evidence to

suggest an affair took place, but we don't believe it has continued.' Henderson replied.

'Illegal?' asked the DG of Five.

'We don't think so.' Zoe answered. 'Her identity's watertight. Facial recognition, mobile phone history, social media, it all checks out. She even had a DNA test while at Leicester.'

'Isn't that how it's all supposed to look, *Ms* Taylor?' Williams said in a condescending tone. 'Her parents die in a car accident. Couldn't the real Charlotte Fisher have also perished and someone paid the local church to lose the death certificate?'

'We think she is who she claims to be.'

'Also a hunch,' Henderson said, causing Jones-Cooper to roll his eyes skyward. 'For one thing she's an amateur. No tradecraft — the Watchers all said the same.'

'I've deemed it prudent to continue our round-the-clock surveillance on both her and Jacques until we know more,' Jones-Cooper interrupted, turning to Henderson to add, 'just in case you're wrong, John.'

Detecting the usual spite in his assistant chief, 'C' let the comment hang in the air. He wondered where the thinly veiled disdain came from. Henderson could be terse, it was true, superior to the point of condescending even, but sometimes the combination of a robust intellect, an intolerance for the petty, and plain speaking in a born field-man like him produced a cocktail a little too potent for a desk warrior like Jones-Cooper. He supposed they were just opposites. John was a shy man really, like many a good spy — a shadow-dweller cocooned in a laborious, unspectacular and plodding world by a closely guarded anonymity. Jones-Cooper on the other hand wore naked ambition and a thrusting desire for self advancement on his sleeve. The privilege his AC aspired to Henderson eschewed, as he did anything elitist or highbrow, thoroughly despising what he considered the "bigotries of the ruling classes" or any whiff of an affectation. 'C' personally thought his head of section could swap the careworn corduroy for a decent suit and get away with it but beyond that he had no criticism of the man. Of course he knew the real reason his AC didn't like John - and that was that he just wouldn't kiss his arse. Quite why he seemed to have developed a personal feud with him though, he didn't know.

The men closed the files in silence and waited for him to speak. 'Gentlemen,' he said, then with a polite tilt of the eagle-like head he turned to Zoe indicating her inclusion without feeling the need to add *and lady*. 'Utmost discretion is required, at least until we may learn more. I propose we pay our right honourable member of parliament a little visit to see how much he really knows about his *assistant*.'

Jones-Cooper had to hurry to catch up with them in the corridor. 'This bug you broke into a woman's hotel room to plant, John. Bit reckless. Irresponsible risk I would've thought. Does what, exactly?'

Zoe sensed she should answer . 'It's the latest in crypto-surveillance tech. Means we can read everything on any device it's inserted into. So when certain keywords are entered into that device, on a desktop computer for example, laptop, external drive, it sends out an encrypted signal which is picked up by GCHQ that they then decrypt and send back to us.'

'Who chose the keywords?'

'I did,' said Henderson, stopping.

'Well, I hope you stuck to the point.' He announced loudly while marching forward as if he had somewhere to be, leaving Zoe to notice the embarrassment register in John's eyes and to wonder if the brazen querulous manner was reserved only for him.

Katya tried again. She had used the time to try to call her husband nine or ten times now. There'd been no answer, but it was still ringing, there was still hope. A shiver went through her again. Her feet were soaked and weren't drying. The walk to the bus stop at Komsomolets, Cinema, had taken an hour and by the time she arrived there her cheeks were blue from the bitter wind. She'd then spent thirty minutes overheating on a crowded bus until twenty-three stops later it arrived at Teatral'naya Square close to the Bolshoi Theatre where she'd walked the last fifteen minutes to Lubyanka Square. Having passed through security, a junior officer with a black eye had accompanied her to the third floor where he told her to wait on the end of a row of chairs in the corridor at 9:45 a.m. At 11:30 she was still there wishing she could dry off, every moment willing her husband to hear her calls.

Answer, she begged, gripping the phone.

Inside his office General Grushenko was listening to the periodic muffled rings of her dead husband's phone coming from his safe. He had been staring at it for nearly two hours, in an attempt to organise the slowly scattering pattern of lies.

His private office was stale and oblong, sparsely furnished and dominated both by a huge antique desk he'd had brought over from The Aquarium, as the GRU building is known, and by the large safe bolted to the far wall. Eight feet in height with both a mechanical dial lock and electronic keypad mounted upon it's six inch thick titanium door, it was state-of-the-art. It was also useful as a high enough surface upon which to secrete numerous bottles of vodka. Finally, he straightened, walked through to the outer office and instructed his secretary to show the woman in, then for her to leave them.

When Katya, clutching her phone, entered the sombre room he barely recognised her. The young, elfin face he remembered seemed to have aged twenty years. She'd clearly been crying a great deal, her eyes were all bloodshot and swollen, and she looked like she'd walked from Siberia. The coat, a cheap-brand windbreaker, was thin, patently inadequate for Moscow winters, and her long blond hair with black roots clung to her head like damp straw.

He cleared his throat of phlegm and addressed the bedraggled figure in front of him. 'Katya, my dear, I'm sorry you had to wait. Would you like to sit down?' He raised a finger to the club chairs near the windows.

From beside his secretary's desk, she stared, unable to ignore the smell of stale booze that clung to him like old petrol. Something caught her eye: a janitor's cart with a mop bucket hooked on to it, by the wall. Was it his? Was it here her husband drew his last free breath? Grushenko, seeing her looking at it, bit his lip, cursing inwardly.

Choking back her tears, in a frail voice she said, 'Where is he? Two days. He has vanished. Where is he? Where is my Dmitri?'

He coughed again. 'I was going to wait until we

knew more before I told you, Katya. I'm afraid I have been on the telephone to the Police all morning . . . ' He gripped his knuckles tightly and stared down at them, fabricating the deception he'd been rehearsing. 'I'm very sorry. I don't know how to tell you this. But there was an automobile accident. A car he was driving, near Yaroslavl. Dmitri is dead. I'm sorry. I've only just been informed.'

She listened to her uncle. To the deep rasp of his voice. Watched him in his thick, grubby uniform desperately acting, hopelessly grasping for realism, and at once she was surer than she'd ever been about anything that he was lying through his stained teeth. 'When?'

'We don't know yet. We're doing all we — '

'Yaroslavl?' she interrupted, 'What was he doing in Yaroslavl?'

'Secret work. For me. I'm sorry but I can't tell you any more than that.'

'I want to see him.'

'I'm afraid that's impossible. The body was very badly burned.'

Lies. Disgusting lies. Secret work? How could he even think of saying such revolting things? But when it dawned on her why the general would lie, tears began tumbling from her eyes uncontrollably and rolling in streams down her cheeks. She knew at that moment that he himself, this man, her own blood relative, had killed Dmitri, or had ordered him dead. It was then that her world splintered and fell apart. She didn't remember turning away from him, falling to her knees and sobbing right there in his office. Nor walking away from the building and across the square. For from that moment on she suddenly found herself submerged in a sea of unimaginable grief, gasping for air, kicking against the raging current.

He had waited awkwardly for her to pick herself up and leave before retreating back to his office where he swivelled the three-pronged handle and heaved the safe door open. Reaching inside he removed two objects. The first was the cell phone, which he pocketed. The second: the miniature Leica camera. At his secretary's desk he arranged a few documents into neat order before photographing them several times. Afterwards he removed the camera's memory card and dropped it into a plain, sealed envelope, just as Dmitri had told Savich was his routine. Later that night, somewhere in the early hours when the traffic had thinned down and night's cover had fallen, he would drive out to the Bolshoy Ustyinskiy Bridge. Once beneath it on its south side he would look for a paint stroke on one of the second columns in from the road, (Dmitri had said there were five), leave the envelope behind it, and throw the phone into the river.

4

The secure line went dead and Igor Savich replaced the receiver. The call from the defence minister had lasted two hours and he was tired as very old men often are. He clicked open the ornate silver pill box, never far from his side, and removed a tablet. The angina was worsening, and the nitrate tablets didn't seem to be helping anymore, still, the tablet went down with a sip of water and he breathed heavily, feeling the log fire's heat reddening his deeply wrinkled face. He was comfortable here, wanted to die here. The exclusive dacha complex of Peredelkino had been his home for decades and he had seen the littérateurs give way to the new rich, yet like an old oak impervious to gusts of changing winds, he remained. Pasternak had written Dr. Zhivago three houses down, and as a young man he'd exchanged pleasantries with the elderly poet, then in his final year of life.

He glanced over at the chess board, letting his mind wander back to other distant days, those spent sitting opposite General Secretary Brezhnev at that very board. Somewhere in the industry boom years of the sixties they'd met while hunting and regularly got drunk together playing the game beneath the fog of strong cigarette smoke that followed the then Soviet leader wherever he went. In those days many believed supremacy at the chess board symbolised Soviet superiority over the capitalist West, though these days he cared less for such notions, feeling the game's comparisons to a military campaign were misguided. In chess, every piece is visible and the player may base his strategy upon his opponent's moves. You may know everything about him. But in battle there is no black and white, only the grey of secrets, and Savich was tired of grey. Recently, he had begun to feel a lifetime of secrets eating away at him, slowly consuming him. Strategic planning required energy, and despite having spent the last two hours assuring the Minister that all preparations were in place, he knew his levels were running low.

The newly formed Directorate would meet on Monday evening to finalise the details, giving him the weekend to prepare. It was time for an old man's afternoon nap, but not before he placed another call. It was to the signalman, Krupin, who awaited orders in a cold radio room in an old gulag. 'Message reads: Proceed to phase one,' he said, before hanging up the phone and drifting off to sleep in front of his waning log fire.

Less than thirty minutes later the two-thousand feet tall radio mast was transmitting the encrypted message on the same 4625 kHz frequency via its powerful two-megawatt towers. Inside his cramped and archaic radio room next to a three-bar fire and surrounded by Soviet-era radio equipment, Krupin had encrypted Savich's telephone instruction with the one-time-pad and sent the message at once. This time he had used a reel-to-reel quarter inch tape machine and an electronic synthesiser, as instructed, and had confirmed that this new number method with musical identifier at the top and tail of the transmission would be adopted for all future communication. He didn't know what "phase one" referred to, or whom the message was meant for — he wasn't supposed to. All he knew was he was bloody miserable. He pulled the headphones down around his neck and began thinking about the vodka-soaked game of poker he'd played with the two sentry guards the night before, and how tonight he'd try to win the money back, which cheered him up a bit. It also crossed his mind whether he should ask either of them if they knew a way of getting some girls up to the camp from the nearest village, wherever the hell that was.

The small paper sheet atop the Murano smoked-glass ashtray fluttered briefly before becoming engulfed in flames and burning quickly into a mound of fine black ash. A man's hand placed a gold lighter on the veneer next to it. Further into the room, resting inharmoniously upon a Sheraton chest of drawers was a short wave radio, a Grundig Satellit 750 model, that emitted a series of low, distorted beeps with an underlying buzzing sound. The figure walked over and switched it off. He then moved over to a drinks cabinet where he poured himself an inch of dark brown liquid and stood in front of a large abstract painting on the wall. He stayed there, staring at the painting for a good few minutes until finally he moved silently away and disappeared from the room.

The receipt of the second transmission by those who could not decipher it was met with different reactions in different quarters. Inside his glass office inside GCHQ David Hedges immediately sat down to type a second email to Henderson in a more urgent tone than the last, stating that a second transmission had been intercepted on the UKV-71 station from the same transmitter on the same frequency and at 18:00 hrs GMT precisely. However, he wrote, the squirt of morse had now been replaced by a fully fledged number transmission that featured a five note musical identifier followed by a lifeless-sounding female voice that began by reading code words, then a seemingly random list of numbers. Mp3 file attached.

By contrast meanwhile, in the attic room in Brottby, like many of his kind around the world, some were positively apoplectic with excitement.

Henderson read Hedge's email first thing Friday morning, wondering why, with all the modern, sophisticated digital methods of communication out there today they would reactivate a giant radio tower like Kolikovo and broadcast an analogue numbers station. The answer jabbed at the old wound deep within him, never allowed to heal. He clicked the mp3 file and listened closely. A few seconds of random electronic noise was broken first by a hurried increase of fluctuating electrical voltages, then by an ascending scale played on what sounded like a Moog-type synthesiser. After one five-note musical phrase, a distant, detached female voice began reading:

'PAPA ECHO CHARLIE NOVEMBER 254 254 254 PAPA ECHO CHARLIE NOVEMBER 254 254 254 1 8 2 1 8 2 22 18 2 18 2 22 . . .'

Several minutes passed before the voice ceased, the same five-note synth phrase repeated once and the transmission ended. He decided to call Hedges. He'd forgotten how passionately the man spoke about his subject, every sentence relayed like a man announcing an exciting new discovery to the Royal Society.

'Very little infrastructure required you see, John. For long-distance two-way communications shortwave is about the most robust means there is. Doesn't rely on satellites or internet — all you need is a pair of transceivers, each with an antenna, and a source of energy. And of course you know that the one-time pad is still today the holy grail of encryption thanks to it being virtually unbreakable.'

The word surprised him. 'Virtually?'

Hedges laughed, 'Ha, no, we haven't got there yet. No, I meant it only works if the numbers *are* truly random. So if machines are used to produce the pads they use an algorithm that can be broken, but otherwise . . . '

'What about tracking the receiver?'

'They emit a bit of unwanted signal but you'd have to be at very close range.'

'And what about jamming?'

'Possible, but they'll always have parallel frequencies as back up so from an operational perspective you not only let the enemy know you're onto them but you just end up chasing them across the frequency band.'

'All right. Look, David, I don't think for a moment we have a chance of decrypting the numbers but I know you'll keep trying. Okay, bye.'

After a few minutes he picked up the phone again and asked to be put through to the Moscow station on the secure line. When Finn answered in his eager twenty-three year old's first overseas posting voice, John asked to speak to the Second Secretary, and a few seconds afterwards when another voice said,

'Sam Donavon', he asked him if he'd heard any murmurings about Kolikovo. The man inside the building at Smolenskaya Embankment, known to a few inside S-Section as Carlo, claimed he hadn't. There followed the usual awkward silence, which Henderson soon ended by thanking him and hanging up, before turning his mind to a pressing question he imagined MI6 would be grateful of an answer to, which was why a nice girl from Buckinghamshire would want to spy for the Russians?

When the Range Rover pulled away from its space outside the luxury stucco townhouse on Eaton Place in London's elegant Belgravia district, the man at the wheel of a dark grey Citroën parked opposite turned the key. It was a dark, drizzly morning of the unpredictable type London is known for, and as the Range Rover circled Hyde Park Corner and was signalling left to join Park Lane, the heaven's fully opened and the man following at a safe distance almost lost sight of it through the Citroën's misted windscreen. Having sped up, he regained sight of the 4x4, which through heavy rain he tailed into Marylebone, through St John's Wood, and then north towards the M1, able to catch a furtive glimpse of the driver's famous profile in the rear view mirror each time the sun found it.

Minutes later at Brent Cross the driver of the Range Rover pressed the pedal down hard and the car surged away onto the M1, leaving the man in the Citroën to continue straight on the North Circular and head back into central London.

Two taps came on Henderson's door. It was

Kesterton, phone pressed into his chest. 'John, Jacques is on the move.'

'Where?'

'Wife's country pile in Bedfordshire for the weekend. With a Lucy Penhaligon.'

'Who?'

'Parliamentary assistant to Aavrav Khan MP. Luton South.'

Bloody hell, the man had women all over the place. 'When's he due back?'

'Sunday morning. For his wife's birthday lunch at the Ham Polo Club in Richmond.'

He thought for a moment. A frustrating delay. 'All right, Brian. Tell the teams to stand-by in case he comes back early. Looks like we'll pick him up on Sunday then.'

Kesterton acknowledged him and retreated back to the corridor, leaving him to concentrate on Charlotte Fisher's file.

Firstly, her history: Parents. The father was a man who sold private pensions for Allied Dunbar while the mother had worked in an antique furniture shop in High Wycombe before becoming a full time housewife when only child Charlotte was born in 1993. Their backgrounds were unremarkable. Then the accident in 1997. Nothing unusual about it, according to the Thames Valley Police report. On a quiet country lane on the way home from a friend's house party in the early hours their Ford Mondeo left the road due to a combination of mildly excessive speed, a moonless night, and non-existent street lighting and hit some unforgiving trees. Father was driving. No other vehicles involved. Within the legal limit of 80 mg of alcohol and no trace of drugs found in his system, no history of unrest between them, no unusual effects in their pockets, car was clean. The girl, aged four, went to live with her aunt, a Hayley Lander, the mother's younger sister, who took in her orphan niece and raised her single-handedly when she herself was only seventeen.

Hayley Lander. Born: High Wycombe, 1980. Nine years younger than her sister. Single, never married. Works in a hairdressers in Guildford called *Prince's*. Electoral records show that apart from the years with her niece, she's always lived alone.

He considered the many motives for betraying one's country and the oft-quoted acronym, courtesy of the CIA: MICE: Money, Ideology, Compromise, (or Coercion), and Ego, (or Extortion). The Americans, they say, always turn for money, the Brits are ideologues. What, he wondered, was her motivation? Her bank account shows no large deposits, her past no clues that would inspire pro-Russian sympathies in her, no criminal record. So why?

At three o'clock precisely a man and a woman dressed in the plain grey uniform of the British Gas Board walked into Durham Close, a narrow cul-de-sac in the Woodbridge Hill area just to the north of the centre of Guildford, and towards number eight, a two-bedroomed semi-detached property with a low wrought-iron gate that led to a white PVC front door. Confident in uniforms that arouse little suspicion if spotted by inquisitive neighbours, the couple walked directly down the side of the house and around into the back garden where, once at the UPVC back door, the woman picked the Chubb lock, allowing them to enter.

While she began searching the house for electronic devices, the man started photographing as much as he could in the few minutes they'd allotted themselves. On the walls of the hallway there were several photographs of Charlotte Fisher - gap-toothed at school, aged about five with the aunt and a young man, one as a baby being held by her parents, and a later image of her in her teens that was lit like a semi-professional modelling headshot. The man photographed them all with his mobile phone.

He walked through into the kitchen then on into the living room where the woman was placing a bug into the receiver of a landline telephone. He scanned the bordered damask wallpaper, peach — coloured floral sofa, black shelving units, and the monolithic rear-projection television set that jutted out onto the carpet and decided the room looked like it had been preserved in time, an homage to the 90's. He moved towards a single framed photograph on a shelf. It was of a girl of ten, and was centred in an overly ornate gold baroque frame. Without touching it, he photographed it.

'No computers at all. Not even a laptop,' said the woman sounding surprised. The man didn't react, but made his way back out into the hall. At the foot of the stairs he spotted another photograph on the wall. It was larger than the others, also in a frame, and was of a young man in army service dress, wearing a navy blue beret, and looking away to one side of the camera. He photographed that too.

Having prowled around the upstairs bedrooms and bathroom and rifled through the closets, cupboards and drawers of each, he then joined his partner in the kitchen where they let themselves out the back door. Minutes later, with plain puffer coats now covering their uniforms and sitting in a car demonstrably not belonging to the Gas Board, the woman eased the vehicle away from the curbside while the man began uploading the photographs of the inside of Hayley Lander's house via secure server to a desk in S-Section.

Later, in the early hours of October 24th, when the temperature had fallen to below freezing, the weighted-down envelope was retrieved from beneath the bridge on the Moskva River. The following morning at 8:50 a.m. it was in the diplomatic bag in the belly of a 737 as Aeroflot flight SU 2576 waited on the runway at Sheremetyevo, and by 2 p.m. the contents, a camera card containing a series of twelve photographs, had been signed for and were waiting on Henderson's desk in London, having already been downloaded by the Technical Analysis section on the fifth floor.

Zoe had already been awake for two hours as she sat on the carpet watching cartoons with Joe at seven a.m. that Saturday morning. Paul had been left to cope for the last three days while she'd been working late into the evenings, so it was her turn to get up and do the *Jake and the Never Land Pirates' shift*, as they'd christened it.

They'd met five years before when as a freelance journalist he had come to the home of the Ministry of Justice that overlooks St James Park on Petty France to interview the Lord Chancellor for a piece about support for victims of terrorism. Zoe had facilitated the meeting, and they'd kept in touch, at first arranging to meet for lunch under the guise of work, but soon because they both realised they enjoyed each other's easy company. Paul was older than she was, and quiet, slight and bookish, unlike her previous boyfriends, and although he'd been married before, like her had long-since been single. For Zoe, whose nordic looks and lissome physique had always drawn male attention — something that had begun with the unwanted advances of her elder brother's arrogant friends at high school — it was a refreshingly uncomplicated coupling, made more comfortable by the fact that he seemed unburdened by jealousy. He trusted her, which in her experience was unusual and a sign of strength. Within a few months of their meeting they were living together in her flat in Crouch End, and Joe was born the week she found out she'd passed the entrance exam and had been security-cleared to start work for MI6. Paul stopped working to stay at home to look after Joe, and although it was a gradual process, it was then that Zoe's husband, quietly and without fuss or fanfare, assigned his life over to hers.

She would let him sleep in today, and they'd spend this Saturday together. Go to Alexandra Palace, sit on their coats on the grass with take-away coffees while watching Joe on the play area, eat sandwiches in the Lakeside cafe and then a wander home where she'd skim the Culture papers while Paul cooked them his famous roast dinner he would graciously bring forward a day to accommodate his wife's work schedule.

Henderson too had awoken early, forced himself to go for a run, and by seven he was leaning against his stove waiting for the coffee to boil. He didn't like exercising, but for the last few years had felt compelled to in a bid to ward off the spread that seemed to accompany middle-age. Later he'd fetch the Saturday papers. Taking them to a bench in Hyde Park was the extent of his Saturday mornings these days. A few years before they hadn't been too dissimilar to Zoe's - but that was before Sarah left. They'd take Leo to the park or zoo, or to their son's firm favourite, the London Sea-Life Aquarium where the ten-year-old's imagination soared. Most magical of all the exhibits was the Falkland Island penguins, the Gentoos, who'd frolic on their artificial glacier while the boy stood mesmerised. This was followed by ice cream in the park, by slow walks home, bath and bed for the boy, and wine and reading books in silence for them.

Eight years later and Sarah had traded them both for a French doctor and moved to Primrose Hill — somewhere so bourgeois she must have chosen it especially to twist the knife in — and the wide-eyed boy had turned into an eighteen-year-old thrash metal and cannabis addict who rarely left his bedroom.

It was too early but he made the effort despite it. 'Leo,' he ventured, knocking on his son's door. 'Want some coffee?'

An unusually short pause before the usual, predictable reply, 'I don't like your coffee.'
He thought about calling her to try to talk about their son and how strained communication had become, but then thought better of it. There had been days when he'd walk or take a bus up to Primrose Hill just to stand out of sight near the house — watching and waiting like he did every day at work — then follow them to see what restaurants they ate in, plays they saw, galleries they visited, what kind of friends they

had, all to try to discern what, precisely, he had failed to provide. But he hadn't done it recently. Only that summer he'd given up sniffing the sleeves of the dresses she'd left behind in the closet, but probably not for good.

He filled a flask with coffee and pulled on a jacket. Papers by the Serpentine then.

The Right Honourable Morris Jacques MP left the clubhouse of The Ham Polo club in Richmond with a conspicuous spring in his step during lunchtime on Sunday, pulling off his club tie and stuffing it into the pocket of his blazer as he went. He had excused himself from his wife's birthday table, around which were gathered her usual cronies, apologising profusely with phone in hand that due to some wretched emergency he'd have to hurry back to the office on urgent parliamentary business.

'On a Sunday?' his wife had exclaimed, her cheeks full of duck breast with chicory and potato dauphinoise.

'Yes, I know, blasted Defence Committee nonsense. Probably Bernard panicking over nothing but he's driving up from Croydon so apparently it can't wait until tomorrow. Sorry darling, I'll make it up. Happy birthday and all that. Sorry.'

'Probably just wants to get out of Croydon and who can blame him,' she quipped, inciting much laughter as he administered a dutiful peck on her bulging face.

In reality, even though they'd spent the last two nights together in the clandestine trysting spot of his wife's country house in Bedfordshire with only an elderly and half-blind gardener as witness, he was planning yet another afternoon liaison with the right honourable member for Luton South's twenty-five year old parliamentary assistant inside her Fulham flat. On occasion he was given to wonder why they all lived in Fulham.

Tall and fit and with a thick head of only slightly greying hair despite his fifty-eight years, Morris Jacques' enthusiasm for the ladies was profound, and he wasn't going to let a niggling little detail like his being married stifle it. He was possessed of a mild stoop that gave him a vaguely military bearing that some women find irresistible, and of a rakish charm and winning smile that he used to full effect in the labyrinth of corridors and passageways that lead to the secret rooms designed for indiscretions deep inside the palace of Westminster. Within the next two minutes, however, the famous smile would disappear.

Outside the grounds he shot a finger up at a cab that was parked in front of The Fox and Duck pub. It performed a U-turn and he climbed in.

'Elm Park Lane Mews, SW3.'

Before he could close the door John Henderson had climbed in and sat down beside him.

'What the hell? Excuse me, this one's taken.'

'Vauxhall Cross, please,' Henderson said to the driver.

'Now look here.'

'Hello, Mr Jacques. Mind if we talk?'

The car pulled out onto the Petersham Road.

'What the bloody hell is this?' snapped Jacques, 'and who the bloody hell are you?'

'Oh, don't worry, I'm on our side,' said Henderson. 'We'd like to have a little chat about your assistant, Miss Fisher. Her, you, and the Russian secret service agent she's been passing top secret NATO documents to.'

The blood drained from Jacques' face and his mouth dropped open.

'Oh, and don't worry about the driver, he's on our side too.'

In the rear view mirror the driver doffed his flat cap.

'The question is, whose side are you on, Mr Jacques?'

Behind the lemon yellow front door that matched the fascia boards of his bungalow in a satellite town to the North East of London, an elderly man put his pencil down on top of the crossword. He was usually able to complete it in under twenty minutes but since the postcard had arrived at 53 Peach Tree Close two days before he hadn't been able to concentrate on anything much. Being sober wasn't helping his powers of cognition, but he owed it to himself to be so. He removed his reading glasses and let his hollowed eyes be drawn to the wedding photograph that rested on the sideboard, of himself smiling back at him with thick, dark hair and skin so recently burnt by the Afghani sun. But a half a lifetime later the smile had long since been lost, the hair had become wispy and white, the skin pallid. The only thing that remained of the day was the suit, bought in a shop near Red Square before leaving for Kabul. Seventy-eight, that was. By 1980 it had all gone wrong.

He stared at Anne. Anne with her grooved smile. Wonderful, devoted, beguiled. There was so much she hadn't known. To her he'd been a real life revolutionary, not just one of the fair weather Communists from the district. But of course what she hadn't known was what a miserable failure he really was. How he'd been little more than a KGB legman, who, having been sent to Kabul, lost his nerve when all hell broke loose there and fled to Beirut before being threatened with desertion, forced to hand back his Russian passport and to return to see out his days in a coward's exile in rural Hertfordshire. But the Communist Party of Great Britain was in mortal decline and pickings were slim, and Anne Warwick had fallen for the new member with the much-embellished tales of derring-do, marrying him only a month after their first meeting. And now you're dead, he thought to himself. And I'm only half-alive. Seventy-eight, soaked in vodka whose days are spent in regret, swearing at and snoring in front of the television.

'*But*, dear Annie,' he continued to his dear, departed wife, waving a finger. 'It seems I am required.'

It had arrived hidden inside the usual mix of junk. On the front was a beautifully lit golden hour photograph of a medieval fortress — a castle upon a hill surrounded by lush green trees that overlooked a European old town, yet it was the text beneath the photograph that his eyes remained fixed upon for three whole minutes. *GREETINGS FROM LJUBLJANA*. From the fog of years, the memory had slowly emerged. At his side table he had used a penknife to remove the back of the postcard that revealed a location, date, and time. He had stared at that too.

Now, two days later, horribly sober, crossword abandoned, he rolled up his sleeves, went out to his garden shed to find a hammer, came back inside the house, and began to remove a large section of the bathroom wall.

At the top of five inconspicuous stone steps set back from the Thames footpath, a pair of shabby brown double doors opened and the two men entered. This entrance to the MI6 building is one of the most private, and as the officer had a famous Tory politician in tow, it was deemed more suitable than the more public, main visitor's entrance.

Henderson seated himself behind his chief, who turned over a photograph of the umbrella man, Bosnik, for Jacques to study. The MP was still clenching his jaw defiantly when 'C' spoke in a measured tone.

'Are you aware of the existence of this man, Mr Jacques?'

The MP looked down at the round face. 'No, who is he?'

The two intelligence men were watching his reaction carefully, Henderson deciding he was the worst of all sorts. Statesmanly, soldierly, diffident, supporters proclaimed. A man on the up. Destined for high-office to be sure. To those not so easily impressed by privilege, he was the kind of flashy, super-exec style politician people chose these days to represent them over the camera-shy, principled and scholarly men of yore, whose Eton vowels alone excused the flagrant lies to journalists' questions. But pit this smarmy playboy in blazer and slacks against 'C', thought Henderson, whose sharp, eagle's eyes could read every minute facial twitch, momentary glance, every imperceptible shift of a body in a chair, and whose ears could detect every little inaudible, guilty sniff of the nose or hesitant stutter in a voice — and he'd be done for. 'C' was more at home in an interrogation room than just about any other room you could think of, having spent his nearly forty-year career in various far-flung corners of the world relieving spies of information so craftily he'd practically turned it into an art form.

'Let's begin at the beginning, shall we? How, and where, did you first come into contact with Charlotte Fisher?'

'We met at a party. Said she was a looking for a job, so I hired her.'

'Very good,' smiled 'C' soothingly, as if congratulating a three year old upon forming his first proper sentence. He raised his eyebrows to invite him to continue.

'Look, I know, we started an affair. But you must understand, my wife, well I mean to say she doesn't, you know . . . I meant, she can't . . . ' he trailed off. 'Look, I'm not bloody proud of it.'

'When did it become clear to you she was working for Russian Intelligence?'

'I didn't know.'

'Didn't?'

He squirmed in his seat. 'No. Until - I tried to have her transferred three months ago.'

'Go on,' ushered 'C'.

He breathed in deeply through his nostrils. 'It was in Leipzig. I was at a trade fair, in August, bloody boring old thing but you know,' he snorted nervously, 'infrared, radar, bloody stand after stand of rescue equipment. Anyway I was approached by someone, probably a Russian - I mean, I suppose. Said he strongly advised that I should keep Charlotte on my staff and not have her transferred. I mean we weren't seeing each other by then, it'd just been a fling really but I thought, you know, better not to have her around.'

'And what did you say to this probable Russian?'

'Well I asked what business it was of his, and . . .'

'Yes?'

A weight appeared to descend upon the cornered man's brow.

'He said he had a video.'

'C' blinked slowly, 'What . . . sort of video?' he asked, though he needn't have, seeing the answer appear before his eyes in giant letters: *Kompromat* – material to compromise, that since time immemorial had been used to coerce, blackmail and extort.

Henderson's expression betrayed nothing, yet he, like 'C', was all too aware of the consequences of another looming scandal. Should his *Overture* report ever see the light of day it should probably be revised to include the allegations that Donald Trump had been blackmailed with compromising material collected on a visit to Moscow prior to the 2016 US elections, making him vulnerable to manipulation by the Russian government. Now a future British cabinet minister could be added also. Another victim of a honey trap.

But Charlotte Fisher was no swallow. It didn't add up.

Jacques addressed the table. 'It was taken in a hotel in Paris a few weeks beforehand. Normally we'd stay in the same one, but when she'd booked she said they only had one room available and that I should take it, that she'd take one in the Marais. It was there that we . . . '

'C' regarded him blankly.

'He showed me some, you know, screen-grabs on his phone as proof.' The MP looked up at 'C' like a helpless puppy. 'I'm afraid there's no doubt. Said that if I ever considered ending my professional relationship with Charlotte that he'd make sure the video got, you know, seen.'

'And you didn't think of coming to us?'

'Of course I shitting-well did but I was at school with half of you,' snapped Jacques. 'I mean, how would it look for Christ's sake?' Agitated, he scraped a hand across his head and held it there, as if trying to contain the embarrassment inside.

'C' sat back in his chair. How little history has taught us, he pondered, remembering when, as a seven-year old boy with a lifetime in Intelligence and his knighthood before him, he'd watched the then Secretary of State for War, John Profumo, admitting on television to having had an affair with a nineteen year old showgirl, Christine Keeler. The parallels with Jacques were stark. He was known to be on the short list for the top job in Defence. Making this disappear wasn't going to be easy.

'What are we to do with you?' Rhetorical though the question was, 'C' would have welcomed an answer. Instead, there was silence in the room as he recalled Henderson's much maligned and universally ignored report that he'd read then with a tinge of sympathy but now couldn't help but hear the thunder of those distant canons. How had he classified it? "Step 2. Political destabilisation of Western governments. The spread of disinformation, slander, to create scandal, mistrust, in-fighting, disruption, division". Among these new weapons of war, as

Henderson had called them, 'C' ventured one could now legitimately add fake news and hacking to the arsenal.

The early defiance had gone. 'I'll be ruined,' he whispered into his lap.

Henderson bit his lip, while even 'C' was taken aback at the man's vanity.

'*You'll* be ruined?' His voice remained soft, yet was spiked with venom. 'I don't suppose you've spared a thought for the men and women who are on active service around the world who are protecting our national security? A security that has been compromised to what degree we can only guess due to your torrid little affair and your blithely assisting in feeding our most sensitive secrets to the enemy. Have you considered that, Mr Jacques?' He left a long pause to let the man squirm. 'No, I don't expect you have. Because although when the press takes a bite out of you you may lose your job, when they spit you out again in a year or two you'll probably end up on the speech circuit happily trousering millions with a new book, or heaven forbid a diary, regaling us all with your sordid exploits. But what of your government? Your wife? Her family name? Your children? Your party? Your nation's security? What of your country, Jacques?'

The man's insouciance had deserted him and he began to shake, the gravity of his position weighing down upon him.

Pathetically, he said, 'What should I do? Tell me. What *can* I do?'

'C' leaned in close, and, adopting the menacing tone of a master about to exact punishment upon an undisciplined fag who'd just burnt his toast, said, 'I'll tell you what you can do. You can listen to me very carefully, you little prick.'

5

With a five o'clock Scotch from the staff bar overlooking the Thames warming his belly, Henderson walked his usual route home to an empty house. Turning the key in the lock, he couldn't help hope against hope that the light of the first floor living room would be on, that he'd be greeted by the scent of perfume in the hall and the sight of a coat draped carelessly over the bannister and handbag on the stair.

The day Sarah left had begun like any other: The Today Programme on the radio, the smell of fried bacon, Leo stuffing his PE kit into his bag as he tore out, and the crack of the letterbox that had sent him downstairs to find suitcases waiting by the door. When she joined them, in her above-the-knee black dress with white polka dots, she'd told him matter-of-factly that she was leaving. She'd met someone. A patron of the gallery, an art lover, a doctor — of what he hadn't thought to ask.

'If you really want know, and god I can't think what good it will do, his name is Fabien. He's French, Parisian, but he practices in Ealing.' Then she was climbing into a taxi, ordering the driver to take her to Primrose Hill, and moments later along with her above-the-knee dress with white polka dots and her morning suitcases were gone.

More details came a week later on the phone. Unfulfilled for years. Of course his work was partly to blame. They'd become strangers. Of course she wasn't *looking* for someone, it just happened. About six months. John hadn't suspected a thing, so consumed by the Trump-Russia investigation and practically living up at Cheltenham, and when at the end of the call he'd told her Leo was taking it badly all she said was that he'd be fine, that fifteen is old enough to understand.

But as he climbed the darkened stairs there were no charcoals of Chelsea on the walls, nor a vase of peonies on the table nor the postcards featuring the works of undiscovered modern artists dotted about. The only evidence of her ever being there at all was the line of paperback romances she'd left, presumably having no need to read about it once she'd found the real thing, and the photograph of the three of them, taken a week before she left. That stupid snapshot of their three beaming faces, waiting for the timer to count down, with frozen smiles. It looked ridiculous, he thought, two of them oblivious like lambs in the slaughterhouse wagon, and would remain there as a reminder of a spy's fallibility.

He read for a few hours until the shouting of a reporter half way through the News at Ten made him close his book and watch. She was being jostled by a sea of tricolour-clad marchers chanting "Frex-it! Frex-it! Frex-it!" while punching the air aggressively in support of independence from Europe. Similar events, she was saying, were happening all over France today in Lyon, Marseilles, Bordeaux, and Toulouse - huge rallies whose hundreds of thousands of demonstrators are calling for France to follow the United Kingdom out of the EU. Henderson watched as they cheered and jeered, chanted slogans and brandished placards.

The same breed that kept vigil outside parliament and held daily demos in Downing Street. They were a different species to him — loud and public. And what cause were they fighting for, or against? Brexit he thought an absurdity: the public conned, fed cheap brand nationalism by people with private interests, but they lapped it up and Britain abandoned her allies and turned them into enemies.

Loathing not only mob culture and such combative displays of nationalism but also those idiotic portmanteaus invented by the press: Brexit, Frexit, Nexit, that sounded to his ears like a lost Henry Miller trilogy, he switched the television off, poured himself another, much larger whiskey to help him sleep, and, in the empty silence of his Kensington mews, went to bed.

Less than three miles away from Kensington in an altogether more expensively furnished flat just across the river in a residence called Overstrand, the news broadcast was coming to a close with a Welsh pro-Brexit politician being interviewed. Motionless in the flickering darkness, holding a crystal tumbler of single malt, the figure watched with cold detachment.

Overlooking Battersea Park, Overstrand was an elegant late-Victorian redbrick and stucco mansion block on the prized Prince of Wales Drive - one of the most sought-after addresses in the SW11 postcode. The owner of ground floor flat number 12 had paid over two million pounds for the property in 2015 and had then spent at least the same amount again filling it with antiques. He was a tall man with very dark brown, almost black hair, and light green eyes with flecks of grey that made them appear slightly opaque. He dealt in property as an independent speculator, but also made a moderate income as an amateur collector and dealer in fine art as well as in antique furniture. Unmarried, aged thirty-seven, he owned the three-bedroomed property outright, as well as the year-old Maserati that was parked outside it. The shoes he wore were hand-made, as were his suits and shirts, all bespoke, meticulously measured and cut by Jermyn Street tailors. When dining out, the food he ate was expertly prepared by internationally renowned chefs and complimented by carefully chosen wines. Indeed, to all outward appearances the owner of flat number 12 shared many similarities with any number of other young, successful executives who populate the more elegant postcodes of the nation's capital.

Any visitor to the flat however would have found their curiosity raised upon noticing the oversized radio-like device sitting incongruously atop an antique chest of drawers — that is if their eye hadn't immediately been drawn to the original Mondrian on the wall above it. Had they been told, they might also have been surprised to learn that he kept over four million pounds hidden around the world in various offshore bank accounts whose account numbers were not written anywhere but that he had memorised.

Upon meeting him there was nothing to suggest he was anything other than either he, or his British passport, claimed. However despite looking and sounding like any other prosperous young Englishman, the owner of the flat was in fact Russian born and possessed three extra passports that he kept beneath a floorboard in the study, each proffering a different identity from a different country. Also unlike most other residents in the area he kept a loaded Beretta 9000S pistol in a side drawer by the bed, another in a bathroom cabinet, a Karatel combat knife in a shoulder holster that was draped over the back of a chair in the bedroom, and a glass vial in the fridge that contained two grams of the deadly nerve agent Novichok A234.

Not yet a full week into her grief, Katya Petrenko's nights were spent crying hot, angry tears and she only managed to snatch a few minutes of sleep during the mornings when the Zelenkos had argued or drunk themselves into a temporary oblivion. Two nights ago there'd been a stabbing in the stairwell and a young policeman had pounded on her door insisting he had to interview her. Although she'd witnessed nothing and was barely able to focus through her swollen eyes, the gruff official wouldn't leave until he had his answers.

She was sure Dmitri was dead. When she called his phone it was now silent, yet still she tried, over and over, sobbing after each attempt until her throat hurt. Her uncle with his filthy lies was responsible, she knew it. Lies that stank like the booze that clung to him, whose smell she couldn't rid from her nostrils. She'd given Natalya to Anya on the ground floor to look after to spare her daughter the sight of her anguish. After all, how was she going to break it to a three-year-old that her father had been killed. With Natalya gone and nothing to distract her, she'd allowed herself to be swept away on her tide of despair wishing she would drown.

On Monday morning she had no choice but to find some strength. She showered, ran tongs through her hair, put some make-up on, and collected her daughter early before cooking them a hot breakfast and making it to the bus stop with a minute to spare. The reason was this Monday they would make their monthly bus journey to 23 Kashirskoe Road.

It always took nearly two hours from Koptevo to reach The N.N. Blokhin Cancer Research Centre in the south of Moscow. The nine a.m. appointment was with the usual doctor, Hanna Perova, a stern-looking professional who wore narrow blue spectacles on the end of her wide nose and her thinning hair in a bun. With chipped black and white linoleum tiles on the floor and mould eating through the peeling walls, the office was like the overcrowded wards along the corridor, and every time Katya saw it she couldn't help but be reminded of the day she and Dmitri had received the news, of the moment their world was torn from its axis. Dr Perova had delivered it with affectless professionalism, like a mechanic would diagnose a fault with a car. Acute myelogenous leukaemia. Antiviral. Antifungal. Then, yes, there was a treatment, a drug called Ponatinib, that although the state should provide, in reality would not. What will it cost? Katya had asked. 663,000 rubles a month, approximately 10,000 dollars, the doctor had said. Katya had gone dizzy, started screaming, became hysterical, then collapsed, landing hard on her knees onto the floor. They didn't have a chance of being able to find such an amount. For two months Natalya's condition worsened while all they could do was fight and argue and look on, helpless.

But then in the spring the miracle happened. One spring day Dmitri appeared in the doorway, soaked to the skin after a sudden, heavy downpour.

His eyes were sore, but wide and determined, and he was barely able to contain his excitement. Beaming, he pulled her close and twirled her around the living room in a frenetic dance while their daughter looked on bemused until they finally fell to their knees laughing in a breathless heap.

He'd found the money, he told her, gasping for breath. She shouldn't ask how, or where it came from, only that from then on Natalya's condition could be treated with the best medicine. She would regain the lost weight, the nausea would cease, the crippling abdominal pain would stop, as would the unexplained fevers. And so it was. The improvement was immediate and continual.

Unfortunately this Monday, 26th October, represented the day when little Natalya had ingested the last capsule, and the money Dmitri had mysteriously acquired had run dry. What Katya Petrenko needed now was another miracle.

Donald Philips glanced over towards the bathroom, to the large hole in its wall where he'd taken the hammer to it. The carpet was still covered in plaster dust that he'd been too tired to vacuum up yesterday. He'd get to that. The tyres would probably need pumping up on the car, and he hadn't worn his dark blue suit since Anne's funeral three years earlier, so he'd have to fish that out today as well.

He reached for the package he'd pulled out of the wall, a large padded envelope of faded yellow that was full of what felt like a wad of paper. The black ink of the frank read 4th July 1984, posted from Colchester. An image came into his mind of the day he'd received it. Anne had been standing right there in the kitchen. She'd not batted an eyelid when he starting hammering at the wall, not complained a bit. She was a good woman, that Anne Warwick.

The lift doors were closing when Stephen Jones-Cooper ran towards them and thrust a maroon briefcase into the gap just in time, forcing them open and allowing him to clamber in. Zoe, holding her Cafe Nero coffee cup up high to avoid losing its precious liquid, smiled politely at his clumsiness.

'Morning, Zoe. Sorry. Third floor?' The sudden, brief, exertion had rendered him out of breath.

She found him a curious toad, naturally unlikable, and was reminded whenever she saw him of something he'd said when she'd first arrived at MI6, something he told anyone who'd listen, that both amused and puzzled her every time she remembered it. He said he'd once cultivated ambitions of joining the Royal Navy's Fleet Air Arm, but that unfortunately he'd failed the naval medical examination on the grounds of childhood asthma. Realised he was, regrettably, destined for the office. She'd never met any fighter pilots, but decided there and then he'd be the least likely looking one if she ever did. It was on record his path into intelligence had been fifteen years at Brown Shipley's merchant bank followed by stints in the Far East until he was headhunted by Crown Exports Ltd – one of a handful of cover names SIS uses to recruit. No hint of anything vaguely physical about the would-be fighter pilot.

'How are you finding working with Henderson?' he asked, catching his breath.

The resentment in his voice, she thought. The

sideways scowl, the chip on the shoulder. She wondered where it was from.

The doors opened and someone got in on the second floor.

He set great store by appearing to be another product of the old-boy's network like all the other mandarins in the various agencies and ministries, yet she wasn't convinced. She doubted he'd been born with the double-barrelled name, and that it was the fact plain old Stephen Jones had never wheezed across the playing fields of Eton with the rest of them, leaped for a high catch in the outfield or punted carefree along the Cam or whatever they did that was the source of the grudge towards those that had — especially those who eschewed such trappings of breeding, like John. He was probably a member of the club, she thought, but he'd never really be accepted as one of them.

The lift door opened silently. 'Well?' he said, maintaining his inability to make eye-contact that made him appear blind.

'Oh, fine.'

'Mmm . . . a word of warning. I think you have a bright future here, Ms Taylor, and I wouldn't want you to be . . . swayed in the wrong direction. Some friendly advice.' He shot her a smile and stepped out of the lift.

The man in question was signing overtime sheets and time in lieu requests for Kesterton and didn't look up as she passed his window. She sat down at a work-station and logged on. The screen awoke, and she began to scroll through the weekend's intel from S-Section's case officers around the world. *What did he mean by that?* She'd read his report, and she'd heard the rumours, knew he had few friends, but seriously?

That same morning Hayley Lander arrived at nine o'clock at the hairdressers where she'd worked for the last seventeen years. It was tucked in-between a butchers and a much-graffitied betting shop on a small parade, and bore the name *Prince's* in dirty lettering above the door and stubborn sellotape marks on the glass. Apart from the mid-height frontage it was otherwise windowless, which made it necessary to keep the pale yellow lights on even in the summer, and cold, with an air of neglect — much like the three women who worked there. Lining the left wall, in front of misting mirrors and formica shelves, were the three swivel chairs of black leather and grey steel, and behind them stood the three women where they'd stood and would always stand, sour-faced and ready to cut and buzz the hair of locals of limited means. Payment was taken at a tall whicker and glass counter, where a small sweet from a large jar would be proffered to those on their way out, designed to inspire customer loyalty. Any developer would estimate no more than a weekend to refit it into a burger bar.

By 11.15 Lander had only done an OAP's short back and sides — there'd been nothing on top to attend to — when her phone rang.

'Hello love. Yes, I'm fine. How was your weekend?' she closed *Hello* magazine and retreated into the back room.

In the back of an unmarked transit van parked in a side street around the corner from the Palace of Westminster, Keith Godwin adjusted his headphones. He could tell it was going to be another dull one, as he later noted in the log that he filed at the end of his shift: . . . *the recipient (HL) and the caller (CF) chatted about nothing of any concern or note until the call ended with CF promising to visit her aunt to celebrate 'Sean's' (unknown?) birthday, on November 7th. Call terminates: 11:27.*

At one p.m. 'C' waited for his lunch companion in a private room inside his club in St James's, the oldest and most exclusive of the Pall Mall clubs. It was silent but for the cheeping of birds from the small courtyard outside the bow window, a distant pneumatic drill, and the odd elderly cough from another room. This was a particular comfort that couldn't be replicated anywhere in the world. The soft, much-repaired, antique leather armchairs, the familiar odour of potted shrimps and partridge coming from the kitchen that mingled with cigar smoke, the archaic committee rules one just had to accept, the same school haircuts from this ministry or that getting quietly pissed on the twenty-five. He had been at school with the Cabinet Secretary and the men shared a genuine fondness for each other, and when Sir Humphrey arrived he ordered a mineral water citing 'bloody doctor's orders'. After the waiter had disappeared, 'C' told his old friend the situation with *Domino* as it stood.

'Christ. And how many people know about this . . . shit-pickle?' It was his job to govern the conduct of her majesty's government ministers with what's known as The Ministerial Code, or more colloquially, *The Rule Book* - and also to oversee the intelligence services and their relationship to the government — therefore blackmail was not a word the country's most senior civil servant liked to use before lunch. During his career, Sir Humphrey Matthews, once a United

Nations Weapons Inspector in Iraq, later the U.K's Ambassador to Afghanistan, had seen his share of challenges, but none more acute than keeping Tory ministers in line.

'As of now, no one. By that I mean us, my Section Head – Henderson, his case officer, Zoe Taylor, and my AC, Stephen Jones-Cooper.'

'God almighty.' Matthews was growing paler. 'Jacques, you absolute turd.'

'My thoughts exactly, Humph.'

'What do you propose? The PM's approval rating's already tanking. Something like this could sound the death knell.'

'C' couldn't recall seeing his friend this perturbed and he thought he looked ripe for a coronary. He knew he was under constant pressure to keep ministers in line, but also, since the party's landslide victory at the polls the year before that things had gone from bad to worse to verging on the catastrophic for the government. For his part, Sir Humphrey felt he couldn't eat his egg these days without seeing another scandal splashed across the newspapers. It was the full rainbow: Far-right infiltration into the Tory core, endless internal quarrels, rogue ministers, (twenty-five of whom had either been sacked or had resigned), accusations of racism, bullying, countless allegations of fraud and endemic corruption, sexual scandals across the spectrum — the list was endless. Add to this a beleaguered electorate who were deeply divided and becoming increasingly distrustful of government having suffered economic decline, a billionaire chancellor raising taxes, a rapid surge in violent hate crime, and a spiralling knife-crime epidemic, and the consensus was that one more gust and the whole house of cards would come crashing down. It was his job to wrestle the bellows from the devil himself if he had to, and, weak heart or not, Sir Humphrey wasn't going to see the Blues go down without a fight.

'Well,' said 'C', 'my assistant chief proposes hanging them both out to dry. Charging them under the official secrets act, living with any potential consequences. I however, believe that would be foolhardy.'

'Jesus H. Christ, Clive, I'm glad you agree.'

'I therefore propose we ask three things of Mr Jacques. Firstly, it's of vital importance than he carries on his parliamentary duties as normal. Keeps to the same routines, attends the same meetings, not does anything to suggest a change in circumstances. Secondly, and this is an obvious one, he will be conveniently passed over for the job of Secretary of State for Defence. But under no circumstances does he resign from the house. If that happens we run the risk of them releasing the tape.'

'Could be difficult, the PM won't even hear of anyone else for the job. But all right. What's the third?'

'It has also come to our attention that he's also been doing a great deal of work in the Luton area, in the South in particular, so number three is easy: to keep him out of the headlines as much as is at all possible he breaks off his relationship with the assistant to Mr Aarav Khan, and promises to keep his thing in his trousers for the foreseeable. This, one imagines, should prove the most difficult of all.'

'Wish we could castrate the bastard,' said Matthews, meaning it.

'You and I both, Humphrey,' 'C' replied with a

smile, 'and while that is always an option I think you'll agree my proposal is a hair closer to the Prime Minister's policy of party unity. Finally, we shall embark on a major mis-information campaign to Moscow. Therefore I see necessitating the formation a sub-committee. We'll keep it as small as we can, six or so: You, myself, Jones-Cooper, Sir Nigel, and someone from the Home Office and Defence should do it. All right?'

'This *cannot* be leaked, Clive,' Sir Humphrey stressed, resolutely. 'This man of yours, Henderson. You're quite sure about him?'

'Oh yes, Humph, quite sure.'

The waiter arrived and set down the drinks. At the sight of the mineral water Sir Humphrey sent it back and ordered a double Scotch. 'That waiter new?' he murmured when the man had gone.

That afternoon a sub-committee with the code-name *Echelon* was established, its number restricted to the six names 'C' had proposed over lunch. *Echelon's* first meeting would be held the following morning in a secret location in Whitehall, its remit being to compile, then monitor the continuing supply of fictitious intelligence to the Russians via the duped MP Mr Jacques and his treasonous assistant Charlotte Fisher.

On Monday lunchtime the resident of Flat 12 Overstrand mansions rented a modest Ford saloon car from an agency in South London. He explained to the attentive female clerk he would need it for two weeks as he'd just relocated from Portsmouth. When she asked why, he told her he'd accepted a new job in the area, in sales, a promotion actually, and had just rented a small house in Camberwell. Yes, a saloon would be fine. Did he have a driving license and credit card? Of course. No, he wouldn't need damage waiver, the credit card would cover it.

The girl handed him the keys. There you are Mister Blake, she said, a crimson flush appearing at her cheeks.

'Russell Blake,' he smiled.

An hour later the Ford pulled up alongside a dark, heavily-graffitied row of Victorian railway arches in the London borough of Southwark. The crescent road followed the railway track above, disused and heavily overgrown due to decades of neglect and London's frequent rainfall. One of the doors had a For Rent sign stuck to it.

He called the number and the owner, an elderly Turkish man, arrived twenty minutes later, took cash for the month without asking for a name or address, and handed the stranger a key for the padlock. When he had gone, Russell Blake reversed the car into the garage and set about removing the car's number plates.

It was at ten past five when Zoe appeared at Henderson's door. 'John, I think we have a problem. Can you come take a look?'

'Come in for a second will you?' He had the phone to his ear, listening to Godwin relay the details of Fisher's phone call to the aunt.

Beside a bookcase she began leafing through a well-thumbed hardback copy of Manifesto of the Communist Party by Marx.

'Yes, thanks Keith. Sean, no I don't. No last name? Seventh of November. Okay, got it. Yes, could be a man or woman. All right, yes you deserve one. Bye. Have you read it?' he asked without looking up.

'Of course.'

'When was the last time?'

'University, I guess.'

'You should re-read it, It's as relevant today as it was a hundred and fifty years ago.'

'No thanks,' She snapped the book shut and slid it back in its row. 'John, I really need you to take a look at something.'

Five minutes later they were in Technical Analysis on the fifth floor sitting either side of Nasha, a young Data Analyst of twenty-six with perfect Russian whose job was to sift through intelligence collected from agents in the field. She had opened up a file marked MOSCOW/CARLO/JACKDAW and was quickly organising a series of photographs in order on her screen, each date-stamped, as she read out the basics in her South London brogue.

'Location: Moscow, Handler: Carlo, Asset: Jackdaw, Status: Active.'

Her tone was unusually solemn, Henderson detected.

'Six month period, roughly one batch a month, and between twelve and twenty-three photographs per batch. Now, all taken with a Minox DCC Leica M3 and sent via the camera's two gigabyte SD card in the diplomatic pouch.'

'Can you show John what we found, Nasha,' said Zoe, moving her chair closer in. She clicked open a sub-folder, chose a photograph that showed a hard-backed planner lying on a desk, and honed in on a small section that showed something blurred and white. With a quick click of the mouse the pixels sharpened to reveal a piece of paper sticking out from beneath the book. Upon it, a part of a name could now be made out: . . . *sper.*

'Sper,' said Henderson, searching his memory.

'Now can you show us the overview shots of each batch?'

Nasha swiftly arranged six separate overview shots on the monitor, each showing paperwork laid out on what was evidently the same desk, in date order. All eyes were immediately drawn to the last photograph on the bottom right.

'See what I mean?' Zoe said.

Henderson squinted. 'Look how neatly arranged everything is.'

'Whoever photographed this had time.'

'Date-stamp 22.10. — the most recent — definitely stands out.' Nasha swallowed, her voice breaking slightly. 'The others from Jackdaw are panicked, against the clock, a lot of them are out of focus. But this one's organised, everything's neatly laid out on the desk, and look, there are four shots the same.' She opened up three other identical photos. 'With the others you only get one shot of each. It's definitely out of rhythm.'

'Oh no,' said Henderson.

They all knew what it meant but if Nasha needed confirmation he'd just given it, causing tears to well up in her dark hazel eyes. She sniffed in quickly. 'And this just came in in the last hour on the TASS website.' When she wasn't closely analysing the Human Intelligence she would be collating Open Source Intel – the routine monitoring of foreign newspapers and broadcasts that, being geolocated, time-stamped and verifiable, were a highly valuable source of intelligence.

She clicked an icon on the screen that opened a page of the Russian news agency's website.

The headline read MAN DIES IN YAROSLAVL CAR BLAZE with the paragraph below stating: *A 32 year-old man was killed on Tuesday evening when his car struck a stationary coal truck and became engulfed in flames on a forest road near the town of Telishchevo, near Yaroslavl. Police have named the victim as Dmitri Petrenko, 32, from Moscow, whose body had to be identified by dental records as it was so badly burned. The driver of the truck was uninjured and Police are not treating the accident as suspicious.*

'That's Jackdaw,' said Nasha, her voice cracking and the tears now tumbling freely down her dark umber cheeks. Although she'd never met the young foreign man called Dmitri, she'd poured over his intelligence for the last six months and felt in a funny sort of way that she'd kept watch over him, like she did the others. She knew it was silly really, but she'd come to think of them as 'her boys'.

They sat in silence. Henderson held his forehead in his palm and squeezed his temples tightly with thumb and middle finger. The shared thought was 'How could a man who died on a Tuesday take photographs and make a dead letter drop two days later?'

With a long, heavy sigh, he said quietly, 'he has a wife and young daughter.'

They left her, and out in the corridor his tone was sombre. 'Colonel General Ivan Ivanovich Grushenko. Head of the Fifth Directorate of the GRU.'

'Responsible for foreign military operations intelligence,' Zoe replied.

'Yes, but his office is inside the Lubyanka.'

'Not in GRU headquarters in Khodinka?'

'No, we don't know why. Jackdaw was a walk-in who claimed he had access to Grushenko. He was a cleaner in the Lubyanka and claimed he'd studied his routine. George Provost ran him — codenamed Carlo.'

'Grushenko discovers Dmitri's working for us and has him killed.'

They reached the lift. 'George spoke of a personal connection Dmitri may have had with Grushenko but that he never admitted to. There was nothing on file — it was the way he talked about him. Wasn't in awe or scared of him — a familiarity maybe, a reason for targeting him. It was just a feeling George had but nothing he could prove. We were keen for intel on this general so we recruited Dmitri even though we knew the risks.'

Zoe swiped her card over the infra-red pad on the wall. 'Specifically?'

'Nowadays Ivan Grushenko is a desk general but his true home was always the battlefield, and for this bastard the bloodier the battle the better. It started when he was a conscript soldier in Chechnya, February 4th 2000 if memory serves, when battle-weary Russian forces departed Grozny after the so-called 'taking' of the city.' They stepped into an empty lift and turned to face the closing doors. 'Well, perhaps we should say battle-weary except for one man — a brawler from the slums of Volgograd called Ivan who chose to stay on in Novye Aldi - a suburb in the south west of the city — to assist in the planned 'mopping-up', or *zachistka*, operation that was to take place after the initial troops had left. Ostensibly it was an operation to check villagers passports and detain suspected fighters who had been left behind, but instead, groups of heavily armed Russian riot police alongside drunken mercenaries and short-contract soldiers took it upon themselves to begin beating and randomly shooting civilians in their homes and in the streets. Most of the violence took place along Matasha-Mazaeva Street, where at least twenty-four people were killed as the attackers went from house to house executing civilians without mercy. Grushenko had been one of the early instigators of the violence.'

'The Novye Aldi massacre,' Zoe said. The lift doors opened and they stepped out.

'Yes, and he made sure he stayed until the end to have his bloody fill. The next day the image of a young soldier hoisting the Russian flag in the ruined city made the front page of the world's press.' They reached his office. He went to a bookcase, pulled out a heavily crumpled Russian magazine and handed it to her. 'See?' The image stared back at her. 'See the red tint to the man's trousers? Legend goes his tunic was borrowed as his own was soaked through with the blood of innocent civilians. That soldier in the photo is Ivan Grushenko.'

She stared at the front page in horror.

6

That same General pulled on his overcoat, pushed the intercom button on his office desk and instructed his secretary to prepare his staff car and driver car at once. He had planned to drive himself but the day's vodka intake had been considerable and he didn't want to risk missing a meeting of such importance because he'd run his car off an icy forest road. Armed with the essential files from the safe, he found the car and within a matter of minutes was being driven through Moscow's freezing rush hour traffic, over the Novoarbatski bridge and out towards the most exclusive of private enclaves near the small town of Usovo.

The driver was a young private of twenty-three, also in military uniform, who had stepped in to replace Grushenko's usual FSB chauffeur, whom the general had been told wasn't available at such short notice. Grushenko knew the change in personnel wouldn't be tolerated so when they arrived he planned to dismiss the stand-in driver at the gate and ride back to Moscow later with Volkov. Now though, he could feel the man's eyes steal glances at him in the rear view mirror as he leafed through his papers. Finally, after twenty minutes, he instructed him to pull over.

'Is there something wrong Comrade Colonel General?' the young man asked nervously when the car had halted.

'What is your name, private?'

'Dukovsky, sir. Anatoly Andreyavich Dukovsky.'

'Are you married Dukovsky? Children?'

'Yes, sir,' he beamed with pride, 'I have three children. All girls. Three, five and nine.'

'If you so much glance at me again I will make sure that they do not reach four, six, and ten. Do you understand?'

The car pulled away from the sludge and continued its journey.

One hour later and sixteen-hundred miles to the west, as the tribal drums signalled the end of the BBC's six o'clock news, Donald Philips got up and switched the television off. He was prepared. He'd been sitting in his navy suit for hours with the package on his lap, and had eaten earlier than usual in a bid to avoid having to make any unwanted stops on the journey due to his unpredictable bowels.

It was dark outside when he turned the key in the garage door lock and twisted the handle. The garage door lifted easily to reveal the brown Lada Riva 1300GL model car he'd bought new in 1983 upon his return from Beirut and kept ever since. Now that I look at it again after so long, he thought as he stood there on the driveway on the estate, perhaps Anne was right. It is pig ugly after all.

With windscreen wipers thumping to clear the persistent evening drizzle, he kept the Lada at a steady forty in the middle lane of the M11 as he travelled southbound, then joined the North Circular at Woodford before turning west to follow the Thames towards the City. He was approaching the very heart of the capital of the small island whose people, freedoms, liberties, and follies, he'd spent a lifetime betraying. With bony hands on the wheel, he kept his hollow eyes locked on the road ahead. Trafalgar Square, Downing Street, Pall Mall, Buckingham Palace, and Marble Arch all crept behind the Lada's rain-streaked windows without a caring glance from its driver, until he turned it into a side street off Knightsbridge and manoeuvred the car into a parking space on Egerton Terrace.

After climbing the six steps at the entrance to the Brompton Oratory, beneath the feast of decorative marbles that adorn the interior of the grand neo-classical Roman Catholic church, he made his way past the rows of empty pews and sat down as the organ began to sound. He had chosen a row in the middle of the church and was facing, but still at a distance from, the thirty-six member chamber choir bedecked in long white robes. After two measures, the sopranos of the senior ensemble began their introductory diatonic progression of Lacrimosa, Mozart's Requiem Mass - their glorious legato reverberating deeply off the cold marble and down from the majestic building's mighty dome.

Lacrimosa dies illa . . .

He didn't hear the footsteps of the man approaching, only felt a presence when he sat down in the shadows next to him. When he turned to look, only the man's profile was lit.

Qua resurget ex favilla . . .

'Religion is the opium of the people,' said Russell Blake in a low voice, looking straight ahead.

'Too often people assume Marx was comparing religion to a worthless opiate that helps one forget and merely numbs the pain, but that's not fair,' replied Philips in clipped English, causing the stranger's eyes to glance sideways at the elderly man beside him. This was not the pre-arranged coded reply. But in a superior tone he continued, 'The sigh of the oppressed creature, the heart of a heartless world, the soul of soulless conditions. Marx is saying that religion is not the cause of a flawed society, merely the result.' Philips raised his white eyebrows. 'Do you agree?'

'You have something for me.' It was not a question, it was a statement.

'Ah, but I see you dogs have little regard for the ideology. A shame.' Philips reached down beside him and slid the padded envelope slowly across his lap. 'I do hope your codes are up to snuff, Rover.'

Blake took the envelope. He opened it quickly, thumbed through the thick wad of papers within, and, feeling something, turned the package upside down that caused a small key to fall into his palm. He regarded it, then slid it into a pocket. In the fingers of his right hand was a tiny platinum pellet. He pressed it, and a small needle sprung from its end. It glinted briefly, then without hesitating he jabbed it into the old man's left thigh.

Dona eis requiem.

The pupils of the narrow eyes immediately dilated, his breath halted, and within twenty-seconds he was experiencing respiratory paralysis and a dangerous slowdown of the heart rate known as bradycardia. Within two minutes he would slip into a coma and within ten he would be dead. His killer placed a bible upon the old man's lap, stood, and walked away as behind him the choir sang out Mozart's final, rousing crescendo.

Amen!

Of the nine men in the world who knew the content of the two messages transmitted over the last seven days, eight were present for a clandestine meeting at the luxurious dacha of Professor Karol Turgenev late that Monday evening, and all knew the true identity of the ninth — the recipient in London who although Godless had just visited a church for the first time in his life.

The eight also had the ear of the President of the Russian Federation, Vladimir Putin, yet it was not upon his instruction that the top secret directorate had been established and assigned the codename *Telepol.* Each member of The *Telepol* Committee had been handpicked by Defence Minister Alexei Sotnik, most holding a senior rank within either the government or the military, and had been chosen for their talent, shared ideology, and for their ambition to put into action a plan so audacious and so dangerous it could not be achieved by overt means. *Telepol's* existence was entirely unofficial. If the Kremlin knew of its existence it would deny all knowledge of it if confidentiality were breached - *Telepol's* success relying upon absolute, unconditional secrecy. As a consequence, General Ivan Ivanovich Grushenko was understandably tense when he entered the giant Swiss chalet-like room and took his seat alongside the other men in expensive Swedish chairs. There, beneath the mansion's wide open-beamed gabled roof, without exchanging salutes or handshakes and with their stern faces warmed by a spitting log fire, the eight formed a semi circle before a low teak table that resembled a giant boomerang. Upon it, in front of each man rested an identical red leather folder with a gold hammer and sickle embossed upon its front and a blood-red ribbon bearing the initials SS - the common abbreviation for Top Secret in Russian – to bind it.

Turgenev was a rare breed in that he was not only a respected academic, but also an oligarch whose value within the committee was his ability to organise the purchase of great swathes of London real-estate, despite the recent public clampdowns by the UK Government. He himself owned several buildings in London's Mayfair - including the club the Chief of MI6 and Prince Charles belonged to — whose ground rents alone netted him over a billion rubles annually. His appearance resembled that of a Scandinavian architect, yet his selection for *Telepol* was a result not only of his devotion to an expansionist policy of world communism, but also because he was a renowned British and European political expert who was possessed of a razor sharp insight, a famously robust intellect and a talent for sophisticated analysis.

Earlier that afternoon unseen hands had prepared and laid out *zakuski* for the guests on an impressive dining table in the form of cold cuts, cured fishes, mixed salads, *pirogs* or *pirozhki*, various pickled vegetables such as tomatoes, beets, and mushrooms, alongside sauerkraut, devilled eggs, cheeses, caviar, and breads. To drink there was beer and vodka.

While armed FSO protection men patrolled the icy grounds of the estate, the stone-faced men waited solemnly for the proceedings to begin, until, with the manner of the cautious politician he was, the Committee's Chairman, Defence Minister Sotnik, began by outlining the order of business before introducing Professor Turgenev. From beneath a thick cloud of cigarette smoke and behind thick tortoiseshell glasses with lenses glinting in the firelight, he opened with some polite formalities, and it was half an hour later when he concluded his introduction by expressing his lifelong devotion to the Socialist doctrine, sitting forward in his billionaire's leather chair and staring at each man around him earnestly.

'In the words of the great political philosopher Nikolai Berdyaev, empire and great power status constitute the *essence* of Russian identity. Russia's defeat of Napoleon in the nineteenth century, and victory over Hitler's Nazi Germany in World War II in the twentieth were the crowning achievements of the Soviet State, the latter saving not merely the Soviet Union and Europe, but the whole world from fascism. Having practised caution, circumspection, flexibility and deception — the most valuable qualities we can possess — the moment will soon arrive for Russia's twenty-first century victory. It will be the greatest victory of all.'

The words were vital, powerful, and delivered with a calm yet brutal passion that no apparatchik present could have spoken better. Each considered their repercussions.

The Professor moved towards specifics, stating that, after a lifetime it seemed, the Labour Party of Great Britain was no longer the primary target of Russian infiltration, and instead the Conservative party, who had ruled since 2010, was the focus. This, he stated, represented one of the vital foundations for Overture. Although Turgenev was a man possessed of many enviable traits — humility was not one.

'The result of the 2019 British general election echoed my own predictions of a Conservative party landslide, and solidified my conclusion that Socialism in the UK is all but dead. It was a gradual decline, but the country's opposition Labour Party became at that moment almost completely decimated, losing over fifty seats, many in areas of traditionally working class communities ravaged by the de-industrialisation of the 1990s who have seen their trade unions neutered, their rights destroyed and their voices ignored. So how did the largest Socialist party in Europe, with a membership of over five-hundred-thousand, lose so disastrously? The answer is two-fold, gentlemen. The surge in party membership and support for leader Jeremy Corbyn came mainly from a new, hard left-leaning demographic, meaning the Socialist leader now had to appease both a Euro sceptic working class as well as an avidly pro-EU metropolitan one. In the end the party swung in favour of these new members, whom comprised the majority of the party's grass-root activists, and in doing so alienated the working-class 'leave' voters. This alone, would not have proven fatal, however the lack of leadership with regard the EU referendum result outraged both Leavers and so-called 'Remainers', so when Corbyn caved in to demands to campaign for a second referendum, many in parts of the country who voted Leave and who already felt disenfranchised deserted both him and the party completely. This is what lost Labour the election. You see gentlemen, the working class vote against Europe was really their way of voting against global capitalism. And I'm sure we may all agree that that is the outcome we all seek here this evening.'

More nods and murmurs from around the room.

'These voices were written off as racist,

ignorant, closeted, by both The Labour Party and the liberal press, yet what happened was that the British electorate voted against unregulated capitalism. The Labour party of today has chosen to ignore the proletariat in favour of the middle class. Chosen to align itself with big business, to get into bed with the capitalism it was created to confront. After Corbyn they even elected a knight of the realm to lead the party. The Labour Party of today, therefore, is irrelevant.'

With the exception of Grushenko the men present had all read the professor's report some months before, whose length was more like a book.

'And so it is in the last ten years we have not only been placing agents of all ranks and positions in every corner of British society, but inside the very heart of the *Conservative* Party, both at a local, civic level, and at a national one.'

The faces in the room were implacable. Although the professor was speaking for at least two of the generals present with regards the placement of sleeper agents on foreign soil, their lips stayed closed, allowing the civilian his moment.

'Socialism from the right is palatable to the British,' he shrugged, 'it looks like good social organisation to them. And so it is with the centrist La République En Marche Party of France, and the centre right Christian Democratic Union of Germany. All successfully infiltrated by our well-established network of agents, whom alongside those placed across other sectors, are ready to assume control when the time comes.'

Later, over food, the talk was off-topic, subdued. It was one a.m. and the necessary absence of staff meant the men helped themselves and ate casually, while Turgenev, as host, topped up the vodka.

Once they were seated again, Turgenev stoked the fire with a 24 carat gold poker while the defence minster invited the oldest man in the room to speak, 'Comrade Igor Mikhailovich, the architect of Operation Overture.'

A few moments as Savich wiped his wire-framed glasses with a handkerchief, and in his own time replaced them on his nose and prepared to address the room. His was the only folder that remained untouched on the boomerang table, its ribbon still tied. *Overture* was his brainchild, born back in the early 1960s at the behest of Nikita Khrushchev. Now the Committee awaited confirmation from its father that conditions were optimal, that the baton was ready to be handed over to the generals to initiate Phase Three.

With the handkerchief at his mouth he coughed gently to clear his throat. 'Phases one and two have been satisfactorily achieved to my mind gentlemen. Economically, socially, politically, and militarily. The limitless liberal democratic capitalist expansion practised by Great Britain, France, Germany, the USA, and the West in general is ecologically unsound, and has failed. What is required is redistribution of the world's wealth. The Western governments are weak, their economies are floundering, their peoples and unions are sufficiently divided, their public's moral is in the doldrums. Widespread frustration with the governing elites ever since the global financial crisis of 2008 has led us to this point. Therefore with the sleeper agents in place I can announce it is time to proceed to Phase Three and

Four simultaneously. In the last hour the Executive Officer in England has received the full briefing by courier, and that courier, according to instruction, has been 'dispatched'.'

The word raised some mirth in the room. Savich continued, stating he would continue to orchestrate the communication with the executive officer via the short wave transmitter, then going on to outline some finer points of the mission at length, listing in detail updates and revisions that had been, or that would have to be made to bring the plan to successful fruition in the twenty-first century. He answered questions, speaking without notes. It was four a.m. when he finished talking, and the embers were dwindling in the hearth. Sotnik gestured to the man beside him.

If the chief of MI6's opposite number in the SVR was Mikhail Smolenko, the Director of Russia's external intelligence service (who was not present), then Stephen Jones-Cooper's was Deputy Director, Yevgeni Kovalevsky. Like his British counterpart he too was a man in his middle age and of small stature, but unlike the sedentary Jones-Cooper, Kovalevsky's background was one spent in the field. With untameable black hair, a cruel mouth and pockmarked grey skin that made his clean ecru collar appear permanently grubby, he was also a formidable presence.

'When Phases Three and Four are implemented it has been decided by this committee that the blame shall be apportioned to right-wing separatist terror group, the OAG, the Organisation Against Globalisation. A very fitting cause, I am sure you will agree. For five years they have claimed responsibility for various atrocities. It is the OAG who will claim responsibility gentlemen.'

'Thank you Yevgeni Petrovich,' Sotnik said to the SVR Deputy Director, using his polite patronymic name. 'Finally, before we conclude this evening, or morning, I should say, I have been told that a breech of security has occurred.'

Grushenko shifted in his chair, feeling the eyes of the most powerful men in Russia burning into him.

'General Grushenko, perhaps you can enlighten us as to the seriousness of this?'

He cleared his throat loudly into his sleeve and swallowed the phlegm. 'You have my steadfast assurance that every document pertaining to Operation Overture has been securely locked in my safe, Comrade Defence Minister,' he said in his deep rasp. 'Petrenko, I later found out this was the man's name, was a chancing thief is all, a cleaner, no more, inside Lubyanka who, because of his position, was able to enter my outer office, *outer* only, don't forget, where he was able to photograph whatever he found on the desk there. Which was chicken feed. Nothing more, I assure you.'

'If you are wrong, General, then the British already know about Overture.'

Sotnik glanced over to SVR Deputy Director Kovalevsky, who almost imperceptibly shook his head, conveying to his minister that there was no risk. No one else would have noticed the exchange, but Igor Savich smiled to himself. As well as a strategic planner he knew where all the bodies were buried, both alive and dead, and this minute gesture told him that the source they had placed high up inside British Intelligence, the jewel in the SVR's crown, had not reported any intel relating to Overture having passed through MI6.

'Impossible, sir. You have my absolute assurance.' Grushenko stressed.

The words hung in the air for all to consider. Was he telling the truth or was he covering something up to protect himself? To every man present Grushenko resembled a wolf with blood on its jowls and claws. He wasn't a man who inspired faith.

Satisfied, the defence minister turned to address the room. 'Then, gentlemen, to the matter of Operation Overture, may we proceed to Steps 3 and 4 concurrently?'

As the unrelenting snow fell outside, the Generals and assembled apparatchiks of the intelligence directorates, along with the civilians — the Professor and Savich — their tired faces now paling with the professor's expiring fire, each gave a slow nod of approval.

With the low glow of morning on the cold horizon the men from *Telepol* dispersed into their staff cars and back towards the capitol. In the back of Volkov's Mercedes, Grushenko felt that yet again he'd escaped the heat of battle unscolded. The weather had turned filthy, the snow into a thick rain that was hammering the windscreen the wipers were barely able to clear, making visibility poor and progress slow on the A-106.

Squeezed into his back seat, Volkov turned to his fellow general. 'What of the widow?'

'What?'

'The widow. The Petrenko woman. You have her under surveillance of course.'

Grushenko swallowed. Fuck. He hadn't though

to do it. 'Of course.'

The deputy head of the Illegal's Directorate turned to face forward, and with the sun beginning to rise before them, the car continued its crawl back to Moscow.

It was while that meeting was in progress, at just past nine p.m. GMT, when the alarm was raised. A call came in to the duty officer at MI6 from the Metropolitan Police saying a deceased male had been found 'foaming at the mouth' in a church in Knightsbridge.

A call also came in to Porton Down, home to the MoD's Defence Science and Technology Laboratory (Dstl), which prompted the quick deployment of a rapid response team to the scene. Blood samples in an on-site lab were taken that identified the presence of A234, a nerve agent from the Novichock family. The Brompton Oratory and surrounding area was cordoned off and the church accessible only to chemical warfare and decontamination experts wearing biohazard suits. On the stone steps outside, the Assistant Commissioner of the Metropolitan Police, Mark Bower, dressed in a dinner suit — having been pulled out of a function — was filled in by Sergeant Tim Royce from the Knightsbridge and Belgravia station, while standing deferentially in the background was the first policeman to attend the scene, Constable Harpreet Singh.

The body had been discovered by a member of the choir, a fifty-two year-old tenor called Gil Farrow, shortly after rehearsals finished at 8:15 p.m., the cause of death at first being a suspected opioid overdose. However it was the keen Constable Singh who recognised signs of a possible poisoning by nerve agent. With quick thinking he alerted his superiors and led the evacuation of the church.

The old man's body had been stripped and was lying on the slab when Henderson arrived at the coroner's office the following morning. Senior coroner, Dr Fiona Carpenter, was in the examination room, so while he waited for her he took the opportunity to look over the personal effects that were laid out on a table. They consisted of a Timex wristwatch with a worn leather strap, a folded page from an old AA map of central London, a Parker pen, a brown faux-leather bifold containing fifteen pounds in cash and a wrinkled paper driving license in the name of Donald Philips. The dead man's suit bore a Russian tailor's label on its inside pocket.

When he talked to the coroner she told him that it was while performing her initial visual inspection of the body that her eye had been drawn towards a small puncture wound in the upper left portion of the thigh. This method of administering a lethal dose of a chemical nerve agent, she said, would explain why the team from Porton Down, who had worked through the night, had found no trace of contamination either inside the church or in the immediate surrounding area.

She excused herself when Henderson's phone rang. Talk of the devil. Professor Harding from the lab at Porton could confirm that the blood samples of the victim being tested in their laboratory matched with what the initial analysis in the on-site lab had shown — the presence of the nerve agent — high-quality and military grade. And no, no further contamination found. He thanked him and hung up. A clean kill, he thought as someone brought him coffee — perhaps

Unit 29155 are improving. Harding had been the lead scientist a few years before when Russian double agent Sergei Skripal and his daughter Yulia were poisoned by the same variant in Salisbury. Henderson had driven down to the village of Porton for a meeting with him to familiarise himself with the nerve agent after it had been discovered that in that case no fewer than eight further sites had required decontamination. 'Novichok was designed as part of a Soviet programme codenamed *Foliant*,' the Professor had said, excited by the presence of a real live MI6 officer. 'It is one of the deadliest ever made, that although has never been used on the battlefield is beginning to upstage the PSS Silent Pistol as the assassin's *'arme de choix'*.' When Henderson had raised his eyebrows, the bespectacled scientist apologised and confessed to being a fan of spy fiction.

He sipped at the polystyrene cup, and remembered that while the fallout had been severe, solving the Skripal investigation had proven disconcertingly easy. Once the passport data from the suspected GRU officers watch list had been cross-checked with CCTV from Salisbury on the day of the attack, two suspects were identified almost immediately. The attack itself though, despite becoming the best-known case of a nerve agent being used on UK soil, was in fact a botched failure resulting in the intended victims surviving. A tragic consequence however was that a woman died after coming into contact with the same substance a month later, after her partner had found a discarded perfume bottle and had given it to the woman, who had sprayed it on her wrist.

Personally he regretted the whole affair.

Politically it had been a disaster: when the British government accused Russia of breaking its obligations under the Chemical Weapons Convention it lead to the expulsion of diplomats, economic sanctions, and created a fallout in the intelligence community that two years later had still not settled, having only succeeded in dismantling some major, and precious, intelligence networks.

He put the cup down and picked up the photograph from the crime scene. The old man's head was hanging limp and the body was slumped in a pew with a bible still on his lap. Donald Philips. Six had no record and the name meant nothing to him personally, but he made a mental note of it in case it was mentioned somewhere — a Soviet defector's confession, an autobiography, Kourdakov's maybe. But whoever this elderly Englishman in a Russian suit was, the Kremlin had left their calling card with him.

Henderson nodded his thanks to the doctor and stepped out onto the street, turned his collar to a sudden gust of westerly wind, and caught a cab back to Vauxhall.

The *Echelon* committee assembled at eleven that morning behind 10 Downing Street in the Cabinet Office, the location of the top secret COBRA Briefing Rooms. It was here, at 70 Whitehall, in Briefing Room A, that the six committee members met to discuss the fabricating of intelligence that would tempt Ms Fisher enough to pass it to the Russians.

At the same time an Airbus A321 taxied towards runway three at Heathrow Airport. Bound for Moscow, flight SU 2581 was only at half capacity, and Zoe Taylor, sitting near the rear of the narrow bodied plane, was wondering if she could break the habit of a lifetime and manage to sleep on a flight. She doubted it. Her mind was on their dead agent, Jackdaw, on the man in the embassy under diplomatic cover with the codename Carlo who had run him, and on the dead man's widow who at that hour was just leaving her apartment.

Katya made her way across the communal area away from her complex, past the parked cars and the teenagers kicking the children's swings, and out onto Ulitsa Generala Rychagova. She wore a suit beneath her coat, and sensible boots, yet was carrying smarter shoes in her handbag to change into when she arrived in the centre. The hour's walk to the bus stop, then the same twenty-three stops to Teatral'naya Square would give her time to prepare for her interview with the employment agency, the first since Natalya was born.

Her journey would also give the two men watching her apartment block plenty of time. She didn't notice the grey GAZ panel van in the line of parked cars, nor the pallid-faced man in the driver's seat whose bored eyes followed her as she walked away. It was forty minutes later, when the teenagers had disappeared, that the van's back door opened. Two FSB men got out and strode towards the block. Within six minutes they had accessed apartment 57 using a simple tension wrench and pick in the door's lock, secreted voice-activated recording devices behind the light switches inside each room and two in the living room, (one beneath a bookshelf), closed the door behind them and were back in the van without being spotted.

On the fifth floor inside the Lubyanka, the

General who'd given the order replaced the telephone receiver. He'd asked for daily reports from the surveillance team, although what he really wanted is for the whole Petrenko affair to just go away.

7

It was nearing lunchtime when Russell Blake approached the counter in the basement vault of Lloyd's Bank and handed the pretty young woman behind it the small key. She stared at him, and for a while she liked what she saw. The visitor was tall with a lean, athletic build without being overly muscular — something she didn't like. His face was lightly tanned, and his almost black hair of medium length was neatly parted. His appearance was unlike other men, she thought, and a bit old fashioned. He was calm, composed, and as he rested well manicured hands upon the table in front of her she imagined he always kept control of himself. She had stared into many men's eyes and was something of an expert on men, but after she had stared into the light green, glassy eyes looking back at her for a few brief moments she felt a chill that she couldn't explain. It was as if there was no emotion behind them at all.

She didn't need to ask for identification, but if she had he would have been able to produce it in the form of a current and perfectly legitimate British passport. Instead, she produced the duplicate key and led him into a long room that housed floor to ceiling security boxes of hardened and tempered steel, some slim and oblong, some medium size, that were set into the deep concrete walls. It was to one of the medium bins the woman led the visitor. She took his key, then along with her duplicate twisted both side by side in their locks. She removed the box, which wasn't heavy, placed it on the long table in the room's centre, smiled politely, and left him alone. He lifted the lid and reached an arm inside. First he pulled out a small metal box that when clicked open revealed three more small keys. Next was several stacks of hundred-dollar bills, five in total and each wrapped with a currency strap stating $10,000 — $50,000 in all. The last item he retrieved was the largest — a metal 16 mm film canister, measuring twelve inches in diameter and with a large faded sticker on its front, featuring a red star at its centre, yellow Cyrillic capitals that read: *TOP SECRET. PROPERTY OF THE USSR,* and a scrawl of unruly blue biro-pen in Cyrillic letters that he knew to mean: *DATE: 07.1984. 1200 Ft REEL, RUNNING TIME: 0:33:00 mins. 24 fps.*

Having walked up from Trafalgar Square into the Charing Cross Road, then continued east through narrow streets in the area of Covent Garden, he found the side road tucked behind a 17th Century church. At number 54, a sign above a cluttered window stated HARRY'S SUPER CINE, and upon entering the shop his nasal senses were treated to a faint yet singularly particular odour of old plastic, faintly pungent nitrate, cats, and four decades of dust. Usually visitors in search of equipment were disappointed, for the dishevelled proprietor's more preferred habitat during working hours was that of the pub opposite. This day though was an exception, and when Harold Finchley-Aames greeted the tall stranger and asked him how he could help him that fine morning he smiled unusually brightly, for not only could he see before him the fine suit and the high quality shoes, but also very large pound signs.

A large tabby cat appeared on the 18th century counter top and, upon regarding the stranger, hissed and spat at him the way old Harry had never witnessed before. He decided there and then that whatever this slick-dick wanted, he would have to pay at least double for. Twenty minutes later Russell Blake left with a Bell and Howell Filmosound Model 535 in exchange for £800 in the Queen's currency, and not five minutes after that Harry shut up shop early and went across the road to the Rose and Crown to begin spending it.

Blake hailed a passing Soho black cab and heaved the heavy projector onto the back seat. He had one stop to make, he told the driver. He could keep the meter running, meet him round on Birdcage Walk, and he'd only be a few minutes. He'd leave this case here and give him an extra fifty for his trouble. Fine, mate, the driver replied.

Sandwiched between Buckingham Palace and the powerful ministries of Whitehall, the Blue Bridge in St James' Park offers views across the park's lake towards the palace to the west and Horse Guards Parade, Big Ben, and London Eye towards the east. The low-arched concrete bridge is a favourite with tourists, and also happens to be bustling enough at most times of the day to host a perfectly anonymous brush pass between intelligence agents. Only someone watching closely would have noticed that the well-dressed man who approached the bridge from the north side empty-handed stepped off its south side a few seconds later holding a 12x8 inch manilla envelope.

Once back home in Battersea he opened the envelope to reveal a slightly soiled pair of car number plates.

As the lesser of two evils Keith Godwin had opted for the day shift, and had let young Hallewell take nights. Nights messed with his equilibrium. As far as he was concerned a week into the surveillance of Charlotte Fisher had yielded little, yet the way he saw it he was another week closer to the retirement he would spend sailing on the Solent in the fresh sea air away from the transit van, the pinch of government-issue headphones, and the pâtisseries that were making him fat. But for now it was his job to monitor every sniff and cough from the woman, every snore, downward dog and mouthful of cereal as well as the dreary meetings with faceless ministers, and constituents complaining about local hospital parking, vandalised public toilets and the pressing need for chevrons outside the newsagent's. She ordered lattes 'with room' — room for what Godwin would ask himself each time — ate lunch from Pret in the office, had no friends, and never deviated from an inevitable routine.

The transcript for a phone call by the target, (CF), to her aunt, (HL), in Guildford on 27th October at 10:58 a.m. was a typical example: *23 minutes of chat about CF's job in Westminster and how monotonous she sometimes finds it,* (at least I'm not alone, thought Godwin)*, then mention of how she may have to postpone the trip to see HL for Sean's birthday on 7.11 due to planned parliamentary business, which upsets HL. Call ends when HL says she has to go as a customer has just come into the shop. Time: 11:36 a.m.*

Inside Prince's' hairdressers in Guildford at

that hour, a woman of around forty-five sat down in the chair. Hayley Lander tucked her phone into her jeans and placed a cape around the woman's front, tying it off loosely behind the neck. Talk of requirements ensued, then production, and the hairdresser began to cut. She wasn't her usual kind of customer, she was classier than the regulars, looked like she could afford somewhere a bit more upmarket, like Toni & Guy in town. Still, she was friendly, if a bit too chatty in the usually silent workplace. Her name was Sally, she said, and they talked solidly for the half an hour it took her to trim her shoulder length hair. Afterwards she seemed very happy with the results of Hayley's work, and after she'd paid her £14.50, tipped, and left, Hayley told her colleague how weird it was that they had so much in common. She didn't have many friends, any really, and secretly she thought Sally was the kind of person she could be friends with.

Once outside, the middle-aged woman brushed the few final hairs from her shoulders and turned towards the station, where she would wait for the next train back to London. On the platform she unlocked her phone and searched for Nikki in the contact's list. When the call was answered inside a deafening hair salon in Soho, she made an emergency appointment for first thing the following morning, then hung up. She touched her hair gingerly with a flat palm, and a short series of colourful expletives left her lips. The things I do for England, she muttered to herself, before pulling a chunky knit bobble hat out of her bag and putting it on her head as the train approached the platform.

When Zoe Taylor landed at Moscow's Sheremetyevo

airport at five-forty that afternoon, Oliver Finn, a young embassy attache, was there to meet her. He led her to his waiting car with distinctive red and white diplomatic plates that read 001 T 106 77 RUS, identifying it as belonging to the British Embassy, specifically a member of the administrative or technical staff. From across the road a blond man from the FSB took photographs, but was under no instruction to approach, merely to observe.

The car crawled through the dense evening traffic beneath billboards and past the airport hotels, before speeding up on the three-lane motorway towards the capital. Zoe had asked to be taken directly to meet Sam Donavon, but when Finn informed her that that wouldn't be possible until the next morning she asked him to take her to her hotel — which, for a brief moment after she said it, excited him. Flanked by tower blocks, a giant Ikea, KFC, Toyota, Kia and Western-built car dealerships and Burger King, she watched Moscow approach, and it occurred to her that were it not for the Cyrillic letters on the signs she could very well have just landed in San Fransisco, London, or Paris.

'I'll be waiting here at eight a.m.,' said Finn with his best smile as he dropped her outside her hotel, a modest place called The President, on the northern edge of Gorky Park.

By seven p.m. she was dressed in a thick coat, and in the back of a taxi, being driven towards Koptevo.

She paid the cab off outside an Apteka pharmacy on a treeless main road called Novomikhalkovsky Drive, then when it had gone, walked to the corner of Ulitsa Generala Rychagova

Street. Neither the communal area that the apartment blocks overlooked, nor the children's playground showed any signs of life as she approached. She did, however, notice a GAZ panel van parked amongst the small family cars in the car park. There was no one in its cab, so she walked closer. It was of the closed type that Watchers the world over prefer, and on its coachwork could be seen the vague outline of a previously applied and later removed sticker that read *Ochistiteli,* or 'Cleaners' in English. The vehicle's identity had been changed, and recently. On the icy ground beneath the rear doors were six curled cigarette butts. She turned towards the apartment block's main entrance.

Minutes later, the FSB man in the back of the van had just put his mug of hot tea down safely when the three door knocks came thundering through his headphones, yet the scare did cause him to fling his *Russian Model Magazine* into the air as the voice-activated recorder on a shelf above him sprang into action.

Katya turned the television's volume down and went out into the hall, Natalya gripping at the leg of her jeans. She opened it to find a blonde, attractive young woman in a full length, expensive-looking, North Face coat who was holding the forefinger of her right hand against her lips and miming 'sshh.' Natalya, not yet conversed in the international language of mime, went to speak, but something told Katya to hush her daughter. Less than a minute later, for reasons she didn't know, the visitor was standing in her small living room and scribbling a note in Russian.

Zoe handed it to her. Katya read it slowly, and though she was trembling, nodded. She took Natalya by the hand and led her out through the hallway to the front door. A few minutes later, having delivered her daughter to her friend's apartment, she returned to find the light switch in the living room hanging from the wall and a small black plastic box with red LED light on its side being held up by her visitor. Zoe beckoned Katya over to the window and pointed at the grey van parked below. She placed the small black box on the window ledge, and held her hands apart directly over it before clapping them together hard. A distant but violent scream came from the van, which shook on its tyres slightly.

A nervous smile flicked across Katya's lips. Zoe stepped back from the window and wrote another note. Katya read it, went over to her closet, and handed Zoe a set of fresh clothes; a pair of jeans, T-shirt, jumper, and boots. Zoe inspected each item thoroughly, then handed them back to Katya who changed into them. Fearing a microdot tracker or mic may have been sewn into it, she shook her head when Katya went to pull on her coat, and instead gave her her long winter coat to wear. Their mobile phones switched off, the two women left the building via the rear exit where the lorries collect the communal refuse bins, and began walking away from the apartment complex through the freezing, colourless back streets. Both women spoke each other's languages - Zoe chose to speak in Russian.

'I'm very sorry for your loss, Katya,'
'Who are you?'
'My name is Samantha Hobbs.'
'Is that your real name?'
'No,' she smiled, 'but I do want to help you.'
'Why are they listening to me?'

'They suspect you know something. Did Dmitri say anything, Katya, about his work? About how he earned money to pay for Natalya's medicine? Anything at all that you remember as being unusual?'

So that was how. She'd known it all along of course, that her husband had been a chancing spy, and that he'd been out of his shallow depth, though she hadn't admitted the fact to herself, hadn't had proof, until now. *Oh Dmitri, what did you do.*

They walked on.

'Did you know that Ivan Grushenko is my uncle?' she asked. 'Nobody knows. He makes sure of it. And did you know that he killed Dmitri? Either he killed him or had someone kill him. Grushenko told me, he looked me in the eye, and told me that Dmitri had been killed when the car he was driving crashed into a truck in Telishchevo. You know how I know this is bullshit, Samantha Hobbs, or whoever you are? Dmitri couldn't drive.'

They came to a main road. On the opposite corner, lit only by a single amber streetlamp, stood a fourteen story tower block. At the foot the concrete monolith, in the darkness of its overhang, was a heavily-graffitied mini grocery store protected by steel shutters, a boarded up launderette with a broken window air-conditioner, and a bar with red, jagged neon lettering above the door that spelt *Berlin*. Katya led the way.

The room was dimly lit, with the doorway and windows sheathed in heavy deep-purple drapes. Once they'd pulled them aside and entered, they sat in a corner and ordered two Baltika beers from the artificially muscled barman. Only low mutters from a few over-coated old men in caps and a group of half-doped teenagers in tracksuits broke the silence. This was not a place to socialise in but to get drunk in. The barman brought the beer and Zoe asked questions, trying to prompt Katya to remember anything Dmitri may have said — any clue at all that would account for his death and her subsequent surveillance. But although her eyes were open they were gazing inward, glazed over with grief. Around them the skin was still sore from the tears and behind them her mind was consumed with fear for her ailing daughter's future and the desperate need for money to lift the curse of illness that plagued them. So they sat in silence until she began to tell her story. Her father, Georgi, was a sailor, her mother had told her.

'A . . . podvodnik, actually, how do you say that in English?'

'Submariner.' Zoe whispered.

'Sub-*mar*-iner, yes. But he left her, us, before I was born. He continued to send money but then he died in a bar brawl when I was two years. Some say it was Ivan Grushenko, his own brother, who killed him with a broken bottle in an argument over a prostitute, but his death left my mother penniless, and she started to drink. Later she fell into street prostitution, and then one day she just didn't come home. Three days later a drunk policeman came to the door to tell a sixteen year-old girl that her mother had frozen to death on the street near Esenin's monument. She died of Hypothermia. It was a Tuesday, I remember. It was eighteen below that night. People see someone on the street they think they are addicts, that they are dangerous. So nobody helped her. She was thirty-three.'

Now alone, Katya said, she had no choice but

to ask her uncle for money. That once she had dreamed of attending the faculty of journalism at the State University, but that it was not to be. Her uncle forbade it, and when she protested, he blocked her path by sending goons to threaten faculty staff. He won. Ten years of menial jobs and unemployment followed.

'Some are sent angels, Samantha, I was sent a demon. He is a psychopath, you know. Will you buy us a bottle of vodka?'

Beneath two-hundred metres of concrete in the musty darkness of Bar Berlin the women sat in silence, and Zoe began to realise that Katya's only solace was the here and now: wrapped in a snug goose-down coat with a giant fur hood that warmed her like a Chanel-scented quilt, being bought drinks by a friendly woman from the other side of the world, while letting her eyelids fall, the bottle empty, the hour become early, and the pain momentarily recede.

With the film projector on a high table at the far end of his double reception room, the man the *Telepol* Committee referred to as the Executive Officer poured himself another brandy and set about threading the film into the machine. Having removed it from the canister, he mounted it on the projector's front reel and unwound five feet of film. Holding the lens rim he swung open the mount and placed the film's perforations firmly under the front roller and sprocket, between the guide rails, under the top stabiliser roller and around the sound drum, before closing the lower sprocket guard. Careful to achieve tension around the sound drum, he stood back and checked, then plugged the machine into the wall socket, clicked the volume knob up, moved the upper knob selector up to FORWARD, flicked the room's light switches off, and sat down with his drink.

Russell Blake stared without expression at the image the flickering shaft of light was projecting onto his wall from behind him — that of a gold hammer and sickle on a red background, with black text that read: TOP SECRET. PROPERTY OF THE KGB. USSR. Accompanying this, the state anthem of the Soviet Union resounded through the projector's speaker. Even so compressed, the rousing power of its melody sung by a choir stirred a feeling of patriotism deep within him, but one that almost immediately became detached, like it belonged to someone else or to a memory buried too far into the past to properly recall.

At the same time, a Cessna 172 light aircraft took off from a small private airfield in Schoenefeld, thirty kilometres south of Potsdam in Germany. It belonged to the pilot, Franz Schäffer, a forty-nine year old teacher from the Rhineland, whose destination, being a country outside of the Schengen zone, meant the air traffic controller had called the federal police to verify Herr Schäffer's passport, which was in order. His luggage remained unchecked either by a metal detector or an X-ray machine, as the airfield possessed neither, so both he and his innocent-looking, if rather heavy, suitcase boarded the single-engined aircraft without inconvenience.

Blake reached behind him to the focusing adjuster dial on the front of the projector and twisted it a fraction. The twenty-four frames-per-second film cut abruptly from the title graphic to a plain white office, into which stepped a middle-aged man wearing round, owlish glasses. His appearance was that of a scientist, yet he was wearing a suit and waiting awkwardly behind a high table with Gerasimov's portrait of Lenin on The Podium looming over him. To the viewer's eye both the film stock and the man's appearance placed him in 1983.

Blake squinted through the sparkling dust lit by the bulb. The resolution was low, and the film had degraded so that the bleached-out square frame that shone upon his wall was barely more colour saturated than monochrome. He suspected he was the only person ever to witness this film.

When the presenter spoke it was in an stiff monotone in the Moscovian dialect. 'This film will provide an overview of the RA-115s tactical nuclear weapon.' The frame widened to show a small dark-grey suitcase upon the table. He lay both hands upon it. 'The RA-115s tactical nuclear weapon, or the RA-115-01s – its submersible derivative. Measuring sixty by forty by twenty centimetres, and weighing approximately sixty-five pounds.'

The pilot flew the Cessna through the moonless night, while wedged behind his seat on the cockpit floor was an identical suitcase.

The presenter unlocked two latches, once on each side. 'The outer shell is that of a common suitcase. Although the edges are reinforced by two inches of hardened steel.' He opened the lid to reveal the contents. They were dominated by a wide metallic tube of seven inches in diameter fixed diagonally inside the case. 'Internally the bomb consists of two Neutron generators, here,' he pointed to each side of the cylinder about a third of the way down, 'and here. And the target, here.' He lifted a finger to the top of the tube, before sliding it further down the metal, 'The gun, the bullet is here, and the high explosive.' His finger now rested on the bottom of the tube.

Blake watched impassively.

'In the case's top right hand corner is the power source — a small twelve volt battery — while the arming switch in red is here on the bottom left. Beneath, here, a small keyhole — the arming key. Plutonium and Tritium produce the yield, which is approximately one to two kilotons, depending on degradation.'

The sole audience member, while being an expert in the use of small firearms and close combat with knives and his fists, knew almost nothing of bombs, let alone those of the thermonuclear variety. Nevertheless, he did know that the blast from a weapon with a yield of one kiloton had the power to completely destroy everything within about a kilometre radius and that the fallout would be many times more powerful, and deadly. Somewhere from his memory he recalled that the Hiroshima bomb in Japan in 1945 had had a fifteen kiloton yield. Flashes of black and white images entered his mind; photographs of screaming children with hideous facial injuries and burns.

He sipped his brandy as the projector continued to whir. The film cut to the presenter at a blackboard with a diagram of the bomb's internals drawn upon it. 'The sequence of events is as follows. The few kilograms of plutonium inside the neutron bomb are ignited by the conventional explosive, and serves as a fission trigger to ignite a fusion explosion in the capsule, that contains several grams of deuterium-tritium. Tritium, when placed inside fission weapons can substantially boost the energy released by the fission explosion.'

The man paused. His explanation of the technicalities of bombs was obviously inside his area of comfort; what he was required to say next, was not. 'In a city the size of London,' he ventured uneasily, 'a one kiloton bomb would completely flatten all buildings within 500 metres, immediately killing 20,000 people, with fatalities up to a one kilometre radius. Within hours the prevailing winds would carry the powerful waves of neutron and gamma radiation up to thirty kilometres, meaning the evacuation of the entire city.'

Above the clouds the Cessna was crossing the border between Germany and The Netherlands when Russell Blake, dressed in dark clothes, left the flat on Prince of Wales Drive. He glanced up and down the street, and at 11:30 got into his Maserati and pulled away.

Forty-five minutes later, at a quarter past midnight, having swapped the car for the rented Ford in the railway arch lock-up, he was driving east.

At ten to one the pilot was just able to make out the beaches of the Kent coastline through the glass of the Cessna window after a foggy but otherwise unremarkable flight across the North Sea. He kept the land in his left-side window for a little over twenty-two miles before he turned the yoke to the left, which banked the small plane westwards. It was 01:11 a.m. on Wednesday morning when he brought the Cessna safely down in a long, unlit farmer's field in Seasalter, only a few metres inland from the beach. Unlit that was, except for the pair of high-beam headlights that shone out from a dark-coloured Ford that partially illuminated the left side of the makeshift runway. When the plane had rolled to a halt and the pilot climbed out, a man in black approached. Without saying a word, he took the small suitcase he was handed, turned, and disappeared back towards the blaze of the car's headlights.

Oliver Finn was waiting in the car outside the hotel at eight a.m. as arranged. He was wearing his favourite shirt and tie and his pink, freshly shaven face beamed when he saw her appear at the passenger door. He was about to rush round to open it but she'd already got in without a word. He knew he didn't stand a chance. She was easily five or six years older, probably married, and several thousand leagues above, but, he thought as he manoeuvred the car away, he owed it to himself to try as she was so perfectly beautiful. Today, however, Zoe felt anything but.

The Bar Berlin bartender had kept the vodka coming and it was around four a.m. when she and Katya finally left. At the back of Katya's building where the lorries collect the refuse bins, they'd hugged like old friends, and against her better judgement Zoe had let her keep her long coat before finding a cab that finally delivered her to her hotel at sometime after five.

Asked to wait in a side office inside the large embassy in the Arbat District, Zoe drank a mug of weak coffee and ate a cold *vatrushka* before she was shown into an office that overlooked the river. The man was on the phone as he beckoned her to sit. The room was a spiritless blend of beige and taupe but for the rosy wooden cheeks and red poppies that adorned the midriffs of a set of six brightly painted Russian matryoshka dolls on a side cupboard. She watched him with the receiver under his chin as he picked at his finger nails and nodded. He was in his late-forties with dark, unblinking eyes and thin, shrewd lips that although were set in a permanent half-smile, gave the impression that no humour had ever left them. So this is Carlo, she thought. The man who had been responsible, operationally at least, for Dmitri. It was precisely how responsible that was giving her cause for her concern.

She'd been given the potted history in the staff bar over whiskeys. He's an undeclared, Henderson had said. While the head of a station is assisted by a number of declared officers known to the host nation's intelligence service who operate in liaison with it, some, like Carlo, were not. His cover name in the embassy was Sam Donavon and his duties in his official role as Second Secretary required him to manage junior diplomats and locally hired staff. The more clandestine ones for Her Majesty required him to run a network of agents inside both Russian energy companies and the FSB. Even the ambassador didn't know Donavon was MI6.

His real name was George Provost, Henderson had told her, mother Spanish, an interpreter who had worked on the famous Burgos Trials, and his father a British banker. 'He's run networks all over the world - Nairobi, Prague, Paris, Washington, Geneva. A polyglot — can pick up languages by ear.' He'd operated under armies of identities over the years yet George could recall word perfectly a long-forgotten conversation in a master's study in Sussex, scuttlebutt in a staff canteen in Mombassa, the finer points of a bordello transaction in Hong Kong, or the minutes of a meeting in a petroleum company in 1990s Kuwait - none of which may ever have actually taken place.

'Dates too. George can give you the exact date of a chance meeting thirty years later and be accurate.'

Somewhere in this intricately patterned past hid rumours of an embarrassment, she'd heard later from a woman called Dawn in Human Resources, possibly with a male agent in London, that may or may not have been his fault but that led to his being packed off again under consular cover back to Moscow only the year before.

'George and I go back a long way,' Henderson had added as they finished their glasses. 'Very long.'

Very long. Whatever that meant, thought Zoe as, with the onset of impatience, she pulled her sleeve back to look at her watch, which prompted Provost to utter a short phrase in a language she couldn't place, and to end his call.

'Samantha Hobbs,' he smiled across his desk. 'Do you have a mobile phone with you registered in that name?'

'Of course. But I left it at reception like I was asked.'

'There's a mini-tower inside the airport operated by the FSB. When you landed yesterday and turned your phone on it would have been automatically intercepted by the tower. If they wish they can download everything on it and use it to track you.'

'That's okay,' she said, unsurprised, 'the contract's over ten years old, and Samantha Hobbs has nothing to hide. They were taking photographs outside the terminal. I assumed it was because I was met in a car with British embassy plates.'

'It's Oliver. I think he thought it would impress you.'

And you're trying to test me, she thought, sensing a deeply buried cruelty in the man. The talk moved to business and began informally — about the old guard being hung out to dry, about Washington State - whose geography Provost seemed to know in surprising detail — about how he had narrowly escaped Jones-Cooper sending him packing to the Tottenham cinema to work for the bully-boys, and about everything except the elephant in the room, until, with another appointment looming and in an act of professional chivalry which took her by surprise, Provost addressed it to save her the trouble.

'Truth is I feel fucking terrible about it. Like I let him walk blindfolded into the jaws of hell.' It sounded like real regret but was closely followed by a but. 'But in this business there's not always time to assess someone's mental state beyond the perfunctory.'

'Or suitability?' she fired back. The question, a bare naked accusation, was greeted with some silence. The sight of Katya's hollow grief was still fresh in her mind.

'You mean whether someone with so desperate a need to save his daughter should have been allowed to put himself in such danger?' Provost replied, accepting the charge. 'The *great game* we play, Ms Taylor, is beset with conundra. The primary one being as secret information is so difficult to value, is it ever worth a man's life? For my part, yes, I believe it is. But rarely will two people agree on when. Unfortunately I'm afraid as an asset Dmitri Petrenko produced little intelligence of any value. Which, I'm sure you would agree with me, makes his death futile and rather inglorious. Now, if you will excuse me, I have another appointment, my day job.'

She stood to leave, and he too raised himself and offered his hand, but she was surprised when he kept talking.

'You know, I always think the mind is like those little Russian dolls, the matryoshkas,' — a glance over to them. 'We've known each other since ninety-four, John and I, we're the same age, did you know that? And yet when I come to think of it I don't think I've ever seen him reveal even the second one, let alone the smallest.

The *sixth* one inside.'

8

The drive back from the Kent coast had been fast. The A2 is a road upon which, until just past Dartford at least, there remain mercifully few speed cameras, and after he had swapped the rental car for his own in Southwark, Blake arrived at his flat at 3:20 a.m. He poured himself a brandy and sat down to examine the case. He noticed a modern digital timer had been added to the bomb's interior, as well as a transmitter affixed to the side of the battery he assumed would emit a signal to a GRU post inside an embassy, or maybe to a satellite, if the charge became low. He took the keys from the small box and tried them in the lock. The second one fitted, and a quarter turn brought the digital display to life: 00:00:00:00. He twisted the knob beside it, causing the red LCD numbers to blur randomly, then moved his finger down over the ominous red arming switch. He held it there, feeling the power in the tip of his finger that was an inch away from detonating the catastrophic device. An act that would the reproduce those same images of Hiroshima. He drew his finger away yet he remained there, deep in thought, and while gradually the sun crept up behind the curtains and began to slowly slash the walls of his apartment, he remained there staring, almost unblinking, into the case's deadly metallic contents.

Sean, Shaun, or Shawn, was proving elusive. All S-section had to go on was the birthday that fell on November 7th, yet despite their thorough trawling through the thousands of names that make up a person's documented life history — lists of friends, family, neighbours past and present, co-tenants, fellow students and lecturers at university, political contacts in Westminster, constituents in Somerset as well as even the most casual of acquaintances from gym owners to the boy that served her coffee in the cafe every morning, by Wednesday lunchtime they had only three possible name matches — two Seans and a Shaun. Of those however, none had the correct birthday.

After a light lunch Russell Blake took a taxi into central London and got out at Oxford Circus. He handed the driver a twenty-pound note, waited until the car had disappeared into Regents Street, then walked for fifteen minutes through the bustle to Tottenham Court Road until he found a small shop selling mobile phones and just about every accessory required to support them. He bought a 'pay-as-you-go' phone, unwrapped it, inserted the SIM card and made one phone call before pulling the SIM out and disposing of it. A few minutes later, by the gated entrance to Soho Square, the new handset was also at the bottom of a litter bin.

'Sally' arrived back at Six from Soho sporting the second, remedial trim that to untrained eyes would have looked uncannily similar to the duteous first. She'd worn a wire for her cut with Hayley Lander and the Fifth Floor had printed out the transcript for Henderson, from which he'd gleaned little except that Lander had moved from High Wycombe to Guildford years ago to be with a boy, then, upon being handed the receipt for the corrective cut, how inexpensive a provincial haircut was compared with a Soho one. There'd been no response when she'd mentioned Sean as a friend's choice of baby name, nor anything of worth to the other set of prompts.

Later, in a corner of the staff bar, managing to avoid the regulars who gathered at five every evening, John Henderson realised the reason Fisher had turned betrayer could remain frustratingly absent no longer. There must be something in her history. Both she and the aunt were clean, and it just didn't make sense. No, the answer had to lie in that house in Guildford. He knocked back the last of his whiskey and decided it was time to use a last resort.

At five-past nine Zoe's plane touched down on the tarmac at Heathrow airport. She called Paul as soon as her phone connected to its network, but didn't make it back to Crouch End until gone midnight. The flat was dark but for the occasional car headlamps from below that danced across her ceiling, its only sound the low hum of the fridge, while in the air the faint aroma of another dinner missed.

Henderson had also managed to miss his son again when he arrived home, so decided to bypass the evening news and head straight to bed. In the final waking hour of that Wednesday before sleep came, his thoughts became occupied with his purpose. Thanks to the *Overture* report, to some he was an alarmist, which after having travelled a few corridors soon became a conspiracy theorist, though few people had actually read it or knew what it contained. Jones-

Cooper just wanted him out, simple, and by any means necessary. His mind drifted back to the time just after the AC's appointment when he'd been asked to report alone to a soundproof room on the fourth floor. An innocent enough request. The two officers the Jones-Cooper had sent to 'question' him had been polite at first, explaining that under the new 'banner of transparency', routine investigations into past missions had been approved in a bid to improve future operational procedure. To identify and analyse any outstanding discrepancies, was the claim. "To tie up any loose ends," they'd added, throwing any hint of seriousness away with jocular eye-rolling and the offer of coffee. Yet it soon transpired the answers they sought were not to help fill textbooks for the new strain to read in their laboratories, nor to keep the lawyers happy, and at almost once he sensed it was a trap. All too soon it became clear they were there to discuss one mission and one mission only, one whose details should never be made transparent. The polite early exchanges became questioning which ended up being a three-day interrogation designed to make him slip up, to reveal, to confess. Of course, they failed, *The Mole Hunter* had failed.

Smiling, he opened his eyes. 'Well, fuck him,' he said to his dark ceiling, before turning his mind to Sarah, to her being pawed by her young doctor with his expert French fingers. One day, he imagined her standing at the top of *his* stairs in Primrose fucking Hill telling *him* how she wasn't fulfilled before slamming the door behind her, dropping a brick through the windscreen of his fatuous Porsche with FA13 IEN as its absurd number plate and yelling how she's going back to her spy called John.

He allowed himself another smile at this version of himself he didn't recognise but rather liked the look of, then turned over and fell asleep.

Thursday began in the lift with a phone call from Hedges at GCHQ. 'One of your Domino keywords, John,' the man was saying, 'flagged up on a computer registered to a law firm in Bern in Switzerland, called Gentzner and Asper.'

'*Sper,*'

'Sorry?'

'Nothing. So the disk drive made it all the way to Bern.' The lift pinged, he stepped out and turned towards his office.

'Right. It was plugged into a 2019 model Dell desktop there on the twenty-third, last Friday. The word was in the title of an email that was sent from Bern directly to someone in Moscow yesterday, no encryption, nothing. If they're FSB it's not exactly Edgehill stuff, if you get my drift.'

He did. Edgehill was the codename for the agency's highly sophisticated decryption program that allowed backdoors, or trapdoors, into commercial encryption software. He reached his office. Zoe was waiting at his desk. 'Who's the recipient?'

'An Igor Savich,' said Hedges.

The name was enough to halt his breath. 'And the message?'

'Package received. Request target location.'

He paused. 'What was the keyword?'

'What? Oh, hang on, here it is. *Overture.* Mean something?'

Zoe watched her section head freeze like one of those human statues in Covent Garden. A six foot two statue in a wrinkled navy raincoat over once-dark brown corduroy who looked like it suddenly bore the weight of the world on its back. 'Jesus Christ,' it said, jaw hanging open and without looking down at her.

'John? What is it?'

For the third time in the space of a week at the same briefing table and with tastebuds reeling from the same stale coffee, 'C' was in a COBRA meeting with Sir Humphrey from the cabinet office and Sir Nigel from the JIC, the DG of MI5, and Sir Jonathon Thurling, the freshly appointed Commissioner of the Metropolitan Police. With *Echelon's* misinformation to Moscow campaign being managed, their assembly this morning was to perform 'a spot of decorating' — a term-of-art meaning whitewashing, meaning the issuance of another DSMA-Notice to the nation's news editors to request that they keep the assassination of a British pensioner by a deadly nerve agent on UK soil out of their pages.

While traffic hummed beneath him, accelerating around onto the embankment from the bridge, second in command Stephen Jones-Cooper sensed the calm of his clinically white office was about to be broken. He had reluctantly agreed to Henderson's 'urgent' meeting, even though his secretary had reported the man sounded agitated, and he feared an impassioned speech. He rolled his eyes thinking about it. Stephen Jones-Cooper hated passion, didn't understand the need for it. He preferred logical, by-the-book, problem-solving. When Henderson strode in without a courtesy knock but with Zoe Taylor in tow refusing to sit he got straight to the point by dropping his *Overture* report onto the desk and sliding it across the glass. Jones-Cooper had been right, his manner was pugnacious.

'Operation Overture.' This wasn't what he wanted at all but it couldn't wait. The man was the AC for Christ's sake he had to take notice this time. Still, it was important to exercise patience, he told himself, take it slowly.

'A KGB-era mission blueprint drawn-up in the sixties and once-resurrected — but never enacted upon — in the autumn of '83 during the 'war scare' when Andropov feared a first strike from the Americans. East-West tensions were at an all time low, the Korean airliner was downed by the Soviets, the threat of Pershing Two being launched by Reagan, and the Able Archer '83 NATO exercise that stretched from Turkey to Britain that led the Politburo to believe were genuine preparations for first strike.'

Zoe stood and watched as Jones-Cooper stared at his desk, his face already displaying a blush she knew meant his hackles were readying to the defence.

'Morning John, bit early for double history isn't it?' The quip was delivered tonelessly, and was ignored. 'Have a seat, Miss Taylor?'

This too was ignored. 'Now *that* was the closest the world had come to nuclear war since the Cuban Missile Crisis in sixty-two when Overture was conceived. Conceived . . . ' he slid a copy of the email across the desk towards his nonchalant superior, ' . . . by the recipient of this email, Igor Savich – long-time Soviet strategic military planner.'

'Yes, yes, Operation *Overture*,' came the droll reply with more than a sprig of sarcasm. 'Do remind us John, perhaps Ms Taylor hasn't heard it.' Zoe didn't react. 'Renegade band of breakaway fanatics,' he added, shooting her a conspiratorial look.

'Operation Overture: a plan of attack in four stages. Stage one: Economic autonomy of the West is undermined. Everybody who reads a newspaper knows Russia is the largest supplier of coal, oil, and gas to Europe and that EU member states' reliance upon Russian gas means we are beholden to Moscow, despite there being myriad historical, political and economic reasons why this is a bad idea. Now, *if* the Nord Stream 2 pipeline gets the go-ahead it'll give Russia even more of a stranglehold over us. And then what. Well, we know, don't we. They've turned the taps off before, and they'll do it again. In January 2015 in an act of revenge Gazprom was ordered to cut gas supplies to Europe by fifty percent. And that wasn't the last time, was it? They've demonstrated they can use gas a political weapon and hold us to ransom. Same with oil — of the OPEC countries Russia is the world's third largest oil producer. Banking, real estate. Do you know how much of London is owned by Russian oligarchs?'

'What possible concern all this of ours is, John, is quite frankly beyond me.'

He took his voice down a tone, determined to stay calm in the face of the man's absurd apathy. 'This, concurrent with Step two: Political destabilisation of Western governments by the spread of disinformation — they use slander, scandal, disgrace, fake news, hacking to create mistrust, in-fighting, and division. Need I say more? Europe's being systematically divided up. Russia's supporting nationalist, ultra-right wing anti-EU parties in Europe - remember the nine million Euro loan to Marine Le Pen's National Front from a Russian Bank in 2014 only a month before the French election? Close talks with right-wing nationalist party Alternative for Germany. Allegations the far-right Freedom Party of Austria received money from Moscow. Britain's out of the EU and anti EU fever is spreading all across Europe. Did Russia interfere with the 2016 UK Independence referendum and support the Leave-dot-EU campaign? What do you think?'

'I think I'm very busy, and that I've heard all this before. Now really, John, we do have more pressing - '

But he'd begun pacing as if blocking the man's path to an early exit. 'Did you know that four-hundred and seventy Facebook accounts are known to have been created by Russian operatives during the 2016 US campaign that posted adverts estimated to have reached ten million users? Of those accounts, six — *six*, generated content that was shared at least three-hundred and forty-million times. Facebook admitted that about one-hundred and twenty-six million Americans may have seen posts published by Russian operatives.'

Zoe watched him wait, somewhat optimistically she thought, for a look of horror to cross Jones-Cooper's face, then his bemusement when it became clear the AC showed nothing but disinterest and disdain towards him. He was little more than a thorn in his side, she thought. But he wasn't finished.

'You know, the EU is so concerned about Russian State media-backed and social-media-led internet trolls that they've established a special unit explicitly tasked with tackling 'fake news' and misinformation? Did you know that?'

'All right, John, thank you, I'll see that your resubmission of your report is duly noted.'

'And the hacking is out of control. Cyber attacks blamed on Russian-linked groups. TV5 Monde taken off air — nearly had its systems destroyed, massive data hack of Germany's lower house of parliament — sixteen gigabytes of data lost – Bulgaria, October 2016. In Estonia in 2007: online banking frozen. Government communication frozen. *And. No. News.*' He stressed, the back of his hand smacking into his palm. 'Ukrainian power plant in 2015, Georgia, Poland, Venezuela . . . the list goes on.'

'All right, all right — '

'Now I think you'll agree,' he interrupted, calming his voice in a last futile attempt to soften his superior's slowly reddening glow of animosity, 'that stages one and two are already, indisputably in progress. Stage three we'll start to see political assassinations: sabotage, subversion of democracy, random terrorist acts apportioned to separatist groups. And step four,' he paused, as if the gravity of the words he was about to say could never find quite the right emphasis, 'the detonation of nuclear devices on key targets across Europe. Bringing about a total collapse of Western democracy. Making way for a totalitarian Communist State across the western hemisphere. Britain, France and Germany under immediate occupation and the capitulation of Europe within a year. Political and Economic conditions are perfect, the weaknesses in the three countries' cyber security systems have been exposed, meaning all online banking will be frozen, government communication, total news blackouts. Hundreds, *thousands* of sleeper agents in the three governments are waiting to assume control when the time comes. This email is a message from the agent in Britain,' he gestured to the paper, 'routed through a law firm in Bern to his controller, Igor Savich. It's clear as day. Can't mean anything else. Package received. Request target location.'

Without glancing down the assistant chief pushed the paper slowly away, his fingers coming to rest on the pen in front of him, which he straightened twice on the desk before speaking. 'Overture, you say.'

'Yes, Overture.'

'Let me express this in the simplest terms I can and then underline it for you. This service deems that the threat level from the findings and claims in this report low. Frankly, and pardon my language here Zoe, but you're making a tit of yourself again with these claims, John, and it won't do your career much good if you continue in this vain. Look at what you have. A five word *unencrypted* email from someone in Switzerland to someone in Moscow? I don't suppose you have anything that even vaguely resembles, sorry to use a word you obviously find so foreign, *evidence*?'

He bit his lip. He wouldn't rise. '*This service* deems the threat level low?' he retorted. 'That's some audacity. What about Dmitri Petrenko?'

'Who?'

'Who? Jesus, c'mon, Jones. *Jackdaw.* An asset who's been passing us intel on General Ivan Grushenko. Petrenko's dead and Grushenko's covering it up. The intel's been arranged, prettied, the date stamps on the files show the photographs were taken days *after* Dmitri disappeared. But what it does include is a part of a name, probably an oversight by whoever took the photographs, I'd bet Grushenko himself, that matches the name of a law firm in Bern that's probably an FSB substation: *'sper'*, Gentzner and

Asper.'

'Mmm, probably.' He made a note of it, though not convincingly. 'Anything else?'

'Well, how about the Kolikovo transmitter that's just gone active again for the first time since the fucking Berlin wall came down?'

Jones-Cooper was ignoring the insubordination but his patience had dwindled and he was glaring. 'So, to sum up,' he said in as businesslike a manner as his quivering voice could manage, and after sitting forward and bringing each of his outstretched fingertips together with their opposites. 'You've got a dead source, a part of a word that may or may not refer to a law firm that may or may not be an FSB outstation, some new radio broadcasts, and a vague, unencrypted email requesting a location for god knows what?'

'Jesus Christ. With the title *Overture*.'

'Ah, yes,' Jones-Cooper announced as if the penny had finally dropped. 'Overture - that likely refers to the musical introduction to an opera. But all you really have is an unstoppable imagination, now if you'll excuse me.'

'Oh, for christ's sake.'

'Look, I think what John's trying to say sir, is —' Zoe attempted.

'You're a fucking relic, Henderson. Why the fantasy, eh? What's the matter? Feeling a bit left behind? Can't work the lift? Miss sending a telegram? Don't feel like a part of the family anymore so you concoct some fantasy about fanatical pensioners intent on obliterating us all? A hard-line faction, yes, that'll do. Plausible deniability cuts both ways. A top secret breakaway committee of communist lunatics: perfect!'

Henderson's jaw had dropped open and he had

to quash the desire for violent strangulation. In one last ditch attempt at calm, studied reason before committing an act of aggression that he knew very well would help no one yet feel more satisfying than anything he had ever felt, he asked, 'How can you not see what's happening here?' in a tone of complete disbelief.

Zoe turned to witness the response, which was accompanied by Jones-Cooper squinting and shaking his head in mock bafflement. 'Oh, listen to yourself. The only thing I *see* is the irony that you have titled your plan Overture when it's never going to get past the introduction.'

'*My* plan? You really think I'm making this stuff up?'

He was shuffling paper like someone about to stand to leave. 'I know the game you're playing here, Henderson. I can see right through your little charade. This illusion you've invented designed to win favour. What is it, eh? You foil the dastardly plan and become Chief. And then what?' He turned to Zoe but kept his eyes on Henderson. They were full of vitriol. 'Perhaps we already know. Ask him what his true intentions are, Zoe. Ask him what the long game is. Ask him where his loyalty *really* lies.'

Just as Jones-Cooper rose behind the desk Henderson snapped. Furious, he sprang forward and brought both fists down hard on the glass table, causing the Montblanc to launch into the air and come crashing down hard on its delicate lid like an impotent rocket and its owner to flinch backwards on his heels. 'What, are you fucking deaf and blind?' he yelled. 'Haven't you listened to a word I've said? We're sitting ducks, there's an agent on British soil requesting the target location for a nuclear bomb and you've got your head buried so far up your arse it's turned you inside out.'

Face now plum with rage and jowls quivering, Stephen Jones-Cooper reached clumsily for the pen before drawing it towards the breast pocket of his jacket. Once he had pushed it down with a forefinger he drew in a strengthening breath, and in a low, trembling voice said, 'You are to take an enforced leave of absence until further notice. And I'm ordering the reinstatement of your psychological sessions.'

Zoe stepped forward but knew it was too late for mediation.

'You are blind,' Henderson added, exasperated. 'Or is it plain stupid?'

'Get out. That's an order.'

That evening the heavens opened. Henderson was already half way across the bridge when the first deluge came and by the time he got north of the river he was soaked to the skin, so decided to continue the solitary traipse home instead of fleeing underground. It was while passing Victoria Station that the contents of a puddle seeped sideways into his left shoe, and he was busy muttering a fresh string of expletives to describe Jones-Cooper when another bus thundered past that created a wave that took care of his right shoe and the whole of his right side. He decided then and there he would resign from the service. Sell the mews house, find a desert island, lick his wounds beneath beach sails somewhere ridiculous, drink whiskey at the end of a bar after long afternoons on humid beaches, play the role of middle-aged eccentric with sunburn before . . . before what? Before picking up his pen to write about what god alone knew. But the muse would come, find him far away from the noise and the stench and the new reptilian men like Jones-Cooper who were taking over. Over the Service, the city, industry, politics — and, it seemed, colonising the whole damn planet.

He stopped navigating the dark puddles and paused by some railings to allow his thoughts to ripen. A minute later, with damp shirt and thoroughly wetted socks, he stepped back onto the pavement to begin to skirt Grosvenor Place opposite the Wellington Arch, then move on west towards his home turf of Kensington.

Forty metres below ground, travelling on a packed Victoria line train that was clattering towards Kings Cross, Zoe stared at the distorted pattern of reflections in the carriage's darkened window. The rain above ground was causing it to steam and the aromas of damp coats to mix with wet hair, perfume, and fast food, but it was what she had heard that really made her feel sick. *Was Overture* real? She asked herself. Was the threat level higher than she or they really knew? Or was Jones-Cooper right — had John invented some fiction: the first piece of a jigsaw whose whole no one yet knew. But if so, christ, then for what possible reason. But it was true, the evidence was scant, and what there was was vague. And now what, now he'd been suspended, muted, unbelieved, and what, accused of treachery? By the assistant chief no less? It was all too -

The doors hissed closed at Kings Cross and a new batch of faces settled. Most were staring blankly at their phones as her eyes flicked from face to face.

But what if he's right? She tried to imagine the horror of his prediction becoming a reality. She remembered reading in his report that the kind of bomb they'd use would mean 20,000 Londoners dead at once, some trapped underground in trains like this one, on platforms, in tunnels, hospitals, parks, schools and cars. Ruptured eardrums and lungs, burns from the firestorms, collapsing buildings and flying debris killing thousands indiscriminately — infants, toddlers, sons, and the elderly. That would be the initial blast. Then the whole city of ten million would have to be evacuated. People would die in the panic. Pandemonium would ensue as people tried to flee from the burning thermal radiation that would sweep uncontrollably, causing cancers and penetrating the food and water supplies without pause or mercy. A country's collapse.

The carriage squealed loudly into Highbury and Islington and jolted to a halt, but she didn't blink. What sort of mind would actually go through with such a thing? She asked herself. What kind of human being would knowingly cause such horror?

In the past forty-eight hours the man whose orders were to do exactly that hadn't tried to sleep. Instead he'd spent them deliberating both his own fate and the fate of millions who would be affected by the mission assigned to him - Overture, whose instructions, passed to him by the old man in the church on Monday, he'd memorised and burned in the hearth. Three cases, three target cities, tens of thousands dead. In a few minutes the numbers would provide him with coordinates of the first target. His orders were to then begin preparations immediately — research, perform reconnaissance, trial runs if possible — then plant the device as close to the target as is viable, to arm, set the timer to detonate — at a time and date as yet unknown to him — then place a call to the number in Switzerland to confirm the first weapon had been readied, and to await further instructions before proceeding to the second target.

Naturally, Blake had asked himself questions: Has the timer been rigged to detonate immediately? To kill him, to destroy all evidence? What then of the other two subsequent bombs? Were there two more agents like him out there? Also waiting for the order to blow themselves up in the name of mother Russia? No, he'd reasoned, for a start he had three keys, and the mission's end was for the three to explode simultaneously. No, it would be him alone.

He cast his memory back to marching the freezing parade ground of The Forest in well-trained lockstep with his platoon eighteen years before. What would young Valentin say if his older self could tell him he would be the one chosen to topple the West, to trigger the great European revolution that would result in a quarter of a million dead? It doesn't matter, the young soldier would say, orders must be obeyed, without question, without hesitation.

The trouble was that although that young major may have once understood that simple concept, Russell Blake's stance on committing mass murder to destroy the capitalist system that had afforded him such an enviable lifestyle was now infinitely more complex.

He had therefore come to the conclusion that the great European revolution would have to be achieved on his own, special terms.

9

His office was empty when she walked past it at eight o'clock the next morning, as of course she knew it would be. Sam Faulds smiled at her in the corridor. They seemed to come as a pair, he and Kesterton, a double act. Roughly the same age, mid-forties, followed the same dress code, had the same air of discrete professionalism, the same round, secret faces. Faulds wore sweet, unpleasant aftershave, nursed a sick mother. Kesterton had come from the Art and Antiques Unit in the Met. Much more than that she hadn't gleaned, except that the head of 'S' had his allies, had his enemies.

It had been another sleepless night, her thoughts still all over the place. There was an envelope waiting on her keyboard at her work station. No name on the front, but sealed, so assuming it was for her she opened it and pulled out a piece of folded paper. Upon it was written a single typed word: *PENDULUM.*

It didn't mean anything to her. She typed it into the database, which drew a blank, then, having spent a restless night deliberating over her Head of Section's past anyway, decided to pull up his file. John Henderson. D.O.B: 2.4.73. Age: 47. Graduated from Cambridge in 1994. Joined MI6 the same year, but, curiously, the word that appeared in the next column for the years 1994 and 1995 simply read CLASSIFIED.

She clicked on George Provost's file. He had said he'd known John since ninety-four. The same — classified between 1994 and 1996. It seemed odd. She wondered if it was unusual for officers to have periods in their history that were classified.

Two days later, on Sunday, at a little before six a.m., an elderly, widowed lady, a sufferer of rheumatoid arthritis, was walking her Chihuahua along George Street in Marylebone in central London. She had just turned left into Montagu Square when she was shocked to discover a man bent over in half, impaled on five foot railings outside a neat four story Georgian house. Possessing no mobile phone, she turned and hurried the few paces back home where she told the police operator that the ambulance should hurry as she'd noticed one of the man's fingers had twitched twice in succession.

When firefighters and the London Ambulance Service arrived however, the twitching had stopped. It was concluded that the man, whom witnesses described as 'white, and probably in his fifties', had plummeted over sixty feet to his death from the luxury fourth floor penthouse apartment. Police covered the scene with a tent to assist firefighters who used angle grinders to remove the railings, while the paramedics who attended the incident later said the man was pronounced dead at the scene.

The assassinations had begun.

Later that same day, whilst driving at dusk towards his home in the village of Brockham in Surrey, a man at the wheel of a silver Ford Focus spotted something lying ahead of him in the road. He pulled over and checked around. He'd heard about a spate of local carjackings and, being in the security business, he was of a suspicious nature. Satisfied, he got out and approached the figure. It was that of a man, pale and cold, who was lying on the damp tarmac in the foetal position holding his stomach and displaying only faint signs of life. Gently, the driver moved him onto his back, tilted his head, and began to perform CPR. After thirty chest compressions he began mouth-to-mouth, and it was then, with each new breath, that the unconscious man began to release a greeny yellow-coloured bile into his attendant's mouth. Later the driver would tell a plant toxicology expert from Kew Royal Botanic Gardens that the liquid tasted like car battery acid, and although he himself would suffer no blistering of the mouth or ill-effects afterwards, the victim, who would be identified as Tristan Moss, would never regain consciousness, having been pronounced dead when the ambulance arrived on the scene.

They would conclude Mr Moss had died from ingesting a deadly poison whose scientific name is gelsemium, that had probably been crumbled into his food earlier the same day. The plant's narrowly ovate leaves and colourful yellow, orange flowers and red petals bely its toxicity. Gelsemium elegans causes paralysis of the spinal cord, physical collapse and death by asphyxiation. It also has a history of being used in assassinations, and thus is known as The Perfect Poison, and more commonly as Heartbreak Grass.

If the news had reached John Henderson - which, considering he had been suspended from duty three days before, it did not — he could have told them that Heartbreak Grass was known to be harvested inside a secret poison laboratory belonging to the Russian Secret Services, known as the *Kamera*. Its job, he would have gone on to say, is to devise poisonous biological and chemical agents that will kill or incapacitate their victims in such a way as to make the death or illness appear natural.

The following day there were three more deaths that were apparently unrelated. The year before, sixty-three year old journalist, Helen Holloway, had written a piece for the Manchester Evening News claiming a radical new pro-communist element had infiltrated the Conservative Party, and three key northern constituencies in particular. She'd received a tip off that a tory whip called Gerald Mayman was acting as chief recruiter for the Kremlin and had even been caught on tape on jocular form saying ' . . .tell your comrade controller for five million sterling you can have the second storming of the winter palace by evensong' into his kitchen telephone. Few took it too seriously but a man who did was a documentary film-maker called Lee Min Kwang, who persuaded Holloway to help him produce an investigative hour-long television documentary profiling the alleged red ingress into the blue Tory heart with the working title *The Russians Are Coming; Who Really Controls Parliament.* Several trips to records offices and town halls followed, and they even attended clandestine meetings in provincial dining rooms and Tory party offices up and down the land in pursuit of more evidence that would prove that a systematic infiltration was indeed taking place.

Funding secure, production about to begin,

with exteriors and establishing shots around Parliament and Whitehall in the can, Holloway and Kwan were about to embark on principal photography that Monday when the speeding taxi appeared. Kwang's Uber driver had dropped him outside Holloway's house in the Castlefield area of Manchester, and as the director also lived locally he had agreed to meet them to share a taxi to the studio. His name was Campbell Hughes.

When they saw the white Prius approach, Kwang waved at the driver from the kerb, although all three were surprised to find the car didn't seem to be slowing down at all. Quite the contrary, in fact.

An hour later, as ambulances were attending to that scene in the north of England, in the small town of Betzdorf that lies twenty-three kilometres outside of Luxembourg City, a man whose nerves had been torn to shreds arrived for work. Set on eighty acres, the neo-baroque style Château de Betzdorf had been his place of employment as Principal Software Engineer for eight years, it being home to the headquarters of SES SA, the world's largest satellite operator. With over seventy satellites in two different orbits that carry not only over 8,100 TV channels to more than one billion people globally but also provide connectivity services to customers in markets including telecommunications, cloud computing, commercial air and shipping, energy, mining, government and institutional areas, air and sea travellers, wind farms, mines, and defence and humanitarian missions, the company relied heavily on the ability of its forests of satellite dishes in their worldwide teleports to communicate with the orbiting satellites.

Unbeknownst to his co-workers however was the fact that their Principal Software Engineer harboured a secret. The year before, his facebook account had been hacked, allowing the perpetrators to access his messenger service and to use the contents to blackmail him. Detailed messages outlining his rather unique sexual predilection would be revealed to his family and colleagues unless he performed a simple task at work. Believing the release of such information would challenge his wife's understanding nature, he agreed. It would be many months before he received the phone call, and when it had come the evening before a Russian female voice spoke the code word that he knew meant he had to act. The act would be despicable, yes, but he knew if he didn't go through with it that he simply couldn't bear the humiliation.

The same day in Vienna, Austria, a Serbian employee of a Chinese Company called ProTechtor received a similar phone call. Over coffee and Cremeschnitten a few months prior in a hotel lobby, he had been offered the sum of $300,000, to be deposited into a numbered account in return for his expertise, should the need arise. That need, the caller said in a brief and business-like manner, had now arisen.

Months prior in an office in Moscow, Savich, Grushenko, and Volkov had the man's dossier open in front of them as the latter, sweating in the summer heat and thumbing its pages with fingers made greasy from the fried chicken bucket in front of them, read aloud.

'Dragan Kosovich, a twenty-three year old Serbian. Responsible for leading the hacking operation to covertly capture the hacking tools used by the US's

157

National Security Agency when they embarked upon a cyber attack into foreign networks in 2016. Aged only nineteen, he co-opted and re-purposed it to enable it to be used against new targets.'

A precedent in cyberwarfare had been set, reported the press, and now the American-developed code could be used to disable software networks across a wide range of industries.

This was their man, the three agreed. Grushenko, who favoured brutal analogies added, 'Like a gunslinger taking and using the rifle of the man he's just felled.'

Unlike the software engineer in Germany, Kosovich felt no burden of guilt nor moral encumbrance when the acquaintance, who had stated his name as Kovač but didn't seem to understand or speak a word of Serbian, outlined his brief requirements in heavily accented English.

What do I care for wind turbines after all? Dragan smiled to himself as he hung up the receiver. All I want is girls. And with $300,000 I can buy a *lot* of girls.

When Zoe finally managed to get Pete Girling on the phone the man in charge of Records apologised. He was alone, he said, and had been at the other side of the room and unable to hear the telephone. Also, he sometimes didn't answer it anyway these days as he was more used to handling emails requesting files. But anyhow, he said, drop by anytime. When she arrived in the basement she was surprised to find a room the size of a football pitch containing endless rows of several rain forests worth of paper records stacked to the ceiling in cages. The sexagenarian climbed down from his mobile ladder to greet her.

'Zoe Taylor?'

'That's right. Peter, it's nice to meet you.'

He pulled his reading glasses up onto his forehead, an elastic headband keeping them firmly in place. 'Pete, please. Welcome to my world beneath the Thames,' he said, attempting a theatrical arch-villain but with an awkward smile, quite unused to such attractive visitors to his vast, lonely domain. 'How can I help you?'

'Well, I'm not sure you can. Does the name Pendulum mean anything to you?'

During the early hours of the next day several insomniac residents of the town of Rehden in Lower Saxony, Germany, were the first to smell the unmistakable odour of rotten-egg-like methyl mercaptan that they knew at once meant Western Europe's largest natural gas storage facility nearby had suffered a serious malfunction. Panic prompted some to attempt to seal windows and doors, others to evacuate the area immediately, yet such was the scale of the catastrophe, neither method would prove successful.

Two thousand meters beneath ground and covering a subterranean area of eight square kilometres, The Rehden Plant was the largest of forty-three underground facilities in Germany with a total storage capacity of about twenty-billion cubic metres. Connecting the Nord Stream pipeline through the Baltic Sea it thus played a central role in supplying Germany and Western Europe with energy. Its shutdown would also prove crippling to those living nearby. The leak of November 3rd was so severe it was enough to result in the hospitalisation of all but nineteen of the 2000 residents of Rehden.

Of the thousands of Russian subjects arriving at Heathrow Airport from Eastern bloc countries on Wednesday 4th November, four names would have flagged up had John Henderson been able to continue his investigation. As it was, without this intervention, the men passed through UK border control without hinderance. The four, who travelled in pairs, were GRU officers and members of an elite Russian assassination squad known as Unit 29155. Each carried only hand luggage in the form of a sports rucksack, inside which was a toilet bag that contained within it between fifty and a hundred nanograms of Polonium-210.

Prior to their trip, each assassin had been handed either a sealed deodorant bottle with a false bottom, a perfume bottle, an atomiser, or a pot of hand or face cream, vessels that contained a tiny glass vial of the deadly substance that had originated at a nuclear reactor in the Urals, passed through a production line in the Russian town of Sarov, and had then been converted into a portable weapon inside a secret FSB laboratory called The Research Institute. A rare radioactive isotope, tiny, invisible, and undetectable, if ingested, Polonium is fatal. Because the alpha particles emitted by Polonium-210 cannot travel through skin or paper, it's easy to smuggle a tiny amount in such a way, and because it emits hardly any gamma radiation, Polonium-210 is invisible to airport scanners.

Having entered Britain with ease, the two teams would set about making their preparations for the murder of three people in the next 48 hours.

In between dodging telephone calls from the Service's in-house clinical phycologist, Henderson had decided to use some of his enforced leave attempting to communicate with his teenage son, Leo. Although the boy was named after Tolstoy, his passion for smoking industrial-strength ganja and listening to loud Deathgrind metal music seemed to suggest he shared few traits with his late, literary namesake.

On Monday he'd broached the future with a chat about university that had begun badly, quickly deteriorated, and that by Tuesday had resulted in Leo locking himself in his room again. Today, in an attempt at what the psychiatrists he loathed and whose phone calls and messages he ignored, called 'bonding', the father had awoken with the idea of taking him skiing for a couple of weeks in Europe. He suggested it to the boy's door.

'Jesus, could you be any more bourgeois,' came the mocking reply from inside the bedroom, leaving Henderson to settle back into his routine which consisted of reluctant early morning runs, a book on the corruption of major British defence contractors and their suspect arms deals, walks through Hyde Park, and online crosswords in Russian that sometimes lasted into the small hours.

With the salt wind lashing her hair Zoe paused for a few moments to take in the scene. A low concrete wall marked the boundary between the esplanade and a dirty sand beach, wet from the flat gunmetal sea a few feet beyond that dissolved into a grey haze above. This was the seaside of her parents's youth of which they spoke so fondly. Of crabbing, of whelks drowned in vinegar, sticky rock and something called 'two-penny shove'. Her dad's eyes lit up when he talked about the English seaside of the 1960s. But this was November, she supposed, out-of-season. Even so, the almost theatrical drabness meant she couldn't help feeling she hadn't missed much. The houses that faced the water were all alike: swollen and white, Victorian domestics over four or five floors, mostly guest houses. She turned back and approached one.

At the top of some concrete steps, and to the sound of a very hesitant Bridge Over Troubled Water being played on a distant piano, Zoe pressed a buzzer marked *Reception / Poe*. When the door was buzzed open she was greeted in what served as a reception area by a tall, heavy woman with bright red lips, a shock of unruly grey hair surrounding her head, a sticky wine glass at her fingers and a scruffy terrier at her feet. An elderly man in green overalls was half way up a ladder poking a screwdriver into a fusebox and counting to himself as Zoe followed the woman through into a living room at the rear of the property where she saw the source of the music — a girl in a school uniform sitting at an upright piano.

'Shall we call it a day, Hilary, dear?' Said the landlady. 'I think so, don't you?'

To the relief of all, the girl stopped playing.

'What do you have to remember?'

'Remind mum about bridge club, Missus Poe.'

'Good girl, now off you go before grass grows around you.'

The girl collected a pile of sheet music and disappeared. 'She's *supposed* to be going for grade four,' the woman muttered, before, 'would you like some tea?

Or, what's the time, shall we have something stronger? Spot of grape juice?' Zoe declined, and Ms Eleanor Poe, Cheltenham Lady, Olympic bronze winner in the dressage event in Rome in 1960, and once one of the longest-serving employees of MI6, invited her to sit on a velveteen settee that wore a top layer of closely woven dog hair.

Zoe gave a version of why Pete Girling had recommended she make the trip to the coast. *Pendulum* had meant nothing to him, he'd never heard it referred to and records had drawn a blank. "There is someone who might be able to help you though. Eleanor Poe - she's the one you should talk to," he'd said. "The font of all knowledge; veritable legend round here, fifty-five years of service beginning at Century House, or Broadway, or one of those anyway. One of the 'Mothers' of old — don't tell her I said that. Or do." His smile had fallen away. "But one of Jones-Cooper's early victims, part of the first cull, three years now, would it be? Shame really, after more than a half a century's loyal service. Still . . . Runs a boarding house out in Southend I think, that her sister left her. Should have her number somewhere."

Mrs Poe had sunk into an arm chair and was pouring herself what she said was 'only day wine, dear'. The path of wear on the carpets betrayed her daily route in a room where the pervading smell was stale dog and the photographs on the walls featured horses she had outlived. Both she, in a hand-knitted jumper beneath an old Barbour jacket, and the soles of her slippers made to pad the threadbare floors had long since become undone by age.

For a half an hour she held court, merrily bemoaning how she was told by Jones-Cooper - whom she called 'the toady' — but doesn't he just look like one with that neck — that her time was up, and knowing it was for no bloody good reason other than her face didn't fit any more. Him and his City shits, she complained, had sucked the lifeblood out of the Service. Zoe didn't interrupt, and was surprised to find in between the bitterness at having been so unceremoniously let go after a lifetime of service, that when she allowed herself to reminisce, gaily fishing each memory out of the great sea of her time in the foreign intelligence service, her smile was as bright as sunbeams and her voice as young as springtime. Yet it took nearly an hour, several more only day-wine top-ups and three or more prompts before Eleanor Poe nodded solemnly and repeated, 'Pendulum, yes.'

'I'll assume you're unaware of this, but for a long time there's been talk of a mole, for want of a better word, inside Six. But not the usual kind, that is to say not the *consistent* kind. Which makes him even more difficult to expose. Various traps have been set over the years but he always slips through them. Now I don't know all the details, but they say he may have been in place since as long ago as the mid-nineties.' She took a wide mouthful of wine, and lowered her voice to barely above a whisper. 'There was a clandestine operation, yes. *Very* hush-hush. The men, and they were all men, were graduates, fresh young idealists ready to leap bare-arsed into the hornet's nest to spy for Queen and country.'

Zoe sat forward in her chair.

'Began around '86 I believe. We'd fiddle with their history to make them look a bit redder — you know, the usual hocus pocus, but subtly, so that when they approached the KGB to offer themselves as double agents it would look more authentic. We'd furnish them with a gift-horse, a juicy carrot that sometimes the Soviets bit at, sometimes they didn't, but they also ran their own networks — and by all accounts had a wild time of it. The Bright Young Things of the SIS – you can imagine. By the time it was shut down, in '95, we had a labour of moles in various holes. Five, it was rumoured.'

'Why was it closed down?' asked Zoe.

'Winter of '95 we received intel that one of our Pendulums was crooked, pointed East, loyalties lying more towards Moscow than London, you see. Source unknown, but when they pulled a woman's body out of the Moskva one morning — a secretary inside the Kremlin who'd been passing minutes of Committee meetings along with detailed biographies of those present — word was it was her. That she'd somehow discovered her contact really was a double agent, that he burned her and that the FSB killed her, but not before she managed to get a telephone message through onto the safe house tape machine with irrefutable proof that one of the pendulums — or is it pendula, I never know — really was working for the Russians, even naming him. But . . . ' she paused for another long sip. 'Legend has it that the safe house landlady said she sent the tape back to London without listening to it — as was her usual procedure, but that that evening the five Pendulum men turned up at the safe house unannounced. One of them to intercept the tape they thought would incriminate them.'

'What happened to the tape?' Zoe asked.

'Never arrived in London.'

Zoe sat back on the couch and thought before

speaking again. 'So there were five possible agents, and one of them got to the tape.'

She raised her eyebrows as if to say, 'we presume so.' 'What happened at the safe house in Moscow that evening in unknown. There were all sorts of rumours floating around. Pacts, threats, unveilings, bullets fired . . . truthfully I don't know.' She shrugged. 'The op was pulled, the men were brought home and questioned, interrogated of course, but . . . ' she reached for the wine bottle. 'Story goes the crooked Pendulum was never found. That he remained inside the SIS and has done ever since.'

'And could still be here today.'

The old woman shrugged. 'Possible. But as I said, just rumours.'

Christ, he's the right age, she thought. Graduated in '94. Classified file until '96.

The old lady turned her head to gaze mournfully out of her window onto the overgrown garden. They sat in silence for a while, until Poe said, 'I heard the toady reopened the investigation two years ago when he was given the okay to delve into past missions, even the highly classified ones, for signs of foul play or treachery, but that it didn't go anywhere. The quisling didn't reveal himself. No one talked.' She turned back to her. 'Stephen Jones-Cooper fancies himself as the great spycatcher. I take it you're with 'S', otherwise you wouldn't be here.' Zoe didn't answer, and the old lady didn't expect her to, so she turned back to her garden just in time to catch sight of a Robin as it landed on her bird feeder. Then after it had flown away, and as Zoe stood to leave she said, 'Be careful, Miss Taylor, is my advice.'

10

On Thursday morning, with two laps of the park's perimeter that made up his daily exercise routine complete, Russell Blake crossed the road and turned right in the direction of his mansion block, slowing his breathing as he walked. His forearm was still slightly sore, but when he pressed the skin he couldn't feel anything beneath it, and the hole made by the needle would heal quickly, rendering the deed invisible. Once back at the flat he ran a bath. His leg muscles still ached after the trial run two nights prior, so he soaked in the hot water for two whole hours, going over in his mind the detailed preparations he'd made over the last several days in readiness for the planting of the bomb, which, he had determined, would take place tonight.

Before work could begin on planning the exact location for the device, his first commitment the week before had been to his own self-preservation. A long time ago in a pine forest an elderly general had promised him he would be welcomed back a hero, awarded the Gold Star medal, and that great wealth and privilege would be bestowed upon him. But General Sorokin had died several years before, and he wondered if his successor knew of those promises, or whether the medals and glory had been forgotten about in the intervening eighteen years.

On the morning of the previous Friday he had written down all four twenty-one digit IBAN numbers that identified each of his secret Swiss bank accounts on a piece of paper, (CH93 0174 6341 9421 6532 5, CH93 9835 2186 4528 0021 6, CH93 3826 9923 0273 3736 0, and CH93 2827 0247 6765 1100 3), then the following day from a shop in Clapham Common he bought a waterproof dry-bag of the type used by surfers to keep their wallets and drugs dry whilst in the sea. He placed the single sheet into it and wrapped the bag with duct tape, rendering it a small, anonymous mass. That lunchtime he dined at Medlar, an upmarket French restaurant on the Kings Road, on guinea fowl washed down by a carafe of Auxey-Duresses from the small hamlet of Melin in Burgundy, then spent the afternoon studying and buying maps in a shop in Beauchamp Place. He waited until it was almost midnight before driving east.

It was only as he stood at the gates to Greenwich Park he cursed himself for not remembering it was Halloween, evidenced by the handfuls of drunken revellers, some in ill-conceived costume, who were spilling out of the closing pubs onto the streets. The gates were locked — the park closed at six p.m. every evening — so he began circling the perimeter on foot for a suitable entry point. When he was satisfied he was alone, he scaled the railings and weaved in and out of the avenues of chestnut trees — that afforded excellent cover — until he found a suitable spot. Here he dug a shallow grave with a small hand shovel and buried the small package near an ancient oak tree thirty paces from the Henry Moore statue. Having noted down the GPS coordinates, he exited as effortlessly as he had entered, slid the shovel into a litter bin, and began walking back towards the rental car he had parked a few streets away. He had just turned into the dark road and spotted the car beneath its small puddle of yellow street light when he saw them. They were three in number, and by the time their eyes had found him it was too late for Blake to turn back. He slowed but kept on moving towards them, sensing this wasn't going to end by diplomacy.

The one who had been keying parked cars began the encounter. 'Hey, hey, hey,' he announced, crossing the road with a swagger to join the other two who had seemed to emerge from nowhere to block the pedestrian's path. They were young, twenty at the most, Blake suspected, and were dressed in what looked like a uniform: jogging pants and expensive trainers, with the hoods of their puffer jackets pulled low over their eyes. Pointing from their right hands: slim, silver blades.

As he approached, they seemed to sense which car was his. All three stood before it.

'Alright, bruv?' said the same youth as he wiped his blade casually across his jogging pants, a dark tattoo on his wrist immediately visible. 'This yours?' the flat of the blade now tapping on the car's roof.

Blake looked at the car. Both he and it must remain anonymous. Whatever happened now he couldn't allow this to escalate. Any noise in the quiet street at this hour could alert a resident, the police could be here any minute, the fallout from which would be severe. He scanned around quickly to asses his options on the narrow pavement. In less than a second he had surmised there was only one. But with three of them, he was outnumbered.

'Nice. Ain't no Maybach, bruv, but . . . worth money.' The leader, the tallest of the three, the carkeyer, continued in mocking admiration of the compact car. The one to his left, a smaller, stockier example, hissed. Then without warning the last, the most vicious-looking of them to Blake's right took a step forwards and jabbed his knife out in front of his face.

'Money, keys and wallet, bitch.' The demand was accompanied by a sucking of the teeth and a particular type of viciousness in the eyes that was desperate, as if the consequences of killing a stranger weighed nothing against a stolen wallet no matter how meagre its contents.

The blade hovered inches away from his face. Blake didn't flinch. While he waited for the repetition of instruction he began to predict what the other two would do.

'And watch. Or I will fuckin' slice open that face.'

The blade came closer and circled in front of Blake's nose. The other two behind him were now upright, clutching their own knives tighter. When, again, the demand was met with silence, the moment came. The one in front brought his arm back, giving Blake a good half-second's warning. When the blade cut through the air Blake pivoted to his left while at the same time grabbing the man's leading arm and pulling him forward and off balance. In the same swift movement Blake stuck a middle knuckle into the man's right eye, leaving him to fall down clutching at his ruined cornea and screaming out in pain like a felled hyena, while he turned his attention to the two behind, tall and short. Short came at him now with an amateur backwards swipe at the face. Without leaving his spot, Blake swivelled again to his left and launched a strong palm at the man's forearm, which knocked the knife from his fist across the bonnet of the car and into the road, followed by another, almost simultaneously, to his nose. But already the tattooed wrist honed into view from behind. Blake grabbed at the stocky one, now weaponless, headbutted him quickly and pushed his wide frame back onto the tall one's knife, the length of which entered his torso between the shoulder blades, while at the same time reaching round a wide fist and slamming it hard into the tall's ear. The stabbed youth's knees collapsed beneath him, causing him to join his half-blind comrade on the pavement, and leaving the tallest one there in shock at having stabbed his friend and inexpertly jabbing his bloody knife in small thrusts towards Blake's chest. But the ease with which the stranger had so effortlessly dispatched his two friends had sent the fear of God, or worse, into him, and when the stranger seemed to snigger at him, to his eternal embarrassment, he actually defecated himself. This was right before he felt his right leg snap at the knee and he too went down like a paper duck on a shooting range to join the other two on the cold concrete slabs. The noise coming from all three was now enough to wake the whole street, so without pausing Blake got into the car and accelerated away without looking back. By two a.m. he had swapped cars in Southwark and was back in Battersea.

The longitude and latitude coordinates of the burial site were 51.475127 0.005045, and it was this number that he then sent via email to a man in Covington in the US State of Virginia. A short reply came back at once: 'Give me 48 hrs. B.'

On the Sunday morning he lifted the floorboards in the study and pulled out three passports. The photograph in each was identical: no moustaches, beards, glasses or dyed hair in an attempt to fool a modern biometric system that cannot be fooled. On the top of the small pile was a burgundy document with the Danish coat of arms emblazoned on its cover and the words DANMARK and PAS below it. Inside, the bearer's name was Peter Iverson. The second, also burgundy, showed a German Eagle with the word REISEPASS on its cover — it belonged to a Bernhardt Müller of Dresden, a schoolteacher. The third was a Swiss passport in its characteristic red and its owner was Mr Gabriel Brunner of Montreux, the resort town on the shoreline of Lake Geneva at the foot of the Alps. None had ever been used to travel with. Of the four in his possession all were entirely legitimate and valid, having been issued by the passport offices of their respective countries and renewed where necessary over the years by anonymous hands using respectable bank accounts. Only three however had been arranged by Moscow. Peter Iverson's document had been conceived at the connivance of its owner eight years beforehand from an expert forger in Rome at a cost of nearly €10,000. He carried all three into the living room and placed them next to Russell Blake's passport, which was sitting beside the Beretta, the $50,000 in cash, and the suitcase.

He considered the collection of identities laid out before him. It was no good, he decided. He would need another.

The next morning, that of Monday 2nd November, he awoke at 06:30 a.m. and walked to

Pimlico underground station where he caught the busy rush hour train heading north. Three stops later he alighted at Oxford Circus station where he spent twenty minutes walking its myriad tunnels with the hordes of commuters and tourists until he spotted someone.

The man stood approximately the right height, had dark brown hair and green eyes, and although he was wearing glasses and was five or so years older, he would, Blake decided, be suitable. He followed him through the tunnel from the Central Line and onto the escalator, and as he exited the station above ground on the south east side and turned into Argyll Street, where he joined a queue outside Costa Coffee. Ten minutes later, carrying a tall cappuccino, he was walking south. It was when he stopped to admire a pair of trainers in the window of a shop on Carnaby Street that his wallet was taken, and although he wouldn't notice its disappearance until lunchtime whilst at the food hall counter in Selfridges, when he thought back he did remember being jostled by someone on his way to work. What did he look like, Geoff? His wife asked him later. Tall-ish, dark hair, with green eyes. You've just described yourself, she said. He thought about it. The man hadn't been too dissimilar in appearance to himself he supposed, now that he came to think about it.

Later that Monday Blake packed two large boxes with eighteen years worth of items and documents that in the event of his cover being blown and the flat being searched he would ensure escape confiscation. These included code books, unused one-time pads, miniature hardware and old discs and computer drives. The most important details pertaining to the secret British Illegals network were committed to memory.

Among the items was a thick red folder that he had acquired the year before that contained the 'lost' plans for the MI6 building. He remembered the temperature that day was cold, even by Russian standards, and that a storm of sleet and freezing rain had been blowing when he arrived for work at eight sharp wearing a high-vis jacket and hard hat. The identity badge he wore bore the name Dean Chapman, an agency replacement for the regular electrician from the construction company Balfour Beatty who had mysteriously been taken ill the evening before. During the major refurbishment work inside MI6 HQ, sensitive documents detailing internal floor plans of the building and the location of alarms and security measures were kept inside a locked room to which only forty contractors had access. Unbeknownst to the company however, despite his qualifications, experience and credentials being spotless, Dean Chapman was not whom he claimed to be, and in fact not even an electrician at all. He was though, given access to the secure room. When questioned thoroughly by the police in the wake of the incident not one employee knew who he was nor had ever seen him. Nor even, had the agency who had allegedly supplied him. Balfour Beatty was sacked as a result, Chapman's name never released, and the incident, much reported in the national press, was put down to carelessness rather than a result of any hostile activity.

The Chapman ID badge lay in a box with the pile of other stolen identity cards he'd used over the years. He'd decided his most prized personal possessions would remain in the flat: the Mondrian, three Kandinsky paintings from the Bauhaus period, a handful of nude still lifes of little monetary value, a Rothko, the furniture, his Wedgwood Jasperware collection, and various other vases and ornaments he cherished.

In the corner of a small storage unit accessed by an underground carpark in Bayswater, behind one of several hundred identical orange doors, he placed the two boxes. When prompted at the reception he produced the stolen driving license as his form of ID, and Mr. Geoffrey Dowler of Clinton Crescent, Hainult, was thanked for his patronage. He paid for two years in advance in cash, swapped cars in the lockup, and that evening dined alone at Berner's Tavern in Fitzrovia on rare steak and Grand Cru Clos de Vougeot.

Tuesday 3rd would see him performing a trial run of events that he had decided were to take place on Thursday 5th. Any obstructions, either geographical or from personnel, to the situating of the bomb could then be addressed on Wednesday. There would be enough time. The many maps and floor plans, blueprints and architectural drawings he'd accumulated had been poured over at length for the past six days. The time had come.

The meticulous planning paid off, and at three a.m. on Wednesday morning, with a sense of great relief, he arrived back in Battersea exhausted, covered in filthy black dust — something he hadn't at all accounted for but that could be addressed easily — but alive. He would take the day to recover. Tomorrow night, with the heavy suitcase, it would be more difficult.

The following morning, D-day, the front door

buzzer awoke him at 08:20. and a woman in a FedEx uniform handed over a package with the postage mark 'Covington, Virginia, USA' upon it. Once the contents were laid out on the kitchen counter, he wondered if he had overpaid. A tiny microchip shaped like a cylinder and about the size of a long grain of rice was accompanied by an auto tuning reader, or scanner, and a large injector needle. The value of the materials was probably less than twenty dollars, he guessed, yet he'd paid $10,000 for these three modest items. The price of discretion on demand was high. He switched the scanner on and held it above the chip. A fifteen digit number appeared on its grey screen: 514751270005045. He smiled, then rolled up his sleeve, inserted the rice-sized chip into the injector needle, and plunged it into his forearm before pulling on training shoes and going for a run.

Two hours of warm bath water had helped relax his aching thigh muscles and focus his mind. Yes, he concluded, he was satisfied with his preparedness. The encounter with the youths had been unfortunate, but he'd been left with no choice but to retaliate as he did. Besides, there'd been no news reports of the incident, which was no surprise. They weren't the type to go crying to the police. Likely they'd turned up wailing at A&E like so many other youths in South London on a Saturday night and no-one had thought much of them.

He sunk beneath the water and held his breath. And there she was. Her face before his eyes. They were back there. Lying together at the edge of a beautiful azure lake in their bleached vignette. Her hair wet after swimming, and she was laughing, almost uncontrollably, but every time he was back there with her he couldn't ask her why. She disappeared into the mist. He raised his head above the surface of the bathwater and opened his eyes.

He would spent the rest of the day going over last minute details of the route in his head, eat lightly, and try to sleep through the evening before having to leave at eleven p.m.

He was shaving when his phone flashed up a message. Finally, groaned Henderson. It was from his last resort. Two hours later, having alighted a Piccadilly line train at Knightsbridge, he was walking up the station's steps into bright sunlight, and five minutes after that was sitting on his Saturday bench by the Serpentine. A pair of young men were having a rowing boat spat on the lake's calm surface, as an ashen-haired cyclist in a Superman T-shirt attempted to inflate a flattened tyre on his bike a few feet away. Henderson looked on, remembering an article he'd read about the infantilism of the western male. Why, the journalist had written, would a grown man would want to watch super beings who can fly, play video games or wear sports wear designed for the playing field? It certainly escaped him. He pictured what his father would make of it today, and was looking incredulously at the cyclist when a soaking wet Labrador appeared at his feet.

'Hello Mister Sullivan,' a lean man in a Crombie and flat cap said. He was chewing gum and taking in the view across the water. 'Sorry about the delay. You know how traffic can be. How's tricks?'

'Fine, Jim,' he lied as the man sat down next to him. 'You?'

The stubbled chin stopped moving. 'Oh no, Superman's in trouble,' he said, before producing a bulging manilla envelope.

Henderson took it, unable to disguise a look of surprise. When it came to black bag jobs — those whose methods were missing from the procedural rulebook and whom one would not wish to burden the Investigatory Powers Tribunal with — and especially not their by-the-book assistant chief who seemed to share a direct line with the intelligence services watchdog - Tottenham usually handled them. Once a legitimate department, these days they were unofficial and operated out of a disused cinema in that borough, although the trusted, age-old methods remained: Always the distasteful, that ranged from the morally questionable to the downright criminal. Put simply, when bribery, burglary, bullying or blackmail were called for, you called Tottenham. Rumours that helped colour some of the flimsier lunchtime conversations included interrogations and torture being performed in the dusty auditorium while the projector flashed Jimmy Cagney gangster films onto the giant screen, were largely exaggerated. When you'd been put on enforced leave however, or when you wanted an added layer of anonymity that outsourcing provided, you called Jim Griffin.

Griffin was a house burglar by trade whose reputation as being the best in the business kept him in high demand. With no form, no prints on file, and no DNA at Scotland Yard he was known as 'the establishment's burglar', and to his immense pride was the only housebreaker royalty had ever used. He'd even considered having the Royal Warrant stamped onto his business cards after that job, but was later discouraged by a pompous palace emissary. His manor was Bermondsey, where he inhabited a very nicely furnished penthouse apartment in a converted biscuit factory that cost a small fortune. But he got by — he considered himself an artist, and charged accordingly. Someone once called him The Invisible Man, honouring both the fact he'd never had his collar felt, and his literary namesake, also named Griffin. He may have suspected it, but he didn't know the man on the bench next to him was a spook, nor even his real name, only his work name of Sullivan.

Henderson turned over the envelope and pulled out a great handful of newspaper cuttings. Finding a trace of Sean in the house had been a long shot that he'd expected would lead to nothing. But this? This was gold.

'Like falling off a log, mister Sullivan,' and with two friendly slaps on Henderson's thigh Griffin threw a ball for the dog, who jumped into the river, and sidled off along the path while he watched it swim out for the ball.

In reality the analogy hadn't been wholly accurate, yet The Invisible Man wasn't about to admit that breaking into a hairdresser's suburban semi had caused him any fuss. The difficulty hadn't been with gaining entry, which had been as simple for him as for the Gas Board team from Tottenham - via the back garden and in through the UPVC back door. No pets with teeth to ward off, alarms to disable, motion sensors, sensor pads, infra-red, not even cameras to contend with. No, the trouble was that after nearly three hours of searching he'd found nothing. Sean, Shaun and Shawn were all proving elusive. He was holding a cup of tea with his feet on the table in front of the monolithic T.V when the reality hit him that he'd have to go up into the loft.

Griffin hated lofts. More precisely he hated rodents, whom he knew, especially in the cold of English Novembers, were regular residents of the place in the home where the rising heat stops. Luckily, after clambering up into the attic he found it almost at once. The cuttings were in a folder inside a storage file box labelled *Edgecut,* that he scanned quickly with the aid of his torch, then stuffed inside his jacket before climbing down and slipping out unnoticed back to Bermondsey.

Fluttering in the breeze in between Henderson's fingers was a grainy photograph of a man's face he recognised. The man in one of the photos the team had taken when they entered. One from the wall in Lander's hallway. The soldier in uniform — in army service dress with the navy blue beret of the Royal Logistics Corps – who was looking away to one side of the camera.

Jesus Christ, he thought as he read the Daily Telegraph's headline above the photograph. Sean is Sean Hubbard. One of The Edgecut Five.

The nurse could have sworn her eyes were deceiving her. How could someone just disappear from a train like that? She distinctly remembered him at the other end of the carriage as she'd thought him attractive — handsome, and dressed all in black like a special forces type, with thick rubber-soled boots on and with that old-fashioned suitcase between his knees. There were only the two of them here and he hadn't got off at Lambeth North, or at Waterloo because she'd been awake then so she must have dozed off, only for a few seconds, and now with the train approaching Embankment, he's gone. She craned her neck to look left and right but there was no sign. After a twelve hour shift at Guy's Hospital that Thursday, her penultimate of the week, she was tired, and it wasn't unusual for her to sleep on the last tube home. Still, it wasn't often people went about disappearing on her like that.

Indeed, the man she sought had left the carriage and was standing on its rear step, clutching the door handle with one hand while holding the case in the other. He was waiting for the train to halt in the station so he could jump down onto the rail and disappear back into the blackness of the tunnel.

The train squealed to a stop. Russell Blake jumped and landed on the track, careful not to touch any of the four lines. He had learned the second and fourth lines are live, with 630 Volts DC running through them, and quickly identified by white insulators. Crouched down, he waited perfectly still for the train's doors to close and for it to pull away from the station. Once its lights had dimmed into the distance and all was quiet, he switched on his torch to illuminate the blackness behind him. He'd also discovered two days before that the gap between the rails is narrow, making walking along it challenging — made even more so now whilst carrying a heavy suitcase. With care, he began placing one foot in front of the other, and making his way slowly back into the tunnel.

Blake had chosen a long and difficult route to Westminster but for good reason, having learned that out of the eleven lines on the Underground network, there are only two, the Bakerloo and the Central line, that have no CCTV cameras inside their carriages. To disappear into the labyrinth of tube tunnels without being caught on camera was therefore only possible from a rear carriage travelling on either of these lines. His journey had begun on the Bakerloo line at Elephant and Castle, its southernmost station, and now, walking back south along that same route, he was looking for a steel door in the tunnel's wall that would bear a small white 'x' above it that he had drawn with an enamel pen two nights before.

During his seven days spent planning he had concluded that a subterranean location would be best. The intended target was one of the city's most prominent public landmarks, placing the device above ground would leave it susceptible to discovery. The bomb needed to be in close enough proximity to the intended target to inflict maximum impact, but also sufficiently hidden as to remain undetected by either passers-by, employees, or the authorities, until its detonation.

Therefore the London beneath London had been settled upon.

He had begun several days before by studying the area close to the target above ground, spending many hours walking the pavements and making particular note of old red brick ventilator shafts that have been merged into modern shopfronts, manhole covers and drains, locked railings and gates, access hatches on the riverbank, and small, steel doors with curious location codes on plates above — all of which are more numerous than the casual observer may notice. The casual observer may also be scarcely aware of what lies beyond, yet Blake had learned that behind these chains, locks, and mysterious cyphers there exists a vast clandestine underworld of tunnels, telephone exchanges, nuclear bunkers, citadels, control centres and lost rivers. Some were not on planners' maps, he had discovered, some were well documented, while the existence of others could be surmised only from thorough scrutiny of government reports or from occasional accidental disclosures in the news media. Perhaps the most enigmatic of those whose existence he unearthed was Q-Whitehall, a communications facility under Whitehall that was built during World War II and that connects the Admiralty, The Old War Office, The MoD, and The Cabinet War Rooms, and that could be accessed either by exit shafts under various government departments, or, more illegally, by a closed entrance below Trafalgar Square.

After three days spent ruminating over this tangle of unmappable interconnecting tunnels, corridors, holes, pipes and passageways that ribbons beneath the soil of the capital, many of which may afford a terrorist wishing to plant a small nuclear bomb any number of viable options, Russell Blake chose to descend into perhaps the most obvious of them all: The 250 miles of track that transports commuters to 270 stations across the city that Londoners call The Tube.

Two night's before he had navigated the dark tunnels looking for the doors in the arched brick walls that provide access to service tunnels that house electrical apparatus and cables and that act like umbilical cords to the tube network. As well as these, also dating back to the 19th Century and normally only seen by technicians and engineers, were the utilities storerooms, often no larger than cupboards and identified by alphabetic cyphers that determine their purpose and location. It was one of these storerooms, hidden in the tunnel's walls a few hundred feet to the east of Westminster station and precisely twenty-eight metres away from London's iconic striking clock, Big Ben, that was Blake's destination.

He trod carefully, one step at a time to the soundtrack of chirping rats until ten minutes later he shone his torch at his small 'x' above a steel door. He pulled it open and began climbing down a steep wrought iron staircase into the blackness. The stairs led to a small room. He crossed it and exited via another metal door onto the south bound track of the District Line. The last train on Thursday stopped at Embankment at 00:31, arriving at Westminster a minute later, so he knew there would be no danger of more trains. He could take his time to navigate carefully the live track for the next 0.8 miles. The air he breathed was thick and stale and smelled of burning metal, and the case, which he held above the tracks with one strong arm, was cumbersome, but by counting his steps he knew that within seventeen minutes he would find another steel door with another small 'x' above it.

With the dust clinging to his sweating skin and the only sound the distant thunder of trains in far away tunnels, he found the door. He stepped inside, descended another steep Victorian staircase, and pulled open a stiff service door to reveal the featureless walls of the Jubilee Line tunnel. Shining his torch down, he stepped out gingerly onto the ground between the rails, turned to face right, and began walking east in the direction of the Thames.

Where it came from or what is was doing in that tunnel at that time of night he would never know, but with less than two minutes to walk he heard the spark of life in the rails, then the tone of the tunnel lower with its rumble. Slowly, accompanied by an electrical whine, it got louder. He quickened his pace. It was coming from behind, from the west. If it reached him he'd have nowhere to hide. He paused for an instant to make sure, then faced forward, heaved the case up to his chest, and began to run. Louder and faster it came, clattering with metallic rhythm and flashing dashes of light against the black bricks. If he laid down he be crushed. Pressed against the curved walls, the same. There was no turning back, and no choice but to keep going. But the locomotive was gaining fast until it was almost upon him. Numbers above walled doors flashed past, 4C, 5C, but where was it? Now fully illuminated by the train's bright headlights and his shadow shortening with it only metres behind, his legs seemed to go into slow motion, become lead, like in a nightmare as he saw the outline of the steel door and the faint '6C' above it. He had just managed to reach it when the train caught him.

11

Joe Taylor was screaming at the top of his little lungs. Moments later the bedroom light went on and his mother rushed over to console her son, who was sitting up in bed and pointing at the walls with the look of sheer terror in his reddened eyes. The monsters were back, more fiery and even more fierce it seemed, yet gradually, as Zoe sat comforting him, the boy's tears seemed to recede. She cuddled and shushed him, waiting patiently before she could lie back down on her own pillow and try to ignore her own nightmares — the ones that had haunted her for the last week.

She had been asking herself if she really believed that somewhere on UK soil there was a Russian agent planting a nuclear warhead, or whether Henderson needed Overture to become real to prove his worth, for validation, or for darker reasons entirely. The more she considered, the weaker the evidence he'd presented seemed, but what also gnawed away at her confidence in him was the suggestion that he, the very man who had drawn their attention to this conspiracy, was guilty of an unnatural loyalty to that same enemy. It may be a contradiction, but just how implausible was it? The overt love he had for Russia was unapologetic, unselfconscious. He was immersed in the country and its history, and what better cover? He wouldn't be the first Englishman to be seduced by the ideology after all.

Then the rumours. The years marked CLASSIFIED. Did that make him a Pendulum man? If so, was he *the* Pendulum man that Eleanor Poe spoke of? The double agent who disappeared back into MI6 and who had been there ever since, quietly, invisibly, betraying his country?

What had George Provost said to her in Moscow? 'I've known him since '94.' And his parting words: "The sixth one inside." Philby was the Third Man inside the infamous cold-war Cambridge spy ring, Blunt the fourth, Cairncross the fifth. Was Provost trying to tell her that John Henderson was the sixth man? And what was it about his relationship with John that troubled her?

She shut her eyes to stop her thoughts from reeling into confusion. Her son's head fell forward as his eyelids became heavy again, so she laid him back down and covered him with the blanket, before kissing him tenderly on his warm forehead, creeping across the carpet, and closing the door.

The driver of the locomotive didn't see the impact but he heard it. A terrible smack off the front of his cab. But he was running late, in a hurry to get the train into Stratford station and home, so he didn't stop, figuring maybe he'd hit a bat.

Blake lay gasping for breath on the ground next to the suitcase, covered in sweat and dirt, heart vibrating, muscles burning, but otherwise unscathed. The room into which he'd flung himself as the train flashed past inches away from his back, was a small, abandoned store room. The impacting train had struck the metal door and slammed it shut and he cursed the fact the driver may report a collision. But what the hell was it doing there anyway? There were no trains scheduled after 00:48. He checked his watch: 01:11.

'Delays,' he said out loud to the filthy little room, 'typical.'

He dragged a sleeve across his forehead, stood up, and with the torch between his teeth, heaved the case onto a high bench. The lid open, he took the small arming key from a zipped pocket of his jacket, inserted it into its lock, gave it a quarter turn clockwise, and turned the knob that adjusted the digital display until it read 07:20:44:00. He moved his finger down to the red arming switch, and with only a brief pause to wonder if his superiors had booby-trapped the timer, pressed it. To his relief, the display began counting down to the moment in seven days time when the bomb would explode:

Saturday 14th November at midnight.

It was the night of 5th November, and in gardens and parks all across Britain people were celebrating the most infamous saboteurs in history, Robert Catesby and co-conspirator Guy Fawkes, for attempting to blow up the very same building, The Palace of Westminster, four hundred years earlier with sticks of dynamite. Meanwhile, in an airless four by six room in the walls of an underground tunnel beneath that building's north east corner, a Russian agent with the same end in mind had just planted an altogether more destructive explosive device.

'Every day it is worse. The pains in her stomach. The nausea. More aggressive than even before the Ponatinib treatment.'

Katya was with Anya on a bench in the

morning shadow of their concrete complex in Koptevo, their arms linked together while their three year-olds played on the slide with the other neighbours' children. The boys jostled each other for their turn, while the two girls waited patiently to climb the steps. The momentary joy of the slide back down was worth it.

Set back from them in frozen corners of the estate there was the telltale milling of hooded youths before the score, the rapid exchange, and after it the fast, eyes to the ground march towards the stairwells, to and from burning spoons or needles, faces gaunt, determined. The grey van kept its vigil in the row of cars, the rising pile of cigarette butts still at its rear door. Katya eyed it every time she came or went, it hadn't moved in ten days.

'We will find a way,' Anya said to her friend.

'That's what Dmitri used to say.'

Anya squeezed her hand. 'She really looks like you.'

'He used to ask me what he had done to get so lucky. He said to be a father to a girl was the highest honour a man could receive.' Katya was studying her daughter's face, noticing the winces of pain cross it with each stab to her small belly.

Anya stroked her friend's arm. 'Where can I get a friend who would give me such a coat?'

Katya recalled the English woman's visit ten days before. Her parting words asking if she remembered anything unusual. She hadn't even thought of it since, being so pre-occupied. She thought back to the arguments she and Dmitri had had. How she regretted them. He'd been so determined to find a way to save Natalya, and all she'd done was belittle him, accuse him of being useless and impotent, yelling at him about how it would take more than blind optimism to save the child's life.

"How? How?" she'd screamed, the futility of it all suffocating her.

"You must trust me," he'd said, "I promise, Katya."

"You say that but it cannot happen. Your basement pay is not going to save her. Where are we going to find thousands of dollars every month? All you do is play with your stupid toys while our daughter lies sick, dying." Sobbing helplessly she jabbed an accusing arm into to the squadron of plastic aeroplanes that hung impotently from their living room ceiling.

Then one day he'd come home drenched and for a reason she didn't know they'd danced like lunatics around the flat while the Zelenkos banged on the wall in protest at their stomping feet and Dmitri's jubilant, and loud, singing. The thought of it made her smile. Where the money came from she didn't know. He worked inside Lubyanka, she was too afraid to ask. But in a matter of weeks as well as being able to afford his daughter's expensive medicine, her husband had bought the family a new fridge to replace the old Saratov, and had even taken her out to dinner one Saturday at White Rabbit, a European restaurant on the river with a glass domed roof that offered such views across the city that it took her breath away. Katya remembered herself sitting there in her new dress as happy as if she was sitting in a field of peonies, happily deceiving herself, captivated. "What kind of place is this?" she asked, gazing about her in wonderment as waiters re-filled their wine glasses without being asked to.

But now she thought back, he'd been nervous that evening, twisting his napkin with thumbs picked raw like half-peeled radishes. Perhaps he could sense whatever he was doing was catching up with him. That his time was running out.

"If anything ever happens to me Katya," he'd said gravely, but she'd interrupted, hushed him and told him not to worry so much and that they should just enjoy the evening.

But he'd reached out and gripped her hands, insisting.

"Listen to me carefully Katya. If anything happens to me, just remember I have named an aeroplane after you. An aeroplane, okay? It's a Wellington Bomber, Katya."

She turned sharply, locking eyes with Anya. 'Oh my god.' Without a second thought, she sprang up from the bench and began running towards the apartment block. At the bottom of the slide Natalya's mouth fall open, wondering why her mother was running away.

Katya burst into her apartment and ran into the living room, to the corner where the plastic aircraft were hanging. She raised a hand and moved them above her, causing each to sway on its fishing wire, plastic noses turning, tails and wings tapping, as she looked for a clue. And there it was. A large twin-engined bomber with a plastic front turret. She held it like it was the head of a snake, staring at the name painted in red letters on its nose - *Katya*. She stroked it for a moment, studying and thinking, then yanked it down from the ceiling, brought it up high beside her head, and smashed it hard down onto the bookcase.

In his headphones the sound of the plane smashing so close to the bug on the bookshelf had been amplified to a deafening level that caused the eavesdropper in the van outside to swear loudly and fling his pornographic magazine at the ceiling. Inside the apartment, picking through the broken plastic splinters of the dark-green fuselage, Katya found two items sellotaped to its inside — a camera memory card, and the SIM card for a mobile phone.

A single Vuitton suitcase waited by the front door next to a hard case that contained the Grundig. The black cab was idling on the street but at 4:45 a.m. the man was early and Blake had one thing left to dispose of, and that was the film.

He pulled it from the canister, unspooled it and pushed it into a small fire pit in his paved garden. Holding his lighter flame to it, it began to burn, but slowly. He had a vague recollection that film was highly flammable, then suspected that this wasn't nitrate but the cellulose acetate that replaced it, making it more difficult to burn. He wished the taxi driver would shut the engine off to avoid attracting unwanted attention. At last the flames began to engulf the film so he left it, locked the French doors, knocked back the last of his coffee, and gave once last glance around the flat.

Only a few hours before, after having pushed the battered suitcase beneath a table in the tunnel store cupboard and covered it over with some black cloth, he had donned a TFL jacket and cap, closed the steel door, and started to make his way back along the track to Westminster station. The platform screen doors had slid open with a press of the green button on the track side, and, with peak pulled low to remain unidentifiable to the CCTV cameras, he had exited the station dressed as a London Underground employee, walked across Westminster Bridge and disappeared into the cold November night. The rental car was waiting at Waterloo, which he then drove back to the railway arches where he swapped the number plates back to their originals, changed his filthy clothes, and returned the car to the drop-off bay outside the agency's glass-fronted premises in Clapham. Having dumped the plates, clothes and the TFL uniform in some bins behind a Chinese restaurant near the Common, he'd arrived home with only time to make a pot of coffee and to shower.

When the taxi arrived at London Victoria he paid the driver in cash and walked into the station to the ticket counter where he bought a one-way ticket to Dover Priory.

It was time for Russell Blake to vanish.

At 08:25 the MS Pride of Canterbury eased slowly out of the harbour. On the top deck of the ferry among a handful of foot passengers was a man with two suitcases at his feet who was looking back at Dover's famous white cliffs as they receded. The sun was illuminating them from a clear blue sky, turning their chalk from alabaster to marble, which caused him to feel a brief pull of regret. By the time he chased the thought it was forgotten, and so with a strengthening wind in his hair and the luminous cliffs now in the distance, he decided to go downstairs to the perfunctory comfort of the Club Class Lounge where he would spend the two-and-a-half hour crossing.

Herr Müller of Dresden liked to travel as comfortably as he could.

As the German schoolteacher was settling into faux leather in the ferry's lounge, two Russian men were taking their seats aboard the morning flight to Moscow at London Heathrow. Their brief trip to the UK had taken them to Leicester, where the morning before they had abducted a Police Inspector on his way to work, made him drink from a plastic bottle, and left him face down on the muddy banks of a canal. During the train journey back to London one of the men had visited the toilet and discarded an innocent-looking deodorant can in a litter bin.

Just to the south of the airport's perimeter, at the counter of a McDonalds restaurant on the London Road in Staines, the two members of Unit 29155's second team were ordering Big Macs and fries. They had five hours to kill before their afternoon flight back to Russia, and would spend them here drinking cola and staring at their phones. Their visit to the UK had taken them no further than the capital. Their first victim was a member of the House of Lords who had very publicly threatened to blow the whistle on fellow members who worked directly for Russian companies and whom he suspected were susceptible to influence. As he had made his way across Westminster Bridge the morning before, he didn't see the face of the passer-by walking towards him, merely felt the spray from the perfume atomiser. Only a few hours later and also in the shadow of the palace of Westminster their second victim, a Labour MP who had made repeated accusations of Russian interference in both the Brexit and Scottish independence referendums, had been walking along the pavement by St James' Park in pursuit of lunch when he was jostled by two men.

Both apologised in heavily accented English as they passed, and he had thought nothing of it, until a few seconds later when he felt a sudden pain in his arm. By nightfall both the peer and the MP had fallen victim to the effects of the radioactive isotope Polonium-210 and were dead, while a perfume atomiser and a pot of face cream lay inside a bathroom pedal bin in a B&B in Staines.

Missions accomplished, the man who received confirmation via cell phone was the commander of Unit 29155, Kuznetsov, whom in turn relayed it to the general who had given the orders, the head of foreign military operations intelligence of the GRU, General Grushenko.

Another assassination would take place that Friday, yet its order had not come from Grushenko on behalf of the *Telepol* committee but from the head of the SVR, Mikhail Smolenko. It was part of a trade: the man's death in return for the placing of a Russian asset inside the very heart of the UK government — as a member of the British cabinet.

This victim of this trade was tall, barrel-chested and in his late fifties with a full military-style moustache who had been fast asleep when a heavyset intruder in a maroon bomber jacket broke into his riverside flat in Rotherhithe in the early hours. Silently, the intruder pulled from his jacket a bottle, then, standing over the sleeping man, he unscrewed the pipette, pinched the rubber nozzle to draw in some liquid, reached down and held the tip to his lips. When he squeezed the rubber nozzle, a droplet touched the man's lips, and he was force fed an amount of the isotope enough to fell a herd of elephants. His mouth was quickly duct-taped — choking him in his own vomit — and he was dragged down the stairs, out into the street and bundled into the back of a rental van. The Russian then drove to China Wharf, where under cover of night he weighted the rapidly dying man down with concrete blocks and without a prayer unceremoniously sunk him in the Thames.

Several hours later, despite being utterly dead, the victim had managed to cast aside his shackles, resurface, and by ten past nine was floating face-up along the River Thames and about to pass under Tower Bridge on his way into town.

Three and a half miles to the west in his art-filled office, 'C' listened patiently as Vanessa Payne, the Minister of State for Business, Energy and Clean growth, accompanied by an expert on international energy markets, delivered more grave news.

'I'm afraid we have it on good authority that three more plants across Germany have suffered similar leaks since,' the minister said. Her now ex-husband and 'C' had been close friends since Oxford and their recent divorce made her presence a little uncomfortable. 'We're still awaiting exact numbers but initial reports coming in estimate around half again of the scale of Tuesday's leak from the Rehden storage facility. It's an ecological catastrophe — over 100,000 metric tonnes of methane into both the atmosphere and the soil, making it a worse ecological disaster than in 2010 - the Deepwater Horizon in the Gulf of Mexico.'

'Of course it could also cost the EU economy billions,' the adviser chipped in.

'We've managed to keep it out of the media for now, but . . .' she tailed off.

'C' listened, expressionless, his mind on the more prescient threat of critically low gas reserves than polluted soil. Moreover, what the minister didn't know yet was that reports were coming through of a major malfunction in the software that controls mainland Europe's wind farms that would threaten the ability to produce electricity. These two combined spelt catastrophe, and soon every country in Europe would be highly vulnerable to, what he was being assured, was already shaping up to be the coldest winter since records began in 1910.

When the scream came from a city smoker, cast into the drizzle by an heartless world, the body had been floating for ten hours before finally arriving at the foot of the river steps directly beneath one of the sphinxes that guards Cleopatra's Needle. The eyes were open, while around the mouth and stuck to his military moustache considerable foam was still in evidence, yet although he had been carried face-up by the river's current from Tower Bridge all the way to the Victoria Embankment, he had managed to complete his solo voyage unnoticed. When the police and ambulance crews arrived they cordoned off the area, which was standard procedure. The prompt arrival of the rapid response team from Porton Down however, was not.

'The Edgecut Five,' Henderson said into the phone, 'mean anything?' It didn't. She was American - well, she was brought up there, so why should it. 'The mysterious Sean is Sean Hubbard, a soldier at Edgecut Barracks, one of five apparent suicides there between 1995 and 2002. They became known in the press as The Edgecut Five. But the families disagreed with the verdicts, said the army had covered up the deaths. There were allegations of assault, violence, bullying, even rape at the barracks. In 2006 a government inquiry upheld the verdicts, but a series of fresh inquests is still underway.'

'So what's the link to Hayley Lander?' Zoe was in the staff canteen inside Vauxhall Cross, nursing a cup of something claiming to be tea.

'Well, there are several photos of him on the wall in her hallway so we can presume he's the boy she moved from High Wycombe to Guildford to be close to way back when. When you check I'll bet he was from the same town. The Edgecut army training barracks are close to where she lives, and has lived since '96.'

'How do you know all this so suddenly, John?'

He decided to spare her the grubby details of Jim Griffin. 'The uniform in the photo on her wall, it didn't register at first. Then I recognised it - Royal Logistics. Knew there was a barracks nearby so did a search and put two and two together.' It sounded believable to him, but her silence told him she was suspicious.

'O-kay, so what's the link?'

'I can't do all the work, Zoe, I thought I'd leave something for you to do. Besides, I've been suspended, or had you forgotten?'

She tipped the undrinkable liquid away and caught the lift up to the third floor. It took her two hours to find what she was looking for. After pouring over every detail of the events at Edgecut barracks in the government's official review of 2006, buried deep within the 508 page document, finally, there it was. A name she recognised.

She caught 'C' as he was about to leave his office. She had *five* minutes, an emphatic Mary told her with as many fingers raised.

When Zoe told the Chief the name, he pulled a hand slowly down his cheek and repeated it slowly, for clarification. 'Lieutenant Colonel Nigel Forbes-Bailey?'

'Yes. Brother of Lady Cecilia Forbes-Bailey, wife of Morris Jacques MP, and the commanding officer of Edgecut barracks at the time of the deaths; the man ultimately responsible for his personnel in the regiment and their behaviour towards the recruits.'

'I'm aware of Edgecut. So he was the CO. The man these families of the deceased soldiers, including Charlotte Fisher and her aunt, blame for the deaths.'

'But he was never charged with any wrongdoing. On the contrary, he received an MBE some years later, a move that provoked anger from the families.'

He circled his desk, unbuttoned his jacket and lowered himself into the taut leather of his chair, thoughts gathering. 'So. Revenge? Fisher steals defence documents and passes them to the Russians in return for his death?'

'It's logical,' she offered. 'Fisher targets Jacques and begins an affair to try to get to his brother-in-law that way, but when she finds out his wife and her brother are estranged and have no contact she has to look for another way. Meantime the Russians, who've probably had Jacques in their sights for years knowing he's destined for cabinet, spot her, see they're close, make their move, and they strike a deal.'

'And as added insurance they shoot the footage of the two of them in bed together. So that when Jacques breaks off the affair, which he does, they can blackmail him with it.'

'Keep the flow of intel or we send the tape to the press.'

A thought entered his mind, and he couldn't help but smile as he considered his opposite number in Moscow being handed the Secretary of State for Defence on a silver platter. 'Smolenko probably leapt at the chance.'

'We have to get to Forbes-Bailey and protect him before it's too late.'

His smile flattened. 'They fished his body out of the Thames this morning. Suspected polonium poisoning.'

'Oh my god.' The words knocked her back. She'd been optimistic.

She watched him as he stood and walked over to a large Tracey Emin painting, an unframed pink and white abstract canvas that hung in the centre of his outside wall: an old iron-grey eagle amid this burst of chaotic colour.

'Charlotte Fisher received a call from a number we triangulated to the address of a known FSB safe house in Kensington,' said 'C'.

'Telling her the job's been done.'

Thinking deeply, he began to brush a slow forefinger over the canvas, tracing the outline of the violent painted scrawl. After a minute, as if addressing the painting, he said, 'Do you know the name Tristan Moss?' She did not. 'He was founder of Neoliberal, anti-communist think Tank *ISS,* promoting capitalist cooperation between the US and Europe. Found dead on Sunday. Death by asphyxiation caused by a toxic plant. How about Scott Warren, successful businessman and vocal critic of the Russian government and supporter and money launderer for one of her main opposition parties. No? Impaled on railings. In the last few days, as well as those — a life peer, a Labour member of parliament, a police inspector from Leicester – all dead by Polonium, a journalist and two film-makers killed in a hit and run in Manchester, and now a Lieutenant Colonel and brother in law to man the prime minister insists will become the next Defence Secretary – despite our best efforts to dissuade him I may add. Not to mention an almost complete shutdown of our gas reserves, and a malfunction in the software that controls Europe's wind farms.' He turned back to her and strode to his desk towards his phone. 'And I presume you've seen the morning editions? SES satellites down?'

The feeling that came over her was one strikingly similar to a shiver of ice cold fear, and it ran from the nape of her neck all the way down her back.

There are two routes of roughly the same length in kilometres from Calais to Paris, yet as he knew it would take him through the medieval town of Amiens where he could stop for lunch in some reasonable café, Russell Blake, now travelling as Bernhardt Müller in a car he rented in Calais, chose the more westerly route of the A16. He would have also liked to stop at the Musée de Picardie to view its art, but there would be time for that after the mission was over.

At quarter to two he dropped the rental car off in a long-stay underground garage and checked into the famous Le Meurice hotel on the Rue De Rivoli - that in itself is a work of art. He'd considered something more understated, more befitting a humble gymnasium schoolteacher from Dresden, but the lure of its history, gilded glory, and Versailles-like splendour was too much to pass over. He showered and changed into a navy blue suit with overcoat, and walked the fourteen minutes to the bank on Avenue de l'opera.

Inside the basement vault of the Credit Lyonnais bank, the female attendant drew the privacy curtain and retreated, leaving him to place the second of the almost identical keys down on the high steel table, and to lift the lid of the security box. There was only one item inside, which he pulled out and placed next to the key. It was a sealed folder with an OB stamp, meaning Top Secret. He sliced open the seal with his penknife, allowing something to fall out onto the table. He picked it up and turned it over. It was a black and white photograph of a young woman. She was smiling, yet somehow looked sad. It was a face he stared at for many minutes in the booth, for she was very beautiful.

When Katya Petrenko arrived on the street the voice on the phone had read out to her she found it deserted. It was bordered on one side by a long patchwork row of high corrugated fences that protected the privacy of gardens belonging to tall houses, and on the other by the 50 feet high, heavily graffitied concrete wall of the Moscow Ring Road. Natalya pulled at her sleeve. The little girl was holding her aching stomach, and tired from all the walking. Katya picked her up, and to the drone of rubber tyres on asphalt high above them, carried her until they reached the rear of number 19 Ulitsa Leninskaya. The door was low, and was unusual in that beside its handle there was an electronic keypad. She put her daughter down, looked around to check they were alone, entered the four digit number the same voice had told her to memorise, and turned the handle.

To greet them in the garden of a house was the lone figure of a woman. She was advanced in years with very pale pink skin and linen-white hair, and wore a thin cardigan wrapped around a long black dress. Katya thought she resembled an English Victorian spinster. With a smile, she beckoned her inside, and as she followed Katya noticed the woman had a slight limp. They were led through a dark hallway and up some creaking stairs onto the first floor where, in the quiet of a drawing room with faded curtains that covered long-ago bricked up windows, the woman introduced herself as Marie. She offered tea, and when she left the room Natalya curled up on an armchair and clutched her belly, leaving Katya's eyes to wander. The furniture consisted of a desk, four steel office chairs and the plum velour armchair whose arms looked like they were used as scratching posts for a cat. Presiding over one of her empire's secret administrative outposts from the chimney breast was the Queen, aloof and regal at twenty-eight in Annigoni's portrait, while upon the desk was a green bankers lamp, an old red rotary telephone, a cassette tape answering machine, and a chipped glass ashtray. It looked to Katya like a cold-war operations room in a museum, which in a way is exactly what it was.

Marie returned with a tea tray, and Katya covered her daughter with her coat, the small three-bar electric heater doing little to warm her. The two women sipped tea, and for an hour sat in silence inspected only by an elderly cat who crossed the doorway once in a while.

Marie got up and left the room when the man arrived. He said his name was Carlo and that he was sorry for her loss, but not very sincerely, Katya thought. Without prompt, beneath a single misty ceiling bulb, she handed him the camera card, knowing she had no choice but to trust whatever stone-faced man with dark eyes stood over her. It was as she was placing it into his palm that she spotted the unmistakable sight of a bullet hole in the chimney breast, and the glimmer of a smile flicker across his face. He disappeared with the card, and when he returned thirty minutes later, pulled the chair from behind the desk, sat down close in front of her directly beneath the bullet hole, and in a flat tone asked her exactly what she wanted.

Inside his deluxe hotel room at an antique desk that overlooked the courtyard, Blake switched on the Grundig. It was a few minutes to seven, and he passed the time until the broadcast by studying the photograph of the girl again. Precisely upon the hour, the sound of the synthesised five-note musical identifier floated from the speaker, followed by the same distant female voice reading aloud his distinct call signal:

'PAPA ECHO CHARLIE NOVEMBER 254 254 254 PAPA ECHO CHARLIE NOVEMBER 254 254 254 . . .'

The voice read the numbers, and the listener wrote down the day's instructions courtesy of Igor Savich whom hours before had called them through from the comfort of his armchair to the lonely operator in the radio room in the gulag. The five-note synth phrase repeated once, and soon the airwaves were again overtaken by interference static. Once he'd de-coded the message he burned the page, then dressed in a black suit, spent an hour in the bar, and later left the hotel to eat one of the best côtes de boeuf in Paris, courtesy of Chez L'Ami Jean.

The deep freeze of winter had not yet arrived, but the snow had come early and the man staring out across the mountain was grateful for that. Good for the skiing, bad for the city, he thought to himself. Sorokin, his predecessor, had drunk and smoked himself to death, but Andrei Vasiliev, who now held the position of Head of S-Directorate, skied often and prided himself on being as fit as any of the Illegals it was his job to control.

He took in a great lungful of clean mountain air and, with ski poles in the snow, basked in the heat of the sun while he waited for the chair-lift to bring his wife and young sons to the crest of the run. He loved Saturdays, loved trading the grime of the city for the freedom of the slopes of Stepanovo.

The boys waved to their father as the chair-lift approached, Ludmila squeezed between them, their six skis hanging down ready to make contact with the snow. They were seven and ten and looked forward to their father teaching them to ski every weekend, while equally he cherished his time with them, knowing their maturity would come all too soon. Stepanovo was perfect too: marked red, but an easy run, and at a kilometre quite long. Also, as Andrei Vasiliev always said, there aren't too many snowboarders. To him, like to many skiers, their lack of etiquette on the slopes was the bane of his weekends.

He skied over to help his wife off the lift. She wasn't used to the sport as much as the boys were, and sometimes she'd end up flat on her face while they slid around her expertly, helpless with laughter. She grabbed his hands and lurched towards him, when out of the corner of his eye he caught sight of someone skiing towards them from the side. The man turned to a halt, jabbed his poles into the powder, and removed his goggles. Vasiliev recognised him as Major General Viktor Kuznetsov, commander of Unit 29155. Thirty years before they'd been friends, new recruits together at the KGB training camp, The Institute, in the final year before the dissolution of the Soviet Union. He was now as he had been, thought Vasiliev, a short, broad, and muscular man with a shaved head and huge hands. At seventeen he'd displayed genuine fondness for hand to hand combat and martial arts, so when Vasiliev heard he'd been appointed head of the secret assassination unit he hadn't been a bit surprised.

'Andrei Borisovich,' the skier said.

'Viktor Grigorovich, what a pleasant surprise.' He turned back to his wife. 'You go ahead, I'll see you at the bottom.' The woman flicked a smile, unable to read if he was in danger. 'It's alright.' he assured her. After a minute the three of them disappeared off down the slope together and left the two men alone at the top.

'How long has it been, Andrei Borisovich?' the dangerous-looking man said.

'It must be thirty years. You are keeping well I trust?'

'I am. And you? Your boys?' He gestured to where his family had been.

'Yes, Oleg and Fyodor.' Vasiliev watched his

old comrade carefully, who was squinting in the sun. He knew this meeting was no coincidence. The man was a natural killer, but a natural skier he wasn't. 'Do you have children?'

'Me?' he said, stern-faced, 'No, no. I am not so blessed.'

The was a silence between them as they stood there. Each respectful of, yet undaunted by the other's rank — for they were the same.

'You are probably thinking that our meeting like this, in this solitary place, is no coincidence.' Kuznetsov said.

'Old friend,' said Vasiliev, 'what can I do for you?'

The short man looked down and bit his lip. Words did not come naturally to his tongue, so he over-compensated. 'You will have to forgive my bluntness. But how well do you know . . . no, let me put it a better way, how much can you *trust* your deputy, Volkov?'

Vasiliev frowned. He had been the head of the Illegals program for nine years, Volkov his deputy for three, and although Kuznetsov's reputation was formidable he didn't take kindly to such impertinence, even from fellow Generals. Even from old friends. Even from killers.

'Why do you ask?'

The man came closer and removed his gloves. The hands looked more like weapons than human appendages. They were heavily scared and the skin upon them was thick like a rhino's. On the right one was a wide shrunken burn, perhaps a scald, a souvenir of a long-forgotten fight. 'I ask you as a friend, Andrei Borisovich. You see, I am receiving orders that while I know *should* come from you, as head of the S directorate, are not.'

'What kind of orders?'

Without smiling, the man laughed. 'The only kind my unit receives Andrei.'

'And who is the target?'

Kuznetsov stepped forward. 'That's the thing. An illegal. One of your own.' He gave a long pause. 'Russell Blake.'

Jesus Christ, what's the man saying? Vasiliev clenched his jaw. How the hell did Kuznetsov know the name of a legend? And not just any legend, but the name of one of the best deep cover sleeper agents they'd ever placed in Britain? Russell Blake - The jewel in the crown of the Illegals program.

'What are you telling me exactly, Comrade General?'

'I'm saying something is going on, comrade, something big is being staged. And I'm saying that when the mission, whatever it is, is over, that your deputy, General Volkov, has ordered one of your Illegals in Britain to be killed.'

12

Well rested and breakfasted after a night cocooned in an enviable blend of eighteenth-century French opulence and modern luxury, Russell Blake went out into a crisp Paris morning. Dressed in a dark grey suit with overcoat, black Oxfords and slim grenadine tie of a very dark blue, he walked through the famous Jardin des Tuileries, whose trees were still lush with golden yellow leaves yet to fall. He felt glad to be in Paris in November for that month's unique light alone. A not unfrequent visitor to the city, he had learned to appreciate its beauty whilst at the same time was able to remain completely detached from its people. It wasn't personal, he was incapable of emotion towards human beings from anywhere.

Soon he found himself in a mobile phone boutique on Avenue de l'Opera, where he spent fifteen Euros on an SFR prepaid 'Carte Connect' using his German passport as means of identification. Having slipped the SIM card into a handset he'd bought second hand in London, he found a quiet back street and entered a number he dialled daily.

As usual, when the line connected he was greeted with a number unobtainable message. He waited while the pre-recorded voice read, 'numéro non reconnu, veuillez réessayer' for ninety-seconds, and for the sound of the tape machine to start. A robotic, synthesised voice said, '*PAPA ECHO CHARLIE*

NOVEMBER 254 254 254 PAPA ECHO CHARLIE NOVEMBER 254 254 254. LEAVE. MESSAGE.'
'Phase two. Contact information received. Send courier. Out.'

The signal had been encrypted and channelled at lightening speed around the world before it reached the forest of radio dishes on a rooftop six hundred kilometres away from Paris in the Swiss capital of Bern. In the office below, on Casinoplatz, whose plaque outside pronounced the occupants as Gentzner and Asper's Law Office, a young man in the employ of the FSB ripped a printout from a fax machine and carried it across the hallway to another junior clerk at a computer. This man put the printout down on his desk and began copying the contents of the fax into the body of an email. In the subject line he wrote the word *Overture*, as he had been implicitly instructed to do with all such communication, while the recipient would as usual be Igor Savich. Neither he, nor his colleague across the hall wondered why when the telephone messages that came in were sent on a dizzying journey of encryption around the globe, the email that he then typed and forwarded was entirely unencrypted.

The day before, their office had been paid a visit by an FSB heavy squad, and the two clerks had stood in amazement as they watched their computers being ripped out of the wall. 'You will get new machines — orders,' the heaviest of the men had barked, seemingly unaware that the machines were only a year old and worked perfectly well. But when one of the heavies held up the two-and-a-half-inch Intel solid state drive that they'd had plugged into one of the computers for the last few weeks for the others to see, they'd all nodded — as if they'd found what they were looking for. The finder then slammed it down onto the desk, asked for a hammer, and began smashing it to pieces.

When the email from Hedges came in, informing them the intercepts from the Intel drive had ceased, Zoe was at her dining table alone with her laptop. It was late, Paul had long-since gone to bed exhausted and complaining of the onset of a cold, and so it was with a silent flickering television, a glass of wine club Pinot Grigio and a bowl of Waitrose banana chips for company that she read the GCHQ man's message.

She sat back in her chair. Why would it cease? Sudden malfunction? Unlikely. Once the drive had infected the machine the signal would continue to emit whether the Intel was plugged in or not, as it had been doing regularly. The bug was invisible, so it could only mean one thing — it had been discovered, which had led The Russians to change the machines. She felt a stab of dread in the pit of her stomach. Someone had told them, and the source either had to be someone in GCHQ, or inside her own department.

It was gone eleven but she decided to call John anyway. When she relayed the news he didn't sound surprised. Probably broke down, he said with Newsnight twittering in the background, that they should wait to see if the communications resumed over the weekend.

She hung up the phone. Maybe it's just his weak grasp of all things technological that had prompted his nonchalant lack of surprise, she wondered for the sake of balance.

The next morning The MS Pride of Bruges moved calmly past the Norfolk coastline bound for the Humber Estuary where she was due to arrive at terminal two in the King George Dock at 09:30 a.m. The captain was on his bridge preparing to steer her into dock, a procedure that involved turning the ship around and reversing her in. The crossing from Zeebrugge had been peaceful and the sky over the East Yorkshire coastline ahead, he noted through his windows that morning, was like a wonderful azure blue painting. A few seconds later with no warning that same sky was ablaze with giant orange flames leaping out of the peninsula. They were accompanied almost at once by plumes of black smoke that quickly rose out of the ground and covered the estuary mouth and surrounding horizon. It took fifteen-seconds for the thunderous sound of the explosion to reach the ship, which in no time became engulfed in a great dense fog.

Two hours later, the narrow entrance gates of the Elysée Palace opened and two police motorcycles with flashing red and blue lights emerged. They were closely followed by the French president's Citroen DS7 Crossback, itself followed by two unmarked police motorcycle outriders who were bringing up the rear. The uniformed police guards saluted as the motorcade turned right onto the rue du Faubourg Saint-Honoré and swept away. Among a small crowd gathered across the road, some people were holding phone-cameras high and smiling with delight at having caught a brief glimpse of the most powerful man in France, while emanating from among them came a few discordant jeers from protestors brandishing anti-EU banners.

Further along the road, having just left the palace to meet a friend for lunch, a young woman paused on the pavement as the motorcade past, she too catching the outline of the French leader's profile as the car flashed by. Yet Sarina Gaubert shared neither the tourists' delight nor the protestor's indignation.

Sarina worked in one of the Elysée Palace's 350 rooms as a part of the administrative staff, a position she had held for almost five years. She lived alone and was single, yet had never known a lack of male attention. Behind her hazel eyes though was a sadness that, despite her having known many lovers, prevented her not only from ever falling in love, but knowing happiness of any kind, however fleeting. Sometimes, whenever she thought of Andrey, the pain would pierce the well of her stomach. Andrey, the only man she ever loved, would ever worship, the brother who would never grow old.

'Hey, Sarina, Ça va?' One of the police guards shouted over, and she was snapped back onto the street. His name was Luc, she thought, and he was waving at her with the tall palace gates closing behind him. He was young, with kind, dark eyes, and in another life she would probably have gone out with him. But in this one she gave a flicker of a smile, then turned around and continued on to the cafe.

When she arrived on the hidden terrace at Minipalais, Marie was waiting at a table amid the giant Roman columns. They kissed on both cheeks, and the man who was watching from a table nearby saw her give a brief shiver, before she said, 'Tu es toujours assis dehors en Novembre?' to her friend as she sat. He studied her further as she took a sip of wine, and by the time the waiter had produced menus he had decided that she was even more beautiful than her photograph.

Later that afternoon inside his Kensington mews house John Henderson's eyes were fixed upon the early evening television news. Like the rest of the nation, he was watching the tragedy unfolding before him.

'Many hundreds now feared dead in what's being described by police and emergency services as the UK's worst gas explosion. The Easington terminal in Yorkshire and its surrounding area have been evacuated as firefighters battle the blaze . . . '

The same sobering scenes were being shown on the large wall screen inside the COBRA crisis room as the first few members of the specially formed committee began to arrive. The broadcast was cutting to shots of a vast coastal facility as fires raged from it, plumes of black smoke engulfing the skies, while a reporter in a helicopter delivered a fervid commentary.   ' T h e Easington terminal processes gas critical to the nation's energy security, and represents *seventy* percent of the UK's total gas storage capacity. What we don't know yet is exactly where the explosion took place within the facility or if the Langeled Pipeline has been compromised in any way. But reports are saying that the Easington terminal will have to be closed until the investigation into the cause of the explosion has taken place. These sites are of course major fire hazards and they are protected by special Ministry of Defence Police Officers, but at the moment at least there is no evidence of this being a terrorist act.'

Among those expected in the Cabinet Office meeting room that evening was the chief of MI6, though his driver had been asked to take a detour. With the black Mercedes parked discreetly around the corner, 'C' walked up to the door of a house in a quiet cobbled cul-de-sac in Kensington, and knocked. The muffled television upstairs became silenced, and the sound of footsteps on stairs could be heard. As he waited he surveyed the mews houses — converted stables built behind large city dwellings before motor cars replaced horses in the early twentieth century — all identical with black glossed front and garage doors and tall trees in matching planters outside. Although still too bohemian for his traditional tastes, he suspected a house here must be worth a small fortune. He made a mental note to remind himself how John Henderson had made so much money to enable him to live in such a smart area. Surely no one could afford to live here on Six's salary alone.

'Sir Clive,' he said surprised when he'd swung the door open.

'What a charming street, John. May I come in?' In the first floor's living room, before a television still flashing images of the burning northern peninsula, 'C's quick grey eyes were greeted with a parade of Russian literature that lined the bookshelves. Like an extension of his office, he thought — he really does live and breathe it. Were it not for the view through the window they could easily have been in a flat in Moscow. The only personal item seemed to be a framed photograph that stood on a sideboard like a lone gravestone, and when 'C's eyes fell upon it he could sense a spike of self-consciousness prick his subordinate, so he came directly to the point.

'Something that hasn't yet reached the newsroom, John,' he said, flicking a glance towards the screen. 'At twenty to six this evening the BBC received a phone call from the OAG, the Organisation Against Globalisation, claiming it was they who caused the explosion.'

'So it's started.'

'Since you've been away there's been a string of fatalities that could also be viewed as convenient. If one was of the mind to fall in line with your theory.'

'Operation Overture.'

'Yes, Operation Overture. Nine that we know of, most likely more of course, as well as the satellites and wind farms down, and now Easington.'

'According to the original mission blueprint it looks to me like the Russians are initiating phases three and four simultaneously. The assassinations, and acts of terrorism apportioned to separatist groups like the OAG – who fit the bill nicely don't they — alongside their mobilising the sleeper.'

'And *three* nuclear devices, isn't it?'

'I believe so, yes. And it's my guess he's already planted the first bomb and is either on his way to Paris or there already to receive and plant the second. Whoever 'he' is of course.'

'Yes, indeed.'

'But we know one thing. He's the best. Ultra deep cover. An invisible. And now with eight days lost I'm afraid our chances of identifying him are slimming fast.' Christ, why had he thought for a minute that Jones-Cooper would believe him. He became drawn towards the window where the low sun was casting a red fog across the chimney pots and tiled roofs, as the last drabs of daylight slowly retreated from the living room. 'You know how many Illegals there are in the United Kingdom, Sir Clive?'

The chief stared at his man.

'No, neither do I. But the estimate is many thousands. Perhaps as many as ten.'

Henderson squinted into the distance. 'He could be anywhere out there. And without a lead I'm afraid I'd approach any sense of optimism with caution.'

The older man produced a document file from his coat. 'I may be able to help you there. Yesterday morning Katya Petrenko walked into the Moscow Station and asked for asylum. In exchange for this.' He handed him the file. 'It's the dossiers of three of Russia's deep cover sleeper agents, with legends.'

He opened the file and stared down at the grainy thumbnail photographs of the Illegals who stared blankly back at him. It was gold. Their real names, and the names of their legends — their fictitious identities Moscow goes to great lengths to create. 'Dmitri's insurance policy,' he said, transfixed. He suddenly had visions of Dmitri at Grushenko's safe. The little man in steamed-up spectacles and a cheap head torch with ear on the door, fingers on the dial, sweat pouring from him, glancing down to a thick instruction book on his knee.

'C' studied him while he scanned the three profiles, his attention gripped. The Illegals were all male, caucasian, and of a similar age in their photographs — eighteen or so — and all had once borne codenames from Greek mythology but were later rechristened after areas of London. 'Seems some were rather incongruously assigned names of *female* figures,' he remarked as Henderson read:

Name: Major Boris Ivanovich Stepanchikov.
Legend: Adrian Ian Parkinson.
Codename: ~~CRONOS~~ / STRAND

Name: Colonel Anton Antonovich Petrov.
Legend: Charles Spencer Dennison.
Codename: ~~ATHENA~~ / KENSINGTON

Name: Major Valentin Gregorievich Baskov.
Legend: Russell Edward Blake.
Codename: ~~EUROPA~~ / MAYFAIR

Then beneath: every detail typed in small black font. Date and place of birth, languages spoken, hair colour, eye colour, height, body type, distinguishing marks, qualifications, rank, special training, awards, occupation in target country, marital status, recruiter name, general remarks — even the fingerprints and the current UK address of each Illegal was there.

'This is top priority, John. Anything you need.' Henderson pulled on his coat, but before the two men parted he told his chief he had an idea. It was a simple one, but one that he thought could prove effective. 'C' thought for a moment. It was irregular, but not unheard of, and must be handled in the strictest confidence. In fact in the spy business where duplicity is the de facto modus operandi, the Chief of MI6 considered it rather clever.

'Worth a shot, Sir Clive, don't you agree?'

'You go ahead and draft it. We'll include it in the next Echelon parcel for Miss Fisher to deliver personally.'

Bloody clever, he thought to himself as the car came to a halt beside the Old Church on Chelsea embankment. Rush hour was in full swing, and while waiting for the traffic to move he glanced left to the statue of Sir Thomas More in front of the 12th Century building. They regarded each other impassively. If this works then it could save us an awful lot of work, not to mention lives. 'Know your enemies and know yourself,' he said to the statue as the driver let out the clutch. 'Sun Tzu', he added, in case the dead saint wasn't familiar.

He dialled a number, and after a few seconds a man's voice answered.

'Mr Jones-Cooper. I've re-instated John Henderson and assigned him Head of Operations. You're to give him anything he needs: personnel, transport, expenses, to respond to any request favourably. Is that understood?'

The line was silent, but 'C' could hear the sound of the man's blood beginning to boil. 'I understand why you saw fit to reject the initial evidence but I'm sure you agree as of now we find ourselves in a different situation altogether. Is that clear?'

In his riverside flat with the Millennium Bridge ahead of him, St Paul's Cathedral behind, and a Polish girl from an overpriced escort agency waiting in the bedroom, Jones-Cooper, barely able to contain his anger, let out a 'yes, sir' and hung up.

When 'C' arrived at COBRA to give his briefing, the Defence Secretary stood to greet him. The man the PM was so intent on replacing with Morris Jacques had been selected to chair the committee that bore the codename *Minerva,* that as well as himself comprised The Home Secretary, The Energy Secretary, Williams from Joint, as well as uniformed General Fieldhouse, who was Chief of the Defence Staff – the government's most senior military advisor. The Foreign Minister, the man to whom MI6 is responsible, was out of the country, therefore the Permanent Under-Secretary at the FCDO was also patched through from King Charles Street. The tension in the air was palpable, and the unfolding of the day's events had etched the same grave expression over the faces of all who were present. When the chief of MI6 began his briefing, no one even coughed, let alone thought to interrupt.

'C' took his time, choosing his words carefully. Firstly, with what they knew: The truth, he was afraid to have to report, was that contrary to recent news reports of it being an accident the Easington disaster had indeed been confirmed as a terrorist act. A group calling itself the OAG, the Organisation Against Globalisation – German born but about whom we admittedly know very little — claimed responsibility earlier today, and that this most heinous attack on British soil when considered alongside the gas leaks, the disarmed satellites, disabled wind-farms and widespread hacking of trading platforms — also no accidents but sabotage — painted a chilling picture. When these events were viewed in conjunction with the alarming number of carefully targeted assassinations, Sir Clive was afraid it was his unenviable duty to draw the committee's attention to the theoretical possibility that Great Britain and the mainland of Europe may be subjected to an imminent and large scale attack. That dark clouds indeed were rolling in from the East.

What sort of an attack? Asked the chief of the defence staff, matter-of-factly.

With all John Henderson's shards of evidence in a pile in the forefront of his mind, Sir Clive Thorpe told them. The high probability, gentlemen, that they were witnessing the initiation of a cold-war-era plan christened *Overture* by the Soviets. *Operation Overture*, a plan in four stages. For those assembled who perhaps hadn't recognised the uniquely vulnerable position the country and the wider continent of Europe now found itself in, he went on to provide the cohesion - Henderson's cohesion: Thanks to prolonged and, one must add, overt Russian foreign policy, the slow disassembly of trust and faith in western governments, in liberal democracies, the European Union, in NATO. The welcoming with open arms extended to Russian oligarchs with links to the Kremlin wishing to wash their corrupt wealth. Billions of pounds worth of properties in Knightsbridge and Belgravia that provide a safe haven — a Russian playground nicknamed Londongrad, Moscow-on Thames. And against this backdrop the terrorist attacks, the silencing of the most vocal dissenting voices of socialism, the vast network of sleepers, more numerous than they even know, crouched in every corner of society like sprinters waiting for the starting pistol.

And this, *Overture* did you say, Clive? Orchestrated by whom exactly? By a terrorist cell of communist extremists, no doubt with links to Russian military Intelligence, perhaps even to the Kremlin, but one operating separately from Putin and the Siloviki who are ready and willing to deliver the final death blow. A committee of hardliners, you say? Indeed, this is what our intelligence tells us. Mmm, based within Russia you think? Our intelligence would suggest almost definitely. Mmm, members we are to assume are high-ranking personnel within the Russian government and military? We have limited intelligence to suggest this but based on my officer's summation of the situation this is the assumption, yes. A terrorist organisation — the Chief of the Defence Staff now — operating independently, immune to recriminations from NATO. Quite so, general. And the death blow being specifically?

'C' braced himself before he responded. 'The detonation of a portable low-yield nuclear device within our shores.'

Initial confusion now turned to stone cold horror as the impact of his words sank in. If none had realised it before, each member was now facing the irrefutable fact that *Minerva* was in fact a war cabinet.

The general reiterated it for everyone. 'Jesus Christ. You mean to say that somewhere outside of these four walls there's a Russian agent armed with a nuclear bomb?'

'More likely three bombs, general. And yes, that is our belief.'

The Home Secretary was disconsolate. 'Jesus God,' he said, visibly shaken. It fell to him to have to break the news to the prime minister. Overture's MO was to attack each country's ability to govern, Clive was saying, therefore thorough searches of the Houses of Parliament and 10 Downing Street and their surrounding areas should commence at once. Yes, prime minister, he responded on the phone after the meeting had concluded, the DG of MI5 has of course been fully briefed as has the Met Commissioner.

However it is Sir Clive's suggestion, sir, that neither premises at least yet should be evacuated.

From his car 'C' placed a call to Sir Humphrey. 'Perhaps some added words of clarity from you, Humph,' he said, imagining how the Prime Minister could react when he received the news from his Home Secretary. 'Hold his hand a bit, ongoing counterintelligence operation, threat level raised from Substantial to Severe, no need just yet to sound the alarm.'

Thirty minutes later 'C's car pulled in through the sliding iron gates on the Albert Embankment and at just before 10 p.m. he was back upstairs on an animated third floor. Kesterton greeted him as the lift doors opened and they began marching in the direction of his office. 'Both Five and the Met have assigned their respective chief officers roles, sir, and they've been drafted in to be briefed by John. Just arrived actually.' He gave a perfunctory knock on a glass door, and led the chief inside where Henderson was standing with two men. 'Gentlemen? Representing MI5, sir, Mike Hewitt.' Hewitt, a fair-haired, lean ex-paratrooper of the 3rd battalion who'd narrowly dodged death in Helmand in Southern Afghanistan, held out his hand and gave a firm military handshake. 'C' then turned to the taller of the two, a six-foot three black police officer whom he knew by reputation. 'While appointed by the Police Commissioner, Chief Inspector Alan Darlington. Chief Inspector, Sir Clive Thorpe.'

'It's a pleasure.' Darlington said. He was of Nigerian descent, but his father, thinking it would give his children a better chance, had chosen to change the family name of Okonkwo by deed poll in 1966 to the name of the town in County Durham where they'd settled. Whether the name change had helped his son attain such a high rank in the Police Force Darlington couldn't know, (at that time he was only the U.K's second black chief inspector), yet those that knew him doubted it.

'Sir Clive, I've been handed the power to mobilise SCO19, the specialist firearms command, at the national level.' said the CI, it having been quickly decided the special firearms units of the police would perform simultaneous dawn raids on the three addresses the electoral role had confirmed as the Illegals' permanent residences — one in a leafy village outside the cathedral city of Chichester in West Sussex, one in the Oxford suburbs, and finally — a flat in Battersea in South London. Henderson's first move that evening had been to get three Watchers teams in place. Introductions over with, 'C' left them to get on with it.

Zoe had again abandoned the dinner table to rush back to Vauxhall. Paul and Joe received a quick kiss on the forehead and the former a mimed 'sorry' from the door in place of an explanation. The poor man, she felt for him. His cold was now fully blown and Joe still wasn't sleeping but what was she supposed to do? As the taxi shuttled her past Crouch Hill station then The Old Dairy pub she thought of Katya, and of brave little Natalya. Full resettlement package, John had said. A new name, certain money, a new start. More importantly a 'remission induction treatment' for the daughter. Zoe, who hadn't cried for years, sniffed the tears quickly away and by Finsbury Park station was instructing the driver to speed up and to never mind the fucking speed cameras.

At eleven p.m., as Six's task force was assembling, Zoe studied the dossiers of the three illegals that were blown up on screens. Cronos who became Strand, Athena, now Kensington, and Europa, now Mayfair, their young faces blank and emotionless, belonging to blunt instruments of state. But Athena? Why would the Russians christen a male agent with a female Greek name? She asked herself.

When Chief Inspector Darlington marched in and the room had settled he began by going over the pros and cons of deploying CS gas canisters in the three planned raids. Having already concluded a preliminary briefing with his recently assigned assault team commanders, it was with his trademark charisma that he outlined tactics the three SCO19 teams would employ.

'The teams will be hand picked at each area commander's discretion, though none will employ the Gold, Silver and Bronze command structure for the assault on the properties as in my view there won't be enough time to establish the temporary control rooms necessary. Each team of eight will comprise four armed officers to perform the assault, and four more to form two cordons, front and rear. Likewise there will be no attempt to evacuate nearby civilians, nor hold them inside their own homes for safety, nor to stop traffic.'

As he spoke the teams of officers from Thames Valley and Sussex Police were gathering in their regional stations' back offices to rehearse the assaults on each property. Each was awaiting architectural plans of the residences that were being hastily obtained from local councils to assist their entries. Their commanders were clear. Take all occupants alive unless any sign of explosives are detected on the premises, in which case they have the license to use any means to prevent detonation. That to expect occupants to be highly trained military or intelligence agents, and to be armed.

With a range of weapons at their own disposal, all three team commanders chose the Glock 17 9 mm pistol — their standard sidearm — known for its reliability and accuracy.

Lying at the foot of the South Downs is the small village of Boxgrove, and it was from a pretty white corner house on the charming Church Lane at 04:53 a.m. precisely that the thunderous crash of a battering ram came to break the calm. The separating of the front door from its frame awoke the whole street. Within a few seconds of entering, the four-officer squad had charged up the stairs, burst into the master bedroom with guns raised and handcuffed the two startled occupants, a man and a woman both in their forties. Less than a minute later the team had bundled them into the back of a waiting van that then drove away at high speed and before a single neighbour had had time to pull on a dressing gown and make it outside, a second van had pulled up, removed the remaining four-man cordon from the scene, and also disappeared.

Strand had been captured.

During the same dawn some minutes later in Summertown, a wealthy suburb to the north of Oxford, team commander Sergeant Haskill felt adrenalin coursing through his veins as he waited in the darkness of a van parked opposite an unlit house. His radio raised, he was about to give the order to go when he spotted a civilian. 'Shit, stand-by all units,' he said, as through the tinted driver's window he watched a figure appear. 'A sodding paper boy.'

The kid was wearing ear buds and rapping out loud to the early morning chill as he stuffed a thick newspaper into the letterbox of the house next door. The sergeant wanted nothing more than to grab him and drag him into the van to shut him up, but instead gave another order to stand by. The boy jumped over a low wall that separated the properties, managing, much to Haskill's eternal regret, not only to hammer out a quick beat on the lid of a wheelie bin as he did so but to allow the letterbox to snap shut with a loud crack after he'd forced a Daily Mirror through. Haskill winced. With the boy on the scene they couldn't move, and if the occupants were awoken the van stood out like a sore thumb. 'Stand by,' he said again slowly as the kid jumped over the next low wall. 'Wait for it . . . '

Invisible in the back garden the two snipers froze, as did the occupants of both vans. The two front cordon men had disappeared back into the shadows.

Haskill waited, eyes glued to the house for the few long seconds it took until the terrible moment came when a light went on in the first floor bedroom. Before he could give the order to go, a man appeared at the window, spotting the van across the street at once. Then, in a flash, he was gone.

'Shit. Go, go!' The four men sprang from the van and bolted across the road, guns raised, while the man in front charged the door with the big red key, as the police term the battering ram. In no time they were inside and while two ascended the stairs in three easy leaps the other two crashed into the rear ground floor living room, through to the kitchen and bathroom beyond. 'Clear,' came the call in the helmet mic's.

Upstairs the sight in the front bedroom was different. The man was now standing upon the bed with his naked back against the wall and holding a tablet to his lips — goading the two armed officers to approach. But he was cornered. They hadn't been briefed to negotiate with suicides and the naked man knew this. With a final defiant snort he smacked the tablet into his mouth and swallowed hard as Her Majesty's intruders surged at him. By the time the cuffs were on, a white foamy discharge had gathered at the corners of his mouth and a minute after the forced entry he stopped breathing.

Kensington was dead.

Overstrand being a mansion block with a communal entrance, and Flat 12 being on the ground floor facing the street, it had been suggested by CI Darlington that entry through the French windows that look out onto the modest paved garden would be more advisable. Henderson disagreed. A dense, six foot high hedge would have to be ascended and the wide windows could be made of strengthened glass. Not to mention there was more chance of a trip wire or booby trap in the yard than in the communal entrance hall. They would enter through the main entrance's double doors, and use the front door. He didn't mention he had a feeling about this one, which told him the place would be empty. We'll pick the lock and go in like gentlemen then, Darlington said, before clarifying that that actually meant having to bypass the communal door entry system before battering the front door to the apartment in.

When the armed squad smashed through Mr Russell Blake's front door and entered Flat 12 they encountered no resistance. Neither in the form of trip wires in the garden nor gunfights with a highly trained Russian agent armed with a Beretta 9000. Henderson and Zoe stepped over the splintered frame with their guns raised and strode into the double reception room. Seconds later the officers came through and confirmed the flat was empty of occupants.

Mayfair had vanished.

Henderson instructed the team commander to cordon off the area and to give them a minute before sending in the search team that was waiting outside.

'And question the neighbours,' he added. 'I don't care what time it is.'

The squad retreated, leaving them to survey the place.

He'd been right, it was empty, but the sight that greeted them he hadn't foreseen: The wealth. The place wreaked of it. High ornamental plaster ceilings with decorative corbels and Greco-Roman panelling, deep-pile cream carpets, a plush hand-knotted Serapi rug flanked by two matching fern green Chesterfield couches. Lalique, Delft, and more Jasperware than he had seen in one place before. He could sense every stick of furniture was antique, every cushion hand-stitched or woven in silk, and that every painting was the real McCoy. And how many! Dotted across the walls, small gilt framed oils of aloof young women, majestic horses and amusing cats, then several nudes, and Kandinskys, Rothkos . . . and more he could pick out just on first glance. The room's centrepiece though was the Mondrian, that Zoe was standing in front of.

She noticed he was sporting an involuntary sneer. 'You resent all this don't you?'

'Something tells me our Mr. Blake's been enjoying his cover a bit too much.' He picked up a porcelain figurine and scowled at it. This was new money. Such cold displays of luxury always raised his hackles but the petit-bourgeois taste for the obvious conventional, expensive crap he despised. If that made him a snob, so be it. 'Material wealth, you mean? It's a weakness.'

An old film projector on an ebonized French campaign desk caught his eye. He turned his head up to the patch of bare wall it would have illuminated.

Zoe went over to look out of the French windows. 'Take a look.'

They peered out into the garden, their faces framed by the rectangles of the window. The sun had yet to rise, and the paving stones glistened from the night's dark rain. Although the fire pit that rested on the ground was small, and the perforated film inside it was partially burned and charred, they could just make it out, fluttering in the early morning breeze.

'Where are you, Mr Blake?' he said, his breath misting the window.

13

From the front of a grey van the shimmering streets of the city now seemed strangely different to her, infected. The threat was suddenly very real. The blast, the trauma, the sheer devastation the bomb would cause to London she'd remembered on the tube that day, the day John was silenced, re-entered her mind. The firestorms, the panic, the burning radiation. There was no stopping now, she told herself, gripping the door handle tight as the van crossed the river back to Vauxhall, we *have* to find this Russian.

Back on the third floor in the operations room, Henderson coughed politely for silence. Russell Blake's passport photograph was emblazoned behind him on a giant video screen, while seated in front of him among his own section were senior officers from both security services and the police force, all clutching coffee cups and reeling at the indecency of a 6 a.m. meeting. Stephen Jones-Cooper kept to the back.

'This is now a manhunt,' Henderson announced. 'But this is no ordinary man. This,' he gestured to the image, 'is a crack Russian agent.'

Zoe, backlit and with her blond hair tied back, took over as the Cafe 89 paninis from next door were unwrapped from foil and began to compete in the malodorous stakes.

'Major Valentin Gregorievich Baskov, born September 19th 1983 in Kursk, Russia. Aged thirty-seven. Six feet two, eyes green, hair brown. Excellent English, good French, excellent German, also has Danish. FSB trained. Expert marksman, close-combat, and proficient in the handling of nerve agents. Recruited into S-Directorate, the Illegals, in 2001 and placed into deep cover under the legend Russell Edward Blake. That was in 2002.'

Unaware that his cover had been blown and his flat invaded by MI6, Russell Blake dropped the napkin on his plate and took the last short sip of cappuccino. It was more like a spring morning in Paris than a winter one, so he'd chosen an outside table a short stroll from the hotel. He noticed a woman at another table and asked himself if she looked familiar, if she could be a tail, but then her husband joined her and they began arguing loudly, which answered that. He thought of the girl from the photograph, the girl he would make contact with tomorrow and wondered if she was married, and that if she was whether that would make a difference. 'L'addition, s'il vous plait,' he said to a passing waiter as he put on sunglasses and began to consider the route it would take him about thirty minutes to walk.

Zoe thumbed the remote, changing the image on-screen. 'Occupation: property developer. Address: 12 Overstrand Mansions, Battersea. A three bed that he paid two point two million for in 2015. Travels a lot for business, mainly in Europe but twice to the Far East, Macau and Hong Kong, both in 2017. Also deals in art, or buys it anyway, mainly at auction. The paintings in the flat alone are thought to be worth over three million. And he's known to have paid nine hundred thousand for a Goya at Christie's in 2006.'

Passing the celebrated Jardin de Tuileries, he

skirted the northern banks of the Seine and on towards the Louvre, the sheer size and majesty of which never failed to impress him. Knowing it contained the world's greatest art treasures helped. He was about to walk under the first of the arches to the entrance to the Place du Carousel when out of nowhere three police cars screamed up behind him, their shrill two-tone sirens piercing the air. It only took him a second to slip into the shadows and quickly bury himself in a doorway behind the grand facade as the cars flashed by, cutting through the Parisian traffic.

'No mortgage, and an Aladdin's cave of antiques at the flat,' Zoe continued. 'Wardrobe full of expensive clothes, Maserati - last year's model, member of two West End clubs and a Lloyds bank account with an agreed £100,000 overdraft. Balance of only nineteen thousand though so we suspect he's got more buried offshore somewhere.'

The sirens became dissonant and distant. Blake let out a breath and checked his watch. Fifteen minutes until the rendezvous. He stepped out of the archway and turned towards the triumphal arch.

'General remarks noted on the dossier say outstanding, high in aptitude, unsurpassed proficiency, considered ruthless, cold, and unable to display emotion.'

'Sounds like my ex,' a lone voice rung out from the middle, causing the room to dissolve into laughter. Henderson stepped back in.

'Thank you, Zoe. We're handing over to Five and the Met to find the London bomb.' Mike Hewitt gave a swift nod of the head. 'If I'm right he's already planted it and set the timer, but where and for when we don't yet know, so while Mike and his team and CI

Darlington here are looking at the CCTV for the last two weeks and building up a pattern of his movements in Britain we need to find our Mr. Blake before he can plant the next one.'

Kesterton raised a palm. 'And you think he's in France, John?'

'Yes, France, Brian. Thanks for reading the report, I know you and Sam alone formed my core readership.' A murmur of embarrassed laughs. 'That's where I believe he's going, or more likely has already gone, given we've lost so much time.' Zoe gave a glance up at Jones-Cooper, whose eyes were glazed over in bored defiance. 'Assuming the Russians are sticking to the original MO there are three devices - London, Paris, and Berlin, and while specific targets were never specified in the original documents we know they'll be the seats of power. At the moment that's all we have. Begin with border control. Although we can assume he's travelling under a different identity already.' He turned back to Hewitt. 'The sooner we can confirm he's left the country, Mike, the better, OK?'

'Copy that, John.'

'Right, let's move.' The room quickly cleared, leaving Zoe to join him in front of the screen, from which stared the pixellated eyes of a killer, the passport image from eight years before having been enlarged from its original two by two inch size. 'Your trip to Moscow worked,' he said, gathering up files.

'Maybe.' She hadn't thought of it like that. That she had helped jog Katya's memory.

'Seems Dmitri wasn't as stupid as Grushenko, or anyone, thought.'

She remembered the despair Katya had felt, too sad to even speak, too weak to stand up to her uncle and the system he controlled. Did she now have hope?

'Check with Interpol. All arrivals at hotels inside the Périphérique. I know, there are a lot. But cross off everything under four star.' He turned to face his quarry's image, 'Seems our Major Baskov has grown a little too fond of his creature comforts.'

When Russell Blake arrived in the bustling Paris square that hosts the giant multi-coloured Centre Pompidou, among those admiring the exposed green pipes and blue plumbing ducts that adorn the exterior of the tubular skeletal building was a man whose appearance suggested he was just another vacationing tourist. He wore sandals, a Dallas Cowboys cap, and a bum bag around his waist that contained a Czech passport identifying him as Viktor Hrabě, who had arrived with his wife Klara two days prior, after having driven from Prague in their camper van. He also happened to be a former officer of the StB, the now-dissolved secret police force in communist Czechoslovakia – yet that information had been erased from his records. His mission was simple, and he didn't question it, nor had any idea of its significance. He didn't know what the suitcase contained, nor did he wish to, so when he saw the man in the suit approach from across the piazza he opened his guidebook, exactly as he had been instructed to do.

The case had been delivered to him in the early hours of the day before, yet since its manufacture in 1976 its journey had been long. Since the dissolution of the USSR in 1991, this particular Atomic Demolition Munition had been lying abandoned inside the 102nd Military Base in the former Soviet Republic of Armenia, one of a handful of military bases Russia maintained abroad. Only a very small group of men knew of the whereabouts of such ADM's, and it wasn't until one September almost thirty years later that one of them, a General of the Russian Army named Voznesensky, paid an unscheduled visit to the base in Gyumri to retrieve it. Voznesensky was deputy director of 12th Directorate – that which is responsible for the country's nuclear arsenal — however it was not upon orders of the Russian government that he acted. For Voznesensky was a member of *Telepol*, a fact that even his Director wasn't aware of, and it was to them he answered and whom he obeyed — hence the clandestine nature of his visit that day. Once he had taken the case from the storage facility he drove himself to meet a contact at the train station, who hid the suitcase inside the wing of his specially modified *marshrutka,* which he then drove without stopping to Istanbul via Georgia. When he arrived he delivered it to an address, as he was paid to do. The elderly recipient was a Turk, known in the criminal underworld as Mehmet the Bomb-maker, who over the next week in a back room somewhere deep in the maze of the Grand Bazaar would overhaul the long-neglected nuclear device — replace the old-style timer with a modern version, attach a new battery with low voltage alert transmitter, re-key the arming switch, and perform myriad other tasks to ensure its readiness for reliable detonation. When the time came, he dialled a number from a pay phone in the bazaar. Three days later a large amount of money arrived by way of a masked courier on a moped, and the day after that the case was collected at his door by a man with a vicious oblong face and the blackest eyes the old bomb-maker had ever seen. No words were exchanged.

The black-eyed smuggler's name was Saladin, and he accompanied the case from Istanbul in a Bombardier Learjet for the 2242 km distance to Paris' Le Bourget, where it was met at 02:30 a.m. by a customs official who had been generously bribed. He had been told a camper van with Czech number plates would be waiting outside the airport terminal with its sliding side door open, and that he was simply to place the suitcase inside. After he'd done so, the door slid closed from the inside and the van pulled away into the night.

Less than forty-eight hours later it sat on the cobblestones next to two sandalled feet as the smartly dressed figure approached and said, 'I hear Dallas has it own share of modernist buildings.'

'They say Dallas City Hall alone is worth the visit,' came the reply.

The tourist closed his guidebook and ambled away into the crowd to look for his wife. Had anyone noticed, which they didn't, they would have spotted that he had forgotten to pick up and take with him his old scuffed suitcase, that a few seconds later had itself also gone, along with the man he had exchanged a few pleasantries with moments before.

Back at the hotel Blake placed the suitcase next to his own more lavish Vuitton grip in the bottom of the room's wide closet, and closed the doors. Unbeknownst to him, He then took the lift down to the lobby where he called a number belonging to a contact he had used before in Paris, called Bastien, one of the best conduits in the business. A minute later, armed with the information he needed, he was waiting for a taxi that would take him into the north of Paris, where Bastien had informed him he could buy the type of camera he required.

As that taxi pulled up outside Le Meurice hotel, back in London a hundred uniformed police officers descended upon the Palace of Westminster - much to the bemusement of our elected officials — while a hundred more began the laborious search of nearby buildings and a further hundred began to comb the area around Downing Street. Also, at the precise moment that he closed the door and gave the address to the driver, Interpol's General Secretariat was approving MI6's Red Notice application that meant by the next morning every policeman in France would be searching for Russell Blake. They had been told he was good — highly trained, a suspected terrorist — but few outside the Illegal's Directorate itself knew just how good. To those inside the GRU's mysterious Directorate S, however, the man who had been assigned the codename *Mayfair* could not be described as 'good' at all.

Mayfair was the best they ever had.

The story of the man who would be *Mayfair* began on 3rd July 1983 on a blustery afternoon in the Cathedral City of Wells in Somerset, when Terry and Julie Blake welcomed the birth of their son. Terry, a railway signalman, and Julie, a seamstress, chose the name Russell in memory of Julie's own recently deceased father, while Edward was added as a middle name to honour Terry's brother who had been killed by a machine gun bullet in the Falklands War the previous year.

The boy was only a year old when his father, a

lifelong train enthusiast, announced the family was to take a week long railway tour of the Scottish Lowlands, and at 17:30 on Monday 30th July 1984 they boarded the westbound express train from Edinburgh to Glasgow. The service consisted of a British Rail Class 47 locomotive and five coaches, and was fronted by a DBSO control car — which was of particular interest to Terry, their being once-standard carriages converted to operate as control cars that used a system known as push-pull, meaning the driver could drive the locomotive even though it was at the rear of the train.

At 17:55 however, to the west of Polmont station, the train driver spotted an adult Ayrshire cow that had made its way onto the cutting and, unable to brake in time due to the heavy locomotive still pushing from behind, hit it, causing the front car to derail and the second carriage to somersault. The accident resulted in the death of thirteen passengers and left sixty-one others injured. The three members of the Blake family were among the dead.

The following evening a mint-green Mini Metro pulled into the carpark of The Wheatsheaf pub in the small village of Stoney Stanton in the middle of England. The dour-faced Slavic-looking woman at the wheel sat staring for a few moments, weary after another long day spent in the July heat. She would take a room there for one night only. The next morning her work would steer her further south, which to her mind was one day closer to her beloved grandchildren back home in the Moscow exclave of Zelenograd. She missed them terribly, a longing made worse by the fact that it was her job as a ghoul to travel the length and breadth of England touring church graveyards and collecting names of dead infants and children the same age as them. By the evening of 31st she was half way through a tour that saw her travel from south to north and back again over the July and August of that year in her car with only an old Baedeker, a WH Smith's notebook, a box of Bic ballpoints and a bag of satsumas for company. That afternoon had been spent stepping among the gravestones in the churchyards of the local church of St. Michael, Saint James' in nearby Nuneaton, and the St Mary Magdalen in Knighton.

Downstairs at the bar she ordered her usual half a stout and traditional fish and chips, then took a table by the window and opened The Telegraph to scan the day's obituaries — which was her habit. That day she didn't get past the front page. A rail crash in Scotland was just the thing. She reported it to her KGB controllers and before too long a birth certificate had been withdrawn from the local Somerset parish. Later, a new passport for Russell Edward Blake was applied for at the passport office, and granted without question.

A legend was born.

By the time Valentin Baskov arrived in England sixteen years later, a full and complete life history had been created for him to assume. A fictitious identity supported by perfectly real documentation. In the creation of his legend, as with all, thousands of man hours had been expended that brought Russell Edward Blake, in all but physical body, back to life. Minutiae details that make a believable background ranging from school reports, exam certificates, job offer letters and rental contracts to gas bills, magazine subscriptions, and pension plans are arranged. Lloyds Bank would confirm he had kept an account with them since the age of eleven, DVLA would record on their system his having bought and sold vehicles, and the records of Rayner and Ashby of Wells would attest to his having insured the first of them under a fully comprehensive policy with them when he turned seventeen — all arranged by long-since forgotten hands inside the KGB and applied for, opened, paid for, bought, upgraded, closed, sold, cancelled, and confirmed by Moscow. The endless mundane paperwork involved in the creation of a believable legend is a junior intelligence officer's lot.

When the British Airways aeroplane landed on the tarmac at Heathrow in 2002 and Mr Blake was welcomed back into the country, his identity, though bogus, appeared concrete and would prove as unbreakable if scrutinised. There was nothing about the Englishman, nor his luggage that day that offered any hint that he was anyone other than he claimed to be, which was a young estate agent returning from a week-long business trip in Hamburg where he'd been attending a property trade fair seeking to meet foreign investors and partners.

As well as this wealth of background information already committed to memory, upon his arrival at a safe house in South London that day he received a preliminary briefing and was given instructions regarding the nuts and bolts of operating in deep cover: familiarisation with procedures, lists of names, places, dates, contacts, codes — methods and transmission times — safe house addresses and entry codes, emergency telephone numbers, couriers, rendezvous sites, and fallback plans. He had memorised it all within two hours.

He slipped effortlessly into English society. The damp flats in Moscow, the instructor, Talbot, the repetition, unending broadcasts and incessant tape machine had done their job. Then one day in early 2004, rich with confidence if not money, the Russian met his handler in St James' Park. He'd applied to his local branch of Lloyds Bank for a small business loan to set himself up as a property speculator, he announced. The handler declared it contemptible, but when the news landed on old General Sorokin's desk, the then Head of Directorate S laughed out loud and roared "you cannot ask a star not to shine." *Mayfair* was special. "If the man wants to start a business and make money," laughed the coughing Head of the Illegals, "why not?"

Sorokin lasted longer than anyone predicted, but sixteen years later he was dead, felled by a lifetime of strong Belomorkanal cigarettes, and the best agent the Illegals' Directorate had ever produced was a multi millionaire dining at one of the finest restaurants in Paris with a nuclear bomb at the foot of his hotel room closet and a Do Not Disturb sign on the door. Later, after the sun had set, he planned to take the last river cruise of the evening along the Seine. As he'd be the only passenger on the top deck, he'd be free to take detailed infrared photographs of every dark outline of every brick interior of every bridge, each mysterious line in the walls of the riverbanks, and every set of haphazardly placed steps that disappear deep, very deep beneath the Seine.

While Blake dined on duck with plans of late evening reconnaissance in his head, back in London, Chief Inspector Darlington had assembled the largest group of police officers New Scotland Yard's Briefing Room A had ever witnessed. Their task: to track the Russian's movements in the last two weeks. As the final few rank and file settled, he knocked on the door to a corner office — the new home to MI5's soon-to-be constant presence, Mike Hewitt.

'Ready for the briefing, Mr Hewitt?'

The ex-para was unpacking as he beckoned Darlington enter. A rudimentary, military-looking camp bed had been erected in the corner, and an electronic espresso coffee machine   of the like Scotland Yard did not possess installed — brought in to provide creature comfort. Someone had brought three bags of shopping — coffee beans, almond milk, fruit, nuts, protein bars, ten packets of wine gums, a two litre bottle of supermarket Scotch and six cartons of Benson and Hedges. Hanging at the window were five shirts, while beside three laptops on the tank desk were six cell phones in case any one of Hewitt's informants called — his day job.

'Call me Mike,' he said as he plugged the coffee machine into a wall socket before he rolled up his sleeves and followed Darlington out into the crowded briefing room.

Due to the manpower required, round the clocks shifts known as 'three by eights' had had to be hastily orchestrated, overtime budgets agreed, holidays suspended, constables drafted in from distant departments from distant provinces, and the technology links set up to allow so many policemen and women access to the capital's closed circuit network that now included the all new facial recognition cameras —— the controversial new tool whose software can immediately identify a face on a police watch list as soon as it is captured on a video camera. Both Russell Blake's passport photos — the 'original' from 2002 and the renewed one in 2012 - had been uploaded to the database a few minutes before and the face digitally mapped. They were ready to start.

The animated hubbub petered out when Darlington entered, the clear timbre of his voice combined with the three Bath stars on his epaulettes demanding attention. 'Russell Blake, IC1, aged thirty-seven, of Overstrand Mansions, Prince of Wales Drive, Battersea. An estate agent.'

There was a sharp intake of breath from the middle of the sea of blue uniforms. 'Nasty piece of work then, gov',' some wag quipped, which brought the house down early. The CI held his hands up and hushed them.

'We need an accurate a biog as we can pull together of this man for the last two weeks, from 25th October. All from closed circuit - ' A wave of groans from the lower ranks filled the room. 'I know, I feel your pain. Closed circuit, dash cams, doorbell cameras — you name it. *Any* sightings at all, report to your team leader and any of the subject carrying a bag of any kind — briefcase, suitcase, attache, rucksack, holdall — gets top priority. Beginning in the areas around Westminster and Whitehall. Okay?'

After the second wave of lesser groans died down Darlington wrapped up and left his sergeants to assign the shifts. The tedious work would commence at once. The arduous process of studying footage from the city's half a million CCTV cameras in an attempt to track one man, and his car's journeys via ANPR, while separate teams on different floors of the building on the Victoria Embankment had already begun studying telephone records and electronic payment receipts to add to the giant, crucial jigsaw. What not one of the uniformed police knew as they embarked upon the gargantuan task was that the bomb they didn't yet know they had been tasked with seeking was ticking down a mere three hundred metres away from them — and that if they failed, in six days time everything they dreamed of spending their overtime on would be incinerated.

Hewitt closed his door and watched through the glass as the crowd of coppers dispersed into the corners of New Scotland Yard, still joking and jostling each other, spirits still light. He didn't have much time for the plod truth be told. He thought them simple. Simple faces, simple work methods. But he could tell instinctively that Alan Darlington was an impressive CI, and besides, they needed the manpower. He tore at a fresh packet of cigarettes and lit one, inhaling the first chestful of many more to come that night. At thirty-three he knew he should quit, and had promised himself he would only last week, but in the meantime if anyone told him it was a non smoking building they could go to hell.

Over in Vauxhall a woman called Lisa Arnold from counter terrorism was doing the talking while the scant few files MI6 had on the OAG were on up the screen that had descended electronically in front of the Patrick Heron on 'C's office wall. Her clipped Glaswegian accent was accompanied by a jabbing with the remote control to punctuate the briefing. 'The Organisation Against Globalisation, or the O - A – G, a group that has its roots in Germany.' She was ex-army, Henderson could tell. Tall, cropped hair, and a face whose only expression was one of critical importance. Impatiently, he checked his watch again. Eight thirty. Every second counted and he didn't know why he'd been pulled into the bloody meeting when he should be out there trying to track a terrorist. But of course, he knew they needed answers. Since the terror organisation, about whom no one seemed to know much of anything, had contacted the German news agency Deutsche Presse-Agentur to claim responsibility for not only the gas leaks in Rehden and the devastating explosion in Easington, but also the disabling of the wind-farm software — claiming they were all deliberate terrorist attacks — the international press had begun asking who the OAG were in thick block capitals.

'Formed in 1996 in opposition to what it regards as large multinational corporations having unregulated political power, deregulated financial markets, and the growing tide of neo-liberalism and a, quote, *worldwide monoculture . . .*' Her stress implied she had little sympathy for any doctrine that even dipped its toe outside the boundaries of establishment waters. ' . . . in recent years their numbers have grown, mainly in areas most affected by so-called *globalisation*, and they recruit and illicit support by tapping into the sense of betrayal and disenfranchisement that some people feel towards companies, corporations and governments who pursue such ends. However, what began as peaceful political protests on the streets of Berlin in the nineties soon turned more radical. They've taken up arms to further their cause, and are now classified as a dissident paramilitary organisation. Now regarded by Western intelligence services as a fully fledged terrorist group, since 2015 it has claimed responsibility for various atrocities in the name of an insular nationalism that has come to be regarded as fascist in nature.'

She gave them a potted history of the group's tyranny with an efficiency of tone that had been drilled into her in Aldershot twenty-years prior, and afterwards invited questions. Yes, she believed the sabotaging of pipes in deep underground gas storage facilities did fit the group's MO. They were tech-savvy, she underlined, sophisticated, and versatile in their methods. Car bombs in French supermarket carparks one day, CEO assassination here, missile fired at an airliner there, and yes, bank software systems hacked the next.

Jones-Cooper, also present, was rolling his pen in his usual way as he listened. He hadn't acknowledged Henderson since his return from exile earlier that evening. He'd likely been taken down a peg or two, Henderson guessed, which made him smile. He looked at his watch again, but Arnold was still talking. Her boss, Reardon, was a formidable man, one of Six's finest; a recognised expert on violent extremism who had led the Counter Terrorism Implementation Task Force. Rumour was he was ill though, terminal. A shame.

Her voice snapped him back into the room. 'Unless Mr Henderson has anything else to offer with regards the group?' He considered for a moment, thinking it would probably prove unpopular if he gave them his opinion which was that the OAG didn't exist at all, but were instead a necessary fiction concocted as a smokescreen, an invented scapegoat. However, John Henderson had a history of not being believed that he preferred remain as such — having learned more than most the hard way that in the world of Intelligence the truth is regarded as an abstract construct — so as he stood to leave he said, 'no, I don't think so, Ms Arnold, you seem to have covered everything. Now if you'll excuse me.'

'Good morning, sir,' she said as Grushenko's heavy overcoat came at her. 'Comrade Major General Volkov is here to see you.'

It was mid-morning, and as usual he blamed his driver for his being late, but his secretary could always smell the fumes on his breath that could strip the paint off the walls. "The eyes get redder," she would tell the others in the canteen, "the bags beneath them get more swollen, like they are full of pus!" They'd laugh and hush each other. "His collar is stained brown," one would add with a look of disgust, "and his skin is like tree bark." Then they huddle closer together and one will say, "They say he killed his own brother." A collective "Sshh."

The obese Volkov was waiting on a low club chair by the window, staring out at a city defenceless to the nights' snowfall. Once they were inside his own office Grushenko answered his ringing desk phone. The deputy head of the Illegals directorate sat down breathlessly and watched as the face opposite him, always hostile, curled in anger in reaction to what he was being told. It was muted, but Volkov distinctly heard the word 'disappeared'.

'What? When?' he said, spitting into the receiver. 'Four days? Why wasn't I informed?' Grushenko's eyes dropped to the pile of papers in front of him and his thick fingers began picking through them. They were surveillance logs - Volkov recognised the layout as well as the backs of his own fat hands — probably from the team on the Petrenko woman. The caller was telling him he *had* informed him. Volkov guessed by Grushenko's stench that he had been off-grid, probably on a bender for the last four days, and hadn't given a shred of thought to his work.

He suddenly became aware of Volkov watching him. 'Very well, yes, thank you for informing me.'

He was a bad liar, he knew that. Grushenko slammed the receiver down, too hard. He's still drunk, he thought.

'Pavel Igorevich, what can I do for you?'

'Trouble?'

'What? No. Just some routine business.'

Volkov regarded his counterpart, who was now studying the surveillance logs more closely. If anyone is going to bring down Overture with their negligence then it will be him. He thought about confronting him about the widow. If she has disappeared then there was a possibility she had defected, which should be investigated at once. What could she have that the British would want enough to take her in? Had the snivelling husband who was now rotting in a shallow grave near a gulag's perimeter wall really accessed his safe after all? If so, then what did he find? Volkov decided, for the sake of the mission, he must find out.

'What is it, I'm a very busy man.'

Volkov leaned in, which made the chair creak in protest. 'Vasiliev has discovered there is an order out to assassinate Mayfair. He confronted me with it. He only stopped short of directly accusing me of ordering the hit.'

'Russell Blake?' The name seemed to pull him

out of his stupor back into the land of the living.

'Yes, that is what I am saying. Someone has informed the Head of the Illegals directorate.'

'Who? Who informed Vasiliev?'

'That I do not know for sure, yet I have my suspicions. When he questioned me about it, I of course pleaded ignorance, told him I had given no such order. That it was ridiculous. Yet the last thing the committee needs is a Major General asking questions about the whereabouts of our executive officer, no?'

'Well, do what you think should be done, Pavel. Just make it clean.'

Grushenko scraped a callused hand over his chin, still lost in the surveillance logs, trying to weave a lie that would admonish him from any blame. The overweight man realised another body in the ground was the last thing on Grushenko's mind and that it wouldn't even snag his conscience. Volkov himself wouldn't do it of course, yet it pained him somewhat. He respected his immediate superior. But whoever had given Vasiliev the nugget of information had signed the man's death warrant.

He hoisted his giant girth off the forever-weakened chair and bade his equal good morning. As he walked back out through the outer office the secretary was on the phone apologising, saying the general had been out sick for a few days. She wasn't a good liar either. The reason the man hadn't been in his office for the last four days was more likely because he'd been drowning in vodka in a whorehouse surrounded by migrant prostitutes — deaf to everything but the sounds of their sham squeals.

Blake skimmed silently through the enlarged

photographs in the centre of the basement studio. The door to the darkroom was open, red safelight burning as a balding man with small round spectacles washed his hands at a sink in the studio's corner, reaching up for soap from a dispenser on top of a filing cabinet beside him. He didn't speak as his customer regarded each print. The ten by eights were better than Blake had hoped for. The man had done well. Bastien had come through again. But then he never failed, he was a professional who only used those whose loyalty was assured and whose silence was guaranteed. Men who wouldn't ask questions, who had no memory, who couldn't be bought. When the balding man had towelled his hands dry he handed Blake a large envelope, into which the Russian placed the prints. He paid, then climbed the narrow staircase back onto the street where he walked for fifteen minutes before taking a taxi back into the centre. He was pleased with his work. There were over forty stills, and the detail in the shots of the riverbanks and access doors beneath the bridges were especially clear.

The knot of protestors at the palace gates had grown in numbers and the anti EU placards they brandished high offered good cover to the well-dressed man at the rear who was in their throng only to wait for a pretty girl to leave the palace on her lunch break. When she appeared, she smiled thinly at a policeman guarding the pedestrian gate, before turning left and walking away. Blake broke away from the protestors and followed. Five minutes later as she crossed the Champs-Élysées near the statue of Charles de Gaulle, he knew she was heading for her usual cafe.

Minipalais was busier than usual when Sarina

arrived. The male customers stole glances up as she was escorted her to a table, but she was used to ignoring them. What she couldn't ignore however was the man who appeared at her table a few seconds later and sat down directly in front of her. He was dressed smartly, clean shaven, and smiling softly as he placed a book down on the table. It had been years since a man had made so bold a move towards her. There was something about him, this staring stranger, that reminded her of the past. She waited for him to speak. Instead, his eyes dropped down to the book. As soon as Sarina saw the name on the dust jacket she knew the moment she'd been dreading for the last several years had arrived.

14

'Do you read Sartre?'

She swallowed, her thoughts in free-fall and her tongue tied up in knots. 'I . . . I - ' She clenched her shoulder muscles and grasped at the memory, then let the words fall from her mouth. 'I prefer Moliere.'

'I find his inconsistency distracting,' came the reply. He was relaxed, and even seemed to be enjoying her discomfort.

'But you can't deny his . . .' she searched for the word, 'excellence?'

He leaned in to her and smiled, fuller this time, and, correcting her, said, 'Brilliance.'
The breath she'd been holding left her in the biggest sigh. Her appetite having rapidly faded she'd declined lunch, and as they walked away from the cafe together he asked her where she lived.

'Not far from here. Madeleine.'

Once inside her small third floor apartment that overlooked the Greek temple style church of L'église de la Madeleine, Sarina waited as the stranger surveyed her simply furnished living space, that with a man inside suddenly felt much smaller to her. He was looking at the framed photo of Andrey with his violin, the only one she had of him, her most cherished possession and the duplicate of which she carried in her purse with her always.

'Café?'

He shook his head, then put the photo down and went over to the window to look out. 'You live alone?'

'Yes.'

'Boyfriend?'

'Just me.'

She was still standing at the front door. He walked to her and stood close, and as his eyes locked on hers she gave a shudder. 'Major Valentin Baskov,' he said.

'Irina Annikova,' she replied. After so long the name sounded foreign to her.

He pulled out an envelope from his inside jacket pocket and handed it to her. 'I have some instructions for you.'

She questioned whether to open it, and, when he nodded, tore at it. Inside were several sheets of paper that she ran her eyes across for a few minutes. He performed the same action upon her, studying every faint line on her face, every freckle, fine hair above her lip, the tiny mole on the long curve of her neck, and every contour of her while her breasts rose and fell with her breathing. He moved over to the small kitchenette area in the corner where pots and pans hung above two electric rings, and a single cup, saucer and breakfast plate were perched neatly on the draining board. He could tell she lived a solo existence.

When she'd finished reading, she looked over at him and said simply, 'all right.'

'Good. Now I'll need a few days to prepare, so that should give you enough time to find out where the entrance is, what security is like, and to find a way of opening the door, or doors, when I'm ready. I'll probably want to move on Wednesday evening. Okay?'

'So soon? But, yes, Okay.'

'Good. Now, I want you to meet me tomorrow night at eight o'clock.'

'Oh,' She brought a hand up to her mouth, 'Wednesday there is a state visit so there will be more security.'

'Don't worry about that,' he answered, walking back over to her, 'just find me the access and if there's a key before tomorrow night and I'll organise the rest.'

'But why do we meet tomorrow?'

He moved in close enough for her to smell his skin, which smelled of soap. 'For dinner,' he smiled.

Twenty-four hours into the investigation saw Mike Hewitt eating a late lunch of cold hamburger and fries at his tank desk while still studying the CCTV on his screen. But the food was proving as difficult to digest as the fact that as yet Scotland Yard had little to go on. In a capital city where in any 24 hour period twenty-million people swarm around like flies, finding one face by scanning thousands of recorded hours captured by 628,000 CCTV cameras was proving no easy task. The undertaking was enormous, the work both painstaking and monotonous, and for a man who had once leapt out of aeroplanes and fought in the open deserts of Afghanistan for a living he was already starting to feel like a caged animal.

CI Darlington had employed the Metropolitan Police Force's squad of 'Super Recognisers', those men and women with a better than average ability to memorise and recall thousands of faces and match them even though they may have only glimpsed them momentarily. As yet, neither they, nor the facial recognition cameras, had yielded a match.

Equally as fruitless were the physical searches for the device, which were generating nothing but ire from MP's at being subjected to hoards of officers inside Parliament, while palace security cameras also drew a blank. A thorough search of every house in Downing Street had proved equally futile, thus the radius was being expanded across Whitehall that was resulting in both budgets and patience becoming rapidly stretched.

The door to door inquiries had proved more useful. Three days before, on 6th November, a neighbour on Prince of Wales Drive had remembered being awoken by a taxi with its engine running outside Overstrand Mansions, and that a man fitting the target's description had got into the vehicle at just after 5 a.m. with two suitcases — one small, about the size of a trumpet case, one larger. Inquiries at taxi companies quickly revealed the car's destination that morning as Victoria Station, yet when officers pulled up the CCTV of the taxi arriving and matched its plates they failed to confirm Blake as the cab's occupant. A search of the security cameras' footage inside the station and on the platforms also failed to yield a match.

In the list of his bank card payments was one to Merlin's Car Rental Agency in Clapham on Monday 26th October for a compact Ford saloon. It took only a few minutes to trace it on CCTV. It was picked it up as it travelled north on the A3 past Borough tube station but then disappeared soon after entering the borough of Southwark. Frustratingly, the Ford wasn't seen again until Blake returned the car in the small hours of the sixth, at 03:13.

Hewitt finished his lunch and decided to leave

the small office for a couple of hours so he got the tube down to Clapham to interview the employees and to see the car. When he arrived he was told the Ford had already had two drivers since Blake, so he didn't hold out much hope for any evidence. Closer study of the number plate screws revealed fresh scratches that could indicate the plates had recently been switched, which would explain its absence for the whole rental period, but it wasn't enough. Inside the agency's office the female clerk told him the customer had claimed he'd moved up to Camberwell from Portsmouth as he'd just received a promotion, but in what line of work she couldn't remember, before adding that Mr Blake, Russell Blake, he'd said was his name, was *very* good-looking.

Henderson put the phone down on Hewitt and stared briefly into the forest of white paper that had once been the bare green baize board until two knocks came on the door's glass.

'John?' It was Zoe. 'Charlotte Fisher's on the move. On her way to King's Cross and she's booked on the next Eurostar to Brussels. Fresh set of illegally downloaded documents on another hard drive in her bag. Godwin says a call was made to the same number registered in Lille as before asking for a gîte in July – same code. You want we should follow her?'

'Mmm?' He turned back to her. 'No, let her go, but have a VSSE Watcher team tail her to the drop.'

'Right.'

'Any word from the Border Agency?'

'No reports of anyone by the name of Russell Blake leaving the country that day or any other — and still nothing on the closed circuit as yet, but we're still looking.'

'What about the hotels in Paris?'

She smiled. Of course not. He walked over to the world map pinned on the wall above the traitors' and double agents' memoirs.

'He's long gone,' he said, staring into the clumps of pink and green continents surrounded by the pale blue sea. 'Victoria on the sixth: that gives him a three-day head start.' Like trying to locate a tiny microdot on the face of Europe. 'That's the last we'll ever see or hear of Mr Blake.'

Kesterton appeared at the door with Faulds. 'John, they're saying Strand's keeping schtum. Same for Mrs Strand. You want we should send them to Tottenham to up the ante?'

'Leave it to you, Brian.'

'Right 'o. Oh, Sam spoke to INTERPOL and someone will be there to meet you at Charles de Gaulle. A Sal Bernier, Okay?'

'Thanks, Sam.'

A mile and a half upriver the black, six-panelled door of a terraced house opened and the four knights of the realm strode out purposefully into the night. Two black Mercedes cars waited at the wet curbside, and bar the armed officers of the PaDP - the Protection Branch within the Specialist Operations Directorate of the Met who are a permanent fixture on Downing Street - no one saw them leave Number 10. A minute later the cars had sped off and disappeared down Whitehall.

'C' was travelling with Williams of Joint. 'Well, I suppose that was all we could hope for,' the JIC man said as, with the car flying past the Cenotaph, he struggled to click his seatbelt into its buckle. 'Buys us time at least. What's wrong with this bloody thing, oh I give up. Probably won't buy us *much* time though, eh. You know what he's like.'

In the preceding hour, beneath the three brass chandeliers that preside over the long boat-shaped table in the cabinet room, the Prime Minister had begun the meeting with the heads of the nation's security services by complaining of the place being overrun by constables who don't wipe their feet, before refusing to evacuate to Chequers, then stressing how sick to the teeth he was of scandal but that he still wouldn't rule out the idea of appointing Morris Jacques as his new Defence Secretary. Sir Humphrey, sitting beside 'C', had locked eyes with his old friend, and shot him a defeated look that said *I told you.*

The MI6 Chief had responded softly. 'Prime Minister, I thought it was understood, Mr Jacques has been compromised. He must never be allowed to hold high office.' It beggared belief. One call to Fleet Street from a man in Leipzig with a video tape was all it would take to bring down the entire government, yet the most powerful man in England was blithely, belligerently expecting them to cover it up and make it all magically disappear. But it was full battle cries and waves of defiant fingers they wished to avoid, so with Walpole gazing down from above the marble fireplace, when the subject of Overture was addressed it was stressed with all the subtlety that the situation demanded that it was a rogue committee of extremists whom the intel suggested was responsible — and that the operation had categorically *not* been rubber-stamped by the Kremlin. Since Russia's invasion of Ukraine, the importance of diplomacy during wartime and how sensitive the vocabulary chosen by politicians of western nations need be had become frighteningly important, so it was with some relief when the PM gave them his assurance that while telephoning the French and German leaders to discuss the intel he would be especially careful in his choice of rhetoric to save us all from accidentally swerving into a full-blown nuclear war with the Russian state.

And so it was with the balance of peace hanging by a gossamer thread and with the car tearing along Millbank that Sir Nigel — flustered, untethered, and most unused to being driven at such speed — said, 'I just hope we can find this bastard, Clive, and soon. And another thing, unless he'd like my kedgeree, half a bottle of Sancerre and two chocolate Swiss fingers to slither down his neck, would you ask Lewis Hamilton to slow down a tad?'

It was midnight in Moscow when Volkov's instruction arrived. The recipient: a stocky, flat-nosed pugilist head to toe in Lonsdale knock-offs who had been drinking heavily with cronies in the local boxers' bar. But being a freelancer meant you had to take the work when it came, so he made up some excuse about being on a promise before turning somewhat sloppily for home before being forced to elaborate. Like many freelance killers of his class it was brute force, not reasoned discourse, that was his preferred means of communication. Yet perhaps surprisingly it was with great dexterity and even a surgeon's delicate touch that once back at his kitchen table he worked. The toolbox beside him contained the basics like wire, cutters, electrical tape, glue, and solder wire, the soldering iron he kept beneath the sink. Luckily the plastic explosive and collection of detonators he already had, and with the components laid out, within thirty minutes he had soldered wires to each terminal of a nine-volt battery, insulated them in tape, attached a detonator, trigger and rudimentary timer circuit, then expertly encased the entire contraption in an elaborately coloured tin that had once housed sticky toffee assortments.

An hour later he arrived, sober enough for his line of work, on the suburban street with the tin beneath his arm. The only sound was that of his once nimble footsteps in the snow. The car was there, and its number plate matched the one on the text message. Beneath it, lying on his back in the slush, he set the timer, and, by flashlight and with only a pair of pliers and some thin galvanised steel wire, he attached the tin inside the engine compartment. His labours accomplished, he vanished unseen back to his bed and to beneath the poster drawing-pinned at a slight angle of Mike Tyson in full throe.

A few hours later, at three minutes to seven, Andrei Vasiliev kissed his wife Ludmilla goodbye and walked to his car. He turned the key, and once the engine had fired into life, twisted the central dial in the console to enable a blast of hot air to blow from the vents, feeling the welcome when it hit his cheeks. He raised a palm to his two boys, Fyodor and Oleg, who were waving with wide, toothless smiles from the living room window with the net curtains pulled back. Waving goodbye to their father as he was leaving for work was a part of their morning ritual.

They were getting older, and as he moved the lever into reverse and felt the tyres of the Mercedes roll beneath him, he wondered if he was a good father, like his own had been. He'd take them to the slopes again on Saturday. An almost imperceptible click came from just beyond the footwell that made him look up. The last thing Vasiliev saw was both boys' faces drop in horror. A fraction of a second later the Mercedes became engulfed in a fireball so ferocious that it blew in every window in the front of the house.

Her ears popped as the Airbus A320 ascended into a blindingly bright blue sky above London's clouds before settling into cruising altitude. Zoe swallowed. She pulled her window blind down and pressed her head back into the headrest — hearing muffled, fears loud and clear. Why had the disk drive failed so soon? Malfunction was unlikely, too much of a coincidence. But the alternative was harder still to believe: that someone had informed the Russians it contained a tracker and that the man responsible was MI6's own head of Russia desk; the man sitting next to her.

When an attendant carrying a coffee pot had moved off along the aisle Zoe turned to him. It was almost too absurd to think that the Head of Russia Section was the man Eleanor Poe had told her the Russians had left behind inside MI6 in ninety-six after Operation Pendulum had been shut down, and could now be about to deliberately fail in this one.

Paul had been asleep again when she'd got home in the early hours. The hastily written note she'd left only saying she'd be away again for a while, but not telling him where, or why. It was hard on him. She saw the worry and felt his frustration in not knowing if his wife was in danger, and in his being unable to ask. Was he, she asked herself, still the same sharp mind she'd met? The journalist with a conscience, whose rich intellect and quiet pursuit of truth at all cost had first attracted her to him? Was *he* still inside the single parent to a boisterous three year old, who'd laid down and sacrificed his own career so she could pursue hers, the details of which she couldn't ever share? They had little left in common anymore. Her day would be spent on a top secret mission abroad to help safeguard international security, his in a flat performing mundane domestic duties in a T-shirt with someone else's breakfast on it. She'd stopped at the door and considered leaving a second note — one telling him to take Joe and get the train up to his mother's in Edinburgh, and to ask no questions, but had decided against it.

'When was the first time you visited Russia?' she asked.

He thought for a moment. Her faith in him was wavering. Jones-Cooper was getting to her. 'Winter of ninety-four. Right after Cambridge.'

It was a room of the past whose door John Henderson had to guard with great care, fearful that whenever it opened the ghosts that still haunted there would be freed again. He pulled it ajar, casting his mind back to that winter. It had been one of the coldest on record — nighttime temperatures were plummeting to forty below and the Main Medical Directorate was begging Muscovites to be "merciful to the intoxicated," which he took to mean those intoxicated by vodka or that filthy bath lotion they drank rather than by Marxist ideology. He arrived in the snow seeking not mercy but quiet redemption and god knows what besides and, under a workname, rented an unheated loft in Kitay-Gorod that wasn't just part of the cover but exactly the squalor he required. In those first months he cut a solitary figure, trudging the streets of Moscow in a long black overcoat like one of Chekhov's tragic antiheroes, numbed to the bone not by the cold but by a thesis on the partition of India. An Englishman derailed, disillusioned, sick to his stomach of one brand of empire and not another; of the pomposity and swagger of those in scarlet tunics who had marched into foreign lands chanting Rule Britannia, *Britannia rules the waves!* Hearts ablaze with christian fire and blades shining as they sought to bring "European culture to those heathen natives of the uncivilised world." He spoke only Russian, for his own mother tongue was branded by the same privilege of those who had idled away the hours with Kipling on the banks of the Cam, cavorted on the polo field or dined and supped in the private rooms of Pall Mall while the sword slashed its way across the map.

Everywhere he went these ghosts clung to him, these square-toed imperialists, these prim colonialists whose inherited guilt pressed down so hard on his narrow shoulders that with every step he took the weight of it only succeeded in deepening his footprints in the Russian snow.

The official version then. 'I went there to write. But after two years of freezing and suffering like a literary hero but without a coherent chapter to my name I traded my pen for seventeen thousand a year, discounted healthcare and a civil service pension. A few years later I was back there recruiting assets and running a network.'

So he was there in ninety-four, Zoe thought, her flat smile betraying nothing.

She'd read his file, of course she had, and would have seen the two missing years marked CLASSIFIED. Had probably told herself that everyone has gaps in their history — that it's the mark of a good spy. But behind her inscrutable smile he saw doubt. What did she want, the truth the whole truth and nothing but? To hear about the late nights in Chapman's cottage at Cambridge the summer before where they'd spend countless hours discussing radical politics over hock and scrambled eggs? To learn that it wasn't the fiery oration of Trotsky or Lenin that sang to them but Stalin who carefully instructed them on the nuts and bolts operations of the revolution from yellowed books in their laps — the same text they'd read at the same boarding school that had produced a long line of Marxists and Communists, including good old Donald Maclean? Did she want him to confess that during those first months in Moscow of course he had been approached, had gone in deep, so deep that his moral compass may well have gone haywire? Or perhaps she expected him to reveal chapter and verse. To smile like a waiter opening a cloche while the secret that he and George Provost had so carefully hidden away in one of the darkest corners of the past all those years ago sat there staring up at her from the silver platter like a bloody filet mignon.

No, the *only* truth he knew of was that it was their job to lie to ensure the preservation of a version of truth in defence of the West, and that the only question worth asking was whether the West was worth defending.

She had turned away and closed her eyes.

And if she asked where his loyalties really lay? Well, he'd say, one night a long time ago in a freezing loft a young man who couldn't feel his ears or his cheeks decided that in this business if your vision of loyalty isn't obscured by the moral fog then you're not paying enough attention.

Some time later his stomach sensed the aircraft drop. When it was nearing touchdown he turned to her and her eyes opened.

'I thought you said you could never sleep on planes.'

'Yeah, I must be tired.' She looked at him and for a moment didn't recognise who she saw. 'You know what's still bothering me? What are the chances of the FSB deactivating a computer three weeks after we bugged it unless they were told it was compromised?'

The plane bumped back to earth with two short screeches.

'I told you. It probably malfunctioned, Zoe. Computers do.'

Once they were outside arrivals a man stepped towards them. 'John Henderson and Zoe Taylor?' he said. 'Capitaine Sal Bernier, National Police, a pleasure to meet you. I assume you want to go directly to INTERPOL? Good, I thought so. My car's outside – I hope,' he smiled. He was Henderson's sort of man — polite by nature, similarly dressed and softly spoken, with bags beneath his eyes like his own that betrayed a tireless devotion to work. Bernier, still handsome in his mid-fifties whose black hair was now peppered with grey but whose blue eyes and gallic good looks had once stopped women in their tracks, guided them to his waiting Peugeot. He nodded to the air transport gendarme who'd been standing beside it, gunned its small engine into life, and pointed it in the direction of Paris.

Contrary to popular belief, INTERPOL is not

a law enforcement agency itself but rather an international organisation that coordinates criminal police work across national boundaries. A quarter of its staff are serving police officers from a wide range of national agencies, including police, gendarmerie and customs services, seconded by their national administrations. Bernier was such a man, a long-serving Parisian police captain who more usually worked inside the large préfecture located in the Place Louis Lépine in the Île de la Cité.

He drove fast along the A1 towards Paris, and asked his passengers to bring him up to speed. Zoe did the talking, and by the time they'd arrived at the bureau's security screening he'd told them in turn what INTERPOL had on Russell Blake – which was precisely nothing. Henderson knew as much, and that Lyon's headquarters' vast database of fingerprints and face photographs, lists of wanted persons, DNA samples and travel documents had drawn a blank came as no surprise.

After the low hum and subdued reflection of the flight, the high-pitched activity of the building's main operations rooms hit them like a wave. With ID's on lanyards around their necks a hundred agents sat in moulded plastic booths in front of three monitor screens each while banks of larger screens lined the walls and a giant flying saucer-like apparatus that clung to the ceiling shot out dark purple LEDs. The same image of the Russian was everywhere, as well as hundreds of street-scenes that were being captured by CCTV video across the city in real time.

Bernier strode in and clapped his hands together. 'Listen up, this is our Operation head,' he announced as the crowded room of INTERPOL agents looked up, 'from MI6 in London.'

'Thank you,' Henderson said, stepping forward, caught slightly of guard, 'Now, we're concentrating the search on the security cameras, but I want you to look at airport lockers, train station's lost property offices, safety deposit boxes, banks, post offices as well. All these locations we've identified as possible drop sites and methods of communicating. He isn't working alone, he uses short wave radio but I'm convinced he's communicating via other means as well, and discovering how is a priority. Also, he has a network of couriers, contacts, fixers, behind him. So anyone we can pull out of the woodwork, okay?'

Grushenko placed the receiver in its cradle. Vasiliev was dead, they were Volkov's Illegals now. It was all going to plan. Kuznetsov's report showed Unit 29155 were working swiftly, and he hadn't enquired why his workload had suddenly increased a hundred fold. Grushenko envied him, the short bald-headed killer with burnt spades for hands. He was lucky enough to be able to kill for a living. The strength of widows and sick children Grushenko had scant regard for — it was killers whom he admired.

The report recorded that in the last ten days six assassinations per day had taken place across the UK, with the same in France, Germany, Italy, Sweden, and Belgium, and between three and five in most other major nations inside the EU. Columns upon columns of carefully compiled names of undesirables: civil servants, lawyers, police officers, judges, journalists, politicians, and local government officials, now with red ink slashed through them as they were removed to make way for more suitable replacements: many hundreds of sleepers, members of a vast interconnected organisation that had been intricately constructed over many decades, and that were spread across all sectors of society: in business, in commerce, in industry, and importantly, in the press. A favourable press publishing carefully curated propaganda was key to the revolution's success.

Regular readers would notice stories that mentioned Russia, Polonium, Novichok, special assassination squads, *Spetsnaz*, and Putin, were becoming fewer, courtesy of the newly installed editors with dubious fortunes and hand-picked executives who were now pulling the strings inside publishing houses and giant social media companies. The editorial policy now was to lay the blame for the deluge of terrorist acts at the feet of subversive, ultra right-wing groups, specifically the mysterious OAG. The OAG, who were finding themselves not only the central focus of investigation but also the subject of in-depth profiles in the Sunday broadsheet magazines that graced the newsstands across Europe.

One such magazine, published in the UK two days before and featuring a three-page spread on the group, lay open on a bamboo table in a pale pink villa somewhere on the north shore of the Caribbean Island of Jamaica. The pages flickered gently in the fragrant breeze that wafted in through the open shutters, while from the white sands below short bursts of laughter could be heard amid mocking quotes from the article in accented English. The voices belonged to two young men and a woman who had been recruited six months before and had spent them travelling the world so as to escape detection. They didn't know for whom they worked, only that they were paid from an odd Swiss bank account at the end of an intricate and untraceable chain of off-shore companies.

The dining table had been taken over by three computers that changed their VPN's every few seconds, machines that today would be put to use in claiming responsibility for an explosion at a water treatment plant in Norway, a viaduct collapse in the Netherlands, and for the deaths of three prominent politicians. A relatively quiet day.

The voices grew louder until the door to the living room flung open and a young man burst in, the sea falling from his olive body as he ran across the sandy floorboards. He was being chased by a young woman who was pulling off her bikini top and laughing, while an already-naked third man followed, dragging back his long wet hair away from his bearded face as the three of them surged towards the bedroom.

On quiet days their early morning swims often ended like this, and in the six months they'd worked together they'd spent a good portion of it in the world's warmest oceans, so they were fit and tanned as well as being young, highly gifted, highly sexed, and very wealthy.

The bedroom doors clattered open and the three of them tumbled onto a bed of white linen and began to kiss and touch each other hungrily in a mess of saltwater and sand, sweat, and lust.

John Henderson had been wrong — the OAG did exist, yet perhaps not quite in the form even he would have imagined.

Another tendril of the same, sophisticated intelligence

network was having less libidinous thoughts as she looked at her watch inside the gilded office in the Élysée Palace. She had barely looked at anything else all morning. Now lunchtime was fast approaching, and she knew this would be her only chance.

Her nerves had got the better of her earlier and she'd had to go off to find some Pastis to drink in an attempt to calm them. It had worked a little, but then she felt sick so had tried to counter the upset with coffee, which tempered neither the sickness nor the nerves.

At five minutes to one a pretty woman with red lips and a head full of chestnut curls appeared around the door to her office, 'Hey, Sarina, Tu viens déjeuner? Au Minipalais?'

She shook her head, and the woman shrugged and left. The worry was making her head ache. She could hear the sound of the palace's offices begin emptying as staff dispersed for lunch. It was time to move.

Thirty-six minutes later she sank back down hard into her office chair and breathed the biggest sigh of her life. She pulled open her handbag and grasped for her make-up, beads of sweat tumbling from her hairline and behind her ears. With the compact open, she stared into its small circular mirror. Her eyes were frightened, but the sickness and head ache were forgotten, drowned by the sweeping waves of adrenalin, so her heaving chest calmed a little and the nerves too began to recede.

Calm, she told herself, calm. Okay, it was all right now. She'd done what Valentin had asked her to do.

'Unfortunately the French government is rather more spread across Paris than the UK one is in London.' In his office that overlooked the giant screens of the operations room, Bernier was at a wide wall map. 'Therefore while you may deduce that your house of parliament is the likely target in England, here in France it could be one of four buildings, as well as various ministries that are also all across the city. More coffee?'

Before they could answer, the police captain pressed the intercom and for the third time that day said, 'Une grande cafetière, trois tasses, s'il vous plaît,' before taking a ruler and carrying it back to over the map. He jabbed it into the centre of Paris. 'The Palais Bourbon, home to the French National Assembly, the lower legislative chamber of the government. Located here, on the left bank of the Seine, across from the Place de la Concorde.'

He scraped the ruler two inches up to the northwest. 'The Upper House, the Senate, meets in Palais du Luxembourg in the sixth arrondissement.' The ruler moved left. 'The Prime Minister's seat is at the Hotel Matignon in the seventh arrondissement at 57 rue de Varenne – now don't forget that the government ministries are located in various parts of the city but many are also located in the seventh arrondissement near the Matignon.'

'And of course the Élysée Palace,' said Zoe.

'Right, the residence of the President of France. It is where his office is and where the council of ministers meet. Location, of course, The Champs Élysées. To my mind also this is the most likely target due to its importance. Its palace and grounds are already the most heavily guarded, but I will ask to increase security at once.'

'And you're sure, only *one* guard?' Blake asked in a subdued tone.

It was later that evening and Sarina hadn't touched her dessert in the sumptuous taupe and white upstairs dining room of Lasserre. She nodded, still uneasy in such surroundings. Before leaving her apartment she had looked up the place and found that over the years the restaurant on the Champs-Élysées had played host to Brigitte Bardot, Audrey Hepburn and Romy Schneider, and while their fame and glamour meant nothing to her she was sure that if anyone looked at her in such a place all they would see was all she could ever see, a plain-looking rural farm girl from Pskov.

Their table was surrounded by white lilies and the retractable roof was open, allowing the stars of the night sky in. He'd ordered for them both, but she'd only picked at the food with her fork. Now, Blake gestured for the waiter to approach, and asked for Rémy Martin. When offered Louis thirteenth he replied, 'of course,' which Sarina thought haughty, and as he warmed the snifter of cognac with his hands she realised that the luxury he surrounded himself in could never replace the love he'd been denied. She wondered when that had been.

'You were telling me about your childhood. In your town near the Latvian border?' he said.

'That's all there is. I miss Russia but since Andrey died there is no reason to go back, even if I wanted to. There's nothing there for me now. He was killed in the theatre siege. Poisoned by the gas.'

Blake looked back at her, coldly over his glass.

'He was a violinist, very talented. He was so happy when he joined the orchestra. He was only twenty-two.' Her hazel eyes came alive, then died almost at once, so she blinked the memory away. 'And what about you? Or am I not supposed to ask?'

He remained silent. She wasn't.

'You know, when you walked into the cafe I had a feeling that it was you. That the day had come. I've been here all my life, well, since I was sixteen, you know, waiting. Never knowing how they would use me.'

He gulped back the cognac. 'I'll take you home,' he said, thinking it was probably time to show her.

15

The springs inside her mattress pinged dissonantly as Blake buried himself inside her. She counted in time to their rhythm, their squeals sounding in sets of threes, and she made up a song. Her hips moved with him but she kept her eyes shut to conceal her seasoned indifference. Usually even the older married ones on the clock tried to please her a bit, but this handsome Russian whom she presumed could pick up women at the drop of a hat seemed passionless to a degree even she had never known in bed. He was, she concluded as he seemed to be nearing completion, like a block of ice. When he had finished he rolled off and reached across her, took a cigarette from a packet on her bedside table, and lit it.

Ten minutes later they were still lying in silence. When she had watched his smoke roll in clouds across her bedroom ceiling then float there like slow swirling fog, she spoke. 'What is it you are taking inside the palace tomorrow?'

His opaque eyes were staring up at a small spot on her stippled ceiling that he was imagining was a part of a miniature mountain range.

'Whatever it is you can't take it into the building. There will be too much security.'

He turned his head over on the pillow to face her.

'I know, I'm not supposed to ask that either.

Just steal the keys, open the doors.'

'It's a listening device,' he said matter-of-factly, 'transmits data back to Moscow. State of the art but we'd never get it through security at the main gate. This way it sits there undetected — untraceable.'

Sarina smiled. She didn't believe him but what couldn't bring her brother back she didn't much care for. At that moment the sound of a church bell chiming rang out. Frowning, she got out of bed, wrapped a robe around herself and opened a window to look out.

'That's strange,' she said to the cold night air. She'd never heard bells before. L'église de la Madeleine had no bell tower and although the chimes were distant she could neither place where they were coming from nor knew what they meant.

She must have slept, for when she glanced at her watch at three a.m. he was gone, though she could have sworn she hadn't. The window was closed now, and the smell of his stale smoke was in her nostrils. She awoke again at five and rose, showered, dressed, and made her coffee for one on the electric stove before leaving her apartment and walking towards the palace on her usual route. It is a day like any other, Valentin had said, so just act naturally. It was easy for him to say.

When she turned and walked through the monumental gate into the palace courtyard anxiety gripped her. She had expected extra security personnel for the German Chancellor's visit, but surely this was extreme. Her feet froze beneath her and she had to catch her breath. There were crowds of them. Huddled in groups, most from the Republican Guard from the Security arm, but she could see officers from the Protection Service also, while dotted around were the regular officers in the uniform of the National Police. All seemed to be armed.

She buried her hands in her coat pockets and walked slowly, trying to breathe deeply, clenching her toes and hoping no one could smell her fear. She could feel eyes heavy upon her as she crossed, and then from the two men exiting the palace as she approached the steps. One, the taller one, was dressed in a thick tweed jacket — to Sarina's eyes obviously British, like a university lecturer.

As he walked down the steps John Henderson looked at the woman who walked past them with her eyes down and assumed she was part of the administrative staff whom they would interview first.

On the south bank of the Seine, Zoe stood facing the grand colonnaded facade of the Palais Bourbon, listening as a police commandant instructed his officers. He was stressing to them that this, the home to the important lower legislative chamber, the French National Assembly, must be protected at all cost, yet during the thorough search and questioning of staff, disruption to its 577 députés must be kept to a minimum.

Bernier descended the palace steps carrying two coffees and when he reached the bottom handed one to Henderson before at once addressing his courtyard of officers. 'Listen, quiet now, listen. Okay? We begin talking with the office and security staff right away.' The assembled, armed with holstered guns and Russell Blake's photograph, began to fill the building.

From her desk Sarina could hear the thrum of footsteps in the corridors and the voices in the courtyard, and could feel the familiar throb of fear swell in her stomach. Why did he pick today? She cursed Valentin for putting her through this. The voices travelled past her door all morning until the fateful knock came. The man from the steps earlier, the Englishman in tweed with thick dark hair whose brown eyes looked clever and sad.

'Hello, Miss Gaubert? I'm with the British security services,' he said, 'do you mind if I ask you some questions?'

Sarina's body tightened with fear as she looked up at the door. 'Yes, it's okay,' she replied in a thin voice.

The man entered, pulled up a chair and sat opposite her. In an even tone he asked her if she minded if they spoke in English, then when she nodded he asked her her name, what her duties were and how long she'd worked there. Was she married? What was her security clearance? What did she think of the President? Had she met anyone new recently? No? Noticed anyone suspicious? And no one had asked her to bring anything inside the palace? His voice turned suspicious.

'Where were you born, Ms Gaubert?'

'Uh, Paris.'

'Your accent doesn't sound Parisian.'

'I was raised in Marseilles.'

He smiled. 'That must be it then. Tell me, have you ever seen this man?'

It caught her completely off-guard. Suddenly she was staring at the face of the man she'd shared her bed with the night before. The photograph was being held up close to her face for study. The fright paralysed her. His cover was blown. They were onto him. And onto her too? Her mind raced to find a reaction. Her face was reddening, probably scarlet as she stared into the glassy eyes of the Russian while the Englishman's bored into her. With every ounce of concentration to stop her head from shaking, finally, in high voice, she said, 'no.'

'You sure?'

Sarina nodded, her nerves in shreds but her face miraculously still.

He thanked her, and he was gone, and she breathed in so hard the air made her dizzy. Suddenly it was twelve o'clock. Julie appeared at the door as usual with the offer of lunch, left disappointed, and soon after the palace erupted into a frenzy of activity for the German dignitary's arrival.

During the hasty consumption of a sandwich and coffee in a palace back office, Henderson conferred with Zoe on the phone and the three other team leaders at the city's other key locations. No suspicious packages or activity reported in the last two weeks, and nothing on the security cameras. As the black Mercedes limousine belonging to the German chancellor crunched up on the gravel of the courtyard outside, John Henderson had a flat nothing.

Upon hearing the clatter of camera shutters of the assembled world's press, Sarina went over to her window to look out. The cavalry regiment of the Republican Guard stood lining both sides of the entry stairs as the French president descended them to greet a man dressed in a marine blue suit and wine red tie but no coat despite a bracing Parisian November day — with a presidential handshake. They exchanged a few friendly words, then walked up the steps, through the columns into the main entrance of the palace and on into the Hall of Honour.

Bernier was working methodically through the almost 800-strong palace employees, and by three-thirty he himself had interviewed nearly thirty members of the admin and security staff, all the time receiving constant updates from the other locations. At four he passed Henderson in a corridor on the first floor outside the door to the famous Salon Doré, the president's study so named for its golden décor. They didn't speak, merely shook their heads as they passed each other.

At five p.m. the palace's staff began to thin, and the two men met again, this time at the foot of the twin Murat Staircase.

'Nothing,' said Henderson.

'Nothing here either,' said Bernier. 'We've searched everywhere, the whole mansion, state rooms, the private apartments, spoken to everyone. My men are combing the gardens and will be finished by around two or three a.m. I don't know what else to tell you, John.'

The police captain said he would relieve the team, Henderson reluctantly agreed.

At the same time, Julie peered around Sarina's door and bade her goodnight, cheerfully adding 'À demain' as she left. At twenty past five the sun went down and by six the voices and the stamping of policemen's feet outside the door had stopped. Sarina closed down her computer and gathered herself. Her day had been long — spent typing up minutes from meetings — yet the work had taken her mind off the moment about to come, the one she'd been dreading.

After dark, the Russian had said. She checked her watch. It was time.

She opened her door and peered into her corridor like a frightened child before stepping out and making for the entrance hall. Over her shoulder hung her large handbag, and clutched to her chest was the pile of typed papers as she moved briskly along the corridor. Just another secretary delivering some minutes, if anyone asked.

At the elevator she waited for the red light to descend to 'G', then as the door opened she sensed a presence on either side of her. She turned, and to her left saw the English detective, to her right another man, who smelled of recently breathed cigarette smoke.

'Going up?' said the Englishman with a polite half smile of recognition.

'Oui, yes.'

'Ladies first,' said Bernier, and the three of them stepped inside and turned to face the steel doors. She could feel droplets of sweat begin springing from her temples. Two floors would take less than a minute, she told herself — breathe. The shrill sound of a ringing phone caused her to her jump. Henderson lifted it out of his pocket.

'Yep.'

Facing the river, with police officers scuttling out of the Bourbon's grand facade behind her like ants, Zoe delivered the result of her day's endeavours.

'We've searched high and low and no sign of anything suspicious, John,'

Henderson pushed the phone into his ear. 'What about security?'

The voice in his ear said, 'turned a blank on all sites in

the last two weeks and nothing on the closed circuit.'

Sarina could hear that it was a woman's voice, speaking in English. She stared hard, unblinkingly at the crack in the door but she couldn't make out the words. But it sounded like bad news for them, as if they hadn't found Valentin.

'All right.' He hung up, turned to Bernier and shook his head.

Finally the lift settled and its doors opened, and without being asked Sarina took a giant step forward and quickly disappeared along the thick carpet of a gilded corridor. The two men watched her walk away. Bernier, ever the ladies man, regarding her with more artistic appreciation than his diffident English colleague.

Zoe went over it again in her head. She was staring into the blackness of the river asking what had they missed, yet the rolling Seine stayed silent.

'Perhaps we made a mistake,' said Bernier as a security guard showed them to a stairway up to the roof of the westernmost salons. 'If you want to take out this place with a bomb all you have to do is rent a room in a hotel nearby.' The guard looked up at him sharply, but the men turned and started to climb the narrow staircase. A minute later they were on the roof in the cold night air. Bernier, more comfortable with heights than his British guest, peered over into the kitchen yard, a small courtyard set in the centre of the rooms below, and held out his hands for balance.

Sarina had waited until there was no sound at all before she'd run back along the corridor and called the lift back to the ground floor where she'd dashed across the entrance hall towards the elevators on the building's western side, entered one and pressed 'B'. A minute later the doors opened onto the polished grey walls of the palace's basement corridors. Still clutching her stack of papers, she began to walk, her heels tapping louder than she would have wished on the concrete floors.

After five minutes of navigating a series of dim corridors she stopped, heaved the papers under her left arm and pulled out a paper map. She was going in the right direction, and would carry on until she heard the sound of the television. When she could just make out its faint echo she knelt down, removed her shoes and placed them into her handbag. As she reached the final corner a loud laugh echoed out, accompanied by the soundtrack to a raucous cartoon that cut through the basement corridors like rapid gunfire. She placed the wad of papers on the ground, swung her bag onto her back, and got down onto her hands and knees and began to crawl out towards the security office.

The guard, a morbidly obese Provençal man in his sixties who'd been watching cartoons in the forgotten palace basement for years without incident, let out another roar as the animated mouse was sliced into a thousand pieces, unaware of either the missing key from his box or the beautiful woman crawling beneath his wide window not five feet in front of him.

Once safely past, Sarina stood again and continued in her stockinged feet away from the television sound and the convulsive laughter for another three minutes until she came to the door, above whose handle was a card reader. She pulled the card from her purse and entered it into the slot, causing the red light to become green, and the door to open to reveal a narrow stone-walled spiralled staircase. Now there was no light at all, so she switched on the small flashlight she'd brought with her, and, stepping carefully down the stone steps with a steadying hand against the wet wall for support, descended deep beneath the Elysée palace.

Up on the roof, Bernier could sense the MI6 man's unease, but wanted to be sure a small locked cupboard with an electrical sign on its door had been searched, so radioed downstairs for another guard to join them with a key. They'd been waiting for twenty minutes. The temperature had dropped. Henderson cursed himself. What had he missed here?

Now far beneath ground, breathing the thick putrid air that the Paris Catacombs offer, and guided only by the slim beam of her torch, Sarina stepped down from the final step onto the cobbled ground. Shining the light to the far wall she gasped as the beam revealed a blanket of skulls and human bones. She was in the centre of the series of ossuaries — all interconnected by the labyrinthine tunnel network built to accommodate Paris' overflowing cemeteries and home to the remains of an estimated six million people. Without thinking, she whispered a small prayer for the dead, and moved on.

The cavernous stone tunnels in this area, unlike much of the Catacomb network, were untrodden due to the sensitive security restrictions of the palace above, and so it was another ten minutes of careful navigation before she found the thick wooden door at the end of a long narrow tunnel. She was sweating freely and could feel the must of centuries cling to her face as she removed the heavy iron key from her bag. She pushed it hard into the lock and turned it, the noise causing a deep echo that no one else heard. No one, except one man.

At last the guard arrived with the key for the box and began to fiddle with it in the lock. To Henderson the container looked too small to contain an attache case, but they'd searched every other inch of the place so figured he had nothing to lose except perhaps the tips of his slowly freezing fingers.

Sarina heaved the heavy door open and stepped over the threshold into a large clearing. The blackness was lit only by a single flame torch hanging on a far wall that was casting a flickering orange glow across the wide ground towards the lapping ripples of the river's edge. Moving gently on the water's surface was a wooden rowing boat, tied by rope to an iron bar that protruded up out of the water next to it. From all corners came the unmistakable high squeal of rats, like faraway discordant violins. As well as being deep beneath the city, the Metro, and the city's sewer systems, she was also now deep inside the river walls.

He appeared out of the shadows, causing her to scream. 'Blyad! You frightened me. I almost didn't make it. The palace is crawling with police today.'

'Never mind about that, we don't have much time.' He reached down to a suitcase at his feet.

She grabbed his arm. 'No, you don't understand. It's not because of the state visit, it's for you. They know who you are.'

Blake stared through her. What was she saying?

'They have your photograph.'

'Who?'

The words tumbled out of her. 'The British, intelligence people, but INTERPOL too, there were hundreds of officers and they questioned everyone and they are searching the entire palace. Still, now, they are still here.'

He looked up, thought for a few moments. He couldn't know what had transpired that had given the British his identity. But for now his mind was on the mission. He shook it off and smiled. 'It's okay, I promise, come.' He took her by the hand and led her back across the clearing and through the open door.

Where the narrow tunnel fanned out, he stopped. A wall, built for what purpose and when was anyone's guess, would prove ample shelter. There was no need to go further back into the Catacombs. Kneeling, he lifted the heavy latches on the case's front and swung the lid up. She stared over his shoulder, pointing her torch at the shiny metal of the contents. He inserted the arming key, set the digital timer, pressed the red arming switch and closed the case's lid before sliding it down behind the wall's damp bricks, rendering it invisible.

He stood to face her.

'A transmitter?'

'Lock the door behind me.'

She hung her head, and cursed herself for being naïve. Then turned and followed him back along the tunnel and out again into the orange glimmer of the clearing. He was at the boat, untying the rope from its mooring.

'I suppose I knew,' she said, her voice echoing. Sarina Gaubert had never seen an atomic bomb before, nor any kind of explosive device, but she could sense that what she had just witnessed was an object that could cause a violence she had never tried to, nor ever wanted to, imagine.

Slowly, Blake placed the rope down inside the boat. He came to her, looked deeply into her hazel eyes, opened his mouth very slightly, and kissed her, pressing her lips apart with his as passionately as she'd ever been kissed before. As the bullet entered her stomach he held her close while he stroked her beautiful face, as if gently ushering her into death.

Approximately six storeys above them, Sal Bernier thanked the guard who was pocketing a ring full of keys, and the three of them made for the door to the stairwell. It was when Henderson stopped to look over the edge that a thought occurred to him.

'Hey Sal, there are Catacombs in Paris?'

'Yes, of course. So what?'

'Is there access anywhere near here?'

'Not that I'm aware of . . . ' A moment later he'd barged the guard out of the way and the two of them were dropping down the staircase as if propelled only by gravity.

He'd laid her lifeless body down on the wet gravel and brushed her eyelids closed before reaching into her handbag for the iron key. Noticing a small pile of rocks at the end of the river's edge, he gathered the largest of them before untying the rope from the boat and retying one end of it around the large rectangular stone.

Henderson and Bernier hurled themselves across the entrance hall. Bernier yelled "Basement – which way" at a guard, who pointed them towards the lift. The Frenchman hammered on its button with his fist. It seemed to take forever for the doors to open, but once inside he hit the button marked 'B'. The doors creaked to a close and the box transported them casually to the basement. Bare grey walls under a yellowish tinge greeted them. They looked left, then right, chose left, and began to run.

The Russian finished tying the rope to her ankles, then stood, heaved the heavy rock to the water's edge and with one lunge pushed it into the water. As it sank it dragged her corpse slowly towards the water's edge feet first, the water enveloping her legs, then her torso, and finally her head as she disappeared beneath the surface.

He watched the ripple on the surface shrink, and vanish.

The two men sprinted along the corridors, making blind lefts and rights and getting nowhere until Bernier grabbed Henderson by the back of his jacket for him to wait.

'You hear that?' he whispered.

They followed the sound, and a minute later had burst into the elderly guard's security office and slammed a fist on his television to silence it.

'Les catacombes. Comment y accéder?' Bernier demanded. The old fat man had fallen off his chair in fright, and from the floor and scared half to death, pointed.

'Is there a key?'

The man pointed to the box on the wall. Henderson tugged it open.

'It's missing,' the guard said, aghast.

Bernier reached down and grabbed him by the collars, 'Take us there.'

The panting guard led them along a series of corridors, his heart pounding and his hands constantly trying to keep his trousers around his wide waist. They reached a door, and he shoved a card into the slider that jolted it open, allowing the two younger, slimmer men to dart inside, and him to gasp and sweat more than he ever had before in his life.

They traversed the spiral staircase and flashed past the skulls and bones without noticing, Henderson leading the way, following his instincts that finally led them to the tunnel. The two men stopped. At its end they could just make out an orange glow in the blackness. It was moving. It was a flame. Henderson bolted, arms scraping the narrow walls and feet pounding the cobbled stones as he ran for the open door. He was only inches away when it started to close, he lunged at it but it slammed shut, the force causing his palms to sting and his head to hit the thick oak. He held his breath and heard the sound of a key being turned in the heavy lock from the other side — a sound of permanence that carried through the tunnel.

Facing him with only three inches of oak between them, Blake stood perfectly still, careful to stay silent. The hunter and the hunted waited. Henderson moved his head closer to the door, waiting for the slightest breath, footstep or creak of movement that would identify the Russian. Staring dead ahead, Blake slowly drew his gun. On the other side of the door was a man whose mission was to find him and to kill him. But how he didn't know. *How had they got so close?* Slowly, he began to step back from the door. He ran over and grabbed the torch from the wall, then at the river's edge threw both it and the key into the river, climbed into the rowing boat, and rowed silently away into the darkness of a Paris night.

The wait for the all clear over the radio was interminable, and when it came a collective sigh of relief was breathed. Zoe went down to the tunnel with her boss and Bernier to where a man called Lambert was waiting for them. The team from the bomb squad had been on stand-by on the street outside the palace all day, and after Bernier called them down to the tunnel it took their Geiger counter less than three minutes to locate the weapon, which had been hidden behind a four foot wall in the tunnel.

'The RA one-fifteen tactical nuclear weapon,' said Lambert, whose full face helmet and ballistic vest lay next to the open suitcase on the ground, 'or, *suitcase nuke* if you prefer. Did you ever seen one, Mr Henderson?'

'Not close up.' They were accompanied by three men in INTERPOL jackets, as well as two uniformed policemen with the lower rank of Keeper of the Peace. The bomb disposal robot sat motionless behind Lambert, its long pincer arm frozen in mid air.

'Luckily there was no anti-tampering mechanism,' said the man, wiping his brow with a sleeve.

'Molniya,' Henderson said. It was not a word anyone recognised except Lambert.

'Right,' said the Frenchman. 'Yes, it means booby-trap. That's why we have the robot with the multimodal sensor suite with the millimetre wave scanner, high-res camera, and a 3D monitoring system so we can create a spatial map of the contents before we touch the case. Also I see no evidence of any mechanism in place to alert whoever planted it that it has been defused.'

He wasn't sure right away whether that was good news or not.

'But they're old, these suitcase nukes — cold war era. Some say there are anywhere between one hundred and five hundred of them still missing after the USSR collapsed.'

You're telling me, thought Henderson.

Zoe stared into the case at the now benign metal cylinders. 'How much damage can they do?'

The bomb squad man scratched his chin and looked down at the weapon, 'the yield is relatively low, only one to two kilotons. To put it into perspective, the bomb that fell on Nagasaki was about twenty. But even so this one could still kill everyone within a one to two mile radius. In a city like Paris that's anywhere up to a hundred thousand people.'

The words hung in the tunnel's musty air, too horrific to imagine.

Henderson spoke. 'When was it due to detonate?'

Lambert looked at the frozen digital display. 'In . . . fifty-one hours, ten minutes and twenty-eight seconds.'

'In two day's time?'

She looked at him. 'Saturday night?' Then at her watch. 'At midnight. Oh my god.'

The light from another flashlight appeared inside the narrow tunnel and a man wearing the uniform of the French police appeared. 'Sir, we've opened the door.'

'Where the hell are we?' said a bemused Bernier as the beams from the police flashlights lit the clearing. He thought he knew his city.

'We're inside the river walls.' Henderson said, moving slowly to the water's edge.

Bernier's phone vibrated in his pocket. 'Oui? D'accord.' He hung up. 'The border road blocks should be in place within the hour.'

A policeman whose nose looked like it had

been broken many times and who had been standing by the door stepped out unnoticed. He moved quickly back along the tunnel and two minutes later was on street level placing a call. He told the voice on the other end of the line that the Paris bomb had been discovered, and that there would be road blocks on all routes out of France within the hour.

Zoe and Bernier joined him at the river's edge. The brown water was lapping at the stoney shore and heavily rusted iron bar.

'How the hell did he find his way down here?' Bernier said.

Zoe looked at him. 'He must have had someone on the inside. But who?'

Henderson squinted. 'A woman.'

'How do you know that?' asked Zoe.

'Because there's make-up floating in the river.'

16

It was two-twenty a.m. and while his wife snored deeply beneath her two gold angels in flowing robes clutching at their wreath, he was sitting on the end of their gilded bed stroking the sleeve of his favourite velvet dressing gown, still wide awake, still deeply troubled. Since its arrival on his desk that morning he had been pondering the meaning of the twenty-first document that had come in the fresh batch from the source in London via Brussels. One document that stood out from the others amid the material that pertained to Britain's nuclear deterrent and her Dreadnought submarines. Once document that had made the hairs on the back of his neck stand up. Smolenko knew it was incendiary, that in handling it one false move could prove fatal and that no-one, not even his deputy director could be informed. For all he knew, he could be involved. Nearly a year ago he'd welcomed Kovalevsky's appointment. The small man was obviously dangerous, with a reputation for brutality, especially in interrogations, yet he was a consummate professional, discrete and loyal, something the Director of the SVR required above all other things in his organisation. Now though, with this, he could trust no one.

He shook his head in despair. Such recklessness, he thought, such mindless egocentricity. Yes, it could prove fatal, but handle it he must.

Extreme caution was required, but he would have to think of something, and, by the sounds of it, fast.

The two MI6 officers were awoken early by their modest hotel's receptionist on the telephone, and at eight sharp they arrived at the morgue on the Île de la Cité, one of the two islands in the Seine, just behind Notre Dame. Bernier was outside to greet them.

The familiar smell of deodorisers, chemicals and formalin assailed their senses as they walked past the wall of drawer coolers towards the autopsy room. Zoe, less used to such environments, clenched her jaw and tried to ignore the signs instructing that bodies and body parts, including foetuses, were to be signed out.

Save for an assistant in face mask and scrubs who awaited instruction should she be required, the room was empty. It was larger than the one in London's where Donald Philips' cadaver had awaited autopsy by Dr Carpenter weeks before, yet shared the similarities all such places share — tiled floors with drains, porcelain sinks, and a stainless steel autopsy table with holes in it that allow blood and fluids to drain into a trough beneath. A sink with garbage disposal was at its head, with a long grey tube attached to one of the faucets that enabled the table to be quickly washed down.

They approached the body of the naked female.

'The girl from the elevator,' Bernier said.

Henderson too recognised her at once as the young woman he'd interviewed the morning before. She'd been nervous, he recalled, and there was a sadness to her. He'd wished he could help ease her pain but wasn't sure why. Now, in death, the sadness had left her, leaving her beautiful face swollen and puffy and unchallenged by pain.

Zoe went to the effects, the contents of Sarina's handbag that had been placed onto a steel table, and sifted through them. She picked up a photograph. It was black and white and showed a young man holding a violin. Turning it over she saw that on the back was written in biro, 'Andrey, 2002'.

At a little after nine a.m., Bernhardt Müller ceased to be. The documents belonging to the quiet schoolteacher from Dresden were burned by the side of a mountain road shortly after the lighter of the match had stopped to urinate behind a signpost for Geneva. He had checked out of Le Meurice early with his two suitcases, retrieved the rental car from the underground parking garage and returned it to the regional office before taking a taxi to a second hand car dealer in Villette, an edgy area in the north of the city. A deal was struck for a fast and modern Alfa Romeo sports car in exchange for cash, and, courtesy of Bastien, no questions were asked nor would official paperwork be declared to the local *Préfecture* until the fifteen day deadline. When it was, written neatly upon the Certificat d'Immatriculation, known as the Carte Grise, would be the new owner's name — one Gabriel Brunner, a Swiss national and a bank employee who had been a resident of Paris for the last twelve years.

That same man gripped the leather steering wheel tightly and aimed the car at 140 km/h into another tunnel, one of many that slice through the mountains on the alpine route towards Switzerland. A minute later the car shot out of the mountain into a blinding sun onto the Nantua viaduct, that vast feat of engineering between Bourg-en-Bresse and Bellegarde-sur-Valserine on the autoroute known as the Highway of the Titans, and less than an hour after that it was on the Autoroute Blanches, passing over the Jura Mountains and on towards the snow-laden alps. By lunchtime, high in the clouds, the little Alfa was parked beside a small bistro set back from the road and nestled into the snow, where, near the bar, its driver was entering a pre-paid telephone card into a payphone.

A minute later the encrypted telephone message had circumnavigated the globe and come to rest upon a radio dish on a roof near Casinoplatz, Bern. When the FSB clerk in the law office below pulled the printout from the fax machine, he knew immediately it was an emergency communication that required him not to send an unencrypted email, but to pick up the phone and dial a number only to be used when a message of such urgency had been received.

He relayed the message concisely into the receiver.

Inside the FSB headquarters on Lubyanka Square, General Grushenko gripped the phone tightly as he listened to the voice say, 'Paris device likely discovered. Mayfair cover blown. British intelligence aware of Overture. Repeat, Operation Overture compromised. Advise.'

He thought for a second. He had received confirmation late last night about the discovery of the Paris bomb and the road blocks — but this was emergency communication from the Executive Officer.

'From now on all Overture communication, I repeat, *all* comes to me only via this number. Understand?'

'Yes, sir,' said the man in Bern without hesitating. Yet he was confused. 'But sir, what of Igor Savich? I thought it was understood we are only to send the messages directly to that gentleman via email.'

'To me only,' he snarled as the plastic cracked in his palm, 'understood?'

'Yes, sir.'

'No one else knows of this, correct?'

'Correct sir.'

'See that it stays that way or you will be shot. Destroy the communication.'

'Yes, sir,' said the junior man without hesitating.

Grushenko slammed the phone into its cradle. For five minutes he sat seething, then, as snow dropped out of a sheer sky through the window behind him, he went to the safe for one of the Stolichnaya bottles and sank a quarter of it to straighten his thoughts. Now I alone will be informed, he told himself. He slumped back in his chair. No one else will know.

He dialled a number. 'Get me Defence Minister Sotnik.' He waited until the line went secure, and when the head of the Telepol committee answered said, 'Yes sir, good news. The devices in both London and Paris are now primed and ready. No sir, no hiccups. Yes, we are ready for the final phase. Thank you sir.'

He pressed 'end call', then dialled the number of the young radio operator in the gulag, and told him he too was to disregard orders that came from anyone but himself or he would be shot.

The radio man too was confused. Every day since the two generals and the elderly civilian had accompanied him to the miserable gulag by helicopter, Savich had telephoned him personally to dictate the messages to be sent to the agent in the field. But the general's voice was dangerous and desperate, so Krupin said he understood. Grushenko then read out the message to be transmitted by numbers to the Executive Officer that evening. It would assure him all was going to plan, and to proceed as arranged to the final target. Nervously, Krupin repeated the message back, and Grushenko hung up.

The general, haunted by his lies, placed the broken phone back in the cradle.

'Good news about Paris sir', announced Jones-Cooper's secretary as bright as the morning sunshine after she'd delivered his coffee. But the man had a face on him, no bloody change there, and instead all he did was bark back at her without looking up, 'no more email intercepts?'

'No sir,' she replied, refusing to let her smile drop while thinking what a very strange fish he was indeed. 'GCHQ are pretty upset.'

When she'd left he'd picked up the phone. 'I want to see the psychological evaluations of an officer. Henderson. John.'

Six-hundred miles south the elderly man waited to be called forward. Beneath a long grey overcoat he wore a finely tailored navy suit of thick wool, and around the deep furrows and crevices of his neck was tied a cashmere scarf in a dark bottle green. His only luggage for his short stay was a small grip made of fine leather that he held in his left hand, while his right held onto a stainless steel barrier to support himself. The angina meant the pain in his chest was almost constant, and when the customs official beckoned him to approach the window he had to pause to lift another pill from the filigree pill box before handing over his passport.

'From Moscow?' the official said, regarding the document's photograph in which the dark age spots on the head weren't as pronounced. The man flipped it and scanned its biometric chip.

'As it states,' replied the old man breathlessly.

'Welcome to Geneva, Mr Savich,' said the border official, closing the Russian passport and sliding it back to the traveller. 'Have a nice stay.'

He stood beside the warm bonnet of his purring sports car and raised the lightweight Zeiss monocular to his eye. The border crossing was a road customs control station called Douane de Bardonnex, and he was watching cars crawl towards Switzerland in lanes designated by green arrows overhead, able make out the officials in their blue shirts who were taking documents from drivers and handing them to their colleagues in the booths.

He brought the lens down and considered his options. They were checking passports at a customs control, which between two Schengen area countries was certainly unusual but was it cause enough for alarm? There were other routes across the border, Thônex was the next closest, only seventeen kilometres further but it would be the same there and with the accident on the A40 the radio had been reporting, could take hours. There were other roads without customs controls but . . .

He got back into the Alfa Romeo, pulled on a wide newsboy cap low over his brow, and joined the slow-moving queue behind a minivan. It was twenty minutes later, when he was three cars lengths away from the checkpoint, when he reached for the Beretta beneath his coat on the passenger seat, and cocked it.

The one taking the identity documents from the drivers and posting them through the sliding window to his colleague at the computer was a short, thick-set man who from beneath the brim of Blake's cap looked to be ex-military — someone with quick reflexes who could handle a weapon. But it was too late to change lane, to pull out or to turn around. Two cars to go. The checks were moving quickly. Blake became aware of an official in the next lane over, who seemed to be as interested in the occupants of both lane's equally. These border guards, he thought. They're the same officious bastards the world over.

Finally, the minivan drove away and he moved the Alfa forward. Pulling up to the barrier, the military-looking official held out his hand and regarded him with suspicion from behind his heavily broken nose, and a glint of recognition seemed to cross his muscular face. Head held low, Blake handed over his red passport while his other hand rested on the trigger of the Beretta. He only needed a moment and he could blow the man's head to pieces.

The man stared at him, but as he went to open the document a voice made him look up. 'Hey, Paul, it's OK,' it said, energetically, 'I've got this one.'

The official from the adjacent lane had jumped across in front of the Alfa and was reaching out to take Blake's passport from the bemused military man with a reassuring smile and a pat on the shoulder to stand down. Leaning in, he rested both elbows on the car's door.

'Hey Johann, how are you? It's been a long time, how's life?' the man said loudly, overacting and slipping the passport back to the driver. 'How is your Luisa?'

The thick-set official stood frowning.

'It's okay,' he said, turning back, 'this is an old friend of mine - Johann. It's okay, you can let him through.' He gestured to the man in the booth whose view of the driver's face was obscured by both his 'friend' and the low roof line of the car. Had it not been it would have matched the one that stared out from his monitor screen with the words *INTERPOL RED NOTICE* beside it.

'Take care, Johann, and my regards to your lovely Luisa, okay?'

Like many in his profession, the man inside the booth despised irregularity in any form, yet as the queue was lengthening, he pressed the button by his knee. The barrier opened, and the Alfa Romeo entered Switzerland.

At three p.m. the old man from Moscow walked into Hall 406, a permanent exhibition room on the second floor of Geneva's Museum of Art and History, and sat down upon a circular blue bench in front of a Rembrandt. He squinted at it, a sober portrait of a half-smiling woman in a shimmering black satin gown with a low-necked bodice, whose museum label, not that the viewer's eyesight was strong enough to read it, stated it to have been painted circa 1639.

Feeling a presence beside him, the father of

Overture turned his head to see a face he knew well but had never seen in person. "The gun that would deliver the final bullet into the belly of the West," he had written sixty years before.

'Mayfair, I presume?' said the old man.

'Mayfair is dead,' came the matter-of-fact reply, 'Or didn't you receive my message?'

Savich considered the meaning of this. 'I did not,' he said finally.

'Well then, it sounds like you have a problem. The Paris device has almost definitely been discovered. The British know about Overture. And at the border I was expected. By both camps.'

The old man frowned.

'I had help getting across,' he stressed.

'I have heard nothing of this,' came the abrupt reply, 'I am informed that both the London and the Paris devices remain in place, undetected,' he lowered his voice as a little girl skipped past them clutching a balloon. 'You are to proceed as planned. The final instructions will be delivered to you.' He let out a sudden cough which shook his frail frame. To Blake, the head poking from the stiff collar and coughing violently into a handkerchief resembled that of a tortoise.

Blake came in close, and pushing an envelope inside Savich's jacket, said, 'Somebody's lying to you.'

The old man jutted his jaw out and pursed his thin lips. 'You will remember your rank, comrade *Major* Baskov.'

The brief meeting was over. He hauled himself to his feet and began to pad slowly across the polished parquet floor. At the top of the grand staircase he paused, withdrew the envelope, scanned

302

the brief information within that gave the precise location details of the London bomb, then screwed up the paper and threw it into a litter bin before holding tightly onto the bannister rail and stepping carefully down the red carpet. He had long suspected that Grushenko had been lying to protect himself, that the Petrenko man had probably accessed his safe and that the widow had traded its contents — that likely included the Mayfair dossier — for her freedom, but that the boorish egotist had clumsily attempted to cover it up.

Now the Executive Officer had confirmed it for him.

Once, Mike Hewitt had been used to not sleeping. During the six-month tour in Sangin in Southern Afghanistan in 2006, his own C. Company had been subjected to such intense fighting against the Taliban - in 50 degree heat no less — that they'd managed only two hours sleep in every 24. Still, the last fourteen years, and especially the last few days, had taken its toll. He stretched his arms out high and wide and hissed in the stale office air like an animal in pain. The Paris bomb had been set to detonate on Saturday at midnight, Henderson had reported, timed to do so concurrently with the other two. The camp bed in the corner hadn't seen any use, the whiskey had been ignored for strong coffee and the six cartons of Benson and Hedges were now just over four. The man who had once experienced some of the most ferocious fighting in one of the most dangerous places on earth was now relegated to being hunched over a laptop craving a grainy glimpse of a man's face — something that so far had proved dishearteningly elusive.

Two taps on the glass door came before it swung open and a female Sergeant said, 'We think we've got him, sir, one of the Supers has picked him up.'

'Christ, about time,' he shouted in relief, bringing both palms down onto the desk to raise himself up. The two of them marched across the building to a room where a woman in her sixties called Jane was waiting excitedly at a monitor screen. A Community Support Officer from Reading, she was also a Super Recogniser with a memory bank of over 5000 faces ready to be identified in a split second. One of them, the only one they all sought, was frozen in a frame on the monitor — the handsome face of the man who had glanced up with light eyes at a security camera as he'd entered a building.

'Subject entered Lloyds Bank on Baker Street on Tuesday, October 27th at eleven fifty a.m.' The Sergeant said, 'And get this sir, that branch has the largest safety deposit vault in London.'

'Son of a bitch,' Hewitt let out. 'Get me John Henderson on the phone immediately.'

Two hours later teams at both Scotland Yard and INTERPOL were viewing the playback from the bank's internal cameras of Russell Blake approaching the reception desk.

The wall of screens inside the INTERPOL operations room flashed up the image of a man standing at the counter in the Paris bank's vault. His head was hairless, his frame razor thin, complexion pale, and eyes little more than black dots. The date and time code on the image's corner read 15.12.2019 15:33:08.

'Franz Hart, born 17.06.1963,' announced Captain Bernier. 'A German from Dortmund. The security boxes in both London and in the Credit Lyonnais on Avenue de l'opera here in Paris are registered to this man.'

Zoe stepped in. 'We believe Blake picks up additional instructions via this method. No match on this man but he is *not* Franz Hart.' Another face flashed across the wall. 'This is. Franz Alfred Hart, aged 57, born with spastic quadriplegia, the most severe form of cerebral palsy. He's lived in a care home in Dortmund since birth, no mobile phone, no bank account, no passport. Someone who requires round the clock care for his most basic needs but whose birth certificate can be used to build an identity upon. And was.'

'We need to find every security box in Europe registered to the name of Franz Hart.'

The assembled agents erupted into activity, as a disgruntled Bernier led Henderson and Zoe into his office. He addressed his wall map. 'So we have a face we don't know and a name that means nothing. No box in Berlin registered to that name, or in Germany at all, so what the hell have we got?'

A young woman appeared at the door. 'Nothing from the roadblocks, sir.'

Henderson brought a hand up and gripped his temples with his fingers. 'Germany. It *has* to be Germany.'

Zoe thought for a minute, but the brief ray of hope had become obscured and once again they stood and stared hopelessly at the map of Europe. 'Okay, Germany,' she said, organising her thoughts. 'You've got Berlin, and the Bundestag, that according to your original Overture blueprint is the most likely target, but there's Frankfurt . . . '

'Home to the European Central Bank,' offered Bernier as a worthy choice for atomic attack, 'that sets monetary policy for the Euro Zone economy. Also the Frankfurt stock exchange is Germany's biggest.'

'Dusseldorf is also a major financial centre. Stuttgart - headquarters to major businesses . . . '

'Hamburg, again for banking, the Hamburg Stock Exchange,' Bernier said, realising they'd probably covered it by now.

The light behind them changed, which caused them to turn to find the operations room in partial darkness. Only the purple of the overhead ceiling light now illuminated it, the banks of wall screens and individual monitors having completely died. Bernier strode back out into the dim confusion. 'What is it?' he shouted at the confused staff who were frantically trying to revive their computers. 'Well?'

An agent close to him spoke. 'The European Space Agency is reporting the loss of three hundred commercial satellites. Cause unknown but looks like SES.'

Zoe took out her phone. No signal.

Bernier scanned the report handed to him. 'This will affect all of Europe.'

Henderson went over to the now blank screens that lined the walls, and with a graveness of tone of a man about to go into war said, 'It's happening.'

'What is happening, John?' All Bernier knew was that he could feel his command slipping away.

'SES, Luxembourg. They provide worldwide video and data connectivity to broadcasters, internet service providers, mobile and fixed network operators, governments and institutions. It means GPS networks and internet communications will be heavily compromised. The effect will lessen our ability to report news, to trade, to defend. It means chaos. It means we're more open to attack. Radio, television and news agencies rely on distributing text, audio and video, voice and data via satellite. As do newspapers and magazines on sending text to printing plants. With the broadband internet and some mobile phone network satellites lost it means banks, water, gas and oil plants will be left critically compromised.'

An agent appeared. 'Mr Henderson,' she said thrusting a folded note at him. 'This came through just before we lost comms. For you, urgent.'

Henderson opened the note. He had to digest the words he was reading slowly, for he couldn't quite believe them.

At 11:15 p.m., with their bags at their feet and wearing headsets, the two MI6 officers sat silently in the rear cabin of a twin-engined Eurocopter EC135 as it swept them away from the sprawling city of lights below and into a starless night towards the snow-frosted alps of Switzerland. Neither spoke over the noise of the four blades that roared above their heads, Zoe imagining the confusion the loss of communications would be causing below, and he, sitting next to her with eyes closed and his hands in his lap, getting his wish to go back in time to the pre-digital age. She wondered if Navigations Satellites would be next. With GPS down, ships would be stranded at sea, planes grounded and those that were in the air would struggle to communicate with air traffic control, as world leaders would fight to combat the catastrophe it would certainly cause.

Henderson was consulting his inner clock: Forty-eight hours and fifteen minutes to find Blake and stop him, and for MI5 and the Met, Hewitt and Darlington, to find the London bomb. *Two days.*

Neither of them spoke for the two hour journey until they were inside Geneva airport.

The almost transparent layer of aluminium encased within the glass pane enabled the three observers to see into the interview room, but the elderly man at a table with a polystyrene cup of airport coffee and a silver pill box before him to see nothing back but his own reflection which, due to his advanced age, he disliked acutely.

'Was he carrying anything?' Henderson was addressing Jules Leutzinger, a high-ranking member of the Swiss Border Guard who'd had orders to hold the man. Two uniformed guards carrying Heckler and Koch P30's in their holsters stood guard in the corridor.

'Only that,' came the reply in accented English as he pointed to a slim leather grip, which was open upon a chair next to the scarf and overcoat. 'But it was empty save for an envelope, that pill box and his passport.'

He opened the envelope, moved it in his hands, then picked up the passport. The man in the photograph was slightly older now, but if Henderson had never met him, he knew the name and the face as well as he knew any of the Soviet Union's most infamous players.

The door to the interview room closed behind him as he pulled out the chair on the other side of the table, and sat. The old man, as still as granite, watched with ageless, bright blue eyes set deep into a wrinkled face that appeared to be in some pain — the discomfort of a long day further weighing on an octogenarian constitution already weakened by angina. But the hairless head, now stippled with dark spots that shone in the harsh strip light was proud and obstinate as the two men regarded each other for some minutes in silence.

Henderson, although showing no emotion, smiled to himself. Igor Mikhailovich Savich. A man whose name he had known only in books was now here in front of him, his captor, the father of Overture. After some time, he said, 'Hello Mr Savich, I'm from MI6.'

Behind the glass, Leutzinger increased the volume to the speakers in the wall. He and Zoe watched closely.

'Well? What of it?'

'Come on, cut the bullshit, Savich. You've got something to say so say it.'

The old man was studying him, this British agent who hadn't shaved for a while. He hated slovenliness. He moved his gaze up to the corner of the room to where a small CCTV camera aimed down, then to its opposite in the other corner. There were eight covering the room in total. All were recording. Henderson too looked up at them. Zoe watched. It was as though he were looking through them. He seemed to be thinking very hard about what to say.

'Igor Savich.' The melody in his voice was as if he were greeting an old friend. 'KGB strategic planner, devoted nationalist, communist, and architect of Operation Overture, flies in from Moscow on his own passport. Why don't you save us all some time and tell me what you're here to tell me, because as you well know my time is very precious right now.'

What was it in his speech Zoe couldn't put her finger on. It was as if he were play acting.

Savich breathed deeply. He chewed at the inside of his mouth, then reached for a pill from his little box and knocked it back into his throat with a sip of cold coffee. He could sense the Englishman's impatience, yet allowed some time to pass before he spoke. When he did, it sounded like to do so was taking all the strength he had.

'My work is . . . analytical. I am a tactician. While it seems death has rather become a way of life these days in Russia, I myself have never killed. No man has died by my hand.'

'But by your pen? You sit behind a desk and contrive ways others can do it for you. Like Major Baskov?'

The old man smiled. 'Ah,' he nodded, 'so Petrenko did access Grushenko's safe.'

'Tell me where the London bomb is.'

'So Grushenko has lied all along. I suspected it, although it makes no difference. The West will yield, either by force or by its own volition. The capitalist model has failed. World socialism is the next step in man's evolution, therefore capitulation is an inevitability.' He leaned forward and lowered his voice into a whisper. 'There are a *million* hidden tendrils in every corner of the West to ensure it. You must know an enemy to defeat one, after all, no? How are you so sure you are even equipped to define who the enemy is, let alone to go about picking the fly shit out of the pepper?' A smile. 'A colourful English expression, is it not?'

'Where is Valentin Baskov?'

'As for me, I do not think I will live to see it. You see, I have a heart condition.'

'You can say that again,' Henderson snapped back. 'Hundreds of thousands of innocent people asphyxiated by polluted air, crippled by cancers, burned and poisoned by radiation — now that's what I call a heart condition.'

The Russian blinked. 'In every war there are unfortunate victims.'

Henderson's chair screeched back as he stood, and started to pace. 'One thing that's always bothered me, Savich. About Overture. Why not America? Why only Europe?'

'It is a long held view in our country that America can manage its own downfall very well without any outside intervention,' he croaked, 'And do you consider it too fantastical to believe that Russia has assets high in the US government?'

Henderson didn't.

'Very high, in fact.'

Zoe stared through the one way glass at the two men. 'Perhaps in the highest office of all. So you see,' he said, 'this is my bloody legacy. What of your conscience . . . mister?'

'Henderson.'

'Ah, yes,' he replied at once, his old head nodding in recognition. 'Cassandra.'

What did he call him? Her thoughts were surging in all directions as she glared at them through the glass, still staring through each other. Savich had recognised him by name, *knew* him, had called him by a codename – Cassandra - a female name from Greek mythology, like on the dossiers. Oh my god. The accusations, the disk drive, the Pendulum man, and now this? She needed answers.

Savich smiled, and in Russian said, 'I think perhaps we would both prefer to talk in private.'

Suddenly at volume. 'Everyone out,' he shouted up to the glass, 'and kill the cameras.'

The chair scraped back across the floor and he burst into the viewing room.

'John? what the hell's going on in there? What did he call you?'

'That includes you, I need you to leave.'
Leutzinger stepped forward. 'Mr Henderson, I do not have the authority to allow you to . . . '

'All of you, and take your men. Wait in the corridor and kill the recording. Now.'

Zoe was chasing him for answers. 'For his benefit or for yours? What exactly is your relationship with this man, John?'

Henderson looked down at her, her brown eyes accusing, and spoke firmly, 'Now.'

Leutzinger looked on at the two agents who stared daggers at each other. He didn't know what was going on, but could see that pulling rank wasn't going to get any of them anywhere, so he switched off the microphones, the speakers and the monitors, and joined his guards in the corridor. A minute later Zoe reluctantly joined them.

Hours went by. Leutzinger was called away, leaving Zoe's mind to run wild under the glare of the buzzing strip-lights. It was him, the mole, the Pendulum man, over and over, until at two-thirty in the morning a blurred figure in a long overcoat and carrying a stiff leather portmanteau bag appeared. 'I am Doctor Becker,' he said in a thick German accent through a full beard.

Zoe led him into the viewing room, and as they approached the glass they could see Henderson and Savich in the room beyond — now in their shirtsleeves, sitting in silence.

The MI6 man, sensing movement behind the glass, got up.

'Thank you for coming at such a late hour, doctor,' he said, 'did you bring it?'

The elderly doctor rested the old medicine bag down and unclasped its hinge. What he lifted out was a green bottle with a label on the side that read SP-117. Inside the room, Igor Savich reached for another pill.

'No, John, no, you can't — ' she said.

Henderson nodded for him to continue. The doctor took out a syringe then stabbed its needle into the top of the bottle, turned it upside down and retracted the plunger, filling it with a clear liquid.

'John, don't. Please, listen to me, you have no right to . . . '

'Go ahead, doctor,' said Henderson, ignoring her and opening the door.

They watched through the glass. Becker was holding the syringe upside down as he entered the room and approached the old man at the table. A moment later he was rolling up the old man's shirt sleeve.

'Please, John, please . . . '

The doctor inserted the long needle into Savich's thin shoulder and squeezed the plunger. As the liquid entered his blood stream the eyelids dropped, his elbows slid out from under him, and he slumped forward onto the table.

'Jesus Christ. What have you done?'

He looked her in the eye. 'Zürich.'

'You have precisely one minute to explain yourself Mister Jones-Cooper,' said 'C' as the lift doors opened. His AC was waiting for him, and the sight of him well-rested and with those big jowls cleanly shaven after an unexplained twenty-four hour absence was enough for the famous Thorpe patience to desert him. He himself had been kept awake most of the night in the wake of the cyber attack on the European Space Agency. Friday 13th was already off to a bad start.

'I'm not following you, Sir Clive.' Jones-Cooper could hardly keep up with the older man as he marched along the corridor. He was also vying for position with several officers and secretaries who were scurrying along behind.

'Would you care to explain where you have been since yesterday morning?'

'If I could just have a moment in private.'

'C' stopped abruptly. 'Have you the slightest notion of what is upon us?' The man was brandishing something, a sheet of paper. 'What's this?' he said, taking it and scanning it. It was a psychological evaluation, three years old, of officer SKV-90323, better known as John S. Henderson. 'C' looked him in the eye. *What the shit are you playing at?*

'Information's come to light. We should pull Henderson off this,' said Jones-Cooper in a low voice so as not to be overheard. 'I've been studying his psychological reports and I've reason to believe Henderson will deliberately fail in this mission.' He stepped in closer. 'Henry Chapman - name ring a bell?'

'Mister Jones-Cooper . . . '

'His tutor at Cambridge. Documents have been unearthed that prove without a doubt Chapman was a member of the Communist Party of Great Britain between fifty-three and fifty-five, until — and listen to this — he was expelled from the party for being considered too radical.' His face was aglow with conspiratorial victory.

'C' stared at him. 'I think you should have a serious think about what it is you're implying here.'

Jones-Cooper snorted, but kept his voice low. 'The psych reports say, look, here, "seems to display deep sympathies for Russia and its people." He's had us all fooled all right. But trust me, sir, *he will deliberately fail,* it's all a part of the plan. It's all been a cover, a ruse, he's the last person anyone would suspect precisely *because* he's been so vocal about the Russian threat all these years. But if you look at the evidence . . . ' He lowered his voice further. 'Operation Pendulum. Winter of ninety-five, now it's my opinion that John Henderson is a double agent and has been for the last twenty-five years — '

'That's enough.' 'C' held up a palm and narrowed his eyes. 'While you've been away embarking upon your absurd personal vendetta for reasons I do not yet know, we've lost the ability to communicate with three-hundred satellites, ostensibly meaning the continent of Europe is careening back towards the Ice Age. Nod if you understand.'

'Of course, I'm aware of that — '

'Good. So go to work immediately, and if after tomorrow at midnight we still have a world, we'll address both your sordid accusations and your own future inside Six then.'

'It will *be too late*,' he seethed through gritted teeth as one of the advisers approached them and whispered something into 'C's ear. 'C' nodded and the man retreated.

'Now I don't suppose you know if we've made any strides with Savich?'

Jones-Cooper squinted.

Christ, the man was incapable, thought 'C'. 'Is he *awake*?'

His mind was jumping. '*Igor* Savich?' he asked, tentatively.

'Yes, for Christ's sake. We're holding him in Geneva airport. You may remember the name from the report you were so keen on burying? Well, he seems to have turned himself in.' 'C' strode away with his gaggle in tow, leaving Jones-Cooper feeling like he'd taken a blow to the solar plexus. He was holding onto the wall, and his mouth had fallen open to give him the expression of an expiring sea bass. His thoughts had been sent into turmoil. Think, he told himself, think. Minutes later he was on the third floor.

'Zürich,' Faulds answered, confused as to why he was being asked. 'That's all Savich said. Shouldn't be too long before he gives us chapter and verse, but . . . Didn't you ?—' But the AC seemed to have suffered some kind of a shock. Appeared somewhat disorientated, Faulds thought. His arms were out to steady himself. He swayed once, then appeared to think of something, turned around, and stumbled back out through the open plan office.

17

With the sun behind him Russell Blake had driven north towards Lausanne around the northern shores of Lake Geneva, seeking to spend the night in as comfortable yet discreet a location as he could find. The town of Vevey on the banks of Lake Geneva is dominated by the alps and the majestic Mont Blanc that rises out of them from the East, and it was here, safely away from the town's tree-lined promenade, old town, museums, statues and the square whose early Saturday market plays host to great local crowds, he had checked into a small guesthouse under the name of Gabriel Brunner. It had been a particularly bracing evening, yet despite the guesthouse being at full capacity, at seven p.m. no guest nor member of the staff had heard numbers emanating from the speaker of a Grundig short wave radio in room twelve. Nor did anyone take any notice later of the unassuming, some would have said taciturn, bank employee, as he dined locally on whitefish caught that morning in the lake, drank a bottle of Sancerre, and retired early back to the warmth of his lodgings.

Friday morning he was gone. The Alfa joined the A12 autoroute that lies a few well-placed kilometres to the north of the town, and was soon carrying its driver in the direction of Bern.

Later that afternoon its hot engine sat cooling in the freezing air behind an ice rink while its driver had set off on foot through light snow towards the centre of a picture-postcard-like resort town. Nestled high in the alpine peaks, its pretty cobbled main street consisted of a series of low, wooden-beamed chalets that housed designer stores, luxury boutiques, and restaurants and cafes with busy terraces. The sun had lowered and was casting long shadows behind groups of chattering Italian women in expensive sunglasses and fur coats, their slim-tailored husbands, and skiers fresh from the piste clutching glasses of gluhwein. Russell Blake came to a stop beside a sign whose gold letters read The Eagle Mountain.

In the large circular bar and restaurant area he chose to sit on one of the calfskin seats, ordered a Vieux Carré cocktail, and gazed out of the full length windows onto the panoramic mountain range that opened up before him and gives everyone in that place the impression of being suspended in the middle of the shimmering bluey white mountains amid the wisping clouds. He glanced around. The clientele was mostly made up of locals: elderly, tanned and wealthy, mixed with some young skiers — trust fund Brits and some Italians - early arrivals for the season, and a German couple who were sitting cross-legged on the central stone fireplace. No one paid any attention to the man sitting alone in a blazer and open-necked shirt who was scanning the room. Had they, they would have assumed he was just another well-travelled sporting European on holiday. He only had to wait fifteen minutes until she walked into the bar and sat down a few degrees away to his left, facing Mount Pilatus.

Blake studied her and decided there and then that she would be the one, a choice based mainly on her looks. Her profile was wonderful, her age around forty-five, which again was perfect. He also noticed her elegant fingers were unadorned by lovers' rings as they lay draped across one knee drumming lightly while she waited for her cocktail. She seemed hypnotised by the view. While everyone else pulled out their phones every few minutes in the hope their precious bars and provider's name would spring up again at any second and save them from this purgatory, she seemed lost contentedly in the clouds.

When he asked if he could join her and she agreed, he introduced himself as Simon Wells from London, a widower who was taking a driving tour of the alps after the death of his wife only some months before. Her name, she told him only slightly warily, was Elisa Freiin Von Kramer, and she was Austrian, and a baroness by birth. A bottle of Lanson and a dozen oysters later, the two people who only an hour and a half earlier had been strangers were now holding hands and sliding happily up the main street towards the ice rink.

With the Alfa Romeo parked in her driveway and two cases sitting unopened in the entrance hall of her alpine chalet, the baroness spinster, coat of arms wrapped in a dust sheet beneath the bed, let herself be kissed by the Englishman she'd met only a few hours before. She found him rather passionless, but it didn't matter — she was content to be held on her long fur couch, her head light from the champagne and their naked skin lit perfectly by the burning orange summit that shone through her tall windows.

Less than 60 kms to the north, in Zürich, in an apartment above a grey flower shop that specialised in purple orchids, two people were having dinner in silence. They were father and daughter — he, a mercenary who killed men and women for a living, and she, his nine year old who visited on Fridays as per the terms of the limited visitation rights enforced upon them by the court. They were chewing their over-boiled ravioli pasta when a light emitted from his phone. Under his daughter's judging glare he read the message that had come in from the secure line. The photograph at the top of the screen was his, with his codename, GERHARD, written underneath. He scrolled down to where the word TARGET was written, and to the name below it. It read JOHN HENDERSON, and appeared above a photograph.

Gerhard looked at the features. Looks like a good guy, he thought. Maybe not, he decided after a few seconds more.

'Why are you so important?' Asked his daughter.

He shot her a quizzical look.

'You're the only one whose phone works.'

Standing on her chalet's wide balcony he brought the vodka to his lips and felt the fire ignite in his stomach as the liquid hit. The village below was shimmering in an incandescent glow while the mountains, lit by the last dregs of sunlight, created a contrast of burning red and bright blue. In the distance he could just make out the last of the day's skiers exiting the cable cars that hung out of the clouds beyond, while the faint sound of traditional folk music floated up. It was difficult to imagine a more beautiful, deadly landscape.

Wearing a robe and with a towel wrapped around her wet hair, Elisa drew up to the window behind him and watched her stranger's back as he stood motionless. She placed her fingers on the glass, then thought better of interrupting his thoughts, drew her hand back, and went back to the bedroom to wait for him.

He knocked back the glass and felt the vodka numb him. The Russian's eyes glazed over, and like Perses standing high above the innocent, he began to plot the final stages for the destruction of the doomed beauty below. A line came to him from somewhere. "Now I am become death, the destroyer of worlds."

What was Cassandra if not a codename? Zoe had been asking herself the question since they'd left the old man slumped over a table in Geneva in the early hours. Savich *knew* him, that was obvious, if not by face then by that name when he told him his name was Henderson. She had decided to confront him — although she was unsure of what she would do with the truth when it came — but moments after the doctor had packed away his bag and disappeared the man from Geneva Station had arrived and her boss then spent forty-five minutes briefing him before a TETRA radio was thrust into his hand and they climbed into the back of the Eurocopter. For the hour long journey she could only watch as, over the noise, he and London tried to find a crack to prize open in Switzerland's strict banking secrecy laws. After the INTERPOL helicopter had them touching down in Switzerland's largest city, they had then spent the day attempting to achieve the same end on the ground, being passed from pillar to post, from bureaucrats to lawyers and to various officials in a series of state buildings. 'C' had spoken to his Station Chief in

Zürich, then to the head of Swiss Intelligence, the FIS, but Swiss banking secrecy being enshrined in federal law and akin to a religion, little could be achieved at Intelligence level before the disclosure was granted.

Dusk found them at the Police headquarters building on the Kasernenstrasse, where they were told blankly that they would have to wait until the following day. The Kommandant for the canton of Zürich was at the opera, and they simply had to understand it was Wagner's Tristan and Isolde. Henderson raised hell in the strip-lit waiting room until the duty officer agreed to try again. Patience with the Swiss authorities had officially run dry.

They waited. Zoe had been staring at a poster on the wall that reminded the public to report suspicious packages when she finally found the moment to ask.

'John, what did I witness last night?' Her question was greeted with silence. 'You have to tell me. You understand? Tell me what I saw.'

'I think you know what you saw.'

There was something inside him, she could sense it, something he kept locked away, perhaps had done for a very long time, that he wanted to say. But he hesitated, and as the hammering of footsteps in the corridor closed in, the time for private confession dissolved.

When Monica Rousseau arrived she had her hair up and was elegantly dressed in a fine black cashmere coat over a black dress, and accompanied by two senior police officers. She greeted the sight of the two British intelligence agents with confused disdain. This was a woman who exuded quiet sophistication, and one who couldn't bear deviations in protocol.

'I am Monica Rousseau, the Kommandant of Zürich police, whatever this is it is most irregular.' She spoke in perfect English with a superior air.

They stood to shake hands, which was reciprocated with icy reluctance. 'John Henderson. This is Zoe Taylor, British security services.'

'I have been informed that I am to afford you every assistance, and unconditionally it seems, which I might tell you I find most irregular.'

'*Most* irregular?' he said sharply, already exasperated by her calm.

Zoe interjected. 'We've reason to believe a suspect we've been following will be arriving in Zürich tomorrow, if he's not already here, to access a safety deposit box in a bank that may be registered under the name of Franz Hart. We need to know which bank.'

'You do understand the strictness of our banking privacy laws here in Switzerland prevents us from disclosing client information, Miss Taylor?'

'We had heard,' said Henderson with more than a hint of contempt. 'but these are extraneous circumstances, and your precious law is not absolute.'

Rousseau lifted her head and regarded the unkempt Brit. It was sarcasm, and his tone was firm but, she decided, not aggressive. Male aggression in any situation was something she wouldn't stand for.

'I thought your co-operation was supposed to be unconditional,' he added.

'Mister - sorry, what was your name again?'

'Henderson.'

'Switzerland's neutrality and privacy it affords the individual in these matters is something we take great pride in. Like an agreement between a priest and penitent, or one that a doctor makes to a patient, our banking act protects unparalleled client confidentiality.'

'Unless you receive an accepted criminal complaint.'

'John?' said Zoe stepping in, sensing his temper rising. 'Madam Kommandant,' she took the woman aside and continued in a calm, but firm voice, 'We're not talking about tax evasion here, we're talking about a terrorist who at some point tomorrow we suspect will receive instructions from a safety deposit box in one of your banks here in Zürich, instructions on where to plant a bomb. A very, very deadly bomb. Now you've already been asked to afford us every assistance. Unconditional assistance were the words you used. So?'

The flicker of a smile crossed the older woman's lips. She admired strength in women. Within thirty minutes they had what they wanted, and the Kommandant what she did, which was to disappear back to the gilded glamour of her opera house and the second act of the tragic romance of its opera.

She watched him next to her with his unblinking eyes focused upon her ceiling. He was a man of few words this Simon, she decided, and that was fine. Better to say nothing if there is nothing to say, her mother had told her. She wasn't used to meeting men at the Eagle Mountain Hotel and bringing them home, and something about it made her feel young, which made her feel happy. She wondered if she should cook for them both tonight or if he would want to leave.

He brought his arm up and looked at his watch. 'I have to make a phone call,' he said, getting out of bed and pulling on trousers.

'You'll be lucky,' she laughed, 'haven't you

heard? Most of the phones are dead — it's all over the news. They think it's a terrorist attack. I don't mind being cut off. I feel safe here with you, Simon.'

He crossed her bedroom, passing its stone fireplace with a gentle log fire that warmed the animal skin rug, and closed the door.

In a spare bedroom he pushed the door to before setting up the Grundig on a desk. With three minutes to wait until 19:00 hrs, he tuned the dial away from the 4625 kHz frequency, and lowered the radio's volume. A man's voice, stilted and formal, read, ' . . . and claims by the OAG that they also have the capability to fire anti-satellite weaponry are also being investigated. This is Radio Sputnik with the voice of Russia. Our top story, the loss of three hundred of Europe's communication satellites has been apportioned to the OAG, the Organization Against Globalisation, who claimed responsibility today. The group has also claimed it was behind other attacks in the past week that include explosions at gas storage plants across Europe, and cyber attacks on banks, corporations and key infrastructure on the continent.'

Blake checked his watch.

In the master bedroom Elisa pulled on her robe and tied it around her.

' . . . Fearing total collapse of the European Union amid widespread unrest in support of closing member countries' borders. The OAG, meanwhile, has seen an unexpected surge in *support* by many people who share the group's sense of disenfranchisement with liberal economic policies by corrupt governments . . . '

She turned on the tap and filled a glass with water. From the open-plan kitchen she noticed the light in the spare room was on. She took a sip, and placed the glass down upon the marble countertop.

' . . . European policy of globalisation, that succeeds in both lowering wages at home while, in poorer nations, exploiting a cheap labour force and depleting agrarian and tribal cultures that creates division among communities . . . '

He twisted the dial, and with pen hovering above the one-time pad, waited for his identifier. At seven precisely the five note synth phrase resounded from the speaker. The few seconds pause that followed was soon broken by the female voice.

'PAPA ECHO CHARLIE NOVEMBER 254 254 254 PAPA ECHO CHARLIE NOVEMBER 254 254 254 . . . '

She trod lightly on the balls of her feet so not to make a noise, and as she drew closer to the small gap in the door, she could see his back, crouched over a large radio set at her father's writing desk. It looked like he was writing something, but the sound emitting from the radio was curious: that of a distant, disembodied, woman's voice reading lists of numbers — *'Two. Seven. Nine. Four. Five. Zero. Two . . . '* over and over.

He knew she was there, behind him, and could feel her gaze on his back. When the numbers stopped and the musical identifier had signalled the message's end, he switched off the machine and sat back in the chair. To let her live was impossible of course. Whether she had seen or overheard anything or not.

It was nine fifteen p.m. Moscow Time, and signalman Krupin too leaned back in his chair after having broadcast the message from his frozen gulag. It was longer than the others and as usual the content meant nothing to him, yet now his orders were coming from a general called Grushenko, and they were getting more garbled and more threatening as the days wore on. He wished he could escape back to Moscow, but he was sure that this Grushenko was the same general who had had that man killed only a few metres away the day they'd arrived.

He remembered seeing the two thugs bury the body in the frozen ground out near the poplar trees, but they hadn't done a very good job for now whenever they were let out, the guards' dogs sniffed around the mound of soil.

In Lubyanka in the nation's capital the man at whose hands Krupin feared he would suffer a similar fate went to his safe and took out every shred of paperwork concerning *Overture*.

His secretary had left for the evening some hours before and he'd been getting progressively drunk since in an attempt to see a way of untangling himself from the web of lies he'd been spinning. Lies Dmitri Petrenko had forced him to tell, that imbecile traitor — he was one who was to blame for all this. Having carried the files to the outer office, he dropped them on the floor near the grate. No-one in the *Telepol* committee knew he had covered up the theft from his safe, knew about Katya who had probably sold the stolen dossiers to the British, and no one knew he had lied about the Paris bomb being discovered. He was in the clear. Volkov's suspicious glowers didn't worry him — he could handle that fat coward. No, he thought as he crouched down, struck a match and lit some thin kindling, tomorrow at midnight the London and Berlin bombs would explode, and Overture would be successful. With a trembling hand he held each file over the flames until they curled and dropped into ash. The faces of Donald Philips, Sarina Gaubert, and Major Valentin Baskov – loyal servants to a malevolent master — burned into dust, cremated without ceremony, erased forever.

Blake took the brass poker from the hanging fireside tools and prodded at the logs in the grate. The bedroom was still warm and the scent of her perfume lingered, which stirred his senses. He would have her again, strangle her, and leave before sunrise. His eyes fell to the rug and he frowned. Where was she? She'd been gone for, how long, forty minutes? He crossed the room and out into the hallway. A door to an interior he had presumed was a cupboard before was ajar. When he opened it there was a staircase, as if to a basement. An unusual smell floated up and flooded his nostrils. It wasn't altogether pleasant. A swampy, organic odour, sometimes sweet then at once a stagnant pond. He stepped down gently until he reached the bottom step and turned into the space. It was entirely pale grey, lit only by the moonlight reflecting off the mountain that cast a diffused light through the vast windows and gave the white brick walls a bluey sheen. As soon as he entered the wide basement he identified the distinctive smell as clay, as emerging from the shadows, from corners, from high shelves and low clay-splashed pine benches stared the frozen figures: Immaculately sculpted lips, eyes and jawlines, breasts and thighs, life-size and human enough as to be real.

The only colour in the studio was courtesy of

a huge vase of red and violet flowers that sat in one of the window sills. Elisa was at the end of the room with her back to him. She was standing still, wearing her robe in the half darkness. When she heard him she turned.

'You found me,' she said through a modest smile.

She stepped to the side to reveal what she'd been studying: a full size female form, a figurative sculpture, towering and strong, yet overwhelmingly feminine. The clay was moist, her skin shimmering, light enough grey to be white. Her hair was long and her neutral expression both enticing and utterly mysterious. Blake's eyes became locked upon it as he drew nearer.

Elisa fidgeted with the loop tool she'd been stroking along the figure's abdomen moments before, and began picking bits of clay from it and rolling them in her fingers, wondering what Simon would make of this. He approached, open-mouthed and apparently lost in thought. For a long time he didn't speak, just stared.

Finally, 'This is your work?' he asked in a soft voice.

Elisa nodded. She lay down the loop tool among used minarettes and spatulas that rested beneath the statue in no particular order. 'I call her Sophia. I think she is wise.'

He circled the sculpture admiringly, then came to face her again, unable to draw his eyes away. She was the most perfect thing he'd ever seen.

'What do you think?'

There was a softness to her, a compassion that he had never witnessed before. A feminine approach, he supposed. The depth of the feeling was both familiar and alien to him, both unsettling and comforting at the same time. 'Extraordinary.'

Elisa smiled.

"No drawings?' he asked, gesturing at the bare walls. 'You don't work from photographs?'

'No. She emerges from the clay. She is born here.'

A few short hours later with the pink glow of early sunrise reflecting through the hallway of the warm chalet, a man's silhouetted figure carried two cases across the hardwood floor to the front door and set them down. He walked back away, and in the background, through the open bedroom door, the figure of a woman could be seen. Elisa was naked, lying motionless on her front, her lower half covered by a white bedsheet and her left arm hanging down from the side of the bed. Her head though was turned unnaturally towards the ceiling and her eyes were open, as though she were staring upwards, yet they were unblinking. Her chest too was still.

The cases were taken away, followed by the sounds of the door closing and the engine of an Alfa Romeo being started, and finally that of its tyres rolling away slowly down the mountain road. When the sound of its engine had disappeared Elisa blinked, closed her eyes, sighed deeply, and wondered to herself if she would ever see her stranger again.

Neither of them slept that night. At 09:30 on Saturday morning with a mere fourteen and a half hours until detonation, Henderson and Zoe were waiting in an unmarked car on the Limmatquai in Zürich, the busy kilometre-long promenade that runs along the Eastern bank of the River Limmat from the train station in the north. Their attention was fixed beyond the usual stir of cars, trams, and weekend shoppers, upon the neoclassical facade of a building fifty metres away with a brass plaque on a column that read First Allied Bank, Zürich. It housed one of the largest, most modern, and closely guarded private vaults in the world.

Designed to provide total privacy for the storage of precious metals, gold bullion, gems, coins, works of art and other valuables one wishes to hide from either the taxman or the authorities, the private vaults here offered storage options ranging from a small drawer to a medium sized room. The man who used the name Hart had registered a box the size of a large airport locker here on 17th December the previous year, two days after he did so at the Credit Lyonnais bank in Paris. Unlike any other countries depositories however, security here in Switzerland was different.

Here, no one but the fake Hart himself would be able to gain access, the reason being that after a complex series of card-swiping and passcode-entering, a retinal scan must be performed. This allows the customer to enter a glass booth that moves him or her towards a room — bare but for a countertop with a rectangular hole in its centre and yet another keypad above that. This final keypad entry enables the required box to be picked in a giant underground facility and to take an elaborate automated journey up to the countertop where it may be accessed it in the old-fashioned way — with two turns of keys in tandem locks. This meant that unless someone had gouged out the eyes of the individual who registered the box originally and transplanted them into his own head, Henderson and Zoe were waiting for a bald, razor thin, black-eyed man to appear that cold morning.

Rousseau had sanctioned a team to be led by a soigné man with neat grey hair named Loubet, one of the Cantonal Police's best. On the roof of the building opposite, the three-storey town hall known as the Rathaus, he had placed two marksmen who had been ordered to fire only in the unlikely event a positive ID of Russell Blake could be made, while two plain clothes police officers, Bravo team, sat in a white Hyundai further along the street, and two female officers from the Federal Intelligence Service acted as pedestrians on the pavement. There were also two inside the bank, one in the vault's basement reception dressed as a bank security guard, and Loubet himself who was seated by the entrance and ensconced behind yesterday's Neue Zürcher Zeitung newspaper. Henderson had also requested a team be put in place at the train station consisting of four FIS Watchers. Although all were armed, their orders were strictly to follow. Hart, they were told, should he appear, was just a messenger.

Henderson checked his watch for the third time in a minute. *Fourteen and a half hours.* He went over it again. Savich had given him one word: Zürich. No one had accessed the box in the past month so Hart *had* to show today to pick up Blake's final instructions. Eight and a half hours to Berlin by train, nine by road, an hour and a half in the air. Based on the fact that communications links had been so severely damaged, he was quite prepared to follow Hart all the way there — his supposition being that the instructions would be delivered in person, that the Russian was likely already in place with the device. 'What if we're wrong?' Zoe had asked, but he couldn't answer her. If he didn't show, if Blake had received or was yet to receive instructions via alternative means then they would fail. But they had nothing else to go on. The Red Notice was impotent when it came to men like Blake, or whatever name he was using now. This was all they had. A man with no name, a box, Zürich. The clock was ticking away valuable minutes and if they were waiting here for no reason then the simple, appalling truth was that following the stroke of midnight tonight millions would die.

Another precious hour ticked by in silence. The snipers were poised, index fingers resting across trigger guards, eyes fixed to crosshairs at the steady flow of Saturday morning activity at the bank's entrance while inside it, beneath the high ceilings of the marble entrance hall the tellers went about their morning, oblivious and smiling. But silence wasn't supplying Zoe with answers, so finally she broke it, slowly and deliberately.

'John, why did Igor Savich call you Cassandra?'

He took a few moments, then turned to look at her. 'In Greek mythology Cassandra was the daughter of the king of Troy. Apollo gave her the power to see the future but he also made sure that no one would believe her, so when she warned the Trojans that the Greeks were hiding inside the Trojan horse to take control of Troy – no one listened. She was cursed to always be disbelieved in spite of her telling the truth. Igor Savich calling me the Cassandra means he knows who I am, which means someone's told him. He's telling me the Russians have a highly placed source inside MI6.'

She slotted the information into the gaps that had formed in the last few weeks. A mole in the Service. That's how they knew to destroy the disc drive. She squinted through the windscreen, at people arm in arm, hands holding their children's hands.

'And this source gave them Dmitri?'

'It''s possible,' he replied. 'Although he was taking irresponsible risks to pay for his daughter's treatment. Luckily he was clever enough to tuck away any Overture intel as insurance for his wife in the event of his death.'

'And Savich's request for the messages from Bern to be sent unencrypted. His way of alerting us from the start?'

'Maybe,' he answered as though he hadn't considered it, which only slightly irked her for a moment. 'I don't suppose we'll ever know *when* he made the decision that Overture couldn't be allowed to succeed.' He drew in a long breath. 'He's a coward. Wants redemption, salvation before he dies, but won't commit to full betrayal. But time was running out so we had to give him something to help loosen the tongue.'

He pulled at his chin with forefinger and thumb. She examined him, the sleepless nights evident in his eyes. Of course, *Cassandra*. Her reaction, she conceded, had been clouded by the fact that the name slotted in with the other Greek names on the sleepers' dossiers: Cronos, Athena, Europa, but of course she knew the meaning and the myth of Cassandra. And of course he was convincing, and of course it made sense. John Henderson always made sense. Always ready with some history to explain away and to educate and patronise and pat you on the shoulder and say there, there, it's okay, while really meaning I'm always one step ahead of you. And Savich was telling us we have a mole inside MI6, was he? Well now that is handy — to have someone to blame when the mission fails. So, now what? Should she treat this as the great revelation he wants her to think it is? Or was this mole Savich hinted at the man from Pendulum the Soviets left behind all those years ago like a bug in an aspidistra that no one remembered to throw out. Left there to live, to secretly suck the oxygen out of the British Secret Service from the corner of the room — hiding in plain sight, undetected for all these years? And of course the real question was, was he really talking about himself? Had the guilt of privilege or whatever he called it that he harboured at Cambridge made him vulnerable enough to fall for the rhetoric or the history or the ideologies or a combination of all of those things, and had that intellectual cocktail been the catalyst to a lifetime of betrayal? Had youthful disillusionment with what he would call the 'democratic empire' spawned a series of actions that led to a woman's death, a cover up, and a legacy of lies and double cross that continued to this day? The answer was, Zoe imagined, and probably always would be, elusive. More pressingly, was he intentionally intending to fail to thwart Russell Blake's mission or was she entirely wrong about him and owed him an apology.

Perhaps. Or perhaps not.

The building three doors to the north of the First Allied should have been empty, for its offices across three floors were home to the weekday business of a large legal firm, yet it was not. The intruder entered unnoticed through a ground floor window to the rear of the property and climbed the central staircase until he found a third floor office window that overlooked the promenade. He had taken his time setting up the long-range rifle upon its tripod, had loaded its barrel, and was waiting for the target to exit the car opposite the bank.

He moved the focus wheel a hair, although he did not have a clear shot for the man was obscured by his passenger, the woman — pretty with blond hair. He would have to wait until he got out of the car. Gerhard was a professional, and a moving target from fifty yards would prove no problem for a marksman of his skill.

'You know that prevailing wisdom says Sodium Pentothal just makes the subject talk more, but not necessarily more accurately?' Zoe said.

'I know, but you know what I think about prevailing wisdom.'

The waiting was hurting. At midday she pushed the button to turn on the car's radio and tuned it to the BBC's World Service.

'Morris Jacques MP, the man tipped to be named as new secretary of state for defence, has resigned after a sex tape was released yesterday in which it is alleged the MP for North East Somerset is seen engaged in sexual activity with his parliamentary assistant.'

It was the scandal, as he'd always proclaimed, that had always been the end game.

Four minutes later a black BMW saloon pulled up slowly to the kerb outside the bank. He was about to order Bravo team to run the plate when a deafening shriek flooded the earpieces of every member of the team. A high-pitched white noise that caused them to tear them out for fear of hearing loss. 'Christ, what the hell?' He yelled. The two pavement female cops were blown, any observer immediately having witnessed their grasping at their heads, while the rooftop marksmen grappled with their full headsets, that in doing so had left their limp rifles to fall downward in the confusion.

The car lay still, its engine running as they gathered their senses and waited for movement. It was obstructing their view of the bank's entrance, but staring into the glass, could he make out a driver's cap through the heavily tinted windows? It was difficult to see with sunlight reflecting off them. A second figure in the back? 'Stand by, everyone,' he whispered, with only Zoe able to hear.

One of the BMW's rear doors swung open. A moment later a man in a black suit, tall and slight and carrying a slim briefcase got out of the car and without pausing strode into the bank. Zoe caught a glimpse of his profile. 'It's him,' she said, 'It's Hart.' The female pedestrian opposite nodded in acknowledgement.

'What's he carrying?'

'It's a briefcase,' she replied.

He tried the radio again, but still the chaotic clamour of white noise emanated across all eight channels. Inside the bank, Loubet lowered his crumpled newspaper and watched the slim man disappear down the marble staircase towards the vault. The vault guard picked him up, watched him enter a passcode into a keypad, then stand rigid as the retinal scan was performed on his black eyes.

Loubet appeared at the entrance and gestured subtly. Zoe raised a palm that he took to mean, 'wait, and watch.' In the vault the guard too waited, while the marksmen aimed at the bank's entrance from above and the two officers on foot innocently perused the nearby shop windows.

'They're using a jammer. It means they're expecting us,' said Zoe.

Another two minutes went by. At the same time as the note of the BMW's revving engine rose a key the thin-framed man reappeared in the entrance carrying something heavy enough to give him a starboard list.

'Oh my God, I think it's the bomb.'

Their hands grabbed the door handles.

'Go, move in,' Henderson called out in the cold air as they charged across the street, causing the two female FIS officers to pull their guns and shout for Hart to freeze.

The engine screamed. Hart dived at the car as the rear tyres squealed, sending black smoke up in a violent plume. His target in the crosshair, Gerhard squeezed his trigger. The BMW veered suddenly towards Henderson. He leapt backwards to avoid being hit and the bullet tore into Zoe's right shoulder. The force spun her around and the instant stab of pain was quickly followed by the cobblestones coming up to smack her in the side of the head. Through the blur she saw him running at her sideways and shouting her name as the car disappeared behind him into the smoke.

'Scheisse.' Gerhard spat. He never missed. He scrambled to reload another bullet into the chamber and took aim.

Henderson reached her and dropped to his knees. 'Zoe, what — ' As shrieking pedestrians scattered around them he looked up to the marksmen, eyes darting left and right along the rooftops.

One of the marksmen hoisted his torso over the edge of the roof. 'It's coming from that building,' he pointed to his colleague.

Gerhard hadn't spotted the marksmen. He thought for a second, took aim, then fired again into the street. The bullet scraped Henderson's upper arm, knocking him backwards onto the hard ground, but he still had hold of Zoe so began dragging her behind a parked car.

'It's coming from the building three doors away, third floor window,' the second marksman yelled into his radio whose frequencies were again clear. The two FIS women looked up. They could just make out the outline of the shooter in the window. They pointed their pistols up and fired in time with the marksmen.

Inside the room the wave of police bullets ripped at Gerhard's head and body propelling him back so hard into the office he was dead before he hit the first lawyer's desk.

'Zoe, hold on, hold on,' He was gripping her face, but the strength was leaving her, her eyes were closing. 'We'll get you to a hospital.'

'Go,' she managed in a whisper, 'get after him.'

18

Hart gripped the back seat as the driver hurled the speeding BMW north, weaving through the heavy traffic on the tram-lined street like every other car was stationary. Several seconds behind, Bravo team's white Hyundai had given chase but was struggling to keep up as the driver was forced to lurch the car across both lanes to avoid cars and cyclists.

He didn't want to leave her there but he had no choice. Numb to his own wound, Henderson scrambled back to the car and in no time was also heading north at speed along the busy promenade past confused and terrified pedestrians. When he reached sight of the Bahnhofbrücke bridge he pulled the wheel sharply to the left, stamped his foot down hard and slid the car across the wide three lane junction before pointing it in the direction of the station.

At the other end of the bridge the Hyundai skidded to a sudden halt, narrowly missing a passing tram. When it cleared they looked to the right and saw Hart, still with the case but now on foot and running north along the road on the eastern edge of the station close to the oncoming traffic. Without waiting the Bravo man in the passenger seat got out and gave chase while the driver accelerated towards the station ahead of him. He passed the grand archway of the main entrance then drove on until he caught a glimpse of the saloon's dark outline on a narrow side street.

He pulled in, and tried the radio again for backup but was greeted with the same white noise. The BMW had come to rest outside a bookshop, wispy smoke from its exhaust visible in the winter air. The cop got out of his car. With gun outstretched, he approached slowly from behind in what he thought would be the driver's blind spot. 'Armed police,' he called out in English, his face tensed.

A minute later Henderson was passing the archway and spotted the Bravo car up ahead, empty of its two occupants, driver's door open, and the BMW close by. He pulled over and got out. There was no sign of the policemen, and the black car had long skid tracks behind its rear tyres, its engine silent. With the jet black windows reflecting only sky, Henderson approached. He reached for the handle and pulled. Something heavy inside forced the door to open, and the Bravo team driver slumped half out the door, a single bullet hole in the side of his head. The dead man's 9 mm Luger was in the footwell, unfired. Henderson took it and began to run back towards the station.

Hart was getting away. He wasn't young but he was thin and fast like a greyhound and the bigger Bravo man behind was losing ground. Sensing a gap, Hart darted into the traffic in a bid to cross, got half way then recoiled as a refuse lorry swiped close to him. He had the case against his chest and tried again to make it out of the centre of the two fast lanes, cars and trucks only inches from him. He looked back down the road — the panting cop was gaining.

Henderson reached the station's entrance and looked around, then into the darkened archway at the throng of people in the hall. At his feet was a homeless man sitting cross-legged on a blanket with a sleeping dog in front of him.

Just around the corner Hart stepped out. A car's horn screamed as its wing narrowly missed him which made him step backwards into the path of a van. It only clipped his shoulder but it was enough to put him directly in the path of a cement lorry that ploughed into him and sent the thin man flying like a weightless mannequin.

The sudden cacophony of tyre squeals and horns blaring that came from the direction of the river made him look up, before he turned back to the man beneath the arch. And then he spotted it. What the fingerless-gloved hands were stroking admiringly: the wearer's new item of headwear — a stiff-peaked chauffeur's cap.

Cars and lorries were screeching to an abrupt standstill, but the Bravo cop had his eye on the flying suitcase. When, having narrowly avoided being run over twice himself, he got to it eight cars' lengths away from the lorry's impact and had separated it from the front suspension of a Volvo, he flicked the latches and opened the lid. It was empty.

Once he was inside the main hall of the Hauptbahnhof Henderson's eyes began flitting from face to face. Ignore women and children, only men, tall, dark hair, dark clothes, and carrying, not pulling, at least one suitcase. But it was useless — the place was teeming and it was clear he hadn't a hope of finding one commuter in amongst thousands all moving in different directions like crazed ants. He pulled the radio from his pocket and turned the knob. Still the interference, and no phone signal. The four-man Watcher team was here somewhere but he had no means of contacting them. He pushed through the sea of people and found the departures board. Berlin, it had to be Berlin. He checked the time. 11:57. There – Berlin Hbf, ICE 72 departing at 11:59, platform 6. Behind the giant board, platforms 3 to 18 were spread out, left to right, before him. There, the 6 on the screen, and one of the distinctive white ICE trains with a red stripe waiting at the platform already awash with people. He crossed towards it fast, scanning the backs of heads and half glimpsed profiles for sight of the Russian. His eye flicked from one head to another, studying and disregarding groups at a time until in the distance an outline held his attention. He slowed to steady his focus. Walking away from him apace at the train's side was a figure, almost in silhouette: broad shoulders, dark jacket, looked like he could be carrying something. The figure turned to look over his shoulder, Henderson's line of sight became suddenly obscured, and then he was gone. The briefest glimpse. Now people were boarding, the platform was thinning and the train's doors were about to close. He had to decide. Had that been the Russian? Or had he tossed the cap at the homeless man and turned away, disappeared into the throng of the old town, hailed a taxi in the street, slipped underground and caught the first U-Bahn train, or worse, maybe Russell Blake hadn't been driving the BMW in the first place and he was already in the German capital.

What to do. Come on, think.

At 11:59 a guard's whistle blew, and the high-pitched whine above the train's electric door accompanied by the warning beeps told him he had two-seconds left. By the time they had passed, John Henderson was on board the train to Berlin.

News of the morning's events reached 'C' as he travelled back from an emergency meeting with his Foreign Minister. It was Kesterton who delivered it.

'Where's Henderson now?'

'We don't know, sir. His car was found near Zürich Hauptbahnhof station.'

'Thank you, Brian, I know what a railway station is. Zoe Taylor?'

'Took a nasty hit — she's in the ambulance now. They're keeping us updated.'

As he ended the call his phone rang again. It was the Permanent Secretary at the MOD with sobering reports that their Skynet 5 fleet of satellites was temporarily down due to a probable malfunction in their anti-jamming software. Critical communication serving the British Armed Forces, Intelligence agencies and government departments was effected. He rung off, then placed a call to Mary to update him on the whereabouts of Stephen Jones-Cooper - who hadn't been seen since mid-morning the previous day. No further developments, she told him just as his car was pulling in.

'C' joined his chief officers, advisors, and representatives from both the government and the military in the largest of the building's high-tech Operation's rooms housed in the giant command centre below ground. From here he would oversee the next twelve critical hours. The image that greeted him on the wall screen was that of an octogenarian babbling inanely inside an interview room in Geneva airport. It was being patched through live from Nasha's desk in Technical Analysis on the fifth floor, where her team of data analysts was attempting to extract any sense whatsoever out of the diatribe. All were fiercely concentrated — the closed circuit image was sharp and the sound quality was clear, but when the man from the Geneva office asked the set of scripted questions he had been briefed to ask, the answers from Igor Savich were nonsensical.

'Where is the London bomb hidden, Mister Savich?'

A long pause. Then finally, 'Bombs. Bloodshed. More unnecessary bloodshed . . . ' His words were slurred, his head hung low and swaying to and fro with an energy of a man half his age.

'The first target is London, Igor.'

'London,' he murmured, 'London. The nightingale sang in Berkeley Square.' The deeply lined face beamed, and he broke out into song. '*London by night is a wonderful sight . . .* '

'Operation Overture. The target is London, comrade?'

' *. . . There is magic abroad in the air . . .* '

'This is getting us nowhere,' said the DG of the Office for Security and Counter-Terrorism, the Home Secretary's direct messenger for the operation. 'His brain's scrambled.'

While he was speaking officers of the Met police were escorting the last few resilient ministers from the palace of Westminster while colleagues were installing concrete roadblocks to halt access to the area around the key government buildings across Whitehall. Officers were climbing stairs of offices, shining torches into the backrooms of commercial premises and questioning occupants of residential dwellings, with others pounding back alleys and footpaths in search of suspicious packages.

Television news that flashed across their screens in Vauxhall stated manpower was at breaking point — that the concentration of police officers required in central London meant regional stations had all but stopped responding to reports of crime, while on the capital's streets a growing sense of discontent from the public was manifesting into demonstrations that, largely un-policed, had begun to include rioting, with opportunistic looters and arsonists attacking commercial businesses in the West End without fear of recourse. Such scenes prompted some news channels to even proclaim society's collapse as imminent.

For MI5's Mike Hewitt over at Scotland Yard, things were no better. The city's ubiquitous CCTV was proving fruitless. Blake's mobile phone records had been scrutinised, as had electronic payments receipts for the last two months yet had still surrendered a flat nothing. The Battersea flat had been turned upside down for clues yet it too was clean. Fragments of 16 mm film salvaged from the embers in a fire pit were too badly burned to yield the content, and despite the solo inhabitant's possession of a cine projector leading them to question local vendors and specifically to a shop in Covent Garden, inquiring constables left disappointed when the proprietor claimed he hadn't sold a Bell and Howell Filmosound in years, nor did he claim to recognise the man in the photograph when presented with it. The fact he had a Category 5 VAT Fraud conviction on the Police database led CI Darlington to suggest a cash transaction may have occurred, but they couldn't prove it and local CCTV pulled up a blank, so the line of enquiry halted. The Chief Inspector and the MI5 man wanted answers and were getting none.

Relentlessly, the three by eight shifts rolled on.

It was only once he was aboard the train that the pain hit. Standing in the vestibule with his back against the rail for balance he winced as he pulled down his jacket and found his shirt was soaked through with blood at the right shoulder. Thankfully the bullet hadn't entered the flesh but gouged a valley that although painful, could wait. Zoe had been hit hard though, had taken a bullet. He squeezed his eyes shut. What the hell had happened? Why had they been targeted? A woman appeared and started when she saw his bloody shirt, so he pulled the jacket back on, which made him wince again. First things first, he had to identify Blake without being seen. He began walking the aisles in search of the once-glimpsed figure, stepping past each seat and each face until ten minutes later he'd covered the four standard class carriages to the rear. Ahead was the bistro-bar car, the next, another economy carriage that he quickly discounted. When he reached first class he paused. If the Russian were on this train he would be effaced here. He made his way forward, receiving blank looks from passengers until the corridor narrowed. These were the first class compartments, three of them, and he could see they had glass sliding doors but that the middle one had its privacy curtains drawn. How to see inside, he asked himself.

'This number is not recognised. Please try again,' the pre-recorded voice stated. Ninety-seconds to wait — he began counting them in his head. His rented car was parked off the road, on a muddy track to some woodland, and as he paced he could feel himself sweating freely through his suit — though not from exertion, from fear. His hands had been shaking when he'd bought the pre-paid SIM card from the newsagent's in the village with the elderly woman buying stamps next to him staring, then getting the tiny bloody thing into his phone had been stressful and now, now ninety-seconds seemed like an eternity. *Come on*, he pressured, the phone pressed to his ear with a soaked palm. Finally the tape machine clicked, and a robotic voice read. 'Five. Four. Nine. Six. Zero. Five. Four. Nine. Six. Zero. Leave. Message.'

He blurted it out in a torrent. 'This is Barclay. For christ's sake, god all-bloody-mighty, Operation Overture is blown — do you understand? Dead in the water. Savich fucking talked, he's betrayed us — all of us, do you hear? The mission is dead. *Dead*. What with Paris – it's over. You must abort immediately. Six are on to me. I'm getting out. You won't hear from me again, this is my final communication.'

He forced a chewed thumb into the red dot to end the call, drew his arm back and hurled the phone as far as he could into a thicket of copper beech trees. Minutes later he was rejoining the M1 a little too fast and heading north to the rendezvous.

'Coach 14,' he said to the steward who was knocking on the door to the driver's cab, 'one of the first class compartments, the middle one with the curtain drawn.'

The glass door opened to a wide man with full moustache who was seated at the display panel. 'Manfred,' said the steward, 'this man is saying he is from British Intelligence.'

The Englishman didn't wait to be asked inside. 'We've reason to believe there's a terrorist on board this train.'

'What?'

'Do you have radio contact with Berlin?' He turned and drew the curtains to block the view of the cabin from the carriage.

'Yes, of course, but you better show some ID first.'

'Radio in and ask them to call to this number.' He scrawled across the bemused man's timetable in front of him. 'Ask to speak to Mr Sullivan in accounts. Someone will call them back and they'll verify who I am.' He turned back to the steward. 'I need your help, okay?'

The young man's eyes lit up. 'Yes, okay.'
The train was climbing. It entered a mountain tunnel and emerged out of the rock two minutes later at almost 250 km/h.

The steward let out a deep lungful of air and said a quick prayer. Remember the details, he told himself. After giving two polite knuckle taps on the glass he slid the door open. 'Drink sir? Or food? I have brought you the menu.'

The compartment was half in darkness, lit only by the snow-covered landscape through the window, and the man was alone. When he stepped inside the steward noticed the small LED displays above each seat were illuminated, indicating all had been reserved for the entirety of the journey. The passenger took the menu, keeping his eyes locked upon him, and there was something about them that was making the young man's bowels tremble. After what seemed like an eternity and still holding his gaze the passenger said, 'Nothing for me.'

Back in the driver's cab Henderson covered the

phone's handset with a palm. 'Well?'

'It's him,' the steward said as he entered, his heart still pounding. 'Seat 86.'

Thank Christ, he thought. 'You're sure.'

'Yes. Like the photograph, for sure I'm sure.'

'And the case?'

'I think so. Old style, brown I think. In the overhead rack but he was staring at me. Like he was suspecting me.'

Henderson took his hand away. 'We have a positive ID, sir. Yes, it's him all right and it looks like he has the bomb with him.'

The Germans' expressions dropped at the sound of the word.

'Yes, sir, Berlin. I'll need backup — a team of four should do. When they board tell them its Seat 86. He almost definitely saw me outside the bank so I'll keep out of sight with the driver for the duration. Yes, direct train due to arrive at 20:26. If he's planning to detonate at midnight like the others then he'll still have time to make his escape as the Bundestag is only a minute from central station. I believe so, sir, yes, I think it'll be as simple as that with this one — he's probably planning to leave the case in a station locker or in lost property.'

Inside Six, 'C' handed the receiver of the rotary telephone to a comms officer.

'Advise the BKA to co-ordinate with the German police and GSG 9 to evacuate and surround the hauptbahnhof immediately.'

'Understood, sir.'

'And get me the Home Secretary. And someone please find Stephen Jones-Cooper or must I do it myself.' The chief turned back to the old man's image on the screen.   'Eleven and a half hours. Come on you bastard . . . enough with the songs.'

At 15:30 in Moscow, instead of preparing for glory, General Grushenko was tight-lipped with anger as he replaced the receiver softly back into its cradle.

'Bad news?' enquired Volkov, who was staring at his back.

He turned in his swivel chair to face his overweight colleague across his desk. 'Yes.' His hand reached up to his desk drawer and without making a sound he pulled it open. 'I have just received word. Comrade Savich has suffered a switch in allegiance.'

'Then Defence Minister Sotnik must be informed at once. We must call an emergency meeting.'

He pushed the cartridge into his PB Makarov pistol and checked the safety was disengaged. It was. 'It is too late for that.'

'What? What are you saying?'

The PB was just a desk gun. It was old but it felt good to hold it again. 'The Paris device was discovered.'

Volkov leaned in. 'So. You lied to protect yourself. To cover up your own incompetence. And now you do not have the guts to admit your mistakes and inform the Defence Minister. You leave me no alternative but to do so.' He made movements that suggested he was going to stand to leave, although hoisting his massive frame from the creaking chair was no swift operation. Finally to his feet, he shook his head in disgust and turned around to go.

Grushenko raised the pistol and pointed it directly at the middle of the man's back. The tip of its integral silencer almost touched his uniform. 'Either victory or else a grave, Pavel.' he said, then pulled the trigger.

When the obese body had crashed to the floor he stood over it and put another bullet in his head for luck, then called his secretary on the intercom and told her to cancel his afternoon.

'Defence Minister Sotnik is requesting your presence immediately, General.' Came the reply.

'Tell him . . . tell him I can't be reached.'

'The name on the ticket credit card receipt is Gabriel Brunner, Swiss. Clean, of course, watertight.' Kesterton said, before 'C's distinctive voice came back on the line.

'Change of plan, John. Word from the FO is it seems the Germans, rather understandably, would prefer not to have a train carrying a nuclear bomb barrelling towards Berlin at 300 km/h, so we've had to have a rethink.'

'This is Dominic, Mister Henderson,' A younger voice, public school, affectless, sounded in John's ear. 'Dominic Mathieson? We're looking at options of interception now.'

Options of interception? For god's sake, who teaches these people to speak? This was someone whose theoretical expertise in operational tactics was being called upon but who Henderson knew better as one of Jones-Cooper's classroom spooks. 'What kind of *options of interception*, Mister Mathieson?' The sarcasm in his voice was uncontainable.

'One would be to put a man on board when the train stops at, say, Freiburg or Offenburg, who has with him some Ketamine you could put in a drink. Another is a man with a chemical weapon, or perhaps, as we understand he's in a compartment, chloroform with a high-pressure sprayer.'

Henderson covered the mouthpiece as the steward entered the cabin and said, 'He has just ordered some food. What do you want me to do?'

'Can you get me a first aid kit?' he whispered. Holding the phone up was causing the stabbing pain in his shoulder to come in waves.

The analyst was still talking. ' . . . looking into the feasibility of evacuating the train of passengers and diverting it into the mountains then having a special forces squad storm it from helicopters or getting a team aboard and forcing it to stop on a disused — '

'Let me stop you there,' he interrupted, thinking where are the bloody generals when you need them? 'This man is a top Russian agent. And he's armed, not only with a gun but with a nuclear weapon. If he suspects something, even for a moment, he could flick the switch in a second. Let alone if he sees fleeing passengers, helicopters with special forces units dangling on wires or men coming at him with fucking garden sprayers.'

The analytical team aside, no one in the command centre could help but smile.

Dominic Mathieson didn't see the funny side. 'Our edict is to attempt to divert you away from metropolitan areas, Mister Henderson.'

'We are approaching Basel.' The driver said as the blur of snow-veiled scenery sharpened to become graffitied sidings and a low stone wall and railings.

Henderson pinched his nose and thought hard. Dammit. The Germans wouldn't allow them near Berlin. His plan had been to see the journey out, watch the Russian but with no intervention until the GSG 9 grab him at the other end when he steps off the train. But now it was out of his hands and he knew if he didn't give them something that a rapid response force from Kommando Spezialkräfte would be sent in. Okay, then what? The drugging was an idea but it would need to be instant. Benzodiazepines in pill form, like Rohypnol. It was risky, but not as risky as an all out assault or diverting the train — the merest hint of either would alert Blake in no time.

A plan for someone to meet the train at Freiburg was agreed — if they could work that fast — a courier with a pill containing a highly concentrated sedative that should be secreted securely in a sandwich wrapper to make it appear like trash that he could pass to a steward on the platform. The steward would be young, tall with short blond hair, with a name badge that would identify him as Max, and he would be holding open a refuse sack. Henderson made a questioning gesture to the man behind him, who swallowed hard and nodded back fervently.

A few minutes later when the train was pulling away from Basel, Max tapped on the glass, slid it back with the curtain and entered holding a tray of food. 'Large leaf salad?' he said, laying it down on the table along with cutlery and a side dressing, before stepping back.

Russell Blake stayed silent, and regarded the food. When he looked up he caught the steward staring directly at the brown suitcase that rested in the overhead rack. The steward's eyes flicked back down quickly and a look of near panic crossed his face until he forced a tense smile.

'Anything else?'

The passenger left a long pause before he answered. 'No,' he said tersely.

Back at the bistro car a woman called Marion who was six months pregnant with her second child was wiping the counter when she saw her colleague return with flushed cheeks. 'Hey, Max, you okay? Something wrong?'

He thought he would act well under such conditions, but had underestimated the level of danger. 'Ya, I'm okay,' he replied, his breaths still short. Moments later when she wasn't looking he took a large mouthful of Riesling straight from the bottle before hurrying back to the driver's cab.

When he got there the Englishman was still on the phone and saying that Freiburg was fine, then he covered the mouthpiece and said, 'Fifteen minutes. You ready, Max?'

'What? No, I think he saw me looking at the case.'

'Okay, calm down,' he said, thinking hard. If Blake was onto him there's a chance he might alight at the next station. But Max would stand outside Coach 14 and could radio the driver if he did. The young man's nerves were jumping. He wasn't from his world. Henderson soothed his voice. 'Listen carefully, Max. Just wait by the train with the plastic sack and people will drop litter in. It couldn't be easier. Max? Are you listening to me?'

At 1:49 p.m. the voice over the intercom announced their arrival in Freiburg im Breisgau and the driver brought the train in alongside an unremarkable platform. Through the driver's curtain the MI6 man kept an eye on the corridor while from his seat Russell Blake was afforded an excellent vantage point of the platform. The steward who had taken a keen interest in his luggage waited outside his window with an open plastic bag for commuters to discard their rubbish into. No steward had done so at Basel, he noted, but more curious was why the man looked to be in such a state of heightened anxiety. Blake regarded him for a few minutes until a man in a motorbike jacket and with a helmet under one arm appeared from the darkness of the underground steps. He waited there, out-of-breath and holding something by his side, an empty sandwich wrapper, and appeared to be looking for someone. When his eyes fell on the man collecting litter he approached him, dropped the wrapper into the sack, turned and walked quickly away. To most people it wouldn't have looked unusual, but to the man watching from the train it was enough to sound an alarm bell in his head. Why had the motorcyclist skirted a litter bin to perform this act? It was an amateur, and obvious pass. He leaned back in his seat and thought about what he had just witnessed until something on the platform made him look out of the window again. This time it wasn't what he saw that alarmed him but what he heard. It was the sound of a child's voice. The boy was about five years old and was pulling his mother eagerly along the platform by the hand. When the child saw his father he shouted excitedly, 'Vater, vater, da unten sind soldaten. Im zug!'

'Papa, papa, there are soldiers down there. On the train!'

It was then that it hit him. Russell Blake knew then that his cover was blown. Feeling the wheels of the train begin to roll beneath him as it eased away from the platform, by instinct, he placed a flat palm on his chest over the holstered Beretta.

Henderson's radio crackled. He brought it to his ear and increased the volume. It was the FIS Watcher team who had boarded and found the frequency.

'Do you read me? Come in?' a hushed voice said. It belonged to a young black man wearing headphones who had joined the first class carriage and seated himself a few rows away from the compartments. He was one of four who now had the target surrounded along with a woman in her fifties with the air of a strict school headmistress, a businessman carrying a newspaper and coffee flask, and a tourist with an expensive camera around his neck, all with a discrete speaker in their ears and a clear view of the corridor.

Henderson was instructing them to stay put when the driver's door slid open.

'I can't do it,' Max said, pushing his way into the cabin. He could feel the sweat on his back, cold where his shirt was sticking to it.

'You're just serving a drink to a passenger, like you do every day.'

'Marion could do it?' offered the driver.

Max was aghast. 'What? No. What if he smells it or tastes it? He will kill her. She's, she's pregnant. With a baby.'

'Then you *have* to do it.' Henderson was firm.

The phone rang and the driver passed it over. 'John?' 'C's voice. 'You've got company.'

'Yes, they've made contact already. Their orders are to watch. We're serving complimentary drinks any time now.'

There was a pause. 'I'm afraid that's not all,

John. A six-man KSK team, special forces command, also boarded at Freiburg.'

His mind galloped. 'What?'

'Its been deemed the best way. The cleanest.'

In the Bistro car Max held the straw in his trembling fingers, stirring the whiskey until he'd counted to thirty. He held it up. All the powder had dissolved away. He wiped the glass as he'd been told to do, then gripped it firmly on the tray all the way back along the aisle until he reached the compartment door. He didn't notice the dancing curtain as he had shut his eyes to say another prayer. Then he knocked twice and slid the door back. The maelstrom hit him. The tray dropped out of his hands, he pulled them up to protect his eyes but with the window gone the blast from the outside had turned the interior of the compartment into a snowstorm blowing through a freezing wind tunnel.

If his fear had been attack from the lone passenger he needn't have worried. Save for a red emergency hammer lying discarded on the carpet, the compartment was empty.

The moment the door opened everyone in the two first class carriages felt the temperature drop as the winter rushed in. It was when Henderson saw the steward stumble out into the corridor that he pulled the gun from his belt and started to run. When he reached him he immediately went over to the open space where the window had been and pushed his head out into the freezing wind with hands shielding his eyes. He couldn't see a thing. He barged out and got to the window in the next compartment, and there on the snow-covered hillside in the distance was the tiny, but distinct, black figure. A man with a suitcase.

Without hesitating he reached up, clenched a fist around the emergency handle and pulled down on it hard. Three seconds later the train's wheels locked, sending a deafening screech through the carriage, coffee cups sliding and passengers and luggage tumbling uncontrollably forwards.

'Radio Berlin our position and call for backup,' he shouted at the steward. Then much to the young man's surprise John Henderson rushed back into the open compartment, climbed up onto the table, tucked his arms in tight by his side, crouched down with his knees pressed together, and jumped out of the open window.

When he hit the embankment his impact was deadened by the thick snow yet the train's speed forced him into an uncontrollable barrel roll along the heavily sloped bank that steered him careening back down towards the razor-like wheels. He spread his fingers and dug them claw-like into the bank in an attempt to slow himself. When he did slide to a stop he was lying face down only inches away from the shrieking rails. He stayed there on his stomach until the train had passed, then began to crawl up the steep bank. When he reached the top and was able to stand, though the snow was almost up to his knees, he caught his breath.

The train had snaked into the distance. The driver must have overridden the brake and continued on, perhaps to get as far away from a bomb as possible, probably under orders — either way, he was now alone in a freezing wilderness with no means of communication, badly bruised, and with an untreated bullet wound that was throbbing like all hell.

Above the tracks the view that opened out before him was uninterrupted. He was in a basin encircled by hills with two towering monoliths standing majestically in the long distance — yet between himself and the peaks was a panorama of forested slopes, valleys, and ridges that form the undulating and deadly snow fields of the Black Forest. Every dusted contour as far as the eye could see was like a shimmering white carpet. It was a degree or two below freezing, as silent as the grave, and blinding in the early afternoon sun, but the slow moving dot in the distance was unmistakable.

He buttoned up his suit jacket and began to walk towards it through the deep snow.

19

The phone line to the Command Centre went dead and ten frustrating minutes of silence passed until communication to the train was restored. When the driver did answer he relayed the news that both the terrorist and the British agent had left the train somewhere in the mountains. There was a mixture of both alarm and guilt in his voice, yet, 'C' noted, the man had the grace to admit he had received orders to continue on with the journey.

The news was met with deathly silence. Finally, standing next to 'C', the country's second most senior government official responsible for counter terrorism spoke for them all when he said, 'God help us.'

At 3 p.m., to the drone of police helicopters that patrolled the skies above, with parliament and much of Whitehall now evacuated, senior members of the Ministry of Defence were invited to begin making their way down to the tunnel that connects the building to the Pindar military bunker. In the event of nuclear war it is from here a full cabinet may not only survive an attack, but communicate with military commanders, thus enabling government to be maintained and authority to prevail. On the kerbside outside 10 Downing Street the Prime Minister's car waited expectantly, yet there was no need for it. Pindar is also accessible by a tunnel from this building, and the nation's premier was already 100 feet below ground in front of his maps in preparation for retaliation, although the advice he was receiving as to whom it should be directed was, to his mind and those of his top aides, still sketchy.

Between 3.30 p.m. and 3.50 p.m. three private jets took off from RAF Brize Norton in Oxfordshire. In the small hours the Prime Minister had given his Home Secretary, on behalf of an executive arm of the Cabinet Office known as the Civil Contingencies Secretariat, the green light to implement Operation Candid, a cold-war era contingency plan to evacuate the Royal Family to safety in a time of emergency. The jets were flying due North-Northwest, to where HDMY Dannebrog, the royal yacht belonging to the Danish Royal Family, was hiding in the lochs of northwest Scotland, closely guarded by a nearby Royal Navy warship.

Inside Scotland Yard at 4 p.m. both Police Chief Inspector Darlington and Mike Hewitt received their hourly updates, and the man seconded from MI5 phoned through his own hourly progress report to Sir David at Thames House. They'd had more sightings, he stated: one late at night on the last day of October near Greenwich Park, the other two days later where multiple cameras had recorded Blake's movement at Oxford Circus tube station. On neither occasion was the target carrying a suitcase. The head of MI5 recommended the immediate thorough searches of both locations, Hewitt told him he'd already ordered it.

From his office on the 21st floor that overlooks Yasenevo, Kovalevsky stared down at the telephone before picking it up. Barclay, their top agent in

London, had called in on the emergency line to report that the Paris device had been discovered after all, meaning Grushenko had lied to him. That, along with the fact that Igor Savich had handed himself in to the British and confessed — to how much and in god's name why he couldn't guess — left him with no alternative but to conclude that the operation was dead.

When his home phone rang, Defence Minister Sotnik turned the television's volume down and answered it himself. The voice on the other end was solemn, and he knew the deputy director of the SVR, once an officer of the First Chief Directorate of the KGB, would not adopt such a tone if the news was anything but dire. He was correct. While Kovalevsky spoke of lies and betrayal at the highest level, Sotnik's screen showed scenes of police helicopters swarming over London, and it now became clear why Paris was not being subjected to the same level of high alert.

When Kovalevsky replaced the receiver he walked over to his window and looked out across the forest that surrounded him. 'Barclay,' he said in despair to the misted glass. Not since Philby had they penetrated so deeply into MI6, and the disaster of it was they would probably never have an agent in such a high position again. Still, he thought to himself as he walked back to the desk and picked up the phone, desertion is desertion. 'Roza, get me Major General Viktor Kuznetsov, commander of Unit 29155,' he said.

He stopped to catch his breath and bent over with palms resting on his knees. He had been going for almost two hours, and in the thin air it was exhausting. The slope was getting steeper, the fresh powder still deep. With each dogged step towards his target a kilometre ahead in the distance, the cold gripped him like a vice and the throb in his shoulder was distracting. Breathing slowed enough, he looked up. Was he gaining on the Russian? Only marginally. Time to move.

The case was getting heavier with each minute, so Blake was glad when he reached the crest. Without stopping he turned to look back. The man was gaining all right, but now the terrain ahead flattened out. He heaved the case into his other hand and pressed forward, breaking into a jog. Water splashed at his feet. A long cracking noise began to accompany the crunch of his shoes as they pounded the thin layer of ice, and with every step he could see rapid water ever more clearly swirling beneath it. A deep crack formed, he stepped widely to avoid it and landed hard, which caused another, the path ahead separated, forcing him to jump sharply to his right like he was navigating stepping stones across a river.

Reaching the crest Henderson saw the Russian had made ground so too increased his pace. The next instant he felt his right foot slide away from him and he was over, balance lost and body slamming into the unforgiving surface like a dead weight. The ground shifted, the sheet of ice broke away and with it his right leg as it plunged into the freezing water and began to pull him under.

Blake turned back. 'Blyad,' he exclaimed, surprised to see the man down — one leg under and clawing frantically at the edge in a desperate attempt to stop being dragged down further. He was probably out of range, but it was worth a try. Blake raised his 9 mm, stepped forward, aimed more precisely, and fired twice.

The cracks rang out and the bullets flew close past his eyes, penetrating the wet ice and narrowly missing his submerged, kicking thigh. He looked up. The bastard was still aiming.

Blake steadied the gun with both hands, closed one eye and fixed the struggling man in his sights. With a twitch of the finger he released a bullet from the chamber.

He was being dragged slowly backwards on his jaw when the bullet exploded in the ice, missing by inches his already injured shoulder. Christ almighty, he was a sitting duck, he thought, more like a floundering seal. There was nothing to hold onto, and with another fragile crack his other leg plunged into the freezing water. In up to his waist with torso about to follow, he reached out and tried to dig his fingers in deeper. He could see the Russian lower the gun and turn. He was out of range to be accurate at least. It was now or never. Forcing his right arm out in front of him followed by the left, he kicked both legs down with every ounce of strength he had while heaving himself forward. With fingers dug into the ice like crampons he pulled himself forward enough to hoist himself up onto his forearms. Luckily the ice beneath them held, and, one knee at a time, he managed to pull his lower body free of the grabbing water. Once out, he lay on his back in the centre of the gelid landscape, flanked by two glimmering hills, one brushed by evening's first shades of pink and the westernmost a cobalt blue, and with heart thumping, it struck Henderson that he had never been so glad to feel the burn of the sun on his face.

At the lake's edge a wide valley opened up. It wasn't so

deep underfoot now and with a gentle descent Blake found he could move faster, even with the cumbersome case, which he did for a half an hour until he paused to rest. He checked the time. It was six minutes past six. Around him the reflection in the snow crystals was gradually dimming, and the only sound was his breathing. There was now no sign of his pursuer, no whir of police helicopters, just this soundless, icy wilderness. He didn't know where he was, where the closest town was where he could maybe steal a car, or if there'd be a reception committee waiting if he did find civilisation. No, one lone pursuer with no radio contact out here was preferable to a village where the man could use a telephone or find a police station to mobilise an army of backup. It was better to keep going, and the more remote the better. He would lose him. Or the man behind him would expire first. He, Valentin Baskov, was the stronger.

The Russian was lucky. When the sun finally became eclipsed behind the tallest of the peaks thirty minutes later, it cast a giant shadow in the valley that left only a small smile of light glowing in the distance. Closer in, he found it belonged to a domed brick building that was nestled into a narrower valley. Strands from its roof disappeared up into the clouds, making it look like a cardboard model suspended on wires, until, having made more ground, Blake smiled to himself when he saw what it was. The station for a gondola lift.

When the figure appeared from the slopes dressed only in a dark suit and carrying a battered suitcase no one was there to witness it. A single 4x4 was parked outside the building that for a moment he considered stealing, yet elected instead to open its bonnet and cut the plug lead with his Kizlyar Korshun tactical knife. He inspected the dome's exterior until he found the telephone junction box and applied the same disability to the wires within, then went inside, paid 12 Euros at the desk, and caught the next gondola up to the mountain.

Twelve minutes later the elderly man in the booth whose car would mysteriously fail to start in an hour's time could hardly believe his eyes when a second man dressed only in a business suit burst in. This one looked worse though, half-mad, like he'd been shot out of a aeroplane and had then hiked crossed the alps. His eyes were wild when he demanded to know if he'd seen the first man.

The elderly German threw his hands up, 'Ya, ya, he was here,' he replied from behind small oval spectacles that gave him the bearing of an old watchmaker, 'suitcase, ya. He took the gondola to the mountain. He was like you — '

'Your phone, give it to me.'
The man presented a heavy telephone with thick cord through the hatch. Dead. Of course.

'How long ago?'
Checking the wall clock behind him the old man shrugged. 'Twenty minutes?'

'How long to the mountain?'
'The same. Twenty minutes.'

There goes thoughts of halting the cars and suspending him in mid-air. 'I think I know the answer but do you have a mobile phone?'

The station master laughed. 'What would I do with such a thing? The operator has one, but he is saying there is no signal since Thursday.'

Henderson hadn't waited. He'd left the counter and was running past the stairwell towards the doors to the boarding area.

'You are crazy, both you and your friend,' the old man shouted after him. 'It is over four thousand feet up there, in these clothes you will freeze to death.'

To the clangour of empty gondolas as they whirred in and out of the terminal and the noisy clatter of the overhead chains that accompanied them, Henderson barged into the central control booth and demanded to know if the operator could increase the speed. When this was met with a flat refusal, he had no choice but to wait patiently for the next approaching cabin, then for its aluminium door to open, then when he'd entered, for the infernal device to circle around the tin shed at a snail's pace until it launched him gently out into the night and up towards the highest peak in Germany.

The old man's sense of time had been blunted by age, for further into the clouds, while Henderson was beginning his slow arial ascent, Blake was only twelve minutes ahead and attempting to survey the topography from his own gondola as it crept up the mountain. The monochrome of black trees in white snow below prevented any precise mapping until, with each supporting tower that passed, the car's higher elevation allowed him to determine his approach to the summit was from the west. A long, straight line of trees arrowed downwards on the crest of a ridge forty-five degrees to the east, which the slope beyond joined to form a valley at the foot of the steep gradient of the main face. As his gondola neared the upper station it was clear that at least a kilometre of thick forest surrounded the summit, and that from it, the slopes of the main face plummeted dramatically through those thick pines. What was beyond that was invisible to him and was anyone's guess.

If he'd wanted remote, he'd got it.

He opened the suitcase on the bench seat and looked over the bomb's components. It would explode at midnight tonight as planned, he told himself in the cold of the cabin. Not in the Bundestag, nor anywhere close, but explode it would and along with the detonation of the London bomb that meant he would have followed orders. He knew somebody had betrayed him, traded or sold his identity that had led the British to Paris, to Zürich. Events that had been out of his control. The reaction from the old man in the museum when he'd told him about Paris was evidence enough that there'd been a break in the chain of command, and it maddened him. He slammed a sideways fist into the cabin's metal door. *He* was a professional, *he* wouldn't fail. He shouted a two-second-long 'fuck' at the window and spat on the floor at the thought they considered him expendable. That there were others like him ready to die for mother Russia. But they were wrong, he said to himself. There was *no one* like Valentin Gregorievich Baskov.

When the gondola had docked in the upper station and he had incapacitated the telephone box on its rear wall, he stood at the edge of the forested mountainside. At 4,213 feet above sea level he could feel every muscle in his body tighten in an attempt to protect their vital organs. But he ignored the cold. The fury had subsided, yet his will remained iron. The priority now was to find a vantage point from which to put a bullet in the man who would be arriving any minute — and to finish this once and for all.

The telephones were dead, of course. As they had been at the base station. When he exited the similarly domed upper station he was struck by the blackness of the mountain that fell away beyond, hidden by thick trees that soon dissolved into total darkness and lit only by pallid ribbons of purple sky. And the silence. Other than the rhythmic echoing of the whirring chains and motors from inside the gondola station, there wasn't a sound. But of course, Henderson knew he wasn't alone. There were fresh footprints, and they were leading only one way: down.

The slope was steep, so with gun in hand he began to climb gingerly down as inaudibly as possible, using each tree to slow his momentum and being careful to avoid cracking branches that would betray him. It was a definite pass, but narrow, and he couldn't see further than twenty feet into the distance. After almost fifteen minutes the footprints stopped. He ducked down fast, shielding behind a tree. He knew it would come, and when it did the bullet exploded an inch from his cheek, ripping the tree bark back with a violent snap.

Blake was lying in the snipers' prone position using the case for stability. Feet flat in the snow, with breathing slowed, he squeezed the trigger again.

Henderson didn't wait for this one. As the bullet left the Beretta's barrel he sprang forward and reached for the tree below, using it to swing around and bury himself behind it for cover.

'Baskov,' he shouted, the sound deadened by the timberland. There was no answer. 'Give it up. The operation's dead in the water. Savich talked.'

The voice was closer. The man had moved position and was now hidden, and now Blake was facing the wrong way. He raised himself very slowly into the kneeling position and swivelled around in an attempt to see.

'You hear me?' Another minute went by. 'Vy menya slyshite, Valentin?'

Immediately the Russian let off two rounds in the direction of the voice.

The shots were wide, but Henderson saw the muzzle flash from the first so fired two back and heard his second ricochet off a tree. No return fire. He kept still and counted. Blake had four remaining bullets: one for the cop, seven for him, but probably at least one spare magazine. He let five more minutes pass before he moved again, clambering down, one tree at a time, each rustling and showering him with silent snow from its branches.

When he found the hole in the tree caused by his own bullet there was, alas, no body, nor blood, only four spent shell casings in the snow. He moved on, quicker now, almost falling from tree to tree, the snow deep and the whistling mountainside wind bitter.

It was three quarters of an hour before he started to catch sight of the Russian below. He was gaining ground. The suitcase would be heavy and cumbersome and in a few minutes he reckoned he'd be close enough to have a clear shot, even though he was rarely called on to fire a gun and was certainly no expert marksman, especially at a moving target.

Out of the terrain vertical drops began to emerge of three feet, five feet, and as Henderson slid down one even deeper step, suddenly from behind a skier raced at him out of the blackness at high speed.

He was crouched in flight and jumped clean over him, coming to land in front with bent knees and carving off expertly into the dark haze below.

'Christ alive,' he said out loud, 'it's a ski run. Who the f — ' but he hadn't finished the expletive when he felt skis slam onto his shoulder blades, the force of which sent him lurching forward and landing on his stomach. Sliding, he looked up at the man's back, who had somehow managed to stay upright, and, clad all in black, was yelling 'Bewegung!' At once, another one appeared out of the black trees above and flew at him, Henderson held up his arms for protection, but a metal-edged ski tore deep into his right sleeve and drew blood as the man whizzed past.

Further down the mountainside, with less than a second to decide, the first skier aimed at a small gap between Blake and a tree but it was too tight. He barged into him, knocking the case from his grip. 'Scheisse! Runter von der fucking piste!' the skier shouted as he shot away and disappeared into the unlit forest beneath them.

Blake lunged for the case but lost his footing and both he and it began falling uncontrollably, with him sliding on his back and the suitcase bouncing from tree to tree like a spinning pinball. From above, Henderson fired into the twitching trees. The bullet landed close enough to launch splinters at the Russian's face just as the second skier came at him already screaming, but unable to get out of the man's path Blake too felt a ski slice across his shoulder with the ferocity of a flying sword.

Every few seconds now skiers came shooting out of the blackness only a few feet above him with no warning and with the speed and ferocity of frozen spears. A brief pause, Henderson made to move, but without even momentary notice to duck came another. A head torched flashed, too close! Henderson sprang right but it was fruitless. Already upon him and only inches off the ground, the skier, a huge man, hit him with full force, sending them both barrelling forwards.

The case had gone. Blake managed to grab a tree, which wrenched him to a sudden stop. He turned his head and looked up, and as if delivered by God, his pursuer appeared on the ridge above, tumbling and sliding uncontrollably towards him in a tangled mess of limbs, skis and poles with a felled skier. Blake saw his chance, drew his Beretta and fired.

The bullet exploded into the ridge as yet another man shot out from the darkness above them, lithe and slender, skilfully slalom-jumping both falling bodies and hurtling past the gunman. Henderson slammed into a tree and felt ribs crack, but found the cover that probably saved his life. Fast, he pulled out the Luger, returned fire, narrowly missing.

His pursuer was too close. Blake let go of his tree again and slid fast. Again he was dropping down the slope on his back with no control when another bullet whizzed past his head. He spotted the case that had become lodged, managed to slow himself by digging his elbows into the snow enough to snatch a hold of the handle as he passed it. Henderson let go of his tree and just managed to duck as another skier came out of nowhere, soared over his head and seconds later struck Blake with such force that the man's skis were wrenched from his boots as he was flung high into the air like a rag doll. Before he could land Blake shot him in the side, causing the man's flying body to twist in mid air before hitting a tree backwards.

Henderson was closing, but speed and the danger of colliding with the trees made it difficult to place an accurate shot. When yet another skier had flashed past dangerously close to Henderson's head, Blake, still sliding fast but hearing the protests above him, reached back, and with face contorted in anger shot the man in the chest the instant he appeared as if he was a swivelling card on a shooting range. The pass was steepening. All he could do was let gravity pull him downwards through the powder. His pace was increasing, while all the time his frozen fingers gripped the handle of the suitcase dragging behind him.

The dangerous trees were thinning out into haphazard clumps and the pass widened, allowing three more skiers to carve easily around Blake. Behind their masks and goggles they may have been traumatised by the sight of dead fellow-sportsmen, but no doubt fearful that the wild-eyed men in suits brandishing guns were to blame. It was clumsy, Blake had little control, while further back where it was still narrow Henderson was stumbling, still able to use the pine trunks for support but hampered by a bleeding arm and the pain of the shoulder wound that was engulfing his whole right side. Also, again, he had lost sight of Blake. He was thinking about launching himself down the mountain in the same way as his quarry when seemingly out of nowhere the silent skier struck him. The impact knocked him instantly forwards like a domino and sent his head into the base of a tree.

The skier dug his pole in deep as he landed and was able to regain control, leaving the man he had struck unconscious.

Blake was now falling uncontrollably, unable to slow his speed and blind to what lay ahead. He felt two sharp bumps beneath him, lost his grip on the case, then the ground beneath vanished. What followed was a sensation he had never felt before. He knew he had gone off the edge of a precipice and was plummeting like a stone back towards the hard ice. He also knew that because the thought had lasted this long, that it was a very long way down.

'Believe me, Sir David, I've got every police officer in London and more working flat out.' Hewitt assured MI5's Director General at 9:32 p.m. as he marched past the operations rooms crowded with policemen and women whose exhausted faces were glued to black and white monitors.

'Greenwich park was a fuck-up,' came the bewailing voice in his ear. 'A waste of valuable time and a bloody waste of manpower and resources that when all this is done with I hold you responsible for. No more wild goose chases, you hear? You've got two and a half hours, man, just give the Met what you've *got*, do you understand?'

The updates were now bi-hourly. Hewitt had taken plenty of abuse from CO's before, but this newly minted knight in his gold cufflinks was irritating him. People react under pressure in different ways, as an ex-soldier he knew that only too well, but Hall had none of the military discipline, which made it hard for him to respect him. But Hewitt was determined to help stop this bomber. He knew what pain and suffering the death of one man can bring. The terrible afternoon when a Taliban mortar landed inside 3 Para's compound was a day he would never forget.

The death of tens of thousands from a nuclear attack was inconceivable to him. The suit was still barking orders at him in his cut glass accent when Hewitt cut him off.

'If you can keep your head,' he breathed to himself as he crashed back down in his chair and hit the spacebar to resume the CCTV video at his laptop. He kept the Kipling poem folded in his wallet at all times. 'You'll be a better man than Sir David fucking Hall my son.'

While 'C' and the brass of the U.K's foreign intelligence agency were watching the live stream from Geneva airport inside the basement Command Centre, on the fifth floor of Vauxhall Cross, Nasha had taken to replaying segments she'd tagged for further review.

'Here, stop,' she ordered a colleague, 'play from there.'

The image of Igor Savich stopped speeding backwards and froze.

'This is from 14:47 this afternoon,' said her assistant as the image began moving to the click of her mouse. The old man was still delirious, yet out of the quagmire of nonsense he was spewing they hoped they could mine the narrowest vein for even a drop of truth.

'Sea sick. Sea sick. Sea sick,' he was repeating over as the Data Analysts watched with blank stares. 'Sea sick, sea sick, sea sick, sea sick . . . ' like he was chanting in rhythm, the head still swinging from side to side like his neck muscles has collapsed.

Nasha bit her lip. 'What does this mean? Is the drug making him feel sea sick? But why *sea* sick? It just doesn't make any sense.'

'Could be the Thames?' ventured the colleague. 'Should we check recent moorings? HMS Belfast?'

'I dunno. Let's go back to the songs again to see if we've missed anything.'

At 9:55 p.m. the small, round figure of the man known inside Russian Intelligence as Barclay paced the asphalt next to a small runway as he waited for the navigation lights from a Cessna aircraft to pierce the leaden clouds. The anxiety he felt was still gut-wrenching — evidenced by two interruptions to the seven hour car journey to pull over and vomit on the hard shoulder. But the journey ended here, both his life as an Englishman and his tenure as Russia's most important, and expensive, agent in fifty years: at a private airfield in a corner of North West England. England, the country of his birth, the place he had always lived, yet the land he had been betraying at the very highest level for ten years from within both the private, corporate world then later from inside her prized foreign intelligence service. But if England had made Stephen Jones-Cooper, it could not repair him, nor would get the chance, for tonight, with virgin passport in inside pocket and €10,000,000 in global bonds waiting in Copenhagen, he would bid a spiteful farewell to all he had ever known and be flown east by someone he had been assured was beyond the vengeful reach of even the SVR.

It was like they had never seen one before, yet for a brief moment when the little girl let the string slip from her fingers and the red balloon floated above the crowd it seemed to capture everyone's attention. It rose quickly above the warm lights of the resort into the night sky, through the cable car lines and then further into the mouth of the mountain peaks, but by then only its bereft owner was still watching. Those gathered in the village had turned their attention back to their beer steins, their gluhwein, hot Kielbasa sausage and pork schnitzel that women in traditional dress served them, and to their jubilant festivities in the carnival atmosphere. Around an outdoor ice rink locals proudly proclaimed as being the largest in the mountain range, many more skated, holding hands and gliding to the traditional waltzes being piped through the tannoy speakers. Near the pretty resort's old church, gathering at the top of the diagonal ramp, was a large contingent of Germany's Federal Police, their livered Range Rovers lining the only access road. They were fifty strong, and were being instructed to group in a circle around a superior.

'Come in, closer. All of you. This man is armed and extremely dangerous,' the officer stated as he handed out the Red Notice bearing Russell Blake's mugshot and description. 'Our orders are to call for backup, and only then to apprehend. He may be carrying a suitcase — if he tries to open it your orders are to shoot to kill, understand? The suitcase must not be touched under any circumstance.'

While the policemen and women dispersed into the animated crowd, body armour over their uniforms and P30 semi-automatics at their side, the man they sought was closer than they knew, having been buried alive a mere two thousand feet above their heads.

It could have been in a training manual, he couldn't remember, but he had read somewhere that if you get hit by an avalanche or buried alive by deep snow you should curl up in a ball to avoid rescuers pulling you star-shaped from your icy grave. Upon impact Blake had done just that. Unable to breathe but able to move his arms, albeit only an inch at a time, he began ramming his fists back and forth into the roof of snow above him, again, and again, and again until he could fully extend his arms and he had punctured the thick ceiling that allowed the sweet mountain air to rush in. Sucking at it greedily, he continued punching until a section fell in on him, then more until he was able to climb out, gasping but alive. He lay perfectly still on the ice. For a few minutes he didn't know why he was there or where there even was. An unknown period of time passed until gradually oxygen returned to his brain, flowing into it like music. But slowly he realised it *was* music he could hear. When he found the strength to climb to his feet he brushed the snow from himself, and approached the edge of the ridge and leaned over. Below, in the foot of a deep valley was an alpine village, whose lights in the darkness made it look like a shimmering jewel set into the distance. The distinctive rhythm of a waltz reechoed up through the mountains, and a yellow gondola glided away from the village on long cables that disappeared away to his right. He made his way further along the ridge. Beneath him was a docking station, unmanned but with a line of eight black-clad skiers with skis held upright at their shoulders as they awaited the next gondola.

His Beretta had been lost in the fall, yet a few minutes' search yielded the hole the case had made on impact, and he managed easily to dig it out with his hands. Carrying it, he began to make his way down the slope in the direction of the station.

One by one in fearful silence they stepped back when they saw him approach. The next cable car was only minutes away, but each skier had witnessed the bodies on the descent and could sense this man who walked towards them with the battered suitcase in one hand and gun in the other, half-frozen in blood-stained clothes and with the dangerous, desperate look of a killer, had to have something to do with the violence. When he reached them no one spoke, and when the gondola finally docked and the doors opened, to a man they were content to wait another twenty minutes for the next car.

When it pulled up and settled, Blake stepped inside and turned around to face the frightened line of skiers as he waited for the aluminium doors to make the first hiss to close. A sound made their heads turn at once, which made him snap his head up the right to see the man who'd been chasing him running at the car.

20

A gasping Henderson slammed his palms on the doors just as they snapped shut. The man inside didn't flinch. Only stared back at him with glassy, emotionless eyes that remained fused together with his own until the car jolted once, swung on its cable, and was pulled away.

The mountains of the Lake District that forced the westerly Atlantic winds to rise made the rain that fell on the airfield relentless. The pilot was late — he would tear into him. Then again, he thought, maybe I'll let him land me in Denmark first. But Jesus, a mercenary pilot being paid £40,000 for a four hour flight, you'd think he'd be on time. He looked at his watch again. 10:30. *Come on*, he growled into the rain. He'd cut it too fine, should have left yesterday. If the bastard doesn't get here soon, the fallout . . . , he paused, how far *would* the fallout from the bomb reach. Scotland? He didn't know. All he knew was the whole bloody British Isles could be obliterated for all he cared. He supposed he could drive further north and get on a boat over the North Sea to – The sound of a Cessna's engine above the thrum of the rain interrupted the thought.

The rotating red beacon tail light became visible, and grew as the plane descended through the thick layer of clouds, flew by once, then made a banked turn and landed against the weather a hundred metres from where he stood. When he reached it the rear cargo door swung open and a wide-skulled man with a face like pounded meat knelt in the opening. He was using both hands to grip a Gsh-18 9 mm handgun.

Jones-Cooper's jaw dropped. He stepped back, gulping in short breaths with thick droplets falling down his face.

The man regarded him blankly from beneath heavy eyelids, and for reasons unknown he let the sodden man turn and run. Maybe he sought more sport, for when he climbed out of the door and stood on the tarmac he knew he would incur a soaking from the good old English rain on his bald head — yet it didn't bother him. The man could barely run, the shot would be too easy. When he fired it, the target fell flat onto his front, but a few seconds later one of his arms twitched so the assassin had to walk over to where he lay to put another slug in the head.

The man from Unit 29155 had obeyed his orders.

At the same time the light aircraft took off, the yellow cable car was descending towards the lights of the alpine resort. Its only occupant stared stoically at his throbbing fingers, the ends of which were plum red and had begun to blister. Also, he noticed his body had stopped shivering which, although he couldn't remember how he knew, he suspected was a warning sign. *Think.* He clenched his right hand into a fist and slammed it hard into his left arm, over and over to try to focus his brain. *The bomb.* He knelt down, unlatched the case and lifted the lid. *The key.* He fished it out of a pocket and inserted it into the lock, then, without pausing, twisted it. The timer sprang to life, its LED zeros in a line. He would leave the key inserted, then the bomb would be primed, ready, meaning a simple press of the red arming trigger would detonate it immediately. *But why wasn't he shaking. What* - The gondola docked. The doors opened. There was a delay to his actions. It took him a few seconds to regather his thoughts, and it was only after he had stepped out and the cold air hit him that he was dragged back into the present.

That, and the sight of so many people in one place, quickly triggered his mind into surveying his surroundings. It was like a carnival. The crowd was thick and vibrant, a cacophony of noise, music and voices from the horde of high-spirited revellers, children with balloons, and jostled waitresses with trays of pretzels and overflowing beer steins. Beyond, he could see there was a line of police 4x4's on the ramp, meaning the place would be overrun with armed Federal officers. Studying the people, he was able to pick out the odd flash of a patented peak cap, a fleeting glimpse of thick body armour over a uniform, and the glint of a holstered firearm, signs that the police had infested the jubilant crowd.

It was twenty to midnight, and at the same time as his pursuer's cable car left the upper station, Russell Blake, with a tight hold of his deadly luggage, stepped into the throng. He shuffled his way through the backs and moving elbows, avoiding eye contact until he reached the ice rink where skaters fifteen deep held hands as they glided around in time to the tinny waltz. A heavy coat lay folded over the barrier, he removed it and put in on, zipping it up to his chin and pulling up the hood. Two police officers approached, he changed direction and pushed back through the crowd, the large case hitting people's knees as it swung behind.

He stopped to look over towards the road. At the base of the ramp parked beneath overhanging rock he could see a ski bus. People were loading equipment onto the roof and climbing into the side door. He moved through the crowd until he reached the road, crossed it and joined the queue of those about to board.

He was six away from boarding the minibus when a police car crawled up and stopped. Two officers got out and approached those at the front of the line, asking to see papers. Slowly, Blake turned to shield the case with his body as he slipped back and away from the line, and with no choice, again back into the crowd.

Trying to keep his face covered he searched for a route out until a police officer stepped out holding a small torch in his rolled fist, and demanding 'Ausweispapiere.' When he turned he saw the command was being directed at a man holding a rucksack some way away, not to him. But there were police everywhere, suspicion and recognition on every face, torches in every hand illuminating proffered ID cards while every other hand rested on holsters ready to kill on sight. A waitress with yellowed teeth beckoned a glass which he snatched and drank in one gulp. Gluhwein, it was too hot and bitter but he realised his body badly craved liquid. A bearded face, a policeman with head tilted in scrutiny, made him swerve to his left and duck down.

Some time later he found himself behind a wooden hut. The case was at his feet and two policemen were inches from his face asking to see identity papers.

The cop noticed his badly swollen and blistered fingers. 'Danish?' he demanded, unfolding the stiff burgundy passport.

The second cop was eyeing him strangely, and his hand was moving towards his holster clip. Before it reached it, the passport's bearer had slashed both officials' throats with two rapid movements. In perfect sync their knees gave way, and they slumped to the ground.

John Henderson was staring through the window of the slowly descending gondola willing the thing to move faster. Unlike his quarry, he was still shivering. Despite having been donated a goose-down jacket by one of the terrified skiers his suit felt like it was fused to his skin with ice. But it was ten minutes to midnight and the car was only half way down, so any thought of his own health or comfort was a long way from his mind. Without a thought for his vertigo he tried to make out details below. Could the tiny rectangles he could see be the roofs of police cars? Had they captured him? Arrested him? He asked himself. Had the Germans received the train's co-ordinates and swarmed the nearest villages with armed officers? Or in ten minutes would there be a giant explosion followed by a pluming mushroom cloud.

The hut was in almost total darkness, but at one end a glint of light reflected off the nosecones of a matching pair of light blue snowmobiles. He peered out through the gap in the wooden slats and watched another police Range Rover circle the resort like a prowling lion, then, turning back to the machines, wondered how far he would get back out into the mountains on one of them. His attention then turned to the two blood-soaked policemen slumped in the corner.

Finally, at midnight Central European Time while still eleven p.m. GMT, at the exact time the bomb was supposed to explode in Berlin, and after the longest twenty minutes he'd ever known, Henderson pulled at the doors of the cable car to prize them open, pushed through the gap, and ran directly into the steaming crowd.

The door to the wooden hut opened and a man in a police uniform carrying a suitcase stepped out. He paused briefly to pull his cap low over his face, then walked away.

Eyes darting left to right, Henderson grappled through them, roughly pulling back shoulders to look at faces. How far could a man have gone from here in twenty minutes? He was asking as he forced his way through the bodies. It looked like the road was blocked, so unless Baskov had caught the next gondola back up the mountain, which was a possibility he didn't want to face, he'd be here. A tray of hot wine was thrust at him, which he dodged.

Blake pulled twice at the Range Rover's door handle. It was the third he'd tried on the ramp that led to the only road out of the resort, but it too was locked. Out of nowhere he felt a presence behind him.

'Hey, was machst du?'

He turned to find a policeman. A young, confused face above a slender, almost feminine frame.

'I found this case,' he replied in German while glancing down at the suitcase, 'I was going to radio it in.'

'Why not use your own radio?' asked the man, moving closer.

Without hesitating Blake plunged his knife into the young man's stomach then immediately hugged him like an old friend, which forced the blade in deeper and stopped the man's arms from waving and drawing attention. When the head slumped upon his shoulder, without checking around him, Blake lowered the body to the ground and dragged it around to the other side of the car. He took in a breath, as though he'd forgotten to inhale for too long. Things were becoming less clear. The delays were worsening. His breathing was shallow, fitful, and he couldn't feel his fingers. Nowhere to run, he kept saying in his head. Nowhere. Once back into the swaying waves of people the music became louder, voices more uproarious, and he found himself being slammed and shoved by elbows swinging beer glasses that belonged to distorted faces, their teeth bared in drunken song. Blake wiped his eyes, and when he opened them again the scene had changed. A waitress holding a tray of glasses high bumps his shoulder hard. Beer is dripping in streams over the heads below like a waterfall. He grabs a glass of gluhwein from the tray and throws it onto the ground, smashing it to try to snap himself out of it. Hypothermia, he knows it is, or Hypoxia, lack of oxygen from almost suffocating. It is what is disorienting him. It will pass.

In the centre of the sea of people, John Henderson stood perfectly still. He was oblivious to the cold, the exhaustion, the thirst and hunger he felt, and instead was entirely focused on the policeman holding a suitcase ten feet away who was moving unevenly towards him.

Though heavily dazed, the Russian's eyes were swerving left and right for an escape as he pushed his way forward. And then he stopped. The man was staring directly at him. His pursuer. Like a frozen ghost but with eyes aflame. Seconds passed as they waited for the next move. A figure swiped in front of them, Blake turned back and charged into the crowd with the ferocity of a bull.

Henderson bolted towards him. People jeered and shouted as they were barged out of the way by both men in a flurry of sudden violence. But Blake was fast, and Henderson lost sight as a group of men stomped out in front of him, clapping and striking the soles of their shoes in a Schuhplattler. He spun around, feverishly searching above the heads.

Two police officers, one using the radio, were kneeling at a Range Rover. They've found the body, Blake told himself, panting. He was trapped. Was the road blocked? He'd checked already, or had he? He swung around clumsily. The case struck a waitress hard on the thigh, sending her full tray of steins crashing to the ground and causing an uproar from those nearby — both the soaked angry and amused. His bearings were shot, senses altered. Turning was putting him off balance. He squeezed his eyes shut tightly, and he is in the centre of a high maze, pleading. Pulling with broken hands and lacerated tendons at the solid iron bars of a cage. A policeman stepped in and thrust a giant palm onto his chest. 'Ausweispapiere!' the cavernous mouth is barking through a thick beard while a rising arm brings a radio close up to it. But before the device has reached the shoulder he feels his finger pull the trigger and he shoots him at point blank range in the chest.

The crack of gunfire caused screams as people in the centre ducked and scattered. Henderson turned to the source of the noise, then began frantically pulling people out of his path to get to it.

Blinking rapidly, Blake quickly backed away, allowing the gun to swing freely at his side. He was struggling again against the barrage of noise and music and drunken shouting, pushing through the bodies with his weakened limbs while his mind was spinning in a kaleidoscope of streaming images that flashed indiscriminately before his eyes: an injection into his arm, poisoned Nagasaki children wailing in pain, a dribbling waiter, an inferno ripping through an auction room. But he is buckling. A giant pretzel looms up to another roar of laughter. Ceaseless robotic numbers, *FIVE. EIGHT. NINE* . . . Mondrian. Disjointed orders from the old man with a tortoise head, soldiers marching in Siberia, "Two, three, four." *PAPA. ECHO. NOVEMBER.* Property of the KGB. A waitress is shrieking '*Gorky Park at Dusk!*' hysterically in his face. Grotesque faces flash before him, beside him, all around him: painted carnival masks screaming. The pungent smell of burning pork flesh. Fasching men dressed as women stream past in a fast flowing rainbow of colour, leering, colourful fools ringing bells, goat heads braying in unison, their arms linked with ugly Kings and peasants in idiotic lockstep procession.

Stumbling towards the ice rink the Russian launched himself at the barrier and crashed over it, the case slamming on the solid ice and sliding into the skaters' path, causing their knees to fold like dropped marionettes and then sending them tumbling away like bowling pins. Henderson had just reached the wounded policeman and was kneeling over him when heard the commotion. He stood, and began to run towards the ice rink.

He is in the centre of them, revolving with them as they glide around him on their scraping blades. His vision smeared, they are flashing past like streams of paint, great slashes of colour circling him in a wide blur, spinning him as the legato cellos and staccato violins propel them around their frozen carousel like demented figures in a music box.

He sank down to his knees.

Henderson vaulted the barrier and on sliding soles began marching through neat waves of moving skaters, who one by one began shouting in objection as they struggled to avoid him.

It came from the centre of the rink: a single high-pitched female scream that pierced the cold air, rapidly followed by a shrill cacophony of them. Panic swept over the witnessing crowd, who began spilling out. Henderson drew the gun and raised it out in front of him. Almost immediately skaters fell away screaming as they fled, collapsing onto their knees and scrambling across the ice towards the barriers. As the rink cleared the sight of the Russian came into view. He was in the centre, gun raised in one hand and kneeling over the open suitcase with a forefinger resting upon the red arming switch. Beneath it, the key was in its keyhole, and the digital figures on the display above read 00:00:00:00.

The slightest pressure from the Russian's blistered forefinger, and the bomb would detonate.

Both men's eyes remained totally fixed on each others, and for a moment they were completely alone. Outside of them, amid the surrounding panic, as the innocent fled, fifty federal German police officers were rushing to the barriers and drawing their weapons.

'Stop, don't shoot — it's a bomb.' Henderson shouted without moving his gaze. Hysteria erupted again, and all he could hear was commotion around them.

He tempered his voice. 'It's over, Baskov. These police officers have orders to kill you. Slowly. Move away, lay the gun down on the ice . . . '

The Russian dared not blink. His senses were addled, sight and hearing muddled, sense of time disjointed and body detached. He had locked his muscles tight to stop himself swaying but didn't know if he was or not.

'Valentin? I know you want to live. And they will let you live. You *want* to live, Valentin.'

The Russian's lip twitched. He allowed himself a momentary glance to his right. Officers lined the circular barrier like the minute graduations around a clock face. Every one of them frozen-faced peak-capped mannequins with 9 mm semi-automatics aimed at him.

There was now almost complete quiet.

'Let me ask you. Have you read the original blueprint of Overture? I don't think you have because if you had you wouldn't be here, doing this, now. But I have.'

Behind him, the sound of a safety catch being switched caught his ear.

'No,' Henderson yelled. 'Hold your fire.'

'You know what Savich wrote in the final paragraphs? The Executive Officer must *not be allowed to live*. You hear that?'

The Russian's face was impassive.

'I've seen the way you live, Valentin. Do you

want to destroy all that, everything you love, just to obey the orders of men who have betrayed you and would kill you themselves if they could? Men like Grushenko, like Savich - to protect themselves from blame? I know you don't believe in mass murder. Trust me, the only way out of this now is for you to take your finger away from that trigger.'

The finger that was touching the arming trigger, its skin red and cracking, began to tremble. The slightest twitch would be enough to activate it.

'Valentin? Can you hear me?' He was unsure if the Russian could comprehend. 'In London, there is a bomb. A bomb that you planted, that in thirty minutes time is going to explode. You have to tell me where the bomb is, Valentin.'

'Major? Can you hear me? Do you understand what it is I'm asking?'

Blake's mouth fell open as if he were about to speak. His eyes fell to the bomb, illuminations from all around reflecting patterns in its metallic cylinders, the timer's luminous digits, zeros all in a row. He watched his shaking forefinger, hovering above the red switch. Raising his eyes he could make out the blurred outline of the Englishman pointing a gun, but closer, in wonderful clarity, is the face of a girl. She is lying beside him at the edge of a beautiful blue lake, laughing. Her hair is wet, and, yes, now he can see, see that she is mocking him.

Very slowly he started to move the finger back, away from the trigger.

The finger had only retreated an inch when the blaze of police gunfire swarmed him from every angle. Henderson screamed in protest, dropped the gun and ran towards the body that was squirming on its knees, already shredded by the hundreds of rounds being launched into it. The torso was falling forward towards the bomb, Henderson launched himself at it and seized it in his arms, leaving only one dangling finger to brush the trigger. Heaving it upwards, he let go of the lifeless body, allowing the Russian to fall backwards hard onto the ice, and to lie there contorted in a gradually widening pool of blood.

To the sound of police sirens whaling below and the throp of helicopters above, the minute hand of Big Ben struck half past eleven, allowing the half-hour chimes from it and its four quarter bells to ring out across the city. Four minutes later, at twenty-six minutes to midnight, at her desk less than a mile and a half downriver, Nasha was still staring at the deeply wrinkled face of the man on her monitor who had so far failed to provide any further clues as to the bomb's location.

She checked her list of time stamps again. There was something in there, she knew it. Her mother had taught her to trust her sense of intuition. It was not ethereal, she'd said in her strong Amharic accent, did not belong to the heavens, but real. As real a part of the brain as chemistry. Nasha had always trusted her ability, and now it was time to dig deep.

For some reason her mind kept flitting back to 14:47 - "Sea sick, sea sick." It was such a strange thing to say, like none of the other stuff he was garbling. She dragged the curser back, clicked the mouse again, and closed her eyes.

'Sea sick. Sea sick. Sea sick,' the old man's now familiar voice repeated. 'Sea sick, sea sick, sea sick, sea sick . . . '

In an instant her hazel eyes opened wide. She tore the buds from her ears and sprang to her feet.

'It's not sea sick,' she announced the to the monitor.

' . . . sea, sick sea, sick sea, six 'C' . . . '

'It's 6C.'

At 11:37 p.m. Mike Hewitt received a knock on his open door. 'Mike, we've got a break,' said a breathless policewoman. 'Subject seen entering Elephant and Castle tube station on November 5th. And guess what — he's carrying a suitcase.'

Hewitt brought his fist down hard onto the metal desk, causing his six cell phones to jump, then sprang to his feet. 'Where's Darlington?' he yelled.

Outside the tube station on the London Road, with its sirens blaring and a trail of rubber behind its tyres, the doors to a police BMW opened and two armed officers from the Met, accompanied by two soldiers from the 11 Explosive Ordnance Disposal Regiment, got out and pounded into the entrance way. Inside the booking hall they were met by two members of staff, the station manager and her deputy, and it was the former who led them trooping down the halted escalators onto the Bakerloo line platform. The tracks of the whole tube network had been disabled, allowing teams to tread the tunnels without fear of electrocution from live rails, but until the order from Scotland Yard had come in five minutes prior, this southernmost station on the Bakerloo line had been out of the search area as it was deemed too far from Westminster and Whitehall. They were about to jump down onto the track when, at 11:42, the senior officer's radio sounded. He shouted for them to wait, and listened.

'Copy that,' he said into the radio. 'Six 'C', for Charlie, mean anything?' he asked the station manager.

The woman shook her head sternly. 'Not on the Bakerloo line, no.'

The sergeant crinkled one eye. 'What do you mean?'

'Well, 'C's are Jubilee. Bakerloo's are 'J's. Don't make sense, but there it is.'

'Spell it out to me,' said the officer.

CI Darlington hadn't earned his three Bath stars by sitting in front of a monitor, so some hours before he'd decided his time would be better spent on the streets hunting the bomb than inside Scotland Yard. As soon as the call came through from the sergeant at Elephant and Castle it was he who took charge and lead a rapidly assembled team underground to find a storeroom or maintenance cupboard marked '6C'.

The manager of Westminster tube station, 46 year-old Masood Khan, had ordered both Eastbound and Westbound platform doors open in preparation and was waiting at the bottom of the long escalators when Darlington and the two soldiers pounded down them.

'6C,' the Chief Inspector was shouting.

'What, sir?'

'6C — maintenance room. Storeroom. Which way? East or West?'

The manager wasn't sure. He held a hand to his head. 'Ah, Eastbound, I think? I'd need to check.'

'There's no time. Don't think. Be sure,' ordered Darlington.

'Yes, okay, Eastbound. I'm sure. But we don't use them, they have been abandoned for years and will all be locked.'

Darlington didn't wait. He turned left and ran through the domed corridor to the platform then jumped through the open platform doors straight onto the track. A police sergeant climbed down after him, followed by the soldiers in their heavy bomb-proof uniforms and carrying cumbersome helmets and equipment on their backs. With their flashlights aimed ahead, they ran. Almost at once in Darlington's beam 2C appeared above a steel door in the tunnel's brick wall. 'How much further?' he called back to Khan.

It was 11:51. It took them another minute before a door marked 3C appeared in his torch's beam, and a further two minutes before 4C honed into view. By the time the five of them reached the steel door marked 6C with a small white x marked above it, it was four minutes to midnight. They were gasping for breath and drenched in sweat.

Darlington pulled at the door. It opened easily, which surprised the manager. Five torch beams cut through the darkness of the tiny room, dust dancing in the strong white light until the CI dropped his flashlight and sank to his hands and knees in the dirt, desperately reaching and grabbing at anything he could find. A black cloth appeared in his hands. Behind it something moved. He clawed at its edges with fingernails.

'That's it, that's it,' he cried out, at once stepping back to let the soldiers take over. They barged in and heaved the case up onto the table, unlatched the lid and opened it. They shared a momentary glance, not quite believing what they saw, then pulled their helmets on and set to work.

'Come on . . . ' Darlington ushered as the man from TFL stood watching in horror. The timer ticked down mercilessly — two-fifty nine, two-fifty-eight, two-fifty-seven — as the 11 EOD major set about diffusing the weapon. Darlington's eyes were locked onto the device's metallic cylinders as the digits on the timer below counted down.

Two-thirty-three, two-thirty-two . . .

'It's where the arming key is inserted,' said the junior man who had removed his thick gloves and was handing his superior a selection of small picks in between unscrewing the plate that held the trigger mechanism in place.

Two-sixteen . . .

'If we can disable the trigger and at the same time — '

'Spare me the commentary,' Darlington cut in. 'Concentrate,' he ordered.

As he worked, two droplets of sweat left the major's forehead, falling onto the metal cylinder, then slid down its curved edge.

Darlington clenched his jaw and his fists together. Their movements were slow, he guessed they had to be, *but for god's sake.*

One-fifty-six . . .

Keeping his hands steady, the junior man pulled up the whole plate that held the timer, lock and trigger switch. Into a gap of less than an inch, and with extreme care, he inserted a pair of cutters beneath the whole mechanism.

One-thirty-five . . .

Finally, the major, working from above, clicked the barrel to the right a quarter turn. No one breathed.

The two soldiers locked eyes, and nodded.

With the digital timer counting backwards reading 00:00:01:21, he said, 'on my count of three.' Then without hesitating, as his assistant waited poised with the cutters below, the major sniffed in a lungful of stale underground air, counted down from three, and at the same moment as his colleague gripped the cutters together with a snap, he pressed his forefinger down on the deadly red trigger switch.

From the back seat of the Mercedes the man in handcuffs could now make out the clear outline of the giant steel lattice mast beyond the familiar barbed-wire fencing that had started to appear along the road's eastern edge. The same orange sun was sinking into the same blurred white horizon as it had done when he had taken the same journey into the freezing plains of the North West not five weeks before, yet in those intervening weeks, much, everything, had changed.

It was the same driver who had been staring at him when he'd driven him out to Usovo for the meeting. The private, Dukovsky or Dukinski, he couldn't remember, whom he had threatened. This time though, since leaving Moscow the man had barely stopped smirking at him in the rear view mirror.

Now there was no hip flask in his tunic. No vodka flowing through his veins to numb him, no authority. Now, stripped of his general's uniform and wearing civilian work-clothes, when the car slowed at the barrier beneath the stone hammer and sickle in the tangled wire, there was no salute in his direction from the guards.

The car crunched slowly into the centre of the compound and ground to a halt. The driver switched off the engine but did not make to walk around to open the door, but only left him to regard the two men in leather bomber jackets who were walking towards the Mercedes from one of the huts. Dogs. One was carrying a PSS-2 silent pistol, the other went over to a pile of rusted tools and reached down to grab two pickaxes.

Ivan Grushenko smiled.

The door opened. The freezing air rushed into the car as they waited silently for him to step out. He had only taken three steps from it when the one with the gun shot him once in the back of the head and he died. Both men then dragged his body two-hundred yards away to where some poplar trees grew, and beside a mound that attracted the noses of the guard dogs, and in the way many men before them had done in that place, they began the exhausting task of digging the frozen soil with only simple pickaxes.

'Shoulder on the mend I trust, John?' The elder man enquired after he had seated himself and taken in the unmistakable scent of petrichor in the park air, announcing to his senses the promise of rain.

'Better, thank you.' After only five days the injury was still sore, but the frostbite had been superficial, the broken ribs would heal, and with no signs of concussion from the blow to the head from an unflinching Scot's pine, he was telling the truth, or as close as he could ever get to such an abstract construct.

'Take as long as you need.' 'C' gazed out across the water. 'Terribly low atmospheric pressure today, isn't there.' They were sitting on Henderson's usual Saturday morning bench by the Serpentine, yet it being a windless Friday, Hyde Park seemed to be as free of people as the river's flat brown surface was bereft of rowing boats. Not even ducks it seemed were inspired to travel in such uninspiring weather.

'I received a communication from Mikhail Smolenko,' said the chief. 'Not directly of course, delivered by George in last night's bag, to say the SVR have no knowledge of a source named Barclay. As far as they're concerned no such agent ever existed.'

Henderson smiled thinly. 'A thank you card. So it worked.'

'In that regard it did, yes. It seems we are to be saved the embarrassment of admitting the presence of a Russian asset inside our organisation for three long years — and I know they felt longer to you,' he added, smiling, 'yet one can only speculate as to how Smolenko acted upon the information sent to him in the Echelon documents telling them Overture had been enacted. At your behest, I hasten to add.'

'We'll never know. It is possible he could have tipped off Savich, knowing the old man's loyalty was fraying anyway, that that prompted him to show up in Switzerland on his own passport.'

'C' turned to him. 'Still, rather a clever stroke on your part, if you'll forgive the flattery. So the Jacques trade wasn't part of Overture at all.'

'Morris Jacques would have proved far too unstable an asset. Scandal has always been a long-standing weapon in the Russian's arsenal, so when Smolenko realised they'd never get him to behave as Defence Secretary they released the tape and let good old fashioned blackmail do the work for them.'

The chief pulled out a packet of mints from his pocket and popped one into his mouth. He didn't bother to offer one. 'Of course, Moscow's denying any involvement in the software malfunction of the satellites. And they've even claimed to have arrested a group they say are the leaders of the OAG and are promising to hand them over to the Court of Justice. Should keep the newspapers happy.'

Henderson, staring at the murky water's surface, did not reply. The players may change, the games would go on.

'As I said, take as much time as you need, John. While you're away I doubt there'll be many takers for your office.'

He smiled, then, spotting his son walking around the lake towards them, raised a hand.

'Your boy? Leo, isn't it?'

He nodded. Leo was the reason he had asked for indefinite leave. To attempt to heal the rift, make peace with his son, become a father to him again. He had spent the morning drafting a letter to Sarah, trying to spell it out to her in a tone that wouldn't make her irate that she needed to be more present for the boy, that not stifling a child is no substitute for encouragement, and, dare he say it, love. But he couldn't organise the words properly so had decided to go it alone, at least for today.

'By the way, John,' he said as if it were an afterthought, or that it were something that had slipped his mind. 'Does the name Pendulum mean anything?'

Henderson appeared to search his memory, then, seemingly drawing a blank, shook his head innocently. 'Doesn't ring a bell, Sir Clive.'

'C' stood slowly, and sniffed the air deeply though his wide nostrils. 'Yes,' he said, raising his shoulders and with a slender smile. 'Definitely rain.'

'Who was that?' asked Leo as he watched the grey-haired man walk away along the river's edge.

'Just someone I used to know,' his father answered. 'Look, sit down, I want to ask you something.'

His son sat beside him, the twinkle in his eye suddenly snuffed in fear of a lecture.

'What have you got planned for the next two weeks?'

Leo looked confused. 'What do you mean?'

'Well, I've got two tickets to Goa in my jacket pocket and I thought we might go together. Get some sun, you know . . . ?'

'Goa?'

'Yes, it's on the coast of — '

'I know where it is, Dad. Bit decadent isn't it?'

'Well, they are economy seats,' he replied with a straight face.

'What happened to the skiing idea?'

He looked out pensively across the water. 'I've gone off the idea of a skiing holiday.'

Leo took a few moments and bit his thumb nail, and when he looked up and smiled it was the first time John Henderson had seen his son do so in a very long time.

Later that day in South London, after the rain the Chief of British Intelligence had predicted had indeed come, and then gone, Katya Petrenko sat on a damp bench in the afternoon shadow of her new housing estate watching Natalya in the play area. Her daughter was waiting to climb the slide but the neighbours' boys pushed in front of her, their voices foreign and boisterous, so her mittened hands remained clenched patiently by her side. Katya glanced over to their mothers chattering on an opposite bench, oblivious to their sons' early displays of boorishness. It had been a week, and so far no one had introduced themselves, or had even said hello. She gestured to her daughter again to go ahead, but the child was scared to. Minutes later, just as her despondent blue eyes looked like tears may burst from them, a little girl of the same age appeared and offered her her hand. Shyly, Natalya took it, and the girl led her to the foot of the slide's steps and invited her to climb, while using her knitted elbows to force the jostling boys behind them to wait.

Katya felt a presence next to her. 'Samantha,' she said when she saw the woman's face. 'What happened to your arm?'

'I'm fine,' said Zoe. She was wearing a sling beneath her new coat, a replica of the one Katya was wearing. 'How are you settling in?'

Katya eyed her new surroundings. It wasn't an easy answer. Koptevo was not such a world away. The building was similar to the one she'd left, the designers and contractors of each equally unblessed by generosity. There were still the hooded figures with gaunt faces slipping in and out of the stale stairwells, the hard-faces of the mothers worried for their children's futures, the elderly residents who swept the paths and scrubbed with bleach the outdoor areas young men who'd gather at night urinated over, too lazy to go inside. The grey van keeping vigil in the car park had been traded for the more overt surveillance cameras clamped to every lamppost, arctic winters for near-constant drizzle, and, more importantly, Natalya's acute suffering for a bathroom cupboard full of

Ponatinib from a healthcare system that, for today at least, promised to provide more.

She looked up at the leaden, iron grey South London sky. 'It rains a lot,' she smiled. 'Dmitri would have liked that. He used to love the rain.'